HEART'S SURRENDER

F. ROSANNE BITTNER

ZEBRA BOOKS
KENSINGTON PUBLISHING CORP.

It is true that the building of America is a great and proud story; that it took strong, courageous people to develop such a great and powerful nation. But there are chapters in the history of this growth that have been quietly left out of the story we learn in school when growing up. One of those chapters belongs to the Cherokee Indian. Perhaps that chapter was left out because of the shame and embarrassment it sheds on our forefathers, and the guilt still carried by the descendants of those who so cruelly and heartlessly exiled a noble, educated, civilized people from their beloved homeland. This story is dedicated to the Cherokee Indians. I hope by the telling of it, people who were formerly unaware will know the truth, and will weep themselves as they go back in history and walk the Trail of Tears.

—Author

Historical events in this novel involving the persecution of the Cherokee Indians are true, as is my depiction of the wealth and education of the Cherokees in northern Georgia in the 1820s and 1830s. However, my basic story and main characters are fictitious, although there are a few references to people who really did exist and were involved in Cherokee removal during this time period. Dialogue given to characters who did exist at this time is not direct quotation, but is merely supposed, according to factual printed records of these events. All such records are available to the public. My primary source of information for this book is from a book entitled *Disinherited: The Lost Birthright of the American Indian*, by Dale Van Every (William Morrow & Company, New York, 1966); with some further factual information taken from *Creek Mary's Blood* by Dee Brown (Holt, Rinehart & Winston, New York, 1980).

Other than my references to historical fact, any resemblance of the author's fictitious characters to actual persons, living or dead, or of the author's fictitious events to any events that may have occurred at that time, are purely coincidental and are the product of the author's imagination.

PART I

"Resolved, that the Committee on Indian Affairs be instructed to inquire into the expediency of providing, by law, for the removal of the various tribes of Indians who have located within the States and Territories of the United States to some eligible situation, west of the Mississippi River. . . ."

—Resolution introduced into Congress on December 13, 1827 by Wilson Lumpkin, a Georgia congressman, in an effort to get the federal government to help Georgia remove all Indians, by force if necessary, from its territory.*

*(Disinherited: The Lost Birthright of the American Indian, Dale Van Every)

CHAPTER ONE

Andrea led her gray pony up the steep embankment. It was late spring in northern Georgia, and the soft, rolling Appalachian Mountains were alive with green forests of oak and pine, walnut and tulip trees, and with wild rhododendron, daisies, and violets. She took a deep breath to enjoy the sweet smell, and a brown thrasher flitted out of a nearby bush and flew away.

Andrea looked up then, studying the top of the ridge before gazing down at the lush, green valley below, where her father's farm lay. She was not supposed to come this far, but, at fourteen, how could one reasonably argue against curiosity? Something lay beyond this ridge, and she wanted to see what it was. Her father had just bought this farm, having moved north from another farm that was sold at a loss, its soil used up and no longer yielding good crops. He had heard talk of better land in the north, with a possibility of someday being able to buy up Indian land, the value of which was steadily growing as more and more people flooded into the state. Some folks even talked of going farther west, perhaps beyond the Mississippi River and into unsettled territory.

The girl picked a daisy and twirled it in her fingers, smelling it and getting yellow pollen on her nose. She decided she would not ever want to go to the strange land in the West, where rumor was there were no green forests and lush soil like here in Georgia. But she wondered, too,

11

how her father or anyone else thought they would get to buy Indian land. Everyone talked about how the Cherokee had been in those mountains for hundreds of years, maybe longer. They had already been pushed out of other parts of Georgia and now had taken a firm hold in the north, with their own government and schools and farms. She didn't really understand it all, except that some grown men complained that the Indians had no right to consider themselves a separate state and to think they had full rights to any land in Georgia. As far as Andrea was concerned, if they were nice people, why shouldn't they get to live wherever they chose?

She climbed higher. Somewhere on the other side of this ridge was Indian land. Her curiosity had plagued her for days after her father had bought this farm right on the border of Cherokee country. She'd never seen a Cherokee. Did they wear regular clothes like her father and brother? Or were they half-naked savages? Everyone knew they were once a violent, fighting people that had done unmentionable things to the white settlers who'd first come to Georgia. "You can never truly tame a bloodthirsty savage," her father had grumbled. "But as long as we'll be living right next to them, if they are as peaceful and settled as folks say, we might as well try to get along with them. Maybe someday they'll move on and that land will be up for grabs."

Was it true? Were all the Cherokee really bloodthirsty savages? Her father had talked of going visiting soon, perhaps inviting the nearest Indian family to supper, as was often the custom along the border. A few of their neighbors actually considered some of the Cherokee their friends.

She slipped on a rock and fell, getting a red scuff on her boot from the clay soil, but she got up and hurried on until she reached the top. Then she tied her pony and walked farther out of the trees to look, pulling her woolen sweater closer around her neck. Although it was nearly always warm in Georgia, it was cooler up here, and still damp, for she had left very early in the morning, in those still-misty

12

hours between the cool of night and the heat of day. The branches of the trees hung heavy with dew, and her hair felt wet as she grasped its long, blond strands and pulled them back behind her shoulders. She wished she knew how to fix her hair in pretty ways, but it was straight and fine and very stubborn, and she usually ended up just brushing it long and loose, or braiding it.

The morning sun glowed against her freckled face, as her blue eyes scanned the green valley below. Far in the distance she saw what must be a town. Was it New Echota, the center of activity and government for the Cherokee? A river meandered in and out of hills and valleys, the Coosa River, her father had said it was. Scattered here and there were homes, some very fine brick ones, with large, red barns and neat outbuildings. Cattle dotted the entire valley, and all looked peaceful and lovely, hardly any different from the white men's farms and buildings on her own side of the ridge. Perhaps she was looking at the wrong thing. Perhaps the Cherokee were many more miles away. The people moving about below were dressed just like her own people, but they were too far away for her to tell if they looked any different, if their faces were shaped differently, if their skin was darker.

She sighed with disappointment. She dared not go any farther, and was not even supposed to be this far away from the house. She puckered her rosy lips and scowled, untying her pony and turning. It was then she saw the old oak farther to her right, a great, gnarled tree that had surely been on that ridge top for a hundred years, maybe two hundred. She had been so curious about what she would see on the other side of the ridge that she had not even looked around and noticed anything else as she'd headed to the top. She stared in awe at the oak, whose branches reached out for many feet sideways before turning upward to meet the sky.

Hurrying over to it, she tied her pony and then walked even closer, touched the curled, gnarled bark. She leaned her head back to look up into the splendid branches, their light green leaves beginning to grow larger now that they

13

had budded out.

"Oh, great tree, how old are you?" she spoke aloud, running her hands over its bark.

"One hundred and fifty years." The voice was deliberately lowered to make it sound like the tree talking.

Andrea's eyes widened and she felt a chill as she stepped back from the tree and looked up in the direction of the voice. A young man of perhaps sixteen or seventeen peeked around the huge trunk behind which he had been crouched. "Hi!" he said in his natural voice, smiling warmly. His teeth were clean and even, his dark eyes danced teasingly. "Who are you?"

She backed away more. Was he one of those Cherokee Indians? Surely he was! His hair and skin were so dark. But he dressed like any other boy, with leather boots and dark, cotton pants and a red checkered shirt that was clean and neat. His face was surprisingly handsome, the cheekbones high, the lips finely etched against smooth, brown skin; his eyes were large and dark, and his dark hair, looking clean, was neatly cut and fell in gentle waves to the collar of his shirt.

Should she run? He reached out for a branch and began to climb down. She stood frozen, watching him. "Not going to talk, huh?" he said, coming farther down and then grasping a slender branch and hanging from it. Then he dropped to the ground, no more than five feet from her, still smiling, his dark eyes looking her over. "I'm Adam Chandler."

She swallowed. Adam Chandler? That didn't sound like an Indian name. He frowned then, and leaned forward a little. "Do you speak?"

She backed away a little more. "I'm Andrea. Andrea Sanders. I . . . we live down there." She pointed to the valley below, but nothing could be seen through the forested slope. "My father just bought a farm here. We're from southern Georgia."

He nodded, grasping a branch again and swinging from it. "I live on the other side. My father farms, too. In fact, I'd better get back home pretty quick. I've got chores to do. I come up here early every morning to say hello to my tree." He jumped down and stepped back then, looking up at the mighty oak. "How do you like it?"

Andrea followed his eyes and studied the tree again herself. "It's a wonderful tree. I've never seen one so big." She looked back at him. She had only recently become infatuated with boys. How different they were. She wondered sometimes about the things men and women did to get babies, though she was hardly able to imagine what it might be like to be kissed by a boy. But there was one boy she hated—Douglas Means. He was eighteen, and whenever he got the chance, he said bad things to her and he was always after her to go to the woods with him. She had hoped to get rid of Douglas when her father moved, but the Meanses were good friends of the family, and they had moved also, buying land not far from her father's. Never had she known such disappointment as when the Meanses had come along, except that she could at least keep one good girl friend, Douglas's sister Mary, who was the same age as Andrea. The two girls had grown up together and were best friends. Andrea was glad Mary had come, but wished Douglas had been left behind. Still, the boy she was looking at now was nothing like Douglas. He had a kinder look in his eyes, and he was most definitely more handsome.

They watched each other awkwardly for several long, strained seconds, Andrea's face reddening as she struggled to find something to say. He folded his arms then. "You are wondering if I am a Cherokee."

She walked to her pony, petting its neck. "Not really."

"Yes, you are."

"Okay then. Are you?"

He grinned and opened his arms. "Every drop of my blood."

She started to untie her pony. "I . . . I'd better be going."

"Why? Do you think I am some wild thing who will attack you?" He laughed, grabbing a branch again. "I dress and act just like your white boys. I have even finished high school and one year of higher learning at Cornwall."

She let go of the reins and stared at him, stepping closer again. "You mean . . . clear up in Connecticut?"

"Sure. Lots of Cherokee kids go to school there. I think I will be a doctor or a lawyer. I don't know yet." He dropped down and sat with his back against the great, gnarled tree trunk, his smile fading to concern. "But I am not sure now how I can continue. They say Cornwall will not be reopened."

She moved a little closer, and he could see that the plain blue cotton of her dress denoted a white girl of moderate means, but not wealthy. His own father was quite wealthy, with many cattle and a fine farm, and he even owned black men who worked for him. He looked up into her pretty face. It irritated him that white girls fascinated him, for his father had warned him to stay away from them. Still, he could not imagine why a man couldn't be interested in whomever he chose, and he was thinking it was about time he found out how wonderful it was to lie naked with a girl. The Cherokee girls were too chaste, and he'd been strictly warned not to go near the wild white girls on the other side of the ridge, those who liked to visit the haylofts with Cherokee boys. Was this girl like that? Somehow he sensed she was not.

"Why won't the school be reopened?" she asked.

He picked up a weed and stuck it in his mouth. "If I tell you, you will be embarrassed and run away. Anyway, it isn't fair, and it makes me very mad to think about it."

Now her curiosity was chomping at the bit. "I won't run away. I promise."

He grinned again and put his head back against the tree. "Promise?"

She nodded and sat down in the grass near his feet, carefully making sure her full dress covered her legs and feet.

He chewed thoughtfully on the weed for a moment. "The white people up there got mad because some of the white girls became interested in Indian boys," he told her.

Andrea reddened again and looked at the ground. "Is that any reason to close a whole school?"

"They thought it was. One of our people, a wealthy Cherokee called Elias Boudinot, he married a white girl from up there. Even now they live near New Echota, and they are very happy. But a newspaper man in Connecticut, he made a big fuss over it, stirred the people up, wrote bad things about the Cherokee and made it look like a terrible sin for a white girl to love a Cherokee man. The people all got angry and demanded the school be closed." He shook his head. "My father says it is a bad sign. Those people in the North have always been our friends, supported us. We can do anything we want, except marry their daughters. Yet it is all right for the white men to marry Cherokee girls. It is a strange set of values you people have."

She toyed with some tiny wildflowers in the grass. "We don't all think that way."

"Oh?"

She met his eyes and reddened again, and he laughed. "I am glad. That means we can be friends, right?"

She shrugged. "I don't know." She pursed her lips and he wanted to kiss them, just to see what it would be like. "How old are you, Adam?"

"Sixteen."

Her eyebrows arched. "Only sixteen? And you've been to Cornwall?"

"They say I am very smart."

Her wide blue eyes studied him. "You must be. I am fourteen and have just finished the eighth grade. My father says I can go to higher school if I want, but he thinks it's foolish for a girl to go farther than the eighth grade. He says girls don't need to know anything except how to cook and clean house and have ba—" She stopped then and looked away. "I like to learn and read. I made him promise I could go to school longer."

He grinned over the fact that she was embarrassed to talk about having babies. "You should go to school longer, Andrea. It's good that you made your father promise."

She smiled then, and it made her even prettier. He could see in her young face a woman struggling to show herself, but there was still a lot of little girl there. "Do you really think so?"

"Sure. We Cherokees think education is very important."

She looked up into the tree, trying to ignore the strange urges he stirred in secret places, gentle, pleasant ripplings she had never before felt. He was so handsome that he seemed almost beautiful. The forearms revealed by the rolled-up sleeves of his shirt showed hard muscle, and the way he'd swung around in the branches, she knew he was strong. "Why do you call this your tree?" she asked, suddenly wanting to talk to him longer.

"I just do. I've been coming here almost since I learned to walk. It was my secret place—until you came along. Now I will have to trust you to keep it a secret for me and not tell anyone else about my tree."

She could tell by the look on his face that he was actually worried.

"I promise not to say a word," she answered.

He nodded. "Thank you, Andrea Sanders."

She looked away again, almost angry at the strange feelings he gave her, wondering if he knew what she was feeling. "What's it like . . . on the other side where you live?"

He shrugged. "Just about the same as your side," he answered. "We farm, go to school, all those things. Elias Boudinot is working on starting our own newspaper. We live in houses just like yours. My father's is a fine brick home two stories high. And he owns black men, who work for him."

Her eyebrows arched. "Slaves?"

"Sure. But not in the way you say the word. They just work for us and get good housing and food. We are not cruel to them."

She picked at the wildflowers again. "Your father must be very wealthy. My father can't afford to own slaves."

He grinned. "See? We are not wild savages like you thought. We read and write and farm, and have our own government and everything. Now you can go home and tell your parents we are just like you."

She smiled and rose. "I wouldn't dare. I wasn't supposed to come up here at all. If my father knew I'd been here—"

"Why? Because a wild Cherokee boy might find you and do terrible things to you?"

She reddened again, looking down at the ground. "Partly. But that's him, not me." She met his eyes. "I came up here anyway, didn't I? If I believed him about the Cherokee, I wouldn't have come."

He nodded, rising himself. "And what if your father was right?"

She met his eyes challengingly, looking ready to run. Then she smiled. "You're just trying to scare me. You just don't want me to come up here by your tree anymore."

He turned and hoisted himself up onto a branch. "You are a smart girl, Andrea Sanders. And I think maybe you are brave, too."

She smiled once more then, going to stand under him. "Why do you come here, Adam?"

He looked up into the branches that spread in glorious splendor above him. "To be alone. To think. To try to figure out white men, Indians, why they are so different. To think about what I want to do with my life. Some of my people whisper that they fear some day the white men will make them leave this land." He sighed deeply. "I would die if I had to leave this land . . . this tree. If white men came and said I had to go . . ." He clenched a fist and hugged a limb with his other arm. "I will never leave this place, except when I have to go away to school. This land is sacred to us, Andrea. Other Indians have roamed the land, but the Cherokee have been in this place for hundreds of years. We love these mountains, the trees, the red earth. We are like the animals here. It is our habitat. To take it from us would bring our death. I myself know every trail, every tree, every cave, every rock of this land. I feel one with it. To leave it would be like cutting out my heart."

There was a long moment of silence, and she watched him stare absently, suddenly in deep thought.

He finally spoke up. "It can't really happen. I think all that is foolish talk. We live good. We are peaceful, and we are educated like the white man. We farm, trade with him. We cause no trouble."

He looked down at her. "It can't really happen, can it? How could they make us leave when we have been here these hundreds of years?"

"I . . . I don't know, Adam. I don't think it will ever happen."

He swung down again, hanging for a moment before dropping. "Nor do I. But my people are worried because more factories are being built, more railroads. Our land is becoming very valuable, and there is nothing the white man loves more than valuable land. I think he loves it more than gold. There was a time when we could fight for it, just physical fighting with the border people. But now the fight will be in the courts, against the white man's government. My father says such a fight will be much harder to win than just fighting hand-to-hand with knives and arrows." He ran his hand over the tree trunk. "I think maybe he is right. Even now my people are having meetings to form their own government just like the United States, to make their own constitution and pick a president."

"My father and some of the others say that's wrong— that you can't make yourselves a separate state. It makes the white men mad."

He turned and kicked at a rock. "Why should it? They do the same thing. They come into a land, kick out the Indians, build it up, settle it, and then call it a state. We have been in this land much, much longer than any of them. Who has more right to claim some of this land as their own state than the Cherokee?"

He met her eyes then. She wanted to look away, but his dark eyes seemed to hypnotize her. "I . . . I don't know," she answered. "But people like me don't have much say."

He smiled, coming even closer, looking her over, noticing her chest was still almost flat but showing small buds of a bosom beginning to blossom. "That is too bad.

They should listen to smart little girls like you, Andrea."

"Andy. My family and friends call me Andy."

He laughed lightly. "I like that. Andy. Okay, that is what I will call you when I see you again."

Andrea wished she could tear her eyes from his, yet deep inside she didn't really want to. "How do you know you'll see me again?"

He studied her fair skin and freckles, the lovely blond hair he wanted to touch. "I just feel it, that's all. Don't you?"

She blushed a little. "I . . . I guess maybe I do. I like talking to you, Adam. And I like this place."

"Then come again—early in the morning or late in the evening. I am almost always here, except Sunday mornings. I have to do my chores extra early because of church."

Her face brightened. "You go to church?"

He laughed and shook his head. "There you go again. Yes, this wild Indian goes to church. We are Christians. This is 1826, you know. Nearly all of us are Christians. Many missionaries live among us."

"What kind of church do you go to?"

"Methodist. Most of us are Methodist."

She smiled. "So are we."

Their eyes held, and both were suddenly warm all over, feeling a vibrant attraction but too new to speak of it. Her chest tightened strangely, and his breathing quickened. She was too tall for fourteen, too pretty. "They say on your side of the ridge some of the white girls let Cherokee boys . . . visit them," he told her cautiously. He had to know.

Her eyes widened and she immediately whirled, walking back to her pony. He hurried after her. "I'm sorry, Andrea . . . I mean Andy. I just wondered—"

"How dare you!" she shot back in hot anger, her eyes brimming with tears. "Is that all you Cherokee boys think about?" She hurriedly untied the reins. "I should have known! I shouldn't be here at all! I just thought I'd see something new. How did I know you'd be here!"

21

"Wait, Andy." He grabbed her arm and she jerked it away.

"Besides that, I'm new here. How could you think . . . I don't even know what those girls do . . . but I'm sure it's something bad, the way you said it." She climbed up on her pony, but he grabbed the bridle.

"Honestly, Andy, I didn't really think that of you. I only . . . I just wondered. I was hoping you wouldn't be like them. I like you . . . like talking to you. Don't go away mad."

She glared at him, her face still red from anger and embarrassment. Much as she wanted to hate him she could not. And what was he to think, she being there all alone and talking to a strange boy so easily? She wished she understood more about boys, how they thought, what they wanted. And was it right to be friends with one, especially when he was a Cherokee?

"I came up here to be alone, too. I didn't know you'd be here," she said in a quivering voice, wiping quickly at her eyes. "I thought it was pretty up here, and I wanted to see the other side. Everybody talks about your people being over there. I just wanted to see."

He nodded. "Sometimes I walk down your side and watch the people. Some of your neighbors have been to our house to eat, and we've been to theirs."

"And they all get along?"

"Of course they get along. Why shouldn't they? It isn't the border people who give us so much trouble anymore. It's the people in the towns and other parts of the state, who don't know anything about us. They still think we're wild Indians, just like you did, and your father does. Make him come and visit us, Andrea, and he'll see how we live."

She raised her chin proudly. "I might ask him." She tossed her long, blond hair. "But I won't tell him I've met a Cherokee. He'd tan my hide."

"You don't have to tell him. Just bring it up, tell him you're curious. Tell him you've heard neighbors visit with us all the time."

She held the reins tightly. "Why do you care if my

folks visit?"

He let go of the bridle. "I just do, that's all." He held her eyes. "Will you come back up here?"

She backed the pony. "I don't know. Maybe. But not if you think I'm like those girls you talked about."

He shook his head. "I don't. Truly I don't."

"Then why do you want me to come back? Surely you have your own friends. And I'll be making friends on my own side. If I make friends with a Cherokee, it should be with a girl, not an older boy."

Shades of anger moved through his dark eyes and he turned away. "Never mind. I just like talking to you, that's all. Go on home. Nobody said you had to be my friend or that I had to be yours." He walked to the tree and hoisted himself up. "Go on with you," he called out. "And don't come back. This is my tree and I like to be alone."

She hesitated, watching him climb up until he was out of sight. "Okay, I'm going, Cherokee boy. You can have your old tree!" She turned her pony and headed down the ridge, going slowly, waiting for him to call to her to come back. But he said nothing. She worked her way down until the big oak was so mixed in with the surrounding forest that it was difficult to distinguish it from the rest of the trees. She stopped and stared back up at it for several quiet seconds. Was he still in it? Perhaps he was perched in such a way that he could see her looking back up at him.

She headed on down, her heart strangely heavy. She hadn't meant to be mean to him. She liked him, wanted to talk to him more, find out more about his people. Perhaps if she went back in the evening, or the next morning— But no. That would be too soon. He'd think she liked him too much, maybe think she really was like those other girls. It would probably please his male pride for her to go back right away. Besides, it wasn't wise of her to see him again at all. The first time had been accident, but anything after that would be deliberate. That cast a different light on everything, deliberately sneaking up a mountain side to see an Indian boy. It sounded bad, looked bad. She would forget Adam Chandler and the big oak tree. But she'd meant to ask if he had an Indian name. Now she'd never know. And how was she to forget his face, his build, the odd feelings he gave her when he stood close to her? They were pleasant sensations that had made her wonder if she'd faint dead away if he touched her. She was thinking thoughts she'd never thought before. That was bad. Maybe Cherokee boys had a way of hypnotizing white girls and making them do bad things. Didn't white people say the Indians had the devil in them? She'd better stay away from Adam Chandler.

She had nearly reached the bottom of the ridge when Douglas Means came riding toward her, from the road that led to his father's farm west of her own. He called out, and her stomach tightened. She trotted her pony toward her own farm.

"Where'd you come from, Andy?" he asked, riding up beside her on his faster Thoroughbred. "You been up that mountain?"

"That's none of your business." She refused to look at his pimpled, ruddy face and steely gray eyes. "I just took my pony for her exercise, that's all."

"You up there looking for Cherokee boys?" he asked with a nasty laugh. "Maybe I'm wasting my time thinking you're a lady, Andrea Sanders. If you won't go to the woods with me, how come you rode up that ridge alone?"

"Because I wanted to *be* alone," she snapped, gritting her teeth. "Which means I want you to go away, too!"

"Aw, poor little Andy. You're fourteen, Andy. It's time to find out about boys. I could show you a few things. It's fun. Don't you want to have fun like that?"

She turned and made a face at him. "Not with an ugly thing like you, Douglas Means. If your sister wasn't my best friend, I could get you in a lot of trouble."

"If you keep going up that ridge, you'll be the one in trouble."

Her house was in sight, and Andrea was glad. She was afraid of Douglas Means. Oddly enough, she suddenly realized she'd never really been afraid of Adam Chandler at all, even though she'd been all alone with him up there on the mountain.

"I heard there are some farm girls around here who like to go to the haylofts with boys," she told Douglas.

"Oh, yeah? Where'd you hear that?"

"I just heard, that's all. Why don't you go find one of them and leave me alone? I don't like you."

"Fact is, Miss Uppity, I've already found one or two. Had me a damned good time."

"Watch your language."

"You'd like it, too, if you tried it. And if you're such a lady, you'd better stuff something in the keyhole the next time you and my sister take a bath. You sure are a skinny, flat-chested thing."

She met his eyes, her own flaring with rage, but he just laughed and turned his horse, riding off while she sat there furious and humiliated. Douglas Means had peeked at her and his own sister with nothing on. How she hated him! She'd tell her father on him, that's what she'd do. But she realized that if she did, Douglas would say she'd been up on the ridge. Hot tears of frustrated anger stung her eyes as she headed her pony toward home. She'd have to be more careful after this, find a different way up the ridge and watch the road when she came down.

She realized with surprise then what she'd been thinking. She'd go back. She'd go back and find Adam Chandler. After talking to Douglas Means, she suddenly wanted to see Adam again, partly for pure spite, partly because he was so different from Douglas. There was a proud air about him that told her Adam would never go around peeking through holes at his own sister, if he had one. He'd never treat a nice girl with the kind of disrespect Douglas showed.

She moved her pony into the barn and dismounted, leading the animal into its stall and unbuckling the saddle strap. Suddenly she was full of excitement and wonder. She would wait a few days so that Adam didn't get the wrong idea. But she would go back, for suddenly to think of him made her stomach so fluttery that food was the last thing she wanted. She should be very hungry by now, but she wasn't. She had a secret, and she'd met someone very new and very different. It was exciting, fascinating. And his handsome face and powerful build were vivid in her mind now. Yes, she would go back up the ridge and find that Cherokee boy again. Adam Chandler. It was a nice name. But she still wondered if he had an Indian name. Would he be thinking about her like she was thinking about him now?

She unsaddled the pony and made sure it had feed. She would brush it down later. She had to get inside and help with breakfast. She walked out of the barn and stared up at the ridge, wondering if he still sat there in the great oak tree.

"You'd best be staying away from that place, girl," came a voice behind her.

She turned to meet her father's stern, discerning eyes, and she reddened slightly. "Yes, Father. But . . . shouldn't we try to meet some of those Cherokees and make friends with them . . . since we live so close and all?"

He scowled and carried a couple of horseshoes toward the barn. "We'll see. Best to keep the doors open, I suppose. Wouldn't want that kind mad at me. Go on in the house now and help your mother."

"Yes, Father." She hurried away, breathing a sigh of relief. He didn't suspect a thing. And she began to wonder how she would stand the wait until she could see Adam Chandler again.

CHAPTER TWO

Andrea adjusted the green ribbon tied into the side of her hair, then took one more look at herself in the hall mirror. Her matching soft green cotton dress was simple but full skirted, with a wide, green satin sash and bow, a high neck, and three-quarter-length puffed sleeves. It was her Sunday best, made by her mother's hands, but a far cry from the stylish, elegant gowns wealthier women were wearing now, according to what she had seen in the store windows of Atlanta on their way north. Morgan Sanders was a simple, hard-working man, to whom fancy clothes were a frivolity. Most of his profits were put back into the farm, and he had taken a loss on the one he had sold in the south. Frugality was the word in the Sanders household, which meant homemade and properly simple clothing.

Never had Andrea been so nervous. The Chandlers had been one of the families her father had ended up visiting on the other side of the ridge, and they had been the ones he'd chosen to invite to Sunday dinner, primarily because they had a daughter just one year younger than Andrea. So, Adam did have a sister.

Adam! He was coming to their very house to eat. It was wonderfully exciting, secretly already knowing Adam Chandler. Apparently the boy had said nothing of having met Andrea on the ridge, or Morgan Sanders would have been furious when he'd returned from his visit.

Andrea had not gone back to the oak tree since that first

encounter, for she'd been worried about what Adam would think of her, though she'd wanted very much to go. His face had haunted her since their meeting, his bright smile and dark eyes, the vibrant feelings he gave her when he stood close to her. Her appetite, which had dwindled, had returned somewhat when Morgan Sanders had come home from visiting the Cherokee to announce that the Chandlers would be their guests at Sunday dinner. It had been almost two weeks since Andrea had seen Adam. She had thought perhaps she should and could forget about him. But now he was coming to dinner, and her stomach was so tight she wondered how she would ever get any food into it.

She studied herself in the mirror. What would Adam think of her today? How would he act? Everything had to be perfect. After all, the Chandlers were very wealthy. It would all be so much easier if she didn't already know Adam and feel this almost painful excitement at seeing him again. What would he think of their simple farm house and their clothing? And had he thought about her, or just laughed her off? After all, he was sixteen and had been to a school of higher learning. Surely he had met older girls more educated and refined than she. Why did that suddenly matter to her? She had not meant to lie at night and think about him, wonder what it would be like to be kissed by that Cherokee boy. Yet such thoughts had come without effort, and she wondered if they were sinful. She couldn't understand why they had come at all, after one short meeting. Were some things brought about by destiny? Adam had said he was sure he would see her again, and now he was coming to Sunday dinner.

She hurried to the kitchen then, where her mother was basting a large turkey.

"Is the table ready, Mother?"

"I think so. Go and check the silverware, Andy." Her mother was a quiet woman, who gave orders that were not questioned. Andrea had always wished she could talk to her more, especially about boys. But there was a sternness about the religious woman that forbade the mention of such things. Andrea was her only child, and, therefore, was expected to be perfect. She felt the pressure of it, tried hard to be good, but lately she had found herself wondering if her mother truly could not have children or if the woman had simply decided that once Andrea was born she would not submit to the indignation of letting her husband bed her again. Mary Means had whispered to her once that she had heard her own mother talking with Andrea's once, and both women had talked of being good wives in every way but sleeping with their husbands, for which they cared little. Lately, Harriet Sanders had taken a separate room.

Andrea walked into the dining room, slowly gazing around the long table to make certain every plate was clean and shiny, every setting just right. Meanwhile she wondered about her mother. Some women had many children, especially Indian women. Many of their friends had five, seven, nine children and more in their families, yet the parents seemed perfectly happy. Why did some women have many babies, and others only one or two, choosing then not to sleep with their husbands? What happened behind those closed doors? What happened to a young woman when she was married? Did she love a man before marriage, and hate him afterward? Was mating with a man something horrible and humiliating? Surely it was, for Andrea had seen animals mate. If a man did something like that to a woman, how could she ever look him in the eyes again, or let him see her that way in the first place? And yet in stark contrast, the thought of Adam Chandler touching her breast with one strong, dark hand brought very pleasant shivers throughout her body. Was it wrong to think of being touched by a boy, kissed by a boy?

She sighed and stood back to study the table. It looked fine, but the only damper on the day was that the Menses had been invited. Not only did Andrea dread the presence of Douglas Means, she wondered if Adam would have eyes for Douglas's sister, Mary. Although Mary and Andrea were best friends, Andrea was sure she could never like Mary quite so much if Adam looked at her admiringly.

Surely she was not as pretty as Andrea, for her hair was a mousy brown and her face was spotted with blemishes like her brother's. But Mary was a nice girl and a devoted friend, and Andrea suddenly felt guilty for her thoughts.

She walked back into the kitchen. "Everything must be perfect, Mother. Father says the Chandlers are very wealthy. I'm so nervous."

"Well, you needn't be. I do not care whether or not I impress Indians, Andrea, but it is possible your father can learn something from Mr. Chandler, and he from your father. After all, we all have farming in common, and one might as well be friends with people like that as enemies."

Andrea scowled and stirred the gravy. "What do you mean, 'people like that'?"

"You know what I mean. Wealthy or not, they're still Indians."

Andrea's heart felt heavy. "Surely if they live so fine and all, they are no different from us, Mother."

The woman put the turkey back into the oven. "They are different, no matter how educated or wealthy, Andrea. Always remember that. But if you want to be friends with Ruth Chandler, we will not forbid it. Just be wary of those Cherokee boys and Ruth's brother. Your father tells me he's a well-educated, fine-looking boy. But it is wrong for those Indian boys to be interested in white girls."

Andrea's stomach tightened more. If only there were someone she could talk to. She hadn't even told Mary about Adam, and usually she told Mary everything. Now her mother had dashed all hopes of her talking about the boy to her parents. There was nowhere she could turn, and having to keep it a secret only seemed to intensify her feelings for Adam. Her mother's remark had made her want to defend him, but she dared not. She tasted the gravy. It was perfect, but she knew she would eat little that day, and at the moment she was struggling not to cry.

She was determined now to make friends with Ruth Chandler, so she would have an excuse to go and visit the Chandlers, a way to see more of Adam. Walking to the hall mirror again, she pinched her cheeks for color and wished she didn't have so many freckles. She smoothed her dress, hoping it hadn't got too wrinkled in the back from sitting in church. They would eat later than usual, for the Chandlers had also attended church, on their own side of the ridge, and had insisted on waiting an hour or so after church before even leaving to allow Andrea's mother plenty of time to prepare things after getting home from services.

Now Andrea could hear the carriage. Why had she imagined the Chandlers arriving on bareback horses and wearing buckskins? She hurried to the door. A fancy double-seated surrey with a fringed canopy top was approaching, drawn by two fine, shiny black horses, and Andrea's entire body suddenly felt warm and limp. It would not be easy pretending she didn't already know Adam. She had been careful to watch her remarks so she would not slip and in some way reveal her secret meeting with him. As the surrey came closer, she stepped outside, followed by her mother. Her father was approaching from the barn, where he had been feeding the horses. His plain, black woolen suit suddenly looked like poor-man's clothing to Andrea, as did her mother's stern black dress. In the distance the Meanses were coming, Mary, Ethel, and Wilson Means in a rattling buggy, Douglas riding alongside on his own horse, a fine red Thoroughbred of which he was boastfully proud.

Andrea's heart tightened. If only Douglas were not coming, it would be a perfect day. She had avoided him since that day she'd come down from the ridge, still hating him for saying he'd peeked at her and Mary while they were bathing. She had invited Mary over many times since, but had not gone to the Meanses' house; she didn't know how to explain that to Mary. Mary had taken offense a few times, but Andrea was afraid to tell on Douglas for he might tell her father she'd been on the ridge. It seemed since she'd met Adam Chandler, everything was changing. Her stomach was always upset and she felt more and more alone. Something was happening that she could not stop, didn't know how to stop, even if she wanted to.

Both buggies came close then, and Morgan Sanders greeted Jonas Chandler with a friendly smile. As the Cherokee man climbed down from the surrey and shook Morgan's hand, Andrea's eyes immediately went to Adam, and her knees felt weak. He smiled that handsome smile, and she smiled in return, trying to thank him with her eyes for not telling on her. She glanced at his father, a handsome man, short and stocky, with kind, brown eyes. His mother was very pretty, but taller than her husband, and his young sister sat looking nervous and timid.

Andrea's father tied the horses to a hitching post in front of the house, and Jonas Chandler helped his wife down. Adam climbed down, then urged his sister to get out also, while Douglas rode up on his fine horse and dismounted with a cocky air. All the Chandlers were dressed in the latest fashion, and Adam looked splendid in a deep blue suit, the pants tightly fitted, the coat cut to the waist in front, but long in back. Andrea had seen such coats displayed in Atlanta. The collar was an even deeper blue and made of velvet. Jonas Chandler was similarly dressed, but his suit was brown. Young Ruth wore a very pretty yellow dress, and Mrs. Chandler a modest light blue dress, fashionable but not gaudy.

Douglas walked up beside Andrea, as though he owned her, but she moved away, going to stand beside her mother. Adam caught the daring look in Douglas's gray eyes, and although he did not know the young man yet, he already didn't like him. He'd run into white boys like this one before. The Meanses climbed out of their own buggy, and Mary ran to Andrea, giggling and staring at the Cherokees.

"Look at the boy!" she whispered in Andrea's ear. "I thought he would surely be ugly. But he's beautiful."

Andrea scowled. She wanted to tell Mary not to look at him, to announce that the Cherokee boy belonged only to her. But she had no such claims on him, nor could she have admitted such a thing if she did. The ache that knowledge brought to her heart almost made her want to cry.

There were introductions all around, and Douglas blatantly refused to shake hands with Adam Chandler. As they all entered the house, Douglas moved next to Andrea, actually putting an arm around her waist, to her horror and embarrassment. She quickly jerked away and gave him a glaring look of hatred, but Douglas only grinned so she moved to the opposite side of the table, finding it almost impossible not to cry. Why had he done that? Adam would think they were— Of course! Douglas Means was jealous of Adam Chandler's good looks and fine build. He had immediately thought Andrea would have an eye for him. She wished she could flirt with Adam to spite Douglas, but she didn't dare. She glanced at Adam again, and he held her eyes for a moment. He knew! He knew she hated Douglas Means, had quickly discerned the situation and was trying to tell her it was all right. She felt better, but properly dropped her eyes, fearful that Douglas would watch and catch every look.

Pies baked by Rose Chandler were carried into the kitchen and there was general visiting and commotion as Morgan Sanders directed the seating, mixing the guests so they could get to know each other better. To Andrea's surprise and relief, Douglas was seated between Rose and Jonas Chandler. Young Ruth was seated to Andrea's left, and Adam to her right. She wondered if she would get through the meal without fainting, and worried she would spill something or do some other foolish thing to make Adam laugh at her. Douglas sat almost directly across from her, his gray eyes watching her like a hawk. He turned away once, and Adam gave Andrea a nudge with his elbow. She turned to meet his dark eyes, and he gave her a quick smile. He wanted to tell her how pretty she looked, to tell her she'd been in his thoughts night and day since he'd met her at the big oak tree. He still longed to kiss her, touch her. But he couldn't tell her anything—not here, not now.

Andrea quickly looked away, turning to Ruth, who looked nervous and bashful. She spoke up. "I'm fourteen. Father says you are thirteen. Do you go to school?"

The girl nodded. "I might go to Brainard Mission this fall. I want to be a teacher."

"Really? I would like to come and see your house someday, and visit your school and see your town. Do you think I could?"

The girl met her eyes, looking a little relieved. "I would like that, Andrea, is it?"

Andrea nodded. "Most people call me Andy. I have a china doll. I'll show it to you after we eat."

Ruth smiled. "I have a big doll collection in my room. You can come and see it."

Andrea smiled. "That would be fun." In her mind she was thinking mostly of getting to see Adam. Mary Means, who sat on the other side of Ruth, leaned forward to look at Andrea.

"We could both go," she declared, her jealousy showing.

Andrea's heart fell. She didn't want to hurt Mary, yet with her along, how could she get away with talking to Adam? "Sure, Mary. We could both go," she answered, but her eyes showed her disappointment, and Mary scowled, interpreting the look as meaning that Andrea would rather be friends with Ruth Chandler than with her. To Andrea, everything was going wrong, but she was reassured when her mother brought out the food, setting the turkey in front of her father to be carved. The Chandlers were all graciousness and proper manners, and Andrea was secretly proud, especially of Adam, who seemed entirely at ease and far outshined Douglas Means.

General visiting prevailed around the table as they ate, and Douglas Means watched Adam carefully as he answered questions about his education, jealous that Adam, at sixteen, far excelled him in learning and refinement, though Douglas was eighteen. Adam was obviously brilliant, and it was rumored that many Cherokee were exceedingly gifted in the field of learning.

"Many of our young women are now teachers themselves," Jonas Chandler was explaining. "And one of our young men has recently finishing translating the New

Testament from Greek into Cherokee. You know, of course, that a few years ago another one of our people, Sequoyah, developed written symbols for the Cherokee language, and now most of our people speak, read, and write in both Cherokee and English."

"It's quite remarkable how far you have come in such a few years," Harriet Sanders spoke up. "Morgan tells me what a fine home and farm you have, and you even own slaves."

Jonas nodded. "We are making every effort, Mrs. Sanders, to cooperate with our neighbors, to live as you live and be just as educated and advanced, so that we can stay in our beloved land. If we cause our neighbors no trouble, and become educated and civilized, there will be no reason for your government to bring us harm or make us leave this land."

Harriet smiled, but there was an odd silence around the table.

"Come on now," Douglas put in. "Don't you still get an urge to do some raiding again, to hunt, maybe take a few scalps—especially your young men?"

"Douglas!" the boy's father snapped. "That was unnecessary."

Douglas was glaring at Adam, who held his eyes steadily, showing no shock or anger.

Adam smiled. "Do you get urges like that?" he answered.

Douglas reddened. "And just how educated are you, Cherokee boy?"

Adam straightened. "I have been to a school of higher learning already, in Connecticut."

Douglas snickered. "The one they're closing because all the white girls fell in love with the Cherokee boys?"

"That will be enough, Douglas!" Wilson Means snapped. "We are guests in this house, as are the Chandlers, and we're here to get along! That remark was uncalled for."

Douglas looked from Adam to Andrea. Her face was red and she looked about ready to cry. He glared at her a moment. Then he sighed deeply, and glanced at his father. "I'm sorry, Father." He looked back at Adam. "But I'll bet the Cherokee boy doesn't know any more than I do. Indians can't be all that smart."

Adam set aside a fork. "Do you speak French?" he asked calmly.

Douglas glared at him. "Of course not. I suppose you do?"

Adam turned and looked at Morgan Sanders. *"Je vous remercie de votre hospitalité. Je vous suis très reconnaissant."* He looked back at Douglas, whose mouth hung open. "I thanked Mr. Sanders for his hospitality and told him I am very grateful. Wouldn't you like to thank him in another language, or do you only speak English?"

Douglas folded his napkin and set it beside his plate, shoved back his chair. "Excuse me," he grumbled. He rose and walked out the door. Inside herself, Andrea was clapping her hands, wishing she could laugh out loud. The table was silent until Jonas Chandler finally turned to Andrea's father.

"I am sorry. My son had no right to boast that way. It is not like him. Perhaps we should go."

"No," Sanders replied. "You are our guests. Douglas goaded him into it." He looked at Wilson Means. "Wilson, I didn't invite these people here to be insulted, nor did I invite you for the same reason. I'd like you to stay the afternoon. I think we should all get to know each other better."

Wilson nodded. "I agree. I apologize for my son, Mr. Chandler," he added, looking at Adam's father. "He's at an age where he gets a bit obstinate—itching to be his own man, you understand—though I must admit that some of us feel a bit threatened by Indians making such fast progress. Perhaps if your people didn't talk so much about their own government and having a separate state, people like us wouldn't be so worried."

Jonas Chandler glanced at his wife, then at Adam, who looked angry. "I fail to understand why this should worry any of you," he answered. "We keep to ourselves, bother no one, make good use of the land. We have been here for many hundreds of years, were here long before any white man set foot here. Why shouldn't we have our own state?"

Wilson Means scowled. "I . . . I don't know. It just doesn't seem right. Why can't you just leave things like they are? You own the land. We live next to each other and get along fine. Why form a separate government and state? Just be a part of Georgia."

Jonas Chandler smiled sadly, while Adam stared at his water glass, looking ready to burst. "We would like nothing better, Mr. Means. But I am afraid your people would find a way to move in on our land and take it from us if we were simply a part of Georgia. We would have no protection, for the Indian seldom has any rights under white man's laws, nor any power in his government. Our only protection is to have our own state, our own government, a place that we can truly call our own, one that others cannot invade."

"That's an impossible dream," Andrea's father stated, and her heart tightened at the remark. "Our people are destined to own this whole country, pompous as that might sound, Mr. Chandler. One only has to look at what has happened since our forefathers first came here. Some Eastern tribes don't even exist anymore."

Rose Chandler remained politely quiet, and her husband kept his composure. "That is true," he answered. "But they fought back, refused to cooperate, refused to change their ways. The Cherokee on the other hand have cooperated in every way, have worked diligently at improving their lot, learned white man's farming. We have schools; we are Christianized. We live in fine homes and some of us are very wealthy. What possible reason could there now be to exile our people or to exterminate them? What possible motive could the white man have for wanting to do such a thing to the Cherokee?"

The table was quiet again. Everyone knew the answer. Douglas had just displayed it—jealousy, combined with a yearning to own the valuable land where the Cherokee now resided.

"Let us not discuss such heavy matters today. We are newly acquainted," Jonas Chandler continued. "I have brought you something, Mr. Sanders—a gift for your hospitality. May I be excused?"

Sanders sighed deeply, and everyone at the table seemed to relax a little. "Certainly," Morgan replied.

Jonas rose, meeting his son's eyes warningly, and Adam knew he had angered his father. But he couldn't have helped showing off in front of the bragging Douglas Means, nor did he like the idea of the young man having eyes for Andrea. He wished he could look at her, talk to her!

Jonas returned shortly with a burlap bag bulging with lumpy forms. He handed it to Morgan Sanders. "Here is something you can keep for many months and enjoy at any time of day."

Morgan frowned and opened the bag, pulling out a handful of brown, rounded pods. "What are they?"

"Peanuts," Jonas replied. "We are learning to grow them, and they grow very well in our soil. Once they are harvested, they are roasted. Then you crack open the shell and eat the hardened pea. They are very good."

Morgan cracked one and tasted it, then grinned. "By golly, they are good!" He passed a handful around, and everyone tasted them, smiling and commenting about how good they were. The attitude was more relaxed again, and Morgan Sanders rose, suggesting that the men go into the parlor and have a smoke while the women cleared the table and laid out new dishes for pie. Soon everyone was bustling. Ruth and Mary both helped Andrea and the other women clear up. But Andrea noticed that Adam walked outside, and she wondered where Douglas was.

Everything was commotion then, the men smoking and discussing peanuts and how to grow them, the women scraping plates and scrubbing dishes. Andrea dumped all the leftovers into one pan and carried them outside to a hole dug for garbage. She heard voices when she neared a shed near the house, and she froze in place. Adam and Douglas were arguing on the other side of the shed.

"Why don't you just go home, white boy!" Adam was saying.

"And leave you to make eyes at Andrea and my sister? I saw you look at Andrea. You Cherokee boys like nothing better than getting under white girls' skirts!"

"I think you're the one with that on your mind most of the time," Adam retorted. "I know your kind, Douglas Means. The Indians have a word for it. Why don't you get on your fine horse and ride home, white boy!"

"Make me, Cherokee!"

"You wouldn't want me to embarrass you like that in front of everybody, would you?"

"How could you embarrass me? I'm older than you are."

"And I'm stronger. You want me to prove it?"

There was a moment of silence, then a scuffling sound, and a grunt. Andrea set down the pan of garbage and peeked around the corner to see Douglas face down on the ground, one arm bent up behind his back, Adam sitting on him. She ducked back, smiling but not wanting them to see her.

"If it were the old days, I would be splitting open your back with a knife right now, white boy! But we are civilized now, remember?" There was another grunt. "Now get out of here, or I'll pick on you in front of everyone, and Andrea Sanders will see what a weak, pitiful thing you are! It's her you're thinking of, isn't it? Don't worry, white trash. You don't need me to keep you from getting her or any other girl. Just be your own, ugly, obnoxious self. That will chase them away every time!"

Andrea could actually hear Douglas weeping then. "Let me up!" he choked out. "You're breaking my arm!"

"And wouldn't I love to truly do so!"

She heard more scuffling, and the sound of someone brushing off clothes. "I'll get you some way, someday, Cherokee!" Douglas blubbered through tears. "Having you and your family wasn't my idea, and my pa wasn't crazy about it either. Someday our people will have your land, Indian, and you'll either be dead or on your way to Indian Territory, where you'll burn up in the desert!"

He walked off, and Andrea peeked around the shed to see Adam brushing himself off. "Are you all right?" she asked.

He looked up at her in surprise. "You heard?"

She nodded and hurried around the corner so they could not be seen. "I'm glad you hurt him. I don't like Douglas. He bothers me all the time. I'm afraid of him."

Adam scowled. "You let me know if he ever hurts you. I'll make him regret it!"

Her heart swelled with a feeling of importance, and something else, a strange, new feeling she didn't yet recognize as love. "You will?"

"Sure I will. It's ones like him who should be exiled, not my people. I saw how he moved beside you. Has he ever touched you? Kissed you?"

Their eyes held. "No," she answered quietly. "I try to stay away from him. But it's hard because his sister and I are very good friends." She could not remove her eyes from his. "Why do you care, Adam?"

He stepped closer. "I . . . I'm not sure. Sometimes I think about you, Andy, ever since I saw you at the oak tree. I think things that are wrong for a Cherokee boy to think about. And I . . . I've wondered . . . if you thought any more about me. I went back every day, waited for you to come. I guess you didn't want to."

Her whole body felt on fire. "Oh, but I did. I was afraid you'd . . . you'd think I was like . . . those other girls."

He shook his head, studying her lovingly. "I wouldn't think that. I want to talk more. Come and see my sister, Andy. I could see you that way. And maybe when you come we could go to the oak tree together. My sister wouldn't say anything."

She put a hand to her aching stomach and nodded. "I will. I'll come soon. If my parents think I'm coming to see Ruth, they'll let me."

He studied the blond hair and blue eyes, his young man's urges and curiosity burning painfully at his insides. "Did you think about me, too, Andy?"

She nodded. "I knew I shouldn't, but I couldn't help it."

"I'll make sure nothing ever happens to you, Andy. Nobody like that Douglas will ever touch you. I . . . I can't stand the thought of another boy . . ." He bent closer and she did not resist when his lips met hers lightly. It was a wonderful kiss, sweet and warm and respectful. A fire ripped through her limbs, waves of wonderful passion and new desires overwhelming her. Why would her mother or any other woman not enjoy this? And as for Adam, his body ached with fierce urges, and he was consumed by manly feelings of protectiveness and desire and possessiveness. He suddenly felt ten feet tall, and in her eyes he was. She thought him instantly the most intelligent, biggest, strongest, bravest most beautiful young man who had ever walked the face of the earth. To him she was the prettiest, sweetest, most understanding girl he'd ever known, but she was just staring at him now. Had he offended her?

"Don't be mad, Andy," he said quietly. "I promise if you don't want me to do that again, I won't. You'll still come, won't you?"

She put her fingers to her lips. "I . . . I've never been . . . kissed. . . ." She turned and ran then, wanting desperately to stay, wanting to throw her arms around him and let him kiss her again, yet shivering at the thought of even looking at him again. She would surely die of embarrassment, for she'd blatantly let his lips actually touch her own. She didn't bother with the pan of garbage. She hurried into the house, telling her mother she felt sick. She hurried to her room and closed the door, throwing herself down on the bed. Being kissed by Adam Chandler was the most wonderful and yet the worst thing that had ever happened to her—wonderful because it was so beautiful and she'd wanted him to kiss her, terrible because he was Cherokee and to have feelings for a Cherokee could only bring both of them disaster. She shouldn't go to his house, should never see him again. Yet she knew she would, just as surely as she breathed.

Her mother came into the room then. "Andrea! Is it something you ate?"

"I . . . I don't know, Mother. Tell Mary and Ruth not to

come up. I'll be all right. Just let me lie here a while."

Harriet Sanders smoothed back Andrea's hair. "Are you sure? We're having pie."

"I don't want any. I just don't feel good. I think it's the heat."

The woman sighed. "All right. I'll be up to check on you in a while."

After her mother left, Andrea longed to be able to talk to her, to anyone. But there was no one. Never had she felt so alone. Wonderful, aching urges surged through her at the memory of Adam's kiss, and she closed her eyes and whispered his name.

Soon she heard people downstairs saying their good-byes, and she heard Ruth Chandler tell her mother that she hoped Andrea would be all right. Then the voices were outside. Andrea got up and went to her window, looked down at the people below. Douglas had already left. The Meanses climbed into their buggy and were off. Then Adam exited the house, apparently having gone back inside, hoping to see her again. She wanted to call out to him but dared not. He looked up before he got into the surrey and saw her standing at the window. Their eyes held.

Oh, how she wanted to go to him, to kiss him again! He looked worried as if he felt he had offended her and she had run away in anger. But when she waved to him from the window, he flashed that lovely smile. He climbed into the surrey then, wishing he had ridden his own horse so he could show her what a fine rider he was. He wanted to show her everything now, all his skills—be a man for her. He wanted to lie under the oak tree with her and kiss her in its shade, touch her breasts. He already wanted to be with her again, so badly that he wasn't sure how he'd bear being away from her. Wrong as he knew his feelings were, he didn't care. What were wisdom and caution and proper-ness to a boy and girl of such youth and passion? They meant nothing. At sixteen a man could conquer the world, and woe to anyone who tried to stop him.

CHAPTER THREE

There was a sweetness in the air, the warmth of summer, the smell of growing things. Birds sang and bees buzzed as Andrea guided her pony along the climbing, winding road that led to the other side of the ridge, a farmhand riding with her for safety. When the letter had come from Ruth, asking her to visit for a weekend, Andrea had feared her parents would refuse. But they had agreed, wanting to make up for the insult Douglas Means had dealt the Chandlers at the Sunday dinner now almost two weeks past.

Andrea's agony over those two weeks had been difficult to hide. Again she had not gone to the ridge, still afraid Adam would get the wrong idea of her, and afraid Douglas would see her, for he seemed to see everything. Now she had an excuse to see Adam again openly. Her heart pounded with anticipation. Was he just teasing her that day behind the shed? Was he laughing at her? Surely not. His eyes were so sincere, the kiss so sweet. She would soon see him, even though she was supposed to be going to visit with Ruth. Somehow they would find a way to be alone together, and maybe he would kiss her again, and then she would know. It would be an exciting weekend indeed, for in the letter Ruth had said there would be a barn dance and that Andrea should bring a dress for it.

It was exciting and even a little frightening to be riding into Cherokee country, to actually be staying at the home of Cherokee Indians. Surely nothing quite so exciting would have happened to her if they had not moved from the south. She was glad now, even though she'd left friends behind.

They approached the fine brick home of the Chandlers, and Andrea suddenly felt out of place. She hoped she wouldn't do anything that might offend Cherokee ways. She looked around at the neat farm, and the well-kept home, with roses and daisies and all kinds of flowers blooming around the porch. Ruth Chandler got up from a porch swing and hurried down the steps, smiling.

"I'm glad you could come, Andrea!" she said excitedly. "I'm also glad you're feeling better. It's too bad you got sick the day we visited. We didn't get to talk."

Andrea looked around, half hoping Adam would come to greet her but afraid to ask about him. Her father's farmhand took down her carpetbag and helped her down, and a black man was walking toward them.

"Take Andrea's pony, John, and tend to her, will you?" Ruth handed the pony's reins to the black man, and Andrea stared. This must be one of the slaves. The man nodded and took the horse, and Ruth turned to the farmhand. "Would you like something to drink, sir, before you return?"

The man looked uncomfortable and glanced at Andrea. "You sure it's okay to leave you here, Miss Sanders?"

"Of course it's all right, Hank."

The man sighed. "Don't know what this world's coming to," he mumbled. He remounted his own horse and looked at Ruth. "No, thanks, ma'am. I'll be going back. I'll come for her Sunday afternoon."

"Fine. Thank you for bringing her, and please thank Mr. Sanders for letting her come and be away from her chores."

"Sure." Hank scowled and shook his head, rode off.

Ruth put a hand out to Andrea. "Come inside. It's cooler."

Andrea picked up her carpetbag and followed the girl inside. Ruth was very pretty, her skin a smooth, unblemished brown, her dark hair hanging to her waist in pretty, rippling waves. Mrs. Chandler greeted them with a warm smile.

"Welcome, Andrea. I hope you'll enjoy being here."

"I'm sure I will, ma'am."

"Ruth will take you up to her room. She wants to show you her doll collection. Come down in a few minutes and have some cookies."

"Thank you, ma'am."

Ruth tugged at her and Andrea followed the girl through a cool hallway decorated with polished tables and fancy vases, its floor covered with a brilliantly colored woven rug. The house smelled clean, and was elegant. They climbed polished mahogany stairs carpeted with a soft, velvety red rug. Ruth excitedly showed Andrea her parents' huge master bedroom, a large, fourposter bed taking up a good share of it.

"Do both your parents sleep in here?" she asked.

"Of course they do! They're husband and wife, aren't they?" Ruth giggled and pulled her on to another room, simply decorated, with many Indian artifacts hanging on the walls. "This is my brother's room. He keeps things from our ancestors and studies Cherokee history. He's always saying he wishes he could be a warrior like our ancestors. I think that's dumb, but he gets mad at me when I tell him so." She tugged at Andrea again, but Andrea just stared.

The room was clean and neat, and all sorts of Indian weapons and religious objects decorated it. She tried to envision Adam here, felt the strange urgings again when she pictured him lying alone in his bed, perhaps thinking about her. She felt a sudden possessiveness. She didn't want Adam Chandler to belong to this room, this family, these people. She wanted him to belong to her, but that might never happen.

"Where is your brother now?"

"Adam? Who cares!" Ruth waved her off. "Actually he's out helping my father brand calves. He won't be in till evening. Come on. I'll show you my dolls."

45

Andrea followed reluctantly. She wanted to just sit in Adam's room and wait for him. But he was not supposed to be the reason she had come, and the Chandlers must not suspect that he was. She followed Ruth, wondering if Mary Means was still mad at her. The girl had been furious when Andrea had gotten an invitation and she hadn't, and she was consumed with jealousy because Andrea had a new friend. She said spiteful things about Indians and warned Andrea not to get too close to "that dirty little girl."

They went into a colorful, brightly decorated room, where a row of dolls lined a long, built-in chest under the windows. Andrea gasped with delight. The little girl, still strong in her, was infatuated by the collection, and she began to study each doll, most of them china.

"Father travels a lot, working for the Indian cause, taking Adam to schools in the North, things like that. He always brings me back a doll," Ruth was telling her. "You can play with any of them you want. Do you want to take one downstairs with you?"

"Oh, yes, I . . ." Andrea hesitated. What if Adam came in? He could not see her sitting with a doll in her hands! He would laugh at her and think her a child, never want to kiss her again. She would die of embarrassment if he saw her with one. "No, I don't think so," she said then. "I might break it. I'll just look at them when we're in your room."

"But it's okay—really."

"I don't think so, Ruth. I'll look at them more tonight." She turned to the girl. "What should we do, after we eat cookies?"

Ruth shrugged. "I thought we could go riding and watch them brand the calves for a while, then maybe go swimming at the stream. We have a special place where we swim, about a mile from here. Tomorrow father is taking us to New Echota, and tomorrow night there will be a dance there."

"Will Adam go to the dance?"

"Sure he will." The girl picked up a doll and began to

make it dance around on the bed. "I heard him and another boy talking about some white girls who might be there, the kind boys say bad things about. They were trying to think of a way to sneak off with them. I told Adam I heard, and I told him if he was mean to me, I'd tell on him."

Andrea's heart took a plunge and her stomach tightened. White girls? There was only one kind of girl they could be. Somehow the thought of Adam visiting a hayloft with one of those girls made her want to cry, and it made her angry, too. How could he think about such things, after kissing her? She almost wished she could be like them, yet knew Adam would not respect her if she was. She vowed not to let Adam out of her sight tomorrow night, and it was all she could do at the moment to keep from crying at the thought of his even talking about those other white girls.

"Let's go have some cookies," Ruth was saying.

Andrea followed her downstairs into a large, bright kitchen, where Mrs. Chandler, still baking, was ordering a heavyset black woman around. Andrea and Ruth stuffed themselves on fresh cookies and milk, then went out to the barn, where a black man readied two gentle horses for them. Andrea's pony would be left behind to rest. Andrea rode out of the barn behind Ruth, and followed the girl for nearly two miles to the camp of several men who were roping and branding cattle.

Even from a distance Andrea spotted Adam riding down a calf. He didn't see her right away, and she watched, a fluttering, burning excitement in her chest, as he roped the calf, then dismounted and quickly tied its feet together. "Got another one for you!" he called out. "She kept running off."

Some men headed toward the calf with a branding iron, and Adam helped hold the animal until the branding was over. Then he untied the rope, let it go. When he turned, he spotted Andrea. Their eyes held fast, and she slowly reddened for he wore no shirt and his dark skin glowed in the hot sun. His shoulders were broad and powerful, hard muscle showing everywhere. He looked every bit a man, at least to Andrea Sanders, even though he did not have the true fullness yet of a grown man. Without a shirt, he was even more beautiful, and she was filled with an aching curiosity about how a man looked wearing nothing at all. Did he look like the cows and the horses?

He smiled and waved to her, and she waved back. "Where are you going?" he called to Ruth.

"Swimming," she answered. "We'll see you at supper tonight. And don't come swimming. I don't want you bothering us."

Andrea wanted to argue with that, but she didn't dare. The usual bickering that went on between brothers and sisters was going to keep her from seeing Adam as often as she would like, but being at the Chandlers was better than nothing at all.

"Don't worry. I won't bother you, baby sister," he called back. He glanced at Andrea again, glad she could see him shirtless and branding cattle. It made him feel more manly. He was anxious for the dance, for his father had given him permission to escort Andrea, even though Ruth would have to come along—but only because Andrea was an honored guest. He had strict orders not to look at her in any other way. But Adam could not help but to look at her in other ways, and he would be proud to take her to the dance.

The girls rode off, and Adam turned back to riding down more strays. In spite of his feelings for Andrea, he was contemplating finding a way to get one of the wild white girls alone later the next night. There were things he had to learn about girls so he would know how to treat Andrea. Maybe if he could share a hayloft with another girl, he could get rid of these terrible needs Andrea had awakened in him and, therefore, not do something insulting and wrong with Andrea, something that might scare her and make her hate him. Emotions and desires were plaguing him lately, ever since he'd kissed Andrea behind the shed. Till then he'd been only mildly interested in girls, more interested in helping his father and getting his education so he could help the Cherokee cause. Suddenly he was aware of his masculinity, aware of a woman's soft curves, curious about his father and mother. He felt a surge of power and pleasant urges when the Cherokee girls looked at him admiringly, and it was a Cherokee girl his father kept telling him he must be interested in, not others. But he could not get Andrea off his mind—her freckles and blue eyes and white blond hair; her pretty smile that seemed part girl's and part woman's; her slender form just awakening to womanhood . . . and the warm, good feeling he had when he was around her. All of it was more than a sixteen-year-old boy should be thinking about, but he'd always been mature for his age, and he did not consider himself a boy any longer. He was a man. He was nearly as strong as one and he was taller than his own father. He could do a man's work and he had a nearly complete education. Already Elias Boudinot talked of letting him help publish the newspaper he planned to print for the Cherokee people.

He wrestled down another calf. Andrea was here and he was happy. After this weekend he would know her better. Maybe he'd even mate with one of those wild girls and know all there was to know, and someday soon he would meet Andrea again on the ridge, under the oak tree, taste her mouth again and make her whisper his name.

Andrea stood nervously among the huge crowd of Cherokees, many of whom spoke to each other in their own tongue. She was introduced to nearly everyone by Adam, who led her around like a proud peacock, and those she met smiled warmly at her. She felt no animosity, and was not the only white there. Several white missionaries mingled with the others, all very gracious, and the white girl from New England, whose marriage to Elias Boudinot had closed Cornwall, was also present, a pretty and obviously a happy and contented woman. Andrea could not help but watch her, wanting to prove to herself that it was certainly possible for a white girl to marry a Cherokee man and live happily among them.

She knew it was foolish to think of marriage at fourteen, yet what young girl did not think of such things? It would not be that many years before she was a wife and a mother, perhaps at sixteen. But it was possible that Adam Chandler had no such thoughts at the moment, and even when she thought of marrying, it was as if she were contemplating some distant fairy tale. Just being here with Adam at the dance was enough for now. She had seen very little of him after riding off the day before to go swimming. He had come home late, after she and Ruth were already in bed. She had heard him go to his room, and now recalled with guilt how she'd wondered if he was undressing, if he slept naked. The next morning he was gone again, early, for more chores. Had he gone to the oak tree first? She hadn't seen him all day, and just before the dance he had attended a meeting with his father.

"The Cherokees are working on a constitution," Ruth had told her. "Father says Adam is old enough to go to the meetings, and smart enough to help write it."

That made Adam seem even more of a man to Andrea. His intelligence and his importance to the Cherokee, despite his youth, were admirable. But she'd been disappointed that she had hardly seen him since coming to visit, until shortly before they were all to leave for the dance, when he had taken her arm and led her into the parlor. He looked wonderful in a dark gray suit and starched cravat, every bit the picture of a wealthy Englishman, but more handsome with his dark Cherokee looks.

"May I escort you tonight?" he had asked, "as my personal date? My father said it was all right, except that I must remember you are just a guest. I am not supposed to be interested in you." He winked then. "He doesn't know I already am."

She had felt faint at the words, and his manliness and maturity had made her feel like a small child. That first time she'd met him, she hadn't cared what he'd thought or how she'd acted. Now, to be around him made her nervous and weak. Why? Why was it suddenly so important that she look perfect, that she not do anything to make him laugh at her? Of course she had agreed to let him escort her, and she felt like a princess as he introduced her to the others, and when they danced together. He danced beautifully, skillfully guiding her own awkward steps.

And never had Adam Chandler felt more manly than this night. He'd been to his first meeting regarding the constitution, and had been afforded great respect for his thoughts and input. Now the girl who had been haunting him was in his arms, and she was the prettiest girl at the dance, as far as he was concerned. As they danced he had a chance to talk to her more privately, his first opportunity since she'd arrived.

"Do you like it here?"

"I love it here," she answered. "Everyone has been very kind. I thought some people might not like my being here."

"Lots of whites come here, especially the missionaries. What did you think of New Echota when my father took you there today?"

She shrugged. "It's just like our own towns. It's very nice."

"We had a meeting there. I wanted to ride in the wagon with you and Ruth and Father, but Father had shopping to do first and I had chores to do, so I rode in later. I regret that I've not been able to see much of you since you've been here. Did you and Ruth have a good time shopping while Father and I were at the meeting?"

"Yes. But I mostly looked. My father didn't give me money to spend. Ruth bought me a hair ribbon. That was very nice of her."

He smiled. They were suddenly both nervous, making small talk, avoiding the urgent passions they had begun to feel for one another.

"The meeting I attended was to help write a Cherokee constitution," he told her. "They wanted my help."

She smiled softly. "Ruth told me. You must be very proud that they asked you."

He shrugged then, looking a little bashful. "I guess I would have to say I was." Their eyes held and his smile faded. "You are not angry with me then, for that day behind the shed?"

She reddened a little, warm waves of desire rippling through her at the memory of his lips on her own. "No."

He moved his arm a little farther around her, wanting to draw her close against him. But that was improper. If only they were alone, he knew she would let him hold her tighter. "And if I kissed you again, you would let me? You would not be angry?"

She dropped her eyes, swallowing. The whining fiddle music stopped and he had to let go of her. Then a peppier tune was played, and a man began calling steps to a square dance. As several couples hollered out and then formed a circle, Adam took Andrea's hand and led her toward a quieter corner of the huge barn where the dance was being held, on the property of one of the wealthiest Cherokees. He squeezed her hand and she looked up at him.

"Come to visit my sister often, Andrea. The next time I will make sure I am not so busy. We'll find a way to be together. I want to talk to you more. I want . . ." He swallowed. "Saturday. Next Saturday. Will you come to the oak tree late in the day, like around four o'clock? You could tell your parents you are just going for a ride again."

Her chest tightened so that she was sure each breath would be her last. She knew what he would do. He would kiss her again, perhaps even hold her in his strong arms. Surely she would die if he did, but it would be a pleasant way to die. "I'll come," she answered.

He smiled the beautiful smile. "Good. It will be a long week for me."

"For me, too."

He squeezed her hand again. "Would you like something to drink?"

She nodded. Her mouth was dry and she felt warm. "Please."

"Wait right here." He left her and headed for the refreshment table. He was wonderful. He had told her he felt better calling her Andrea, because Andy sounded too childish for a girl turning into such a pretty woman. She breathed deeply at the thought of that remark. At least he saw her as a mature young lady and not a child. She wished she would begin to round out into a woman, but she was still skinny as a stick and so flat chested that she needed no undergarment over her breasts. But if Adam didn't care about such things, she wouldn't worry about it.

She heard a screech and some laughter then, and looked toward the barn entrance. Four white girls had just come in. Surrounded by several Cherokee boys, they were giggling and flirting. Their hair, hanging long, was tangled, and they didn't look very clean. Andrea noticed that some of the older people scowled as they watched the girls and then began to talk among themselves. The girls quickly joined the square dancers, each having picked out a boy, and they deliberately whirled their skirts high, revealing bare legs. They were barefoot, and had generous bosoms.

Andrea's eyes shifted to Adam, who had turned to watch the girls for a moment. One eyed him as she circled by, and turned her head to keep looking at him as the dance led her away from him again. When she whispered something to the boy with her, he turned and looked back at Adam, then said something in reply. Andrea, filled with a most painful jealousy, was relieved when Adam finally turned away, picked up two glasses of punch, and brought them over to her. "Drink up so we can dance again," he told her.

She took a sip. "Who are those girls?" she asked.

He grinned. "They are from the other side. Some of the ones I told you about."

The jealousy burned at her stomach. "Do they . . . is each one with . . . with a special boy tonight?"

Adam laughed lightly. "That kind is never with one special boy. I have heard each girl sometimes walks off with two or three boys. I have friends who have been with them. They tell some pretty good stories."

A lump formed in Andrea's throat and she kept trying to swallow it back. "You wouldn't go off with one of those wild, dirty things, would you, Adam?"

When he didn't reply she looked up at him. He was watching the girls, then he looked down at her. "No," he lied, knowing she'd get angry and walk away if he said anything else. But his blood was hot and his curiosity too strong and urgent now for him to promise he'd never go off with one of the easy girls, in spite of how he felt about Andrea. She was special, innocent. Maybe someday he'd mate with her. How could he do that if he didn't know anything? Maybe he'd hurt her in some way and make a mess of things. "Drink your punch," he told her. "I want to dance again."

She hurriedly drank it down, wanting to dance herself, and show those wild girls that Adam Chandler belonged to her. She was his honored chosen one, and she was much nicer and prettier than any of those pigs who whirled their skirts and danced around on bare feet.

They rejoined the dancing as the fiddlers changed from square-dancing music to a slower tune. Andrea caught Adam watching that same girl again, as she danced flagrantly close to the boy who held her, whispering things in his ear and making him laugh nervously. Once Andrea even saw the girl move her hand over the boy's hips, then throw her head back and laugh. Andrea looked up at Adam, who had also seen. He moved his eyes back to meet hers, and she suddenly felt like crying. He was going to do something. She sensed it with every bone in her little body; yet she had no right to order him not to touch some other girl, nor did she have the right or the maturity or the brazenness to flaunt herself before him and to offer herself in their place. It would be wrong, and she wouldn't even know where to begin. She suddenly felt helpless and stupid and desperate. But then he squeezed her hand and she felt better.

"You do want me to meet you at the oak tree, don't you?" she asked, feeling like a silly child.

"Of course I do."

"You do like me, don't you, Adam? I like you so very much." She reddened then. Why had she said it? She was acting like a fool. But his eyes warmed and he smiled.

"You know I like you." He swallowed. "Maybe I like you too much for your own good. You're a nice girl, and you're hardly any older than my sister."

"Oh, but I am older! I'll be fifteen in October." She swallowed. "Don't let anything stop you from meeting me at the oak tree next Saturday."

He laughed lightly. "Now you're being silly. I asked you, remember? Why would I ask you and then not be there?"

She reddened more. Adam's father came up to him then, putting a hand on the boy's shoulder. "Are you being a gentleman to our guest, Adam?" he asked as the music stopped.

"Of course I am, Father," Adam answered with a smile.

Jonas Chandler looked warmly at Andrea. "Are you enjoying yourself, Miss Sanders?"

Andrea was grateful for the sudden interruption. "Yes, sir. Everyone has been very nice. I'd like to come back. And you must have Ruth come and stay the night with me sometime, although we don't live in quite so grand a fashion."

"Nonsense. You have a lovely home. Ruth would be glad to come." Jonas frowned and put his arm around Ruth, who had come to stand beside them. "It is very important that we show you people how we live, Miss Sanders, that you understand we are no different. The Georgia government, as you know, is trying to get us removed and sent to a barren land. Do you see any reason why we should be forced out of Georgia?"

Andrea looked up at Adam, then to his father. Seeing anger and worry in their eyes, she replied, "No, sir. They can't really make you go, can they?"

Jonas sighed deeply. "One would not think so, but when it comes to the leaders of Georgia, anything can happen." He looked at his son. "The men are meeting outside for a few minutes, Adam. Come with me."

"What is wrong, Father?"

"Just come with me. We will talk outside."

Adam looked at Andrea. "Stay with Ruth. Have some more punch if you wish. I'll be right back."

He followed his father outside, along with several other men. Andrea met Ruth's eyes. "What's wrong?"

Ruth shrugged. "Who knows? Those men are always having meetings. I heard talk that things look bad for the Creeks. The Georgia Militia might come in and force them all out of their homes. But we have been smarter than the Creeks. Father says we have to stay one step ahead of the government all the time, so they don't have any legal way of making us leave Georgia."

It seemed incredible to Andrea that Adam might have to leave his beautiful home and farm. How could the Georgia Militia just come in and order people to leave their homeland? A chill went through her. Whatever happened, Adam would be involved. He was eager to fight for the Cherokee cause.

The crowd quieted somewhat, and three of the wild white girls left with some Cherokee boys, but the one who had been eying Adam was still there, much to Andrea's dismay. Women talked among themselves, looking worried, and after several minutes the men returned, rejoining their wives and girl friends while Elias Boudinot stood on a crate and shouted for their attention.

"I have some sad news," he told them. "But no need to be alarmed for yourselves. As in the past, we have continued to stay legally ahead of Congressman Wilson Lumpkin and his efforts to force us out of our homeland. But you should know that we've learned the Georgia Militia has begun to move in on the Creeks. Many have already been forcibly removed from their homes and farms. We're told it's a very sorry situation—injuries, sickness. Already whites are coming in to claim the Creeks' land and homes."

There were gasps and mumbles among the crowd, and Andrea hung her head, feeling suddenly out of place. "Dear God!" someone behind her whispered.

"I think we should offer prayers for our friends among the Creeks," a missionary spoke up. "How about a hymn?" The man started singing "Amazing Grace" then, and several joined in. Andrea looked up at Adam; the warmth was gone from his eyes.

"Bastards!" he muttered through gritted teeth. "They'll never make me leave my home, my mountains, my oak tree!" His eyes were teared, and Andrea wanted to hug him.

"It will be all right, Adam." She touched his arm, but he pulled away and strode outside. The wild white girl quickly followed.

Andrea's heart felt like lead. She had not seen Adam anymore that night; when his father had come to take his family home in the buggy, he had only said that Adam had told him he'd come along later. "He is sixteen," Jonas had declared when his wife had protested. "He is old enough to make up his own mind about things."

"You know where he went!" she had retorted angrily.

But Jonas had only grinned. "He only goes the way of all young Cherokee boys who have things to learn. Now be still, Rose, and do not question him in the morning."

Andrea had known then why Adam had left, and she'd hated him. She had never hated anyone so much as she hated Adam Chandler at that very moment. She'd wished she didn't have to stay another night in his house. In fact, she wished she could go home right now, and she wondered if she was going to be sick. Everything had turned out horribly, after a beautiful beginning. Everyone was angry and upset over the Creeks, afraid the same thing would happen to them. And Adam had surely gone off with that wild white girl.

The thought of him doing bad things with that girl, of the girl touching Adam, brought a horrible, aching jealousy to Andrea that made her want to scream. She wanted to be the one to touch him, and to be touched by him. She wanted to be the one to please him and take pleasure in him. Instead it would be that awful white girl who would probably do things Andrea couldn't even imagine doing. She felt stupid, ignorant, frustrated. Tonight Adam Chandler would be frolicking in the hay with that wild girl, and Andrea Sanders would be sleeping with his little sister and all her dolls! Never had she struggled so hard not to cry, and when they reached the Chandlers' home she hurried into the changing room where she could be alone and cry quietly into a towel.

Ruth was soon asleep, but Andrea lay awake, staring into the quiet blackness of the night. It seemed hours before she heard a horse coming. Quietly, she got out of bed and hurried to the window.

"Take my horse, John." The voice came from below. It was Adam's. Andrea heard footsteps come inside, a door close. She hurried to her bedroom door then and opened it a crack. She could see him in the light of the burning oil lamp in the hallway. He carried his suit jacket, and his shirt hung outside his pants, partially unbuttoned. His hair was going in all directions, and a piece of hay was still stuck in it. She could not resist letting him know that she knew, and she stepped out into the hallway.

He looked at her, startled. Then his eyes moved over her, taking in the flimsy summer nightgown she wore, and she realized she hadn't even put on a robe first. She folded her arms self-consciously, blinked back angry tears, wanting to shout at him but unable to because everyone was asleep. He came closer; then, to her surprise, he bent down and kissed her lips lightly. She could smell cheap perfume and straw.

"Will you still come next Saturday?" he whispered.

She was amazed that he'd even consider she would. "No!" she whispered in reply. "I know where you went, and I hate you, Adam Chandler!" She whirled and went back into Ruth's room, closing the door.

Adam only grinned. She'd be there, he was sure. And he was sure of something else. He loved Andrea Sanders, no matter how young and silly she was. He loved her. And someday she'd be his wife.

CHAPTER FOUR

Andrea brushed her pony, wanting nothing more than to keep busy, busier than she had ever been. It was the only way she could stand the hurt of knowing Adam had gone off with that wild girl. Sometimes she regretted telling him she hated him, but mostly she was glad, even though she knew down deep inside it wasn't true. She didn't hate Adam Chandler at all. In fact, she was beginning to wonder more and more if she loved him. Why else would she get these weak feelings when thinking about him? Why else would she dream about letting him touch her, wonder how it would feel for her own naked body to touch his. Why else would she feel this horrible fury at the thought of his being with some other girl?

She was home again. Adam had not joined his family at the breakfast table, nor gone to church with them. When they returned from church, Joe was there to take Andrea back, and she only got a glimpse of Adam when he looked up at her from a corral where he was working with a new horse. He'd waved, but she had turned her head and refused to wave back. That had been the end of it.

Now she was wishing more and more that she could have had one last chance to talk to him. Maybe all boys went to those wild girls, just to learn things. That was what his father had said. Surely it was a sign of respect for her that Adam had picked one of those girls to learn such things with, rather than to insult her. Her feelings were wildly mixed. She wanted to be touched that way, yet she didn't. She found the thought of it both fascinating and frightening. And now Adam was even more of a man. What had he learned? What would he do with her under the oak tree? She would be wise to keep her vow to him and not go next Saturday. But already she knew that by then she would be crazy with the desire to see him again, and with curiosity over whether or not he still liked her. She was so confused, and yet there was no one with whom she could talk.

She heard a carriage then, and looked out to see the Meanses coming to visit. It was late Sunday afternoon, and they almost always came then. She scowled. It would be fun to see Mary and tell her of her experiences with the Cherokees, if the girl wasn't too mad and too jealous to talk to her. But she never looked forward to seeing Douglas. He would have prying questions, now that she had been on the "other side." He would tease her about liking Cherokee boys, and she would have to deny it, even though it was partly true.

She kept brushing her pony. She had to finish that before going to the house. Maybe she wouldn't go at all. She didn't want to answer their questions, to see Douglas's prying gray eyes. She didn't want anything right now but to be alone, to think, to dream about Adam, to wonder. But after a few minutes she heard the hated voice behind her.

"Hello there, Cherokee girl," Douglas spoke up sneeringly. "Did those Indian boys teach you anything? Maybe now you know how much fun it would be to roll in a haystack with me."

She turned and scowled at him. "Shut up, Douglas Means! You make me sick!" She threw down her brush. "I'm going inside."

He grabbed her arm, painfully. "Your folks said you were out here, so I just casually stepped out the back door. Thought I'd pay you a little visit before you go in. What was it like, Andy? Did that girl's brother play around with you?"

She kicked his leg and he grunted, letting go of her. She

60

started to run, but a second later he grabbed her again, throwing her into some hay. "Come on, Andy. You can tell me. It's him you went to see, isn't it? It wasn't for Ruth."

"You're a dirty-minded—" Her words were cut off by a cold, wet kiss. She tossed her head violently to get away from his lips, but he only laughed, running a hand over her breast. "Andy, Andy. I know you want it. You just pretend you don't."

"You let me up or I'll scream so loud everybody in the house will come running!" she spit at him. "I don't care what you tell them, Douglas Means! Tell them anything you want! But you'll still look bad and be in a lot of trouble!"

His eyes turned icy and he got up. "You're a cold bitch, you know that? Someday I'll catch you at the right time, and I'll get under those skirts, Andrea Sanders." He brushed himself off. "And don't think your Cherokee boy is going to come and beat me up or something. He wouldn't dare! Indians get in a lot of trouble when they bring harm to whites, and then everybody would know you've been laying with him."

Her eyes filled with angry tears. "You rotten liar! I hate you, Douglas Means. And I'd rather die than let you touch me!"

He just grinned. "Your sweet Cherokee boy has to be more careful now, little girl. They all do. You heard what's happening to the Creeks?"

"I've heard."

"I'll bet," he sneered. "Makes no difference to me. It's about time this land was opened up to respectable white settlers. Fact is, I'm joining the Georgia Militia. I want to get in on some of the action." He smoothed back his hair. "I've heard sometimes there are opportunities to carry some of those young Creek girls behind the woodshed and spank their bare bottoms."

She felt ill at the remark. "You're sick, Douglas Means. You get sicker all the time. Go ahead and join the militia. I hope you get killed!"

He just snickered. "I expect I'll have me a good time before I do. I leave next Friday for Atlanta. Won't you miss me, Andy?"

She brushed off her dress and pulled hay from her hair. "It will be the happiest day of my life!" She whirled and walked out. How she hated him! Now she didn't blame Adam so much for the wild girl. Surely he'd done that so he wouldn't treat her roughly when they were together. He'd learned from someone else so he would be kind and patient with her. He'd never treat her the way Douglas had just treated her.

She knew she should tell her parents and Douglas's parents about what he was like, but she was afraid they wouldn't believe her. Douglas had a way of turning things around and looking innocent. They'd brand her as a bad girl, maybe even punish her. And Douglas would just laugh. He'd love to see her get in trouble over him—poor, innocent Douglas, whose tender young man's needs were tempted by naughty Andrea. She could just hear his story.

Her eyes stung from angry tears. She felt more and more alone, and more drawn to Adam, who seemed to be becoming her only real friend. She was anxious now for Saturday to come, glad Douglas was leaving on Friday. That was good. He wouldn't see her go up the ridge.

She went inside and was greeted like some kind of celebrity. Everyone wanted to know all about her experiences, except Mary. She sat in a chair, glaring at Andrea with jealous eyes. She didn't like her being the center of attention. It seemed that as Mary got older, she got more and more like her brother, and Andrea felt she was losing her best friend. She kept smiling at Mary, trying to warm the girl, but Mary would have none of it.

"What do the Cherokee have to say about the Creek?" Wilson Means asked her.

Andrea shrugged. "I think they're a little bit afraid. They had a meeting about it last night, and are having a big one this afternoon."

Her father spoke up. "They're smart people. So far they've made every right move to keep from being included in the Removal Policy. But it will catch up to them eventually."

Andrea looked at him in surprise. It was an oddly threatening statement. Were her father and Wilson Means plotting against the Cherokee after all? Was their offer of friendship only a pretense? Had she been sent to stay with Ruth just to find things out for them? Perhaps her father had only bought this land in order to be close to Cherokee land, to move in and take some of it over once the Cherokee were banished. It made her heart sad.

"Are they still working on a constitution and talking about being a separate state?" Wilson asked.

She met his eyes. They were too eager. "I . . . I don't know."

The man sighed and looked at her father. "You're going to have to send her back there at least once a month, Morgan. To me, setting up a Constitution and a separate state are nothing short of treason, and good reason to raise a public outcry against the Cherokee. I know it seems like we're grabbing at anything, but they're so damned smart, we have to look for any little thing we can use against them."

Andrea's eyes widened. "Use against them? What are you talking about?"

Her mother rose. "Never you mind, Andrea. You take Mary up to your room now and play. You'll have to help me with supper soon."

Andrea wanted to ask more questions. But her mother's instructions could never be questioned. "Come on, Mary." She turned and went up the stairs, and Mary reluctantly followed, half stomping her feet on the way to show she was mad.

"Why don't you send Mary once in a while, Wilson?" Andrea's father was asking. "I don't like using my daughter like a spy."

"Well, neither do I. I'd share the responsibility if I could get her to go. She refuses to stay in a house where Indians live. What can I do to make her go? She's a stubborn little thing. I can't force her."

"Well, for now I guess we have to keep up the visiting and trading. No sense letting on about anything. Just let things happen as they will. First the Creek, then the Cherokee. It's only a matter of time. Is Douglas still joining the militia?"

"Yes," Wilson answered proudly. "He leaves Friday for Atlanta."

"You must be very proud of him. That's a brave thing to do."

"Oh, I am proud! I'm sure he'll do fine."

Andrea closed her door, and Mary sat down on the bed, pouting. "Oh, Andrea, what was it like? Did they have meetings? Is their house pretty?" The girl asked the questions mockingly.

"Mary, I'm sorry you didn't get an invitation, too," Andrea said politely.

"I don't care! I didn't want to go stay in a dirty Indian's house anyway."

"It wasn't dirty at all. It was quite grand, Mary, all clean and polished, expensive rugs and furniture. It's a huge house, and Ruth has a great big collection of china dolls."

Mary folded her arms. "Good for her. And what about her brother? Did he try to be friends with you?"

Andrea took off her shoes. "Don't be silly. He's sixteen, almost a man. He was very polite, and I hardly saw him at all. He was working all the time, or else going to meetings."

Mary sighed. "He is good-looking. I'll admit to that. But he's Indian." She made a face.

"So what? I bet if he liked you, you'd faint dead away, Mary Means."

The girl put her chin in her hand and thought, then grinned. "Maybe."

They both started giggling then, and Andrea felt better. Mary was still her friend, at least for a while.

*　　*　　*

Andrea led her pony up the ridge again. It was Saturday! It was finally Saturday! She had never been happier. Not only was she going to see Adam, but Douglas Means had gone away. Maybe things would work out after all. Her parents would highly disapprove of what she was doing, but she didn't care. She would not let anything stop her from seeing Adam again. She'd suffer anything to be with him, to find out if he still liked her, to tell him she was sorry for what she'd said. Maybe he would have some explanation, and he would kiss her again; then she could get rid of the awful anxiety and jealousy that had plagued her since that night he went to be with that wild girl. Maybe he'd promise not to go anymore.

It was a pretty day, warm but not too hot. Everything smelled sweet, birds sang, and there was a gentle breeze. As far as her parents knew, she had just gone riding. They'd never find her on the ridge, never find the secret oak tree. From below it was impossible to spot it.

Would he be there? She'd told him she would not. Would he come anyway? If he did, it would mean he still liked her, that he was wishing she'd come so he could see her again. She climbed higher and higher, leaving the farm behind, leaving her problems behind. When she finally came out on top, she panicked for a moment. The oak tree was not there. She had taken a different direction. Should she go left or right? If she didn't get there soon, Adam might think she wasn't coming at all and go back down. She tried to get her bearings and decided to walk to the right. She walked nearly a half-mile before she saw it, but she didn't see Adam. Her heart quickened, and she tied her pony and walked to the great tree.

"Adam?" she called out.

He moved from behind a huge branch, behind which he'd been hiding like the first time. He smiled. "Here I am."

She smiled back. "I was afraid you'd already left."

He swung down. "I waited extra long, hoping you'd show up."

Their eyes held then as he walked closer. "I missed

you, Andrea."

She swallowed. "I missed you, too."

He looked ready to kiss her, but he just took her hand, leading her to the soft grass beneath the tree. "Sit down, Andrea. We'll talk."

She hesitated, still standing and looking down at him. "Why did you go off with that girl, Adam?" She could not help asking it, bold as it might be.

He sighed. He'd had a good time with that wild girl, that was sure. She'd shown him things he'd never dreamed men and women did. But he'd come away still hungry. He met Andrea's eyes.

"There were things I had to know, if I'm to be a man," he told her. "How could I learn them with somebody like you? You're the nicest girl I've ever known. I don't ever want to hurt you." He looked away, actually seeming embarrassed. "I was wishing that girl was you the whole time. And I knew then that . . . that I love you, even though we haven't known each other long."

She just stood staring at him, unable to find her voice at first. He met her eyes again and reached up. When she took his hand, he drew her down beside him. "You probably think I'm crazy, don't you?"

He slipped an arm around her shoulders, and she looked at her lap and shook her head. "No," she said quietly. "I feel the same way. But I thought, when you went with that girl . . ." She sniffed and a tear slipped down her cheek. "I thought you didn't like me anymore, and the thought of . . . of you . . . and her . . . It hurt bad. I wanted to hate you."

He rubbed her shoulder. "I never want you to hate me, Andrea." He bent over and kissed her cheek. "I'm sorry. Please don't cry."

She turned her face to his, and instantly his lips were on hers. This kiss was different. It was sweet like before, yet more searching, perhaps more experienced. He parted her lips and put a hand to the side of her face, running his tongue along her lips and making her feel limp and passionate. He finally released the kiss, and all her hatred and jealousy were instantly gone when she looked into his dark eyes.

"I love you, too, Adam," she said softly. "Can a girl my age be in love?"

He smiled. "Why not? Some girls get married at your age, sometimes younger."

Their eyes held, and she saw the worry in his. "I think we are going to have some big problems, Andrea. But if we love each other, we can always be together, can't we?"

She rested her head on his shoulder. "I hope so." She wondered if she should tell him her own father and his friend were speaking against the Indians. She was afraid to tell, afraid he wouldn't trust her then.

"Things look bad, Andrea. The stories we are getting about the Creek . . ." He sighed and let her nestle into his shoulder. "They stripped and beat the women, raided their homes and took whatever they wanted. The people were loaded into their wagons with whatever they could carry. Many things were left behind, furnishings, cattle, almost everything. Everything." The last word was choked and he squeezed her shoulders. "I feel a great darkness coming, Andrea. I pretend that I am not afraid, but I am. But I will fight. We will fight to the last man, the last law; make the last effort we can to stay here."

"Oh, Adam, I'm so sorry," she declared. "I don't know what else to say."

"There is nothing anyone can say. We can only keep fighting in Washington. We have some good men on our side, men like Daniel Webster, and some of our own fine men—Elias Boudinot, John Ross. And the North is still in our favor, so are the missionaries who live among us. What frightens me is the lust the white man has to own valuable land, as much of it as he can get. He'll use any underhanded means he can to get it. And with so many more people coming into Georgia, our land has become priceless. The white man tries every legal means to get what he wants, in order to soothe his conscience. But if that doesn't work, he just comes in and takes it anyway. That is what is happening with the Creek. They say there is some legal basis, but it all amounts to trickery and deceit." He kissed her hair. Oh, how he wanted to do more! "Speaking of trickery and deceit, have you had any more trouble with that Douglas Means?"

She swallowed and sat forward. "A little. He tried to kiss me, and he . . . touched me."

Adam clenched his fists. "I'll kill him!"

She turned to face him. "It's all right now. He's gone."

"Gone? Gone where?"

She looked down at the grass. "He's gone to join the Georgia Militia. He said a bad thing about the Creek women. I hope he gets killed."

Adam picked up a small rock and threw it angrily. "Bastard! I do not like the idea of him being with the militia, but at least he is away from you." He leaned forward and put his face in his hands. "I can hardly stand to think of it, Andrea, of what is happening. Many Creeks have already died. Old women are made to walk westward. Young women are raped. Homes and farms are left behind. Little children die of disease. They say the land where they go is very different from here—hot and dry and barren—hard to farm. Some of our people went right away, when Georgia first threatened to make us go by force. Many of them died. A few came back with terrible stories. I do not want to go there, Andrea. I do not want to leave this place. It is home. The trees are my friends, and so are the animals. I'm so scared, Andrea."

He raised his head and their eyes met, and there were tears on his cheeks. Her heart shattered into a hundred pieces and she threw her arms around him.

"Oh, Adam, don't! It will work out. I know it will! You won't have to go. And if you do, I'll go, too. I couldn't bear to stay behind and watch you go! I never want you to go away!"

His arms encircled her and he held her tightly. He kissed her cheek, moving his mouth to her lips then, kissing her with all the eager passion of a frightened, passionate young man wanting to hang on to all that was dear and familiar to him. And at the moment she never wanted to let go of him. He laid her back, his desires fired by the urgency of impending disaster, and she returned his kiss with equal fervor. He left her lips then, moving his own to her neck, breathing in the sweet scent of her.

"God, Andrea, I love you," he groaned, moving a hand carefully over one small breast, bringing a gasp to her lips.

Her body felt on fire, and she didn't know what to do with her hands, whether she should stop him, hold him. No, she didn't want to stop him from touching her this way. Never had such wonderful passions engulfed her, such pleasant urges, such utter ecstasy as to have Adam Chandler touch her breast and tell her he loved her. She ran her hands through his hair, closing his eyes and whimpering when he moved his face down and nuzzled it against her breasts. His hand went to her skirt and began to push it up, and his fingers brushed along her bare leg as he moved his lips back to her neck. Suddenly she grabbed his wrist.

"Adam, don't. I can't." He took his hand away and embraced her, kissing her hard again, understanding her fears, glad now he'd been with that wild girl. It helped him restrain himself now. But even though he'd been with her, it was poor preparation for uniting with a virgin That was an entirely different matter and something that would take time. It should be withheld for marriage, but with neither parents ready to accept such a union, it could be months before that could happen. How could he wait that long? He loved her. He wanted her. His need of her was immediate and urgent, his youthful passions difficult to control.

She let him kiss her again, her desires wildly mixed. She wanted to run, but she wanted to stay. She was afraid of being intimate, but wildly curious about it, her joy at his touch knowing no bounds. They kissed with hot passion, grasping almost awkwardly at each other, touching but afraid to go too far, petting, enjoying. She was lost in him, for to her he was all man and more, experienced, intelligent, handsome, brave, strong, everything a girl wanted in a man. She did not resist when he gently grasped her hand and moved it down to touch that part of him that made him a man. It was large and firm, reminding her of the male horses and dogs she had seen. Surely it would hurt to mate with him. She pulled her lips away from his, reddening.

"Don't, Adam."

"It's all right. I don't want you to be afraid, Andrea. Some day I'm going to make you a woman. It will be me and nobody else, understand? I don't want anybody else to touch you. You belong to me. And when I get inside you, I won't hurt you. I promise I won't hurt you. It will feel so good, Andrea, and it will be so beautiful. You'll see."

He kissed her again, content for the moment just to press against her, to fondle a small breast through her dress, to touch and rub and kiss. A little at a time. That's how he had to handle Andrea. A little at a time, or she'd run away and maybe hate him. For several minutes they were lost in one another, fondling, touching, their breathing coming in quick, hot gasps until suddenly he pulled away from her and sat up.

"I . . . I'll be right back," he said, his voice husky. He hurried away.

"Adam, where are you going?" she called out to him.

"Never mind. Just wait there for me." He disappeared behind some shrubbery. Minutes later he returned, his shirt retucked, his hair smoothed back with his hands. He came and sat down beside her, leaning against the tree trunk and reaching out for her. She moved beside him, resting her head on his shoulder, her face still flushed.

"Why did you go off?"

"I just . . . I didn't want to make you do something you aren't ready for. I had to . . . get away from you for a minute, that's all."

Her eyes teared. "Do you think I'm bad, Adam?"

He sighed. "Hell, no. If I thought you were bad I wouldn't have gone behind the bushes. I'd have . . . Never mind. I told you I love you, didn't I?"

She wrapped an arm around his middle. "I don't want

to leave here, Adam. I want to be with you for ever and ever."

"That's how I feel, too. But we have to try to make it work the right way first. Someday I'll have to tell my father, and you'll have to tell yours. Surely when they know how much we love each other, they'll consent to letting us see each other."

"I don't know if my father will ever consent. I don't think his friendship is real, Adam. Some white people have one way of thinking of Indians, no matter what."

"We won't let that stop us. Right now, for a while, we have to keep this a secret, okay? I'll tell you when I think it's time we told our parents."

"Whatever you say, Adam. I'll let you make the decisions. That's how it's supposed to be."

She kissed his neck, and he put a big hand to her face. "I liked you that first time I saw you up here, Andrea. I don't know why. I guess maybe because I saw how you looked at my tree. You loved it right away, and I could tell you liked being alone and thinking about things. Most white girls I've met talk too much, and they're silly and only care about wearing pretty dresses. They don't seem to think seriously about anything." He looked up at the gnarled branches of the old tree. "You do like this tree, don't you?"

She looked up also, feeling dizzy when she stared through the branches that reached skyward. "I love it. Big trees seem almost like God—so strong and immovable. I feel safe under a big tree, and I can talk to God better."

"I talk to Him a lot when I am up here. I pray that I will never have to leave here. But there is so much devil in the white man, I am not sure I will get my wish."

She hugged him tighter. "Surely you will, Adam. Everything is so peaceful, and your people are so successful. To move them out of Georgia would surely be illegal and impossible. It simply can't happen."

He studied the great tree's branches again. "That's what the Creeks thought, and the Choctaws, and the great nations of Indians farther east, many of whom are com-

71

pletely gone now."

They both sat quietly then, thinking, praying, wanting only to be together and cherish this precious moment they had stolen. For another half-hour or better they talked very little, resting in each other's arms, wishing they could stay all day. But then he sighed deeply and kissed her hair. "I have to be getting back, Andrea. I sure don't want to, but I'd better."

"I know. I'd better go back, too. If I stay too long, Father will send someone looking for me."

She raised her face to meet his and they kissed again, hungrily, urgently, his hand moving over her breast again. It seemed so natural, so right, as though it was all meant to be. They were in love. Why shouldn't they kiss and touch and share? What better way to show affection and love than to please and be pleased through the glory of sweet sexual encounters? How could that be bad when it was done out of love, rather than just an animalistic drive as it was with those wild girls?

She hugged him tightly. "Promise me you won't see one of those girls again."

He kissed her hair. "I won't. And you won't date any other boys, will you?"

"You know I won't."

They kissed again. "I convinced my father to let me stay home this winter and not go back to school someplace else for a while," he told her then. "My uncle, Leonard Tallman, also approved. You met him at the dance. He has much to say in what I do, as is Cherokee custom. Both agreed I need to stay this year and help with the constitution and other things that will be happening as we declare ourselves a nation. There is much work ahead if we are to remain in Georgia." He smoothed back her hair. "There will be times when I have to be away, carrying messages to other Cherokee villages. Somehow I will let you know when I can meet you here, *agiya*."

"*Agiya*? What does that mean?"

"It simply means woman, only lovingly."

Her eyes teared. "Am I your woman then?"

"If you want to be." He kissed her eyes.

"You know I want to be. And what is the Cherokee word for man—lovingly?"

"*Asgaya.*"

"*Asgaya,*" she repeated. "You are my man."

He nodded. "I am your man." He stood up reluctantly, pulling her up with him. "We had better go back. Be careful on your way down. Come again next Saturday. Can you?"

"If I don't die of loneliness before then."

He smiled, his eyes sad. "Neither of us will die. We have too much to live for." He pulled her tight against himself, kissing her once more. She ran her hands over the young, hard muscle of his arms and shoulders, finding it hard to believe that this beautiful Cherokee man had chosen her for his own. He pulled away again. "If I do not go now, we will never leave here at all." He backed away.

"Where is your horse?" she asked.

"I run up here and run back, to stay strong," he replied.

Her eyes widened. "All this way?"

He grinned, throwing out his arms. "It keeps a man strong." Their eyes held a moment longer. "Good-bye, Andrea. Please be here next Saturday."

"You know I will."

He stared at her a moment longer, then was off, quickly disappearing into the underbrush. She could not stop the tears then, tears of both joy and sadness. She was in love! And the beautiful man she loved, loved her in return. He had kissed her! He had touched her breast, and she had touched his most private place and was not afraid. He belonged to her. Adam Chandler belonged to her! Waiting a whole week to see him again was going to be torture. She hugged herself, crying.

"Oh, please, God, please let it work. Please don't ever let me lose him!" she prayed aloud. "Don't be mad at me for letting him touch me. I do love him so. Please let us be together forever!"

She wiped at her eyes and took one last look at the big oak tree, his tree, and at the matted grass beneath it where she had been kissed and touched by a boy for the first time. But not really a boy. Adam. Adam was a man, and she no longer felt like a little girl.

She untied her pony and headed down the ridge toward home, while miles away, farther west, more Creek Indians were herded by whips and at gunpoint into wagons, clinging to their little children and the few possessions they were allowed to take with them to the new land, where nearly half of them would die.

CHAPTER FIVE

Their young love could not be denied. Nothing would stop it. At what age is passion and love more painful than in those years that hang between childhood and adulthood, especially when spiced by being a forbidden love, and intensified by the thought that every moment together could be the last. They became more bold in meeting, not caring about the risks or consequences, for to be together was the only important thing in their lives. Everything else took second place.

To Andrea's unwitting parents, the girl seemed moody, a little more stubborn, more quiet, except when she returned from her frequent long rides. Then she would be flushed and happy, almost too eager to do her chores. Both parents attributed her changing moods to "growing up." But Mary Means didn't bother to reason out Andrea's changed behavior. Suddenly her friend hardly ever came to visit her, and Andrea had stopped asking her to come and stay on weekends. She now seemed more interested in riding and being alone. Mary was beginning to hate her. Ever since she'd gone to stay with Ruth Chandler that weekend, she had not been as friendly. Mary felt that she had been replaced, just because Ruth was richer—and because Andrea felt special for having stayed in a Cherokee home.

Andrea was oblivious to all of it, just as Adam was oblivious to the fact that he, too, was different, suddenly more mature, wanting to know about his father's farm and businesses, talking of staying right there at New Echota and perhaps doing some kind of work for the Cherokee in the way of writing and editing. The constitution was fast taking form, and questions and suggestions were run from village to village by Adam, who welcomed the trips, for he always arranged to be back at a certain time to meet Andrea under the tree, having given his parents a vague answer as to when he would return so they would not question the time of his arrival. Doing that gave him all the time he wanted with Andrea, as long as she could get away herself.

Andrea! How he ached to mate with her; how he wondered what it was like to break in a virgin. He must be the one to do it, and no one else. Yet their relationship had to be kept secret, meaning marriage was out of the question yet. Her parents would never allow it, she was sure. But how long would he have to wait for her? For a full month they had been meeting beneath the oak tree, and he had touched her everywhere, but was always afraid to remove her clothes for fear that she would jump up and run away. Still, the last time . . . His breathing quickened at the thought of it, and he curled up painfully against his pillow. He had unbuttoned the front of her dress and reached inside, and she had not stopped him. His fingers had touched the small swelling of a young breast, the round nipple. The memory of her tiny gasps of bashful delight drove into him like a sword. She hadn't stopped him from pulling the dress aside and looking at the lovely whiteness of her skin, the pink fruit of her breast. In hot agony he had kissed it, and only then had she suddenly stiffened. Both knew things were getting out of hand, as both knew that in time it would be impossible to keep from sharing their love through the ultimate consummation; for their driving need for each other was overwhelming. Every touch, every kiss, every whisper was ecstasy, and he wanted nothing more than to see Andrea Sanders lying naked beneath him. The thought of it brought a manly pride and possessiveness to his soul. So what if they were young? A lot of people married young. It was common among some whites, and among most Indians.

But he knew with a terrible hurt that it would not be age that would make her parents force them apart if they knew. It would be the fact that he was a Cherokee. Andrea didn't look at him as a Cherokee, but merely as a young man she loved. And he had stopped thinking of her as white, but simply as the young girl he loved, who was fun to be with, who understood him, to whom he could talk. He wanted to do all the things with her he'd done with that wild girl, only more gently, more lovingly, with real passion and concern. And he was sure that with just the right prodding, touching, kissing, he could do more than touch her breast. She was ready. She wanted him. But she was afraid.

He sat up, wide awake. How could he sleep when his mind and body were so full of Andrea Sanders? How could he rest when he ached constantly from a need to be inside of her. The moment he left her he felt tense and confused, anxious for the next time they could be together. He got up from his bed and went out into the hall. A light came from beneath the door in his father's study. He was close to his father. He loved the man very much, and had always been able to talk to him. Perhaps it was time.

He went back to his room and pulled on a pair of pants, then went out again, down the stairs to the door of the study. He hesitated, taking a deep breath for courage, then knocked on the door.

His father's gentle voice told him to enter, but Jonas Chandler looked surprised when he saw Adam. "I thought it was your mother," he told him.

Adam swallowed and closed the door. "No. I . . . couldn't sleep. I need to talk to you, Father."

Jonas leaned back in his chair and motioned for Adam to sit down in a chair across the desk from him. "Let me guess," he said. "This is about a girl."

Adam looked at him in surprise, and felt a flush coming to his cheeks. "How did you know?"

"I am a man, once a boy, remember? I have seen how different you are lately. I sometimes see a very troubled look on your face; at other times you are very happy. Something has been going on in your life, Adam. Who is she? I know that pretty little Cherokee girl, Cynthia Washington, has been eying you."

Adam looked down at his lap. "It isn't Cindy, Father." He sat there for several quiet seconds, trying to get up his courage. His father waited patiently, a tiny alarm building in him. "She's . . . she's white."

There was a long period of silence. But when Adam finally raised his eyes to meet his father's, he saw no anger there. "Please tell me it isn't one of those promiscuous, unkempt whores from the other side of the ridge, my son."

"Oh, no! Not one of those girls. How could you think that?"

The man sighed deeply, as though relieved. "What else was I to think? You went off with one the night of the dance and left poor Andrea Sanders—" He stopped, eying his son closely when the boy looked away at the mention of Andrea's name. "Not Andrea!"

The boy looked at him defiantly. "Why not Andrea? She is beautiful and sweet and I can talk to her. Yes, it is Andrea Sanders. I love her, Father, and she loves me. I'm tired of hiding it. I want the whole world to know!"

His father rubbed at his eyes and ran a hand through his hair. "Adam. Adam. Why couldn't you have made my life easy and chosen a Cherokee girl?"

"A man has to follow his heart, Father."

Jonas Chandler studied his son's dark, sincere eyes, seeing the love there, the fear, the desperation. "You're right, son. And when the leaves fall from the trees, you will be seventeen. With your size, your education, your dependability and the hard work you do, you are every bit a man. Therefore, I cannot rule your ways any longer, cannot tell you yes or no. You must make your own decisions. But your uncle will not be pleased, Adam."

"He also can no longer rule me. I love her, Father. I don't know what to do. I think . . . I think if she knew her parents would approve, she would marry me right now. I want her to be my wife, but she is afraid to tell her father.

They would not approve of a Cherokee boy marrying their daughter, she is sure."

His father rose, looking suddenly tired. "And she is probably right. The Sanderses were hospitable to us, but I could sense their deeper feelings when we visited them. I do not fully trust them, nor do I trust their friends, the Meanses, especially that boy Douglas."

"Andrea says Douglas is gone now. He joined the Georgia Militia."

The man turned, anger in his eyes. "The militia! Of course. I would have expected that. He's probably among those who continue to raid Creek villages." He clasped his hands behind him and began to pace. "Tell me, how have you been able to see Andrea? How long have you been seeing her? How . . . how serious is this?"

"We are very serious. We have been . . . meeting at a secret place only we know about. She goes riding and meets me there."

"That is deceitful, son. You have both been sneaking around behind our backs. You should have told me from the beginning."

Adam hung his head. "I am sorry, Father. But how could I tell you? I thought you would disapprove just as her own father does."

"I do disapprove! Not because Andrea is white, but because of the harm this could bring to both of you. I would never stop you from marrying any girl you love, no matter what her race is. If she were a slave girl, I still would not stop you, if it meant your happiness. It is you I am concerned about. You know the implications of this, Adam. Our friendship with the border whites is very tentative. If we arouse them against us, it will make our cause even more difficult. Already half the state of Georgia wants our land. They all look for excuses to make us leave. To sneak around with this girl and be found out—or even to bring it into the open deliberately—could bring disaster. I think you should stop seeing her, for your sake, for the sake of the People."

"No!" Adam rose then, tears in his eyes. "You can't ask

me to stop seeing her. It . . . it's impossible, Father! I couldn't stop seeing Andrea any more than I could stop breathing. I would go crazy."

Their gazes held and his father sighed deeply, closing his eyes for a moment. "Yes. How foolish of me to think I can stop young love. The dam is cracked. Soon the waters will rush through, and woe to those who are in the way."

Adam swallowed, blinking back tears. "What should I do, Father?"

The man stepped forward, grasping his son's arms. "I will not forbid you to see her, but give it a little more time, son. Perhaps your feelings will change and you will each go your own way. If you feel the same a month from now, come to me. We will go together to the Sanderses' home and speak with her parents. They might consider it disgraceful, but it is more disgraceful to have your daughter seeing a boy secretly, perhaps living in sin. I am sure they would rather have her legally married, and happy. Surely her happiness is all that is truly important to them."

Adam turned away. "I am not so sure. The whites seem to think more of how things look than of how happy a person is."

Jonas studied his handsome son. "Are the two of you already living in sin, Adam?"

The boy remained turned away, quickly wiping at his eyes. "No. Not yet. But I do not know how long I can . . . can keep myself from her. I want her. If this were the old days, I could take her the Cherokee way, just take her to my dwelling and make love to her, and she would then be my wife. Things were simple then—simple and good and right—until the whites came and complicated everything. I might be educated their way, but my heart is still Indian, Father, and the way we live, sometimes I think it is all mockery."

Jonas put a hand on the boy's shoulder. "I agree with you, Adam. But if we are to survive, it must be this way. You know that. We play the game their way. That is the only way we can win. Remember that. Try to be strong,

Adam. Don't do something foolish. You are young and handsome, and in love. I know it is hard. But to take this girl could bring many consequences. She is old enough to bear children, and it only takes one union. Remember that your own birthday is almost nine months to the day from when I married your mother."

The boy turned, and there was a sly grin on his father's face. Adam took a deep breath and smiled bashfully. "I will remember. I wouldn't want to bring her harm, Father. I would never want to hurt Andrea." He turned away again. "Besides, she's never . . . I mean . . . she's afraid. I've never touched her that way."

"Ah, but young love can be very persuasive, and there is a first time for everything. Be careful, Adam. Try to think clearly, objectively. If, in another month, as I said, you still feel this way, we will have to do something about it, for your sake and for hers." The man moved back behind his desk. "You'd better get some rest now, son. You have a lot of riding to do tomorrow, more messages to deliver and votes to pick up."

The boy nodded. "Thank you for talking to me, Father. I feel better."

"It is very lonely not being able to tell anyone what troubles you, and not being able to share the joy of your love."

Adam walked to the door. "You are right. I feel more sorry for Andrea. She cannot talk to her parents at all. She is afraid of them." He shook his head. "And she is their only child. This will not be easy, Father."

"Nothing has ever been easy for us since the white man came here. We can only take one problem at a time, Adam, and hope for the best. Pray about it, son. Have courage."

Adam quietly exited. He would try to sleep. It was true he had a lot of riding to do the next day, and the morning after that he was to meet her again . . . under the great oak. It wasn't just his tree now. It was their tree, his and Andrea's. It sheltered them, protected them, hid them from the outside world with its massive arms, its foliage; and it smiled down on their sweet love. Perhaps they could just stay there forever and no one would ever find them.

The moment Andrea dismounted from her pony and ran to him, Adam's common sense and his promises to his father vanished. He wrapped his arms around her, whirling her around, meeting her sweet lips, wanting her as much as ever. She laughed as he carried her in his arms to the tree and set her on a blanket, then laid her back, pressing against her, imprisoning her beneath him.

"I missed you," he said, studying her blue eyes lovingly, fingering her blond hair.

"I can hardly stand it when we're apart, Adam."

"Nor can I. That's why I . . . we have to do something, Andrea. It's too hard this way. I . . . I told my father . . . about us."

Her eyes widened and her smile faded. "What did he say?"

"He was good about it. He does not object to our being together, but he is worried it would bring trouble to our family, to the Cherokee. We do not want to make any more enemies than we already have. He thought I should stop seeing you because of that, but I told him I would never stop seeing you."

Her eyes teared. "He doesn't like me."

"That isn't true! He likes you very much. He understands how we feel, Andrea. He is just afraid of what might happen. He said I could keep seeing you, that if we still feel this way in another month, he will go and talk to your father so that the honorable thing is done."

Panic showed in her eyes then. "No! He must never tell my father. We . . . we could run away or something. But don't go to my father!"

"Surely your parents want you to be happy, Andrea. I cannot run away with you. It would disgrace you. We should do it the right way, Andrea."

"But father would never—" She hugged him tightly. "Oh, Adam, they're sending someone right now to invite Ruth to our home for the weekend. That means I can't meet you Saturday. But worse than that, I heard them talking.''

"Who?"

"My father, and Mr. Means. They only want Ruth to come so they can question her about what your people are up to. It isn't to be friendly. I truly like Ruth. I would enjoy having her visit. Please believe me that I have no reason to ask her except as a friend. But I want you to warn her not to say too much to my father and Mr. Means.''

His dark eyes filled with anger and disappointment. "So, that is the way it is then. Even some of the border people are plotting against us. I'll bet some of them can't wait to get their hands on our land.''

"Don't you see, Adam? I thought in the beginning I could one day tell my parents, once they knew all of you better. But I know what's in my father's heart, and there is no love there for the Cherokee. I don't know what to do, Adam. I love you so.''

Their eyes held, a desperate, hopeless desire building; and fear began to grip their young hearts, fear that they might never openly display their love, never be able to share their joy with their loved ones or share their love through marriage. Suddenly time and circumstances were pressing in on them, and all of Jonas Chandler's advice to his son was quickly forgotten. Nothing and no one was going to stop Adam Chandler from having the girl he loved. He met her lips, wanting to brand her, overwhelmed by a need to be sure he was her first man, desperately praying he would be her only man for the rest of her life.

Their salty tears mixed together as they kissed, and both could taste them. Their burning love and the hopelessness of it all only made everything more urgent now, more natural and necessary. Suddenly petting, touching, rubbing, kissing, were not enough. They were not children any longer. After all, in just three months she would be fifteen, and soon thereafter he would be seventeen.

Passion and a desire to prove adulthood consumed them both. They needed to show their elders that they could

83

make their own decisions, choose their own partners, share their bodies whenever they wished. It was their right, for they were in love. And now it seemed every moment just might be their last. They could no longer waste these precious visits.

He moved his lips to her neck, fumbling at the buttons of her dress, wanting to again touch the breast he had seen and kissed a few days before. "God, Andrea, I love you. I want you so bad."

"I want you, too," she whimpered. "I'm so scared, Adam. But ever since the last time . . . when you touched me." She shivered with passion. "Adam, I want to be your woman. I want it so bad. Just don't hurt me. Please don't hurt me."

He met her lips again as his hand slid inside her dress. He kissed her with a hot passion that made him seem ready to explode. The touch of his fingers on her breast made her feel faint, but she had decided and nothing was going to stop her. She was terrified but ecstatic at the same time. After hearing her father talking about ways to get rid of the Cherokees, she would cling to every moment like this. She would no longer deny this man she loved his pleasure. She would be one with him, and nothing her father or anyone else did could change that ever.

Jonas Chandler's words were just a faint ring in Adam's ears now. He was his own man. He would make his own decisions. Andrea was telling him he could make love to her. He wanted to see her naked, wanted to be inside her, wanted the privilege of the manly duty of being the first to invade her. That would make her his forever, no matter what anyone on the outside tried to do. That one thing could never be changed. She would belong to him for the rest of her life, and once her parents knew they would have no choice but to let them marry the Christian way and be together. Yes! This was the answer! He would take her and show them all.

He slipped the dress off her shoulder and her heart pounded furiously. Then he raised himself on one elbow, his eyes glazed with love and desire. "I love you so much,

Andrea," he said quietly as he unbuttoned the front of her dress. "I would never hurt you." He carefully pulled the other side of the dress away, baring both her breasts. When she closed her eyes and reddened, he leaned down and kissed each pink nipple.

"Adam," she whimpered. "Oh, Adam."

He groaned her name in reply, tasting each breast more fully then. They were small and undeveloped, like budding fruits not yet fully ripened. But it was enough to be touching them, tasting them. He moved off her then, gently raising her up and slipping the dress off her shoulders and arms. She hung her head in bashfulness, her blond hair drifting over her shoulders and teasingly hiding her breasts.

"I have dreamed of doing this for so long, Andrea," he told her. She rose to her knees and he pulled the dress and her slip and underpants down to her knees, sucking in his breath at the ecstasy of seeing the soft blond hairs that hid her secret, womanly place; her slender, white thighs; her flat tummy. He leaned forward and kissed her stomach, and she shuddered, whimpering his name again, not sure what to do, terrified but excited. He eased her back down again and pulled the clothes completely away from her. Warm sun glittered through the branches of the great oak, warming her skin in patches, shading her in other places. She closed her eyes as Adam moved a trembling hand over her slender legs, wondering if she might lose her breath when his fingers lightly touched that most private place.

"God, you're beautiful, Andrea," he told her. "I can't believe how beautiful you are."

Every nerve in her body seemed to be alive and on fire. He stood up then and removed his shirt and boots, unlaced his pants and pulled them down along with his underwear. Daringly, she watched, and then swallowed her fear at the sight of him. He was just like the male animals, only to her he seemed even bigger. He saw the fear building in her eyes, and he took her hands.

"Please don't be afraid, Andrea. It has to start somewhere. Surely it gets better, or those wild girls wouldn't like it so much, and husbands and wives wouldn't have so many children like a lot of them do." He lay down beside her. "It's right, Andrea. I know it is. We love each other. That's all that matters. If we wait and tell our parents, they might never let us be together again. This way, they'll have to."

Her eyes revealed total trust as she reached up to touch his handsome face. "Adam, I . . . don't know what to do. What if you . . . what if I don't . . . please you?"

He pulled her close, pressing against her stomach with the huge hardness that brought a frantic beat to her heart. "How could a beautiful angel like you not please me?"

He met her lips again and she was determined now that nothing would make her stop. This was Adam, beautiful, sweet, loving Adam. She closed her eyes and his hand moved over her breasts, down over her flat belly to that secret place no other person had ever touched. She whimpered as his fingers explored, touching something that made her feel wild and free and bursting with love and desire. Her breathing was frantic then, every breath bringing a panting whimper. What was he doing? It was wonderful! She floated on a cloud of ecstasy, an ecstasy she had never known before, now returning his kisses with a wild frenzy, digging her fingers into his arms and shoulders. Her legs were parting daringly, as though she could not control their reaction. His lips moved from her mouth to her neck, her shoulder, her breasts; tasting, lightly sucking, while his fingers worked their wonderful magic until she didn't care anymore what he saw, what he touched, what he did with her. She was his, fully surrendered, totally willing to let him take whatever pleasure he wanted with her. Surely he was every bit a man, for he knew just what to do with her.

It all seemed so natural after that. Two people in love ought to do this, ought to share bodies and enjoy these delightful feelings, ought to please each other this way. A wonderful explosion engulfed her, made his dark form above her seem obscure, like a mist surrounding her with kisses and warmth, enveloping her with warm moistness.

She felt him moving on top of her, and now it was too late. She could not close her legs, nor did she want to. She would be Adam Chandler's woman, no matter what else happened to her for the rest of her life. Never would she belong to another. This was how it must be.

She gasped, and some of the misty ecstasy was suddenly interrupted by a sharp pain. Her fingers dug into him then, and he uttered something in Cherokee, pushing hard as she cried out.

"Hang on, Andrea. Do not be afraid," he groaned, lost in her now, unable to stop it in spite of her sudden tears. He enveloped her in his arms, feeling her sudden fright and knowing she was in pain. He moved rhythmically, automatically, quickly spilling his life into her, unable to hold back for the excitement of it.

He stayed on top of her then, holding her tightly. She was crying. He rocked her in his arms. "Please don't cry. I'm sorry, Andrea. I'm sorry. I did not mean to hurt you. It will go away, I promise."

"That isn't . . . what I'm crying about," she answered between sobs. "I love you so much, Adam. What will I do if they take you away from me!"

"No one will take me away from you. Not ever." He kissed her several times over, slowly moving off her. Then he looked down at himself and saw blood. Yes, she was a virgin; he had been her first. That knowledge brought a burst of manly pride to his soul, and new love to his heart. She belonged to him now. "Lie still, Andrea. I will get some water and help you wash." He kissed her eyes. "The next time it will be better, until it is as wonderful for you as it was for me."

She put a hand to his face. "Was it truly wonderful?"

He smiled the provocative smile. "What do you think? Look how fast it happened. I could not hold myself back, it felt so good."

She reddened some then. "I never . . . what you did . . . it made me feel wonderful, too . . . the way you touched me."

He ran a big hand over her belly. "Are you in pain?"

"Just a little. It will go away, I'm sure."

He kissed her lips lightly. "There is blood on me. Don't be afraid. I have heard sometimes it makes a girl bleed, but it's just like your time of month. It will stop."

She curled up in embarrassment. How did he know all those things? He pulled her dress over her and got up, walking away with the canteen and his clothes. She watched the hard muscle of his thighs and buttocks as he walked. He was all hard power, youthful strength. He was her man now. He returned moments later, dressed. He brought the canteen to her, and a towel. He wet the towel and pulled the dress away. She grasped his wrist.

"Turn around, Adam, please. I . . . I'll wash myself."

Their eyes held a moment. He handed the towel to her and rose, walking a few feet away, looking up at the tree. What had he done? Why hadn't he had more self-control? He'd taken her virginity without any thought to the consequences. And now that it was done, he knew. He'd do it again and again, every time he saw her here alone, for to keep himself from her was like trying not to breathe. But where would it lead them?

"It's all right now, Adam," she finally told him. He turned around to see her buttoning her dress. He hurried over to her side.

"Are you angry with me?"

She looked at him with trust and total love, her face almost childlike. "Why should I be angry? I wanted you to do it," she answered. "I wanted to before this, but I was scared." She put a hand to her stomach. "I was just surprised . . . that it hurt that much."

He sighed deeply, went to his parfleche and took out another towel. He had his horse with him this time, for he'd not yet returned home after delivering the messages.

"Let me wash your face," he told her. "One can tell you have been crying. You'd better brush the tangles from your hair, too. You want to look normal when you get home."

Their eyes held in sadness and love as he gently washed her face. Home. She didn't want to go home. She wanted to stay with him forever, be his wife, go home with Adam

Chandler. "Oh, Adam, I don't want to leave here," she whimpered. He pulled her into his arms.

"And I don't want to let you go. But I must, for now. You can't come Saturday if Ruth is at your house. Meet me Monday morning." He kissed her hair, running his hands over her back and hips. "I will worry about you. I hope I did not harm you. It is not good that you have to ride that pony home. You should lie and rest."

"I can't. I've been here too long already." She raised her eyes to meet his. "I'll be all right, Adam. If anything goes wrong, my mother will just think I'm having my"—she looked down—"my time."

He took her chin and raised her face to his. "I am your man now. You do not need to be afraid to talk of those things around me. Someday you will be my wife. No one will stop us." He kissed her lips lightly. "I will think hard on all of this for a while. I will meet you Monday and we will talk." Already he wanted her again. "And we will do this thing again. Do not be afraid, Andrea. Nothing will keep us apart."

She looked up at the oak tree. It seemed that as long as she stood here beneath it, all was well. She didn't want to leave it. She felt alone and vulnerable away from the tree, away from Adam. "Be sure to tell Ruth not to say too much to my father," she warned him. "Does . . . does she know about us?"

"No. She is too young to understand. Only my father knows for now. Do not tell her. And I am sure my father will warn her not to say too much." He kissed her then, a long, hard kiss of good-bye, the urgency in it telling her already that he was ready to mate with her again. She had never dreamed it could be this wonderful, this beautiful. Why had her mother chosen to sleep apart from her father? If she were Adam's wife, she would never leave his bed, never tire of sleeping in his arms.

He walked her to her pony then, and lifted her up onto it as though she weighed nothing at all. "I still don't like you riding."

"I'll be fine." Their eyes held and he clasped her hand.

"God be with you, Andrea. I love you. I will be waiting for you here Monday at the same time. It will not be easy to wait."

"Oh, Adam, it doesn't seem right . . . to do what we just did and then just . . . just tell each other good-bye."

"I know. I would stay here forever with you if I could. I don't like it either. If I were your husband, I would put you in a nice hot bath and then put you to bed and sleep with my arms around you all night. And in my mind and heart I am your husband, Andrea. I truly am, the Cherokee way. I have claimed you as my own. Nothing can change that now."

She squeezed his hand. "Oh, Adam, I don't want to go."

He pulled away, walking over to gather up his blanket. He rolled the towels into it and tied it onto his horse, hanging the canteen over his saddle horn. Then he pulled on his boots and mounted up. "We have no choice," he told her. Riding up beside her, he leaned over and kissed her again. "My loves goes with you until the next time, *agiya*."

"And mine with you, *asgaya*."

He turned his horse. "Go now. And be careful."

She studied him a moment longer, wanting to remember everything about him. Was it true that this handsome, wonderful Cherokee man had just made her his woman? It didn't seem right to be riding away from him now. She should stay and sleep in his arms. How much longer could she stand this torture? "Good-bye," she choked out. She turned her pony. How would she hide her red, swollen eyes when she got home? She must stop crying. She must. She breathed deeply. Refusing to turn back and look at him again, she then headed down the ridge, toward a place she didn't want to be, to a people she no longer felt a part of. She belonged someplace else now, on the other side of the ridge, to another people. Somehow, someday, that was where she would be. Whether or not her parents approved no longer mattered.

CHAPTER SIX

Andrea polished a glass until all the water spots were gone, then picked up another to dry it, rubbing it also to get off all the water spots.

"Andrea, the glass is surely dry." Her mother was watching her closely. "Why do you keep rubbing it?"

The girl held the glass up to the light. "I want it to be perfect—no water spots." She set the glass down. "Oh, and I cleaned my room, Mother, and I dusted everything, and—"

"Andrea, why are you going to all this fuss for an Indian girl?"

Andrea frowned, turning to look at her mother. "They have a beautiful home, Mother, and servants and everything. I just . . . I want everything to be as nice as it can be."

"We aren't inviting her here to make a fancy impression, Andrea, nor is it important to us what she thinks of our home. She is an Indian. You act as though she were the President's daughter. Now stop polishing every glass so hard and finish the dishes."

The woman went back to rolling out pie crust, and Andrea picked up another dish. She still hurt some inside, but the memory of Adam Chandler taking her virginity was worth it. The bleeding had almost stopped already. Still, she longed to talk to someone about it. But there was no one. Was she a sinful girl? Would she go to hell? Her mother would certainly tell her so. It was torture knowing her parents hated the Cherokee, when she herself was in love with one, had given herself to a Cherokee man freely and willingly.

Adam! Oh, how it hurt not to be able to tell the whole world. How awful it was to be afraid to tell anyone, to wonder if the day would ever come when they could be husband and wife, and she could stay in his arms forever. Adam! Adam! Adam! Everything was Adam—every thought, every dream, every waking moment. He had seen her naked, had touched her, done wonderful things to her, invaded her, claimed her. She was his woman, and he was her man. What a terribly exciting, wonderful yet sometimes terrifying, secret it was. If only her parents could see things differently. Weren't they ever truly in love? Had her mother ever given herself to her father with the same sweet, wonderful abandon that Andrea had given herself to Adam? And how could that possibly be wrong and sinful when they loved each other so much?

"Why haven't you been eating lately, Andrea?" her mother asked. "You go about the house as though you're in a daze half the time."

The girl reddened a little and looked away. "I . . . I just have to get used to our new place, new friends and all. I'm wondering about school, meeting new kids and everything."

The woman eyed her closely. "Is that all? Have you been sick?"

Andrea shook her head, turned her back to her mother. "No."

"Well, I think I should take you to a doctor."

"No!" The girl turned and begged with her eyes. A doctor might be able to tell! Doctors knew everything! He'd take one look at her and know she wasn't a virgin anymore! She reddened more when she saw the stern and discerning look on her mother's face, prompted by her quick and almost impudent reply.

"I beg your pardon!" the woman said slowly.

Andrea swallowed. "I . . . I'm sorry, Mother. But I don't

like doctors, and here I'd have to go to a new one, that's all. I . . . I don't need a doctor. I'm not sick."

The woman sighed deeply. "If you don't start eating better, you'll see a doctor."

"I'll eat better. I promise." How could she eat when her heart was so full of Adam and her body was in a state of constant ecstasy?

"See that you do." The woman put a piece of pie crust into a pie tin. "I hope you aren't mooning over some worthless boy, Andrea. At your age you should not even be thinking about boys."

Andrea turned around, a lump swelling in her throat. She picked up another plate. "There aren't any boys around here to moon over. I haven't been to school yet to meet any . . . and the only one around is Douglas Means. He's gone now, and I hate him anyway."

Her mother poured some berries into the pie crust. "Why should you hate Douglas Means?"

"Because he fits his name," the girl said glumly. "He's mean. I'm glad he's gone."

"Well, don't be telling Mary or her parents that. Douglas seems like a fine boy, but a little immature. I'm sure service in the Georgia Militia will straighten him out. But that is beside the point. He's too old for you, and you're too young for any boy at this time. Fact of the matter is, you'd be better off never thinking about men. It's too bad we can't have children without them, but such is our fate."

Andrea set down the dish towel and studied her mother. "Don't you . . . don't you love Father?"

The woman's dark eyes flashed her a warning look. "A girl your age has no right getting personal with her parents," she chided. She began rolling out another piece of dough. "The fact of the matter is, Andrea, our marriage was arranged, by our parents. It was always understood that I would marry Morgan. Love is a frivolous feeling, here today and gone tomorrow. A woman who thinks she loves a man only gets used by him. A practical and honorable marriage is the best, choosing a man or woman for their strength and the way they work, and nothing more. Then, once you marry, you do what a woman is designed to do—give a man children, at least one anyway. You suffer indignities and pain to give him that child, and then you get on with household things and he gets on with his man's work. Once you've suffered the man's invasion of your personals long enough to realize you'll have no more children, then those things stop and you simply become a housekeeper and mother. Men have certain . . . animal desires, Andrea—desires that a proper woman does not satisfy if she has any honor. She allows a man his pleasures only for the sake of having children and for no other reason. If he continues to have uncontrollable desires after that, the woman looks the other way when she sees him riding off to town to visit the kind of women who get paid to give men their pleasure. It is a weakness men have that a woman sometimes has to overlook, as long as her husband is a good provider, a hard-working man, and one who is there when she needs him. Your father is that kind of a man.''

She put the pie dough into a second pan, and Andrea stared at her dumbfounded. Surely it didn't have to be that way. Adam's parents still slept together. And the way she felt about Adam, the way she'd wanted him, enjoyed pleasing him . . . Something was wrong about her mother's thinking, wasn't it? It couldn't be true that all marriages were loveless and that all women slept with their men simply out of duty, that to do so willingly and joyfully was a sin. Why had God designed men and women the way He did, if He didn't mean for them to be together in that way out of love?

"Now, I've told you everything you need to know—and more than I should have," her mother said curtly. "I just want to warn you against having feelings for a boy. It's wrong and sinful and lustful, and leads only to disaster. When you are old enough, your father and I will choose a husband for you, a man of property and honor.''

Andrea's heart hurt so bad she wondered if it would burst. Her last hope of ever discussing Adam with her parents was gone, and now a new fear had begun to build in her soul. What if they picked out someone and forced her to marry him? No! She would never do it!

"I'm going to my room to change," she told her mother. She hurried out of the room, feeling suddenly smothered. She refused to believe marriage had to be the way her mother described it. She almost felt sorry for her mother, who had never felt about a man the way Andrea felt about Adam. She refused to believe such feelings were wrong. What better reason to marry than to feel as though you could never live without the other, to want to die for the other, to want to spend the rest of your life in the arms of the other—to want to touch him, sleep with him, make him happy. Something that beautiful and wonderful had to be right.

She went to her room and flung herself on her bed, crying into the pillow. Never had she been so confused, so sick with love, so lonely. Adam! How could she ever really have him? If she ran away with him, it might bring a lot of trouble to his people. Her head ached. There was so much to think about. She couldn't wait to see him again on Monday so they could talk about it. She hugged her pillow tightly. Wrong as it was, she knew that when she saw him again they would lie naked together, share bodies, touch and kiss and do all those wonderful things that made her shiver with love for him.

She got up then, and washed her face. Ruth would arrive soon. Andrea changed into a clean dress and brushed out her hair, then heard a carriage coming. She put a hand to her stomach. Would Adam bring her? She hurried to the window to see the carriage approaching. Adam's father drove it. His father! She had not seen the man since Adam had talked with him. Now he knew! What if he? . . . No, surely he wouldn't say anything to her parents, not yet. Her chest hurt as she hurried down the stairs and to the door. Her father was far out in the fields, unable to come and greet them, and her mother was still busy with pies. Andrea walked out onto the porch as Jonas Chandler helped his daughter down and walked her up to Andrea.

Their eyes held for a moment, and then Jonas bowed. When he rose he smiled, and in his dark eyes, Andrea saw the same kindness that shone in Adam's. "Good morning, Miss Sanders," he told her.

She swallowed. "Hello, Mr. Chandler."

"I have brought Ruth to accept your kind invitation to stay the weekend."

Ruth spoke up. "I brought four of my dolls, Andrea!" She hurried to the carriage to get them from where they sat in the back seat. Never had dolls seemed more juvenile to Andrea than they did now. She'd been with a man. There was no more room for dolls in her life, but she must act as though there were.

Adam's father grinned. "One day it is a young man that interests you, and the next, dolls," he declared. "Life is not easy at fourteen, is it, Miss Sanders?"

She reddened, and he laughed lightly and winked. "Don't worry," he said softly. "Your secret it still a secret. It will be Adam's decision as to whether to reveal it, not mine."

Her eyes teared, and he was struck by the love in them. Perhaps this was more serious even than he'd realized. He'd known Adam was serious, but he hadn't been sure Andrea was.

"Is Adam all right?" she asked. "I worry about him, riding into all those villages, with all the trouble going on—the militia and all."

Chandler sobered and nodded. "Adam is fine." He sighed deeply. "You must be very careful—"

"Look, Andrea!" Ruth interrupted. "You can have these two."

Andrea tore her eyes from Jonas Chandler and took the dolls. "Thank you, Ruth."

Jonas straightened. "I will get her bag." He walked to the carriage, and by then Harriet Sanders was at the door.

"Welcome, Ruth," she said in a kind voice. Andrea noticed Jonas glance at the woman warily. Had Adam told him the real reason Ruth had been invited? Of course he had. Perhaps that had made Jonas Chandler respect

Andrea more, for warning them. The man looked at his daughter.

"You remember everything I told you, Ruth," he said.

"Yes, Father." His eyes held hers for a moment as he handed her the bag; then he looked at Andrea's mother.

"Good morning, Mrs. Sanders. I hope the day finds you well."

"Very well, Mr. Chandler. And you and your wife?"

"We are both fine."

"Good. We shall all have to picnic together sometime."

"That would be very nice. I have to run now. I have lots of chores to do. I should have let one of my men bring Ruth, but I felt like going for a ride this morning." He tipped his hat. "Good day."

"Good-bye, Mr. Chandler." Andrea's mother forced a smile, then put her hand out to shoo the two girls back into the house. Andrea quickly glanced back at Jonas Chandler, and he winked and smiled. She smiled back. She felt better now. Perhaps everything was hopeless, but at least Adam's father seemed to like her. That was one tiny accomplishment. And seeing Jonas Chandler had made her feel a little closer to Adam. Perhaps having Ruth here would make the weekend go faster. Then it would be Monday. Monday! She would see Adam again on Monday!

Mary Means came that same afternoon. It was Andrea's mother's idea, not her own. Mary had not been very friendly since Andrea had first spent a weekend at the Chandler home, and Andrea knew she would be unpleasant. She suddenly saw Mary in a different light, saw a lot of Douglas in the girl, saw many things she had not seen before she'd fallen in love with Adam Chandler.

Mary's jealousy was obvious. She looked triumphant when her mother first brought her, gave Andrea haughty looks, which clearly said Andrea could not have Ruth Chandler all to herself. And the rest of the day was miserable, with Mary contradicting everything Ruth said. She asked Ruth if her skin got any "cleaner" when she scrubbed it hard, and she told the girl her china dolls were nothing special. She even managed to "accidentally" break one of the doll's faces, which brought tears to Ruth's eyes. But Ruth tried to be polite and said nothing. Andrea, however, was furious.

"You did that on purpose, Mary Means!"

"I did not!"

"Yes you did! You're as mean as your brother!"

"Don't you talk about my brother! He's in the militia! You always try to make Douglas look bad. It's you who's bad! He told me you let him look under your dress!"

Andrea's eyes widened, and Ruth sat back against the wall blinking back tears.

"Douglas Means is a liar!" Andrea shouted at Mary. "He's a dirty-minded liar who is always trying to make me do bad things! I hate him!"

Mary shoved her, and Andrea shoved back. Just then Andrea's mother came into the room, shouting for them both to stop. "What is going on here!"

"She broke Ruth's doll on purpose!" Andrea answered, pointing to the doll.

"And she said bad things about Douglas!" Mary retorted.

"Both of you stop this right now! Andrea, both these girls are your guests, and you will treat them as such or I'll have your father take you behind the shed and use a stick on you! Do you understand?"

Andrea glared at Mary, then plopped down onto her bed. "I understand. But why did you invite Mary? It was supposed to be just Ruth."

"That will be enough! Mary has always been your best friend, and you know it. I just thought the three of you would have a good time. You have neglected Mary since you started seeing Ruth. I think you should apologize for that, and all three of you should try to get along. Mary, you apologize to Ruth for breaking her doll. You've both made the poor girl feel unwelcome. We'll be having supper soon, and I want you all to come down with happy faces. Your father wants to . . . talk with Ruth."

Ruth looked darkly at the woman. She would do as her father had told her and say nothing about anything, pretend she had no idea of what her people might be involved in. She liked Andrea, and had come for that reason only, no other. She sensed that she was not considered an equal by these people, but that only brought out her pride. Andrea's mother was still insisting that Mary apologize to Ruth.

"I'm sorry about your doll," the girl finally mumbled. Harriet Sanders picked up the pieces.

"I will put these in a bag for you, Ruth. Perhaps someone can fix it when you get it home."

The woman left then, and the three girls sat pouting.

"I think you like Ruth only because you like her brother," Mary grumbled to Andrea.

Andrea scowled at her. "I do not!"

"Yes you do! I saw the way you looked at him that day we had Sunday dinner here. You think he's cute."

Andrea swallowed back a lump in her throat. "So what if I did? You did too. You said so."

"I know it. But he's an Indian. I'd never let an Indian boy touch me." She made a face and looked at Ruth. "I only mean in naughty ways, Ruth. I don't mind having Indians for friends." Her eyes widened wickedly. "Have you ever seen your brother naked, Ruth? What do Indian boys look like? Are they big like the horses? Douglas said he heard they were."

"Stop that!" Andrea ordered. "That's ugly, Mary Means! How dare you ask her something like that!"

Mary grinned slyly. "I saw Douglas's once. He showed it to me."

Andrea's eyes widened, as did Ruth's. Something had changed about Mary. The girl had a strange look in her eyes now. "Don't you ever wonder about boys, Andrea?"

Andrea reddened and looked away. She suddenly didn't trust Mary Means. What had the girl been up to? "No," she answered. She met the girl's eyes again. "And you shouldn't, either."

Mary folded her arms victoriously. "I know something

neither one of you knows. I know all about sex. Douglas took me with him one night when he went to see one of those wild girls north of here. He let me watch. I saw everything. That girl even touched me and showed me how to feel good. Now I know everything, and when the right boy comes along, I'm going to let him do those things to me and I'll be a woman."

Andrea just stared at her, while Ruth hugged a doll. Mary grinned.

"You're jealous, aren't you?" She sneered.

"That's bad, Mary. How can you be like that? You never used to be."

"I didn't know before. Now I do." She raised her nose haughtily. "Maybe I'll go over the ridge sometime and find me a Cherokee boy. I want to see if they look any different. Maybe I'll even look up Adam Chandler and let him take my clothes off."

"Shut up!" Andrea snapped. "Adam is mine!"

She reddened quickly then. The words had come out quickly and easily. Mary's eyes widened and she moved closer. "I knew it! Has he kissed you, Andrea? Did he get under your dress?"

Andrea shoved her away. "It's none of your business! It's . . . we're just friends, that's all! And if you say anything, Mary Means, I'll scratch your eyes out, and I'll tell your mother what you and Douglas did! I'll tell!"

Mary smiled. "Okay. I won't say anything, if you don't. But you'd better let me come over more after this, and be nicer to me."

Andrea wanted to scream and run, to cry, to kill Mary Means. Why? Why had she said that? Her love for Adam was too strong. It made her too quick to speak in defense of that love.

"Don't worry, Andy. I won't say anything. It's more fun this way." Mary giggled then. "Isn't this exciting? We never talked about boys before." She went to the door. "I'm going downstairs to get a drink. And your mother wants us to come down for supper. We'd better go."

Andrea hesitated, looking at Ruth. "I'll be right there,"

she answered. "I have to find my ribbon."

"Well, hurry up."

Mary left, and Andrea turned to Ruth. "I'm sorry, Ruth. I didn't want her to come."

Ruth shrugged. "It's okay."

Andrea blinked back tears. "I'm sorry about those bad things she said about Adam. You . . . you won't say anything, will you? I mean . . . I like Adam a lot, but we're just friends. My parents would be mad if they knew. I'm not supposed to like boys yet."

Ruth stood up, still clinging to her doll. "I won't say anything. I like you, Andy. You aren't like her. I know that. Will she go home pretty soon?"

Andrea nodded. "She's going home after supper. She used to be real nice. I think it's that awful brother of hers and that wild girl she met that made her like this. She used to be my best friend, but now you will be."

Ruth smiled then. "Really?"

Andrea nodded and put her arm around the girl's shoulders. "Really."

Just outside the door Mary listened, her eyes hardening with hatred and jealousy.

Andrea did not even reach the oak tree before Adam was there, running down her side of the ridge to greet her. *"Siyu, agiya!"* he called out, just before grabbing her down from her pony and hugging her hard, then swinging her around. How wonderful it felt to be held! Surely her mother was wrong about everything she had said.

"Adam! Oh, Adam!" She burst into tears right away. "I did a terrible thing! I told Mary Means that we were friends, but I think she knew it was more than that. I didn't mean to, Adam. It just happened."

He kissed her cheek. "Do not cry, *agiya*. Ruth told me what happened with Mary. She is a bad girl. She tricked you."

"But she's getting mean like Douglas," Andrea wept,

hugging him tightly. "She'll find a way to tell. She's jealous, Adam."

He sighed deeply, setting her on her feet and keeping an arm around her while he picked up the reins of her pony and walked her the rest of the way up.

"Maybe she won't tell," he told her. "Ruth told me what she said—about going with her brother and all. You have something you can tell on her, too. She knows that. You probably will just have to keep being friendly with her, at least for now. Once we decide how we can be together, it won't matter anymore what she says."

Andrea wiped at her eyes. "What about Ruth? What did you say to her?"

"Just what you said—that we are just friends. Her mind still thinks in too young a way for her to see it otherwise." He gave her a squeeze. "Don't fret about it, Andrea. Everything will work out. I just know it will. It has to." He tied her pony and turned to her, hesitating a moment, drinking in her beauty. "It has to," he repeated.

It was all too new and wonderful. Both had an aching need to reexperience the wonders they had found in one another. He drew her into his arms, kissing her in a torrent of furious, youthful passion, then picking her up and carrying her to the blanket he'd already prepared. Neither of them wanted to talk first. The keen sexual urgings of youth were too demanding; their sweet, innocent love was too strong. It hurt too much to be apart.

His kisses soon pulled her into the misty madness of desire, and she let him remove her clothes, afraid it might hurt as badly as the first time yet not truly caring if it did. For this was Adam—beautiful, sweet, strong, brave, wonderful Adam, her Cherokee man. Yes, man. Surely he was no longer a boy, and she was no longer a girl. The shivering wonder of lying naked in the open air, his dark eyes drinking in her nakedness, his strong hands moving over her and feeling every curve, every inch of her skin, exploring secret cavities—this brought on a kind of hypnotic state only Adam could induce.

In minutes she felt his naked body touching her own.

She drew his head down and offered small breasts for his pleasure, crying out his name when he again worked magic with his fingers, touching her in places which only that most special of men—the man she truly loved—must be allowed to touch. And she truly loved Adam Chandler. As his lips moved to her neck, she leaned up and kissed his muscular shoulder, her tears a mixture of joy and fear. His lips moved back down again, tasting each breast, moving over her belly, lightly kissing the blond hairs as he groaned her name. This was something new. She was too bashful for this, and she drew up her knees.

"Adam, don't . . ."

He moved back up, relaxing her again with his fingers, his mouth skimming her breasts before moving to her lips. "Someday we will do more," he whispered. "You will see, when you are ready."

His suggestion brought on the explosion that ripped through her insides then, as his hot kiss nearly cut off her breath. He was between her legs again, that most manly part of him searching, probing for its bed. Then she felt the pain, only not as badly this time. She cried out at first, but a moment later such waves of pleasure went through her that she cried out in ecstasy rather than pain. He could see that this time she was enjoying it more, and he felt proud and manly. He was pleasing his woman.

He moved in a natural rhythm, and this time she moved with him. He held back as long as he could, a difficult feat when watching the pleasure and wild abandon evident on her face, when aware of her slender legs and flat belly, and of the blond hair that lay in tangles about her head. It was all done so quickly, but necessarily so, for they had been apart five whole days! His life spilled into her and he groaned something in the Cherokee tongue; then he came down on her, embracing her, remaining inside her.

"God, I love you, Andrea," he whispered. "Tell me it didn't hurt. Tell me I can do it again. I want to stay inside you."

Her eyes were closed. He kissed her cheek, her neck; and

she ran her fingers through his dark hair. "It didn't hurt as bad," she said softly. "I want to do it again, too. I miss you so when we're apart, Adam."

"I miss you, too. It almost hurts."

She opened her eyes and looked up into the great tree. They were safe here—alone, together, in love. How she loved this tree. Beneath it, she had found Adam Chandler and love; she had become a woman. It was like being protected by God.

"We have to do something, Adam. We can't go on like this."

"I know." He kissed her lips. "I will think of something. Do not worry."

She smiled and looked into his dark eyes. "I'm not worried, not when I'm with you this way. It's when we're apart and I'm alone that I get scared. In your arms, under the oak tree, I'm never afraid."

He smiled. "I am glad you found my tree."

"Our tree," she reminded him.

He laughed lightly. "Our tree." He sobered then, and she felt a slight surging inside of her. "Andrea . . ."

"It's all right, Adam. I'm ready."

He kissed her hungrily then, began to move rhythmically again. Her own passions mounted as she felt his manhood growing inside of her, and soon her breathing was as rhythmic as her movements. She could whimper and cry out up here, and there was no one to hear. He could groan her name and voice his pleasure in her, tell her sweet, teasing things that made her blood run hot.

This time it took longer for him to rid himself of his seed. Now he could hold back better, and she was still moist and willing from the first time. They moved in rhythmic splendor, both enjoying, neither able to get quite enough of the other. Slightly raised up, he watched her, studying her beauty, the small breasts that were his alone. She reached up and felt the hard muscles of his arms and shoulders, running her fingers down over his chest to his strong thighs and then circling his hips and tracing his belly and chest before touching his face, running her fingers through his hair. It was the longest they had ever been joined, and it was their most enjoyable union yet.

Finally he found release, in a shuddering moment of pure glory. Gently, he moved away from her then, to lie down beside her and draw her into his arms.

For several minutes they simply lay there, neither of them talking. Finally he drew another blanket over them.

"Are you all right?" he finally asked.

"I'm fine," she answered in a small voice.

He kissed her hair and sighed. "There is quarreling among my own people now," he told her. "Some of the wealthier ones argue that if we leave right now, before the Georgia citizens start coming down on us, we can avoid losing everything we have, avoid losing our wealth."

"What does your father say?"

"He says never, and so do I. We will not sell ourselves out like that. Pride comes first. Our love for the land comes first. Let them do what they will. They will not get us out of Georgia."

She kissed his chest. "It's all so horrible, especially knowing my own father would like to see you go. Ruth didn't tell them anything. They asked plenty of questions, but she acted like she was ignorant of everything."

"Ruth is a good girl. We fight sometimes, but we love each other. She is smart."

Andrea choked back a sob. "Oh, Adam, what are we going to do?"

He kissed her hair. "We are going to love each other. That's all. Just love each other and trust in that love. It will keep us together."

"Maybe that's not enough, Adam. I feel outside forces pulling at us. It scares me."

He squeezed her close. "You just wait. By the end of summer it will all be straightened out. Your parents will have no choice but to let you marry me. Our being together is as natural as the sun rising. We have joined just the way the animals do, naturally, a male and female drawn to each other by the hand of God. We are all one, you know—the land, the air, the animals. This is all just a part of the joy of life, and it is right. God approves of it. That is why men and women were made like the animals, why they mate almost the same way. It is all just part of nature, except that we think."

"My mother says it's wrong to enjoy a man."

"She has never known this kind of joy. She was brought up under those silly white man's rules that say to enjoy our bodies is a sin. It is not a sin. It is good and right. Otherwise we would not have been made this way." He kissed her again then, gently fondling a breast. "It might be another whole week this time, Andrea."

"Oh, Adam!"

He moved over her again, and the tree sheltered them from the outside world.

Later the same day Mary washed her face of the sweat that had resulted from her long walk. Her curiosity over Andrea's frequent long rides had gotten the better of her. She'd waited and watched, sneaking along behind Andrea that morning when her pony went by and started its ascent of the ridge. The climb had slowed the animal enough to allow Mary to follow. But when the Cherokee boy had come running down to greet Andrea, Mary had ducked behind a bush and had quickly descended, afraid the Indian boy would somehow sense her presence. She'd feared he might kill her and scalp her for following.

So, it was true! Andrea was meeting Adam Chandler on the ridge! It was more than friendship. Maybe Andrea even knew about boys now. Maybe she'd been . . . Mary's jealousy knew no bounds. She wanted to be the first to have an Indian boy. Yet there was Andrea with Adam though she acted so innocent and good.

She wiped off her face and went into the kitchen.

"Where have you been all morning?" her mother asked.

"Just walking." The girl sat down at the table and picked up a peach. "Mother, if a girl is really a good friend, shouldn't she tell on a friend she thinks is doing something that is bad for her?"

Ethel Means frowned. "What do you mean?"

"I mean . . . well . . . I think you should tell Andrea's parents to watch her better . . . maybe follow her and see where she goes when she rides in the morning."

The woman eyed her closely. "What has Andrea been up to?"

"Oh, Mother, she's my best friend! I don't want her to get into trouble!"

"Mary Means, you tell me what's going on!"

"Well, she just . . . I saw her go up the ridge, that's all. Maybe it's nothing. Oh, please don't tell her parents I'm the one who told."

Her mother sighed deeply. "I won't tell. But I'll try to suggest that her father watch her for a while."

"Well, I wouldn't have said anything if she weren't my best friend."

"I know, dear. You're a good girl."

Mary smiled.

CHAPTER SEVEN

Andrea saddled her pony. She had met Adam five times since the first time he'd made love to her under the oak tree. Each time seemed more wonderful than the last. And she didn't doubt his sincerity. There was not a treacherous bone in Adam Chandler's body. In her heart she knew their love was good and right. Somehow, someday they would tell the whole world about it. But it was nearly August now. Something had to be done before school started. How could a woman like herself think about school now?

She tightened the cinch, then heard footsteps behind her. Her father stood at the doorway to the stall.

"Where are you going?"

She could not help reddening at his sudden appearance and the all-knowing look in his dark eyes. He had caught her off guard. Never before had she been questioned when taking her pony out for exercise.

She swallowed. "Just . . . just riding, Father. All my chores are done."

"You stay home today."

She could feel herself sweating, and she was suddenly weak. Adam! He was waiting for her!

"Why? I said I did all my chores. My room is clean and—"

"You'll stay home today and not question it," the man snapped. "If you want to exercise your pony, ride him around in the back field, within sight of the house."

He knew! Somehow he knew, or at least suspected! But how much did he know? "I don't understand, Father. I . . . I've done nothing wrong."

"Haven't you?"

She swallowed again, trying not to shake visibly. "No, I haven't."

The man nodded slowly. "Then don't start now by disobeying me. Stay close to the house. And I suggest you do some thinking, girl, about not bringing shame upon this family and falling into sinful ways."

"I . . . I don't know what you mean."

"You think about it, daughter. Go and think about it, and pray about it, and remember your Bible lessons. You're a child, with a child's mind, too ignorant to know when you might be being foolishly used. I'll not question you. I'll give you this one chance to think about . . . things . . . and to start acting in an honorable and Christian manner. No more will be said about it. But there will be no more riding alone, understand? This country is too dangerous, and right over that ridge are Indian boys just itching to get their hands on pretty little girls like you. Now stay close to the house and say no more about it." He turned and walked out.

Andrea's eyes brimmed with hot tears of anger and panic. Adam! What would he think when she didn't show up? How could she bear not being able to see him again? How could she explain?

She climbed up onto her pony, backed the animal out of the stall and trotted it out of the barn. She headed to the back field. She had to be alone. She had to think. Adam! Adam! She rode hard, all the way to the back fence, where she dismounted and walked to the railing. Leaning on it, she burst into bitter sobbing. If only she were older. If only she had some kind of help, someone to talk to. Should she just jump the fence and keep riding? Should she head for the ridge and ride over it, never to return? What would her father do? Would that bring a lot of trouble to the Cherokee, make them hate her? And was she truly a bad girl for lying naked with Adam Chandler? She loved him. Adam didn't think it was bad. He already considered her his wife, the Cherokee way. Things were once so simple for the Indians. Why did her people have to make everything so complicated? How could a piece of paper signed by a preacher make a marriage any more right and valid? Some people who married that way weren't happy at all. But Andrea knew she could be blissfully happy living with Adam.

She sat down in the grass, unable to stop her crying, and prayed with all her might that something would happen that would let her be with Adam. She prayed he would understand, when she didn't show up, that it was only because she couldn't, not because she didn't love him anymore. But what if he didn't?

"Oh, Adam!" she sobbed. "I love you so much. Please don't be mad at me."

How long she sat there crying, she wasn't sure. She couldn't go back to the house. She never wanted to go back. They knew something, and they would look at her with those eyes, those accusing eyes. But how did they know? Where had she gone wrong? She wiped her eyes and tried to think. What had happened the last few days? On Saturday she had met Adam again. Yesterday was Sunday, and the Meanses had come for dinner, as they always did. Mary had been more friendly than she'd been since they'd argued in front of Ruth.

Andrea's eyes widened, and her heart filled with hatred. Mary! She was nicer because she knew inside she had betrayed her best friend. Surely Mary had said something. That was the only way Andrea's parents would suspect anything. Maybe Mary had dropped some kind of devious hint to her own parents, and they had said something to Andrea's. She got to her feet, her fury almost unbearable, tears coming again, this time tears of anger and hatred.

Mary! Jealous, deceitful Mary. She was just like her brother! She broke into renewed sobbing, for on top of everything else, it was obvious she had lost the loyalty of the girl who had once been her best friend. Mary had betrayed her. It all made sense now, the quiet dinner table yesterday, the way the Meanses had kept looking at her, as though she had stolen something or shot someone. What had they been thinking? Dirty, lurid things, no doubt. They thought her simply a "bad girl" who liked to do naughty things with Indian boys. Whatever Mary said, she had surely made Andrea's behavior sound terrible. And no matter what Andrea said now, she knew she could never make herself look any better. She had been sneaking around behind her parents' backs, and that was enough to make them disbelieve anything she said.

How many more tears were left in her? How could she ever stop crying? Everything was going wrong. Maybe she would never see Adam again. Somehow she had to get a message to him. Somehow she had to see him once more.

She heard her mother's voice calling then, and she shivered. She blew her nose on a handkerchief she kept tucked into her belt, and wiped her eyes. They would know she'd been crying, but she didn't care. What did it matter anymore? She mounted her pony, her legs suddenly tired and weak, and rode slowly toward the house.

"It's nearly lunch time," her mother called when she came closer. "You've been sitting out there for nearly four hours! What's wrong with you, child? Are you sick?"

The woman looked startled upon seeing Andrea's swollen eyes and puckered face. "You've been crying. Are you in pain or something? I knew there was something wrong."

"Nothing's wrong," she answered sullenly. "Father told me I couldn't go riding anymore. Why, Mother? I've been good."

The woman's eyes hardened slightly. "So, that's it. Well, we both discussed it and agreed you should stay closer to home. For heaven's sake, Andy, it isn't something to make such a fuss over. Is all that crying just because you can't go riding?"

The girl just hung her head, and wiped at her eyes again.

"There is something you aren't telling us, Andrea

112

Sanders," her mother chided. "And I think it has to do with a boy. That's why the long rides will stop. I only hope you haven't done something foolish and shamed yourself before God. I think you have some praying to do, daughter. If you've had feelings for a boy, you'd better ask God's forgiveness and just forget those feelings. They're useless and sinful, and you're just a child. It is a boy, isn't it? Have you been meeting someone up on the ridge?"

Andrea reddened and swallowed. Adam! Poor Adam! "No," she answered quietly. "I just like being alone."

The woman studied her daughter closely. "So. You have chosen to add lying to your list of sins!"

Andrea met her eyes pleadingly. If only she could talk to the woman. "Mother, I haven't done anything bad. I—"

"Unsaddle that pony and go into the house! I'll hear no more of your lies! Maybe staying in your room for the next two weeks, and ten lashes across your thighs with your father's leather belt, will rid you of your sinful ways, Andrea Sanders! I never thought a daughter of mine would stoop to sneaking behind our backs. We know you've gone to the ridge, so don't deny it. I've seen how you look when you get back, all starry-eyed and flushed." It suddenly struck Andrea that the woman seemed almost jealous. "The only thing we don't know is who you've been meeting up there. I only pray that he is a white boy! Now get that pony to the barn!"

Andrea's chest felt as if something were crushing it. What should she do? How could she talk to Adam? Never had she seen her mother so angry. If she could get away with murder, she'd go and kill Mary Means. This was her doing, Andrea was sure. How else would her parents know she'd been up on the ridge? Mary had planted a seed of distrust, and it had sprouted. The only saving grace was that they didn't know who the boy was. Maybe they didn't even suspect Adam. Her heart lightened a little, and she headed her pony to the barn. If they didn't suspect Adam, maybe she could talk them into letting Ruth come to stay. Then she could get a message to Adam!

Of course! That was the answer! She would say it was a

white boy but wouldn't give a name. Then she would say she was sorry and would never do it again, and she'd ask if Ruth could come and stay. They still wanted to find out everything the Cherokee were up to. They'd surely let Ruth come, and then she could get a message to Adam!

She unbridled and unsaddled her pony, brushed her down and then hurried back to the house. She didn't relish seeing the look in her mother's eyes, and she could already feel the awful sting of the leather belt on her thighs. It wasn't used often, but when it was, the pain was long remembered. But she would not tell. She'd never tell who the boy was. They'd never know—not until she was safe in Adam's arms and in his home, where she would stay forever.

Adam paced nervously. Where was she? Something had gone wrong! Did her parents know? Had they found out somehow? Or perhaps Andrea was hurt. Perhaps her pony had stumbled and thrown her somewhere along the way.

He grabbed his own horse and headed it down the ridge. Maybe he should look for her on her side, just to be sure she wasn't hurt. He carefully made his way through the thick, forested hillside. It was a beautiful summer day, and the sweet smell of wildflowers filled his nostrils, while singing birds serenaded the sun. But he saw and heard nothing. His heart was heavy with dread. What had happened to Andrea? She would never deliberately not come. He was too sure of her love and loyalty. She was his wife by all Cherokee standards.

He carefully led his horse over rocks and fallen trees until he was nearly at the bottom of the ridge. He looked out at the distant farms, then moved carefully behind thick foliage and, in deep shadow, headed toward the Sanderses' farm, deciding it would not be wise to be spotted. Finally he tied his horse and proceeded on foot until he was close enough to see people and movement. Her father was working on a plow, banging a hammer against the metal, but Andrea was not in sight. He worked his way farther around to the other side of the house.

Then he saw her, sitting far out in the back field near the fence, her pony beside her. Why was she there? The pony was saddled and ready to ride. Something was very wrong, and his heart beat wildly. What had happened that kept them apart? He felt sick inside. He moved through growing corn, stooping low so as not to be seen, making his way toward the fence. He would call out to her, find out what had happened. He had nearly reached Andrea when he heard her mother calling for her. He cursed himself then for not having come sooner. By the time he'd reached the spot from which he would have called to her, she was already mounted and riding toward the house.

He crept closer and watched from the cornstalks. She was close to her mother now, and the woman seemed to be shouting something. He caught only pieces of words and sentences: "sneaking behind our backs . . . ridge . . . at least a white boy . . . across your thighs with a leather belt . . ."

His lips tightened. They knew! Somehow they knew, but apparently they did not know who she'd met. Andrea! Poor Andrea! Were they going to beat her? What did they mean about a leather belt? Was she going to suffer on his account? He felt as though he would burst with rage. Yet he could not go over there and tell them anything. That might make things worse, them finding out it was a Cherokee boy she'd been seeing. And as long as they didn't know that, there might be a way he could see her, go to the house on a casual visit and somehow get a message to her. He hated leaving her, but he had no choice. At least the problem was caused by her parents. If it were due to someone dangerous, he would have ridden right in there and killed him. Perhaps in the end he would have to ride away with her against her parents' will. There seemed to be no other way.

He turned and went back through the corn and the underbrush, making his way back to his horse. He would get to her. Somehow he would get to her, talk to her. Andrea! Poor Andrea! They were going to meet, make love, be together again. How had the day turned out so terrible? How could he stand not knowing what had happened, and what was happening to her now? And how had they found out? Mary? He'd like to get his hands around Mary Means's neck. He wished this was the old days, and he could just go and murder the girl slowly! Poor Andrea, suffering her parents' angry tirades all alone, being made to look and feel bad and sinful. He could just imagine what they were saying to her. And if they knew her lover was a Cherokee boy . . . He blinked back angry tears. Nothing hurt so deeply as unwarranted prejudice and hatred. They loved each other. Why shouldn't they be together? It was all so simple. Why did everyone else have to complicate it, just because she was young and he was Cherokee?

He reached his horse and hugged its neck, weeping against its mane. "Andrea!" he sobbed. "Damn them! Damn them all!" He mounted up and headed back up the ridge. There would be no Andrea today, no sweet love under the oak tree. Perhaps they would never be together that way again.

Two long, lonely weeks passed. Every day Adam went to the oak tree, hoping that by some miracle Andrea would show up. But she never came. She was suddenly gone out of his life, and the emptiness was almost more than he could bear. The only way to end this agony was to have her near him always. He thought about sneaking to her house in the night and stealing her away. But that would give her parents an excuse to have him arrested. Maybe something even worse would happen. And he had to think about the consequences for the Cherokee. Still, if doing things the right way did not work, he knew he would eventually resort to stealing her and taking the risks.

The right way. What was the right way? He knew the answer. He must go to the Sanderses' house, admit his love for their daughter, and ask for her hand in marriage. Maybe it wouldn't be as bad as he thought. Maybe now that they knew she had been seeing someone, when they found out who it was, they would consent for the sake of her honor. Yes! Of course! He'd been sitting here every day under the oak tree and praying for an answer. This was the answer. He would bring it out into the open once and for all. He laughed out loud and started to run home. He would talk to his father. They would go together to get Andrea and bring her home with them. Surely now that her parents had had time to think about everything, they would know it was the right thing to do. His own father had once told him that if he still loved Andrea after a time, he should go and tell her parents. And he most certainly did still love her!

Andrea! How tempted he had been to try to see her. But common sense had told him he must bear the pain of being apart, for to go to her too soon would only make her parents more angry. Andrea! What was she thinking? Was she wondering if he would ever come for her . . . if he had forgotten about her? He hadn't! He loved her and she belonged to him. He was her first man and he'd be her only man. She was his wife, and it was time to go and claim her.

He was breathless when he reached his farm. He ran to one of his father's huge storage barns, where he found Jonas Chandler inspecting some peanuts. Chandler looked at his son. During the last two weeks, Adam had lost weight, had had little to say, and had smiled at no one. Now to his surprise the boy was smiling. Jonas suspected his son's downcast mood had had something to do with the white girl, and he wondered what had just happened.

"Father, we have to talk," Adam told him.

"Right now? I am in the middle of something, son."

"It's important, Father. More important than the peanuts. I need your help, before I go crazy and do something foolish."

The man sighed over the trials and tribulations of trying to raise a handsome, intelligent, energetic son who was now madly in love with a white girl. He dropped the peanuts, ordered a hand to pick out any that were too small, then walked outside with Adam, away from any who might hear them talking. He leaned against a fence and studied his son, seeing more desperation in the boy's eyes than he had realized was there. He lit a pipe, his heart filled with dread and warnings.

"I have been worried about you ever since you told me about that girl, Adam," he spoke up. "And the last couple of weeks I have been especially worried. Did she change her mind about you?"

Adam took on a proud, defensive look. "Never, Father! Not Andrea. She is not that kind. She is . . . I love her . . . truly love her. And she loves me." He turned away then, watching some cattle graze. "She is my wife, Father . . . by Cherokee law."

There was a long moment of silence, and when he faced his father again, the man's eyes were sad and concerned. "I warned you not to touch her that way."

Adam swallowed. "We could not help it, Father. It seemed so . . . so right. And we were always so scared, having to meet secretly and all. It just made it seem more urgent . . . more necessary. I couldn't bear the thought of maybe never having her that way. And she wanted me, too. I was . . ." He looked down, leaning against the fence himself. "I was her first. I made her my woman, Father, and I'm glad. She is good and sweet and beautiful, and she loves me just for me. She doesn't care that I am Cherokee."

"Her parents will care. We know that now more than the first time we talked."

The boy nodded. "Yes, sir. But that will not stop us." He looked at his father, determined and possessive. "Nothing will stop us! I want her, Father. I want to be with her always, to sleep with her at night and provide for her and take care of her like a man is supposed to do for his wife!"

Jonas put a hand on the boy's arm. "Calm down, son." He set the pipe on the fence railing. "What has happened?"

Adam turned away. "I am not sure. I think somehow her parents found out she was meeting someone on the ridge. Suddenly she stopped coming. I snuck down to her house that first day she didn't show up, and I saw her crying out in the field. I started to go to her, but then her mother called her, and I heard shouting, something about a boy and the ridge and beating her with a belt. I don't think they know who the boy is, but they suspect she has been meeting someone. I have not seen her since. That was about two weeks ago." He turned then, his eyes teared. "Father, I can't stand this. If they don't let me have her, I'll go and steal her! I'll—"

"You'll do no such thing! We're hanging on to our land by a thread as it is, Adam! Don't do something stupid!"

The boy swallowed, one tear slipping down his cheek. "I don't care anymore what happens. I want Andrea. I want . . . I want to go to their house and tell them I love her and wish to marry her. Will you come with me?"

Jonas Chandler's heart was breaking into pieces as he watched the agony on his son's face. How painful was young love, how passionate and possessive. What choice did he have but to go and at least try, for his son's sake? The boy had been suffering alone for the last two weeks, unsure what to do. He was such a man, yet in many ways still a boy who needed his father's help and approval. Chandler nodded.

"I will go with you. But I must have your promise that whatever they say, you will remain calm and will not cause trouble. Promise me, Adam."

The boy breathed deeply for control. "I promise, Father."

They embraced then, and Jonas could feel the boy shaking. How long had it been since he'd first walked? Wasn't it only yesterday? It irritated him that just because Adam was Cherokee, he could not have the girl he loved. It wasn't right. But worse things could happen. Being Cherokee might mean they could not own land and have their own government. What was so wrong about being an Indian? It wasn't just his son's love he worried about. It was the whole Cherokee Nation, more and more threatened by white invasion. He looked past his son at the cattle, the farm, their lovely home. How long would he be able to hang on to all that he loved?

*   *   *

Andrea's heart pounded wildly when she went to the window at the sound of approaching horses. It was nearly dusk, but there was no mistaking who the riders were. "Adam!" she whispered.

There could only be one reason why he had come. It would be out now. They would have to tell. He must think her parents would consider letting them be together, but she knew otherwise, and never had she been so afraid, not for herself, but for Adam.

She ran to her closet, ripped out a pretty pink dress, and quickly removed the one she'd worn all day. She slipped on the pink one, wishing she'd known they were coming so she could have been ready. Hurriedly, pulling a brush through her hair, she then leaned forward and pinched her cheeks. She looked terrible, for she'd hardly eaten during the past two weeks and she'd cried so much she wasn't sure she had any tears left. She had considered running away several times, but something had told her to wait for Adam. She'd been certain he would come, that he could know what to do, once he'd figured out she could not come to him.

She heard footsteps on the porch, the door opening . . . voices. What were they saying! They came inside. He was here with his father. What other reason would bring him to her home? He had come for her. Adam! Her beautiful, wonderful Adam! He'd come for her, like the man that he was. Andrea's heart pounded furiously. Her one glimpse of him told her he looked wonderful but that he, too, had lost weight. He was dressed in a fine black suit and wore a round, felt hat. He and his father both rode fine Thoroughbreds, sleek animals of quality breeding.

The voices moved to the parlor, and Andrea went to the door of her room. There was still a little pain in her legs from her father's beating, but the welts and redness were mostly gone, with only faint bruises remaining. She opened the door and started out, but her mother met her at the top of the stairs, her dark eyes stern and angry.

"Stay up here. Don't come downstairs."

"But . . . we have company."

"Get back to your room!" her mother ordered.

Andrea backed up, and Mrs. Sanders turned and went back downstairs. Then Andrea snuck to the railing, trying to hear but unable to discern much of the conversation until her father's voice was raised.

"So, it was you!"

"Yes, sir." Adam's reply was calm. "I love your daughter, as much as any man can love a woman. I wish to marry her, in a proper Christian wedding. I am a Christian, a Methodist—"

"You are a heathen!" Sanders interrupted. "What vile things did you do to my daughter? What devil's play have you been up to?"

Andrea began to shake, and a lump swelled in her throat.

"I have done nothing vile with your daughter," Adam replied, his own anger now burning inside.

"My son is a good boy," Jonas Chandler spoke in Adam's defense. "And not really a boy. He is a man. He is educated, strong, intelligent. He is handsome and hardworking. Someday he will inherit all that I have, be a rich man in his own right. He can provide well for your daughter, and I know he would take good care of her."

"Do you really think I care about those things? You are Indians! My daughter will not marry any Indian. And what makes you think that by the time you die you'll own anything at all, Chandler? When you die, it will be in Indian Territory. Yes, your land might belong to my daughter someday—through me—because I'll own it!"

Andrea's eyes widened in shock and horror. How could her own father talk that way?

Downstairs Adam grabbed Morgan Sanders's lapels and shook the man. "I love Andrea! Don't do this to us! She's mine! Mine by right! I have already claimed her!"

"Adam!" Jonas Chandler pulled at the boy, but Adam was bigger than his own father and would not let go. He shoved Andrea's father onto a couch. Sanders drew back a big fist then and landed it in Adam's face. There was a loud crash.

"Adam!" Andrea cried out. She flew down the stairs and into the parlor, running to where Adam lay against the wall, his lower lip split and bleeding. "Adam!" she repeated. She turned wild eyes to her father. "I hate you! I never dreamed you could be this way!"

"You get to your room, you slut!" he roared, heading for Adam, who was struggling to his feet.

"No! Don't you touch him!" Andrea threw herself over him, but her father yanked her away by the hair of the head, throwing her sideways. Her head struck a table, and she slumped to the floor.

"Andrea!" Adam looked from her to Sanders, who was already bent over, ready to land another blow on Adam. Adam butted the older man with his head, knocking him back.

"Adam!" Again Jonas grabbed at his son. "You made me a promise! This is not the way!"

"I don't care!" Adam shouted, struggling against his hold, tears in his eyes. "She belongs to me! And now he's hurt her!" He yanked himself away and charged into Sanders, punching wildly at the man, but Sanders was bigger and full grown. He brought a booted foot up hard into Adam's privates and the boy buckled in black pain.

"I'll teach you to use that thing on my daughter!" Sanders growled, licking at blood on his lip.

Jonas bent over his son, then looked up at Sanders. "I took a vow against violence, Mr. Sanders, but don't count on such a vow after this. We came here to speak to you in the proper way, to ask for your daughter's hand in respectable marriage. You once opened your home to us, and to my daughter—"

"Only because it was the best way to find out what you've got, Chandler, and to find out what the Cherokee are up to. If your heathen son had kept his hands off my daughter, things might have been fine. Just because I offered our friendship and our food, that didn't mean I was offering my daughter for your son's pleasure! Now get him out of here, and don't ever let me see him again!"

Adam struggled to his feet, groaning Andrea's name. He

stumbled over to her, bending over her unconscious body. "Andrea!" He touched her face, bending down and kissing her forehead.

"Get him away from her!" Morgan Sanders roared. He stormed to a corner of the room and picked up a rifle. "This thing is loaded. Get him out of here before I shoot him! I can tell the law anything I like, and they'll believe it because you're Cherokee, so don't think I can't kill him and get away with it! Now get out!"

Jonas Chandler wanted nothing more than to murder Morgan Sanders at that moment. But Sanders had acted much worse than he had expected, and at the moment the man had the upper hand. Adam was bent over Andrea, rocking in his own pain but weeping over her as she lay still and unconscious.

Jonas went to the boy. "Adam, come with me. He'll kill you if you don't," he told him urgently. "Please, Adam. What use would you be to her dead?"

"No! I won't leave her! Bring her with us, Father! Bring her with us!"

"We can't, Adam. Not right now. Trust in the Lord, Adam, and in your love."

Sanders moved closer, pointing the rifle at Adam. "Get up, boy, or I'll splatter your brains all over this room!"

Adam patted Andrea's face once more, then slowly got to his feet. His father was right—for now. What good was he to her if he was dead? But he would be back. He would be back!

"I will go, Father, but only because I do not want you to get hurt."

Jonas Chandler's eyes teared. "I am sorry, son. I did not think it would be quite this way."

"You thought wrong, Chandler!" Sanders roared. "Your dirty-minded son messed with my innocent daughter. That's all your Cherokee boys are good for. I thought it might be different, thought a fine family like yours could be trusted. That just goes to show that no matter how educated and refined an Indian pretends to be, he's still an Indian! Now get out."

123

Jonas took his son's arm, but Adam still stared down at Andrea. How could he leave her behind? Would her father beat her? "Andrea!" he groaned.

"Come, Adam. There will be a right time."

"Not as long as I'm alive!" Sanders growled.

Adam glared at him. "My love for your daughter will win, Mr. Sanders," he hissed. "You will see! She will be my wife, and you can't stop us!"

"Don't bet on it, Cherokee!"

"Adam, come away now," his father urged. "Let them get a doctor for Andrea. The longer we stay, the worse it is for her."

Adam looked down at her. "I should be with her."

"Give it time, Adam. Come. Do not bring harm to these people. It will only hurt the cause."

"My only cause is Andrea!" the boy growled, jerking away.

Sanders rammed his rifle barrel into the boy's stomach. "This is my last warning. Do like your pa says, boy. I've reached my limit!"

Adam was not afraid, only wise. If someone got killed over this, Andrea would be ruined forever, and a war could come out of it. There would be another time. He would see to it. He turned and quickly walked out, ignoring the pain that still engulfed him. Andrea! He should not ride away from her, but what else could he do? He had not come prepared for such hatred. He had not known it was so bad.

He mounted up, bending over in pain then.

"Hang on, son," his father told him, picking up the reins of his horse and leading it. Then they rode off, Sanders watching until they were out of sight.

When they'd gone, the angry man went back inside. His wife was bent over Andrea.

"She is hurt, Morgan."

"I'll take her upstairs. You pack her bags and I'll ride for that woman we met Sunday at church—the one from the Christian school up north, where we talked about sending Andrea this fall. She's going right now."

"What?" The woman looked at her husband curiously. "Tonight?"

"Tonight. She's just got a bump on her head. By the time she comes to and gets rid of her headache, she'll be well on her way north, away from Adam Chandler! Maybe two or three years away from home will straighten her out and make her forget him. I only hope this doesn't get out and that some day she can marry a respectable man." He picked her up and carried her up the stairs to her bed, placed her on it. "Get packing. I'll be back in a couple of hours. If she comes to, give her some whiskey or something to relax her. Don't let her come fully awake, or she might try to run to that bastard." He stared down at his daughter disgustedly. "Imagine, our Andrea lying in sin with that . . . that . . ." He turned away. "My God! I just wanted to make friends with them, to find out what the Cherokee were doing. How did this happen?"

"The devil works in devious ways," his wife replied, a strange sadness in her voice.

Sanders sighed. "Well, his work is finished. Andrea Sanders will be a mature woman with some sense the next time she sees Adam Chandler, if she ever sees him at all. She'll change her tune when she grows up some. I just hope she can forgive herself."

Andrea lay still, hearing but unable to speak or react, an odd blackness swimming over her eyes, her body weak and lifeless. Adam! Where was Adam? Where was she going?

"Do you think Mrs. Endicott will take her in the middle of the night like this?"

"She will for the right price." He went to the door. "Keep the doors locked. I'll have a couple of hands keep watch in case that young heathen comes back. After tonight it won't matter. Andrea won't be here."

CHAPTER EIGHT

"Father, I cannot leave her there."

"You must for now. They are her parents. They can't bring her any real harm. We need time to plan, Adam."

"He wasn't even upset when her head struck the table! What if she dies or something." Adam halted his horse. "Father, I have to go back. I have a terrible sick feeling inside. I can't just . . . just leave."

"He would have killed you, and gladly. Don't go back and give him reason to do so. What good would you be to her then? We'll go home and send back one of the white missionaries. Maybe Sanders will listen to one of them."

Adam swallowed back an urge to cry. His groin screamed with pain, his mouth hurt. But he would gladly go back and beat on Morgan Sanders again, and take a licking himself if necessary. But the gun . . . Sanders meant business. He had not been prepared for quite so much hatred. He'd never dreamed it could be that bad. Andrea! Andrea!

"Do you really think one of our missionary friends could help?"

"It is worth a try, son. At least they are white. And surely the Sanderses would have respect for good, Christian people of their own kind."

Adam kept staring backward. "There is nothing good and Christian about Morgan Sanders. He might pretend to be a Christian, but that is not the kind of Christianity we

127

have been taught. All I can see is Andrea . . . lying there. It isn't right. I should be with her."

"Adam, if you go back there he'll shoot you. Please, son, come home now. We'll give them a few days to calm down, then send a missionary."

"What if he hurts her!" The boy's voice was choked.

"She's his daughter, Adam. She'll be all right." He reached over and put a hand on the boy's arm. "What about you? Everything happened so fast. I should have done more—"

"No. Someone had to stay calm. I broke my promise to you, Father." The boy turned to meet his father's eyes in the moonlight. "I never meant to break it. I just . . . when he said someday he would own our land—"

"I know. It is for that very reason I did not fight him, Adam. It is a hard lesson for the young, to know when to fight and when to keep still. Right now we all must keep still, fight this thing legally. There are a lot of people on our side, important people like Daniel Webster, and a lot of people in the North. We cannot do anything foolish. One small wrong move can ruin it all, Adam. If Andrea loves you, she will also understand this. She will want you to do whatever is right to keep our Cherokee land."

The boy swallowed back tears, still shaking. "And does that mean we must sacrifice our love for it?"

Jonas sighed deeply. "I can't answer that, Adam. Sometimes we must think beyond our own personal needs and wants."

"I won't give her up!"

Jonas squeezed the boy's arm. "I can see that. But things do not always work out the way we want them to, Adam."

"Why? Because I am a Cherokee? What is so different about that? What is so horrible about being an Indian?"

His father smiled sadly and shook his head. "That question will be asked for many years to come, I am afraid. There is something about the white man that makes him think if a man's skin is very much darker than his own, there is something unworthy about him. But it is more than that, Adam. We Indians have something the white man wants—land. He has a lust for this land many times greater even than the desire you feel for your Andrea. That should tell you just how great is his desire. And we will have our hands full fighting it. Keeping our land from the whites will be many times harder than it will be for Morgan Sanders to keep Andrea from you. Now do you understand the danger?"

The boy sniffed and took a deep breath. He wished he were older, more powerful. "No white man will take what is mine—not my woman and not my land. He might get them both for a while, Father. But one day they will both be mine again. I make that vow tonight, before God and my father. Both will belong to me someday, and I'll not breathe my last breath until that happens."

Jonas nodded. "Somehow I feel it will, son. I might no longer be alive, but you'll make it happen. Come now. Come home and take care of your wounds. We'll talk to Reverend Jessup in the morning. He's a good man. He'll help us."

Adam turned his horse reluctantly. He was supposed to be with her, to protect her. In his heart Andrea was his wife. He should have brought her with him. But his father was right. Sanders was itching to shoot him. He had no choice but to leave. Still, if this were the old days . . . He spent the rest of the ride contemplating all the ways he could torture Morgan Sanders before killing him . . . if it were the old days.

Andrea awoke feeling ill. What was wrong with her bed? It was moving, bumping and jostling. She rubbed at her eyes, at first not remembering anything, certainly not remembering going to bed. She lay quietly for a moment, pretending she was in Adam's arms, as she always did when waking. But then another bump startled her and her eyes popped open to stare into the face of an older woman who was watching her with cold blue eyes. The girl's heart pounded faster. Where was she! She sat up slightly, but fierce pain swept through her head, forcing her to groan and lie back down.

"It would be wise not to sit up at all for a while, according to the doctor I talked to before coming for you," the woman stated.

Andrea put a hand to her forehead and opened her eyes again, trying to think, to stay calm and keep the awful pain from getting worse. Adam! Where was she, and what had happened to Adam? It all came back to her now, the night Adam came to tell her father—

She sat up in spite of the pain. She was in some kind of coach. The shades were drawn, but she could see sunshine peeping through the sides. "Where am I? Who are you? What happened to Adam?" Never had she known such fear and panic. Nothing was familiar. Why wasn't she in her room?

The woman leaned over and pushed her back down. "You just relax, Andrea. We have a long ride ahead of us. Considering what you've done, I think your father has made a very wise choice. You'll forget that sinful Cherokee boy soon and regret your waywardness. I think you're young enough that the Lord will understand and forgive you."

Pain seared through her, and she could not help the tears. "Please! Where am I? Who are you?"

"Don't you remember me? I'm Mrs. Endicott. I spoke with you in church Sunday—you and your parents. Your father was considering sending you to a Christian finishing school in the North. That's where we're going now."

Andrea choked back a sob. No! This couldn't be! "It's only the first of August. School doesn't start for another month. And I . . . I wasn't going to go. No one asked me."

"At your age you have no hand in such decisions," the woman said in an authoritative voice. "You're going early so that you will not be able to run to that Cherokee boy. And mind you, if you see him again, he'll be killed. Don't doubt that for one minute. So you might as well start forgetting about him right now. It will be a good two years before you're allowed to return home."

"No! I have to go to Adam! He'll be waiting for me—"

"You'll go nowhere. You certainly can't get out of this coach while it's moving, and once we reach our destination you'll be in a locked room until you come to your senses, child. And I told you, if you care anything for this Cherokee boy, you'll stay away from him, to protect his life. If you want him to stay alive, do as you're told. You're lucky your father didn't shoot him last night. He had the chance."

Andrea just stared at her. Mrs. Endicott suddenly seemed like nothing more than a witch to her. She felt as if she were living out some kind of horror story. Far away? A locked room? Adam almost shot? She was being taken away from Adam, her head screaming with pain from her own father's mistreatment, a virtual prisoner of a witch in a black coach. The child in her became terrified and she threw off the blankets. She'd leap out of the coach no matter how fast it was going!

She almost screamed in horror when she realized she was naked. Her eyes widened and she drew back onto the seat, pulling the blankets back over her. Mrs. Endicott only smiled. "A precautionary measure, in case you thought of running off. You can't go anywhere in that condition, now can you?" Her eyes darkened then. "Perhaps as you lie there in your nakedness you will remember how you lay naked for an Indian boy, Andrea Sanders, and you will realize what a sinful thing you've done. You'll have some extra hard work to do once you get to our school, to atone for your many sins. There will be little sleep for the likes of you for a while, so you'd better lie back and get what rest you can."

A cold fear crawled through Andrea's skin. Was it true Adam would be killed if she tried to get to him? What terrible things lay in wait for her? And what had happened to Adam? Poor Adam! She wondered what he would do when he found out what had become of her. Would he just try to forget her, marry some Cherokee girl? Would she ever see him again?

Mrs. Endicott pulled a small bottle from her handbag

and handed it to Andrea. "Drink some of this. It will make you sleep. You have a head injury and need your rest."

Andrea's blue eyes narrowed with distrust, and she cringed into the corner of the seat, huddling under the blanket. "I don't want it. And I don't want to sleep."

The woman's face hardened again. "Take it, or I'll rip that blanket off you and tell the driver to stop the coach and come back and take a look at you. You deserve to be shamed and humiliated like your parents. You're lucky they're going to try to keep your affair with that Indian trash a secret! In time you'll see for yourself what a fool you've been. Now drink some of this or I'll stop the coach and a strange man will be getting his eyes full of your nakedness. And he'll know what a slut you are!"

Andrea felt sick. She could see the woman meant it. She reached out and took the bottle. "I'm not a slut. I love Adam Chandler, and nothing you or the school can do will change that—not ever! And Adam will never stop loving me! Someday I'll be big enough to leave the school of my own accord, and I'll go right back to Adam Chandler."

The woman smiled haughtily. "You'll forget him soon enough. A child your age knows nothing about love."

Andrea took a drink of the bitter medicine and shivered. "If you knew anything about love, you'd let me go. You'd understand," she said sullenly, handing back the bottle. Mrs. Endicott jerked it from her hand and capped it.

"You have a disrespectful mouth, Andrea Sanders—something you acquired from that Cherokee, no doubt. Now get some rest."

She didn't want to sleep, but minutes later a grogginess came over her. She could not fight it. Her head drooped with the motion of the coach, and vivid visions of Adam came into her mind. She could see him so clearly. He was smiling the brilliant smile, sweeping her into his arms, kissing her warmly. They were lying under the oak tree. The oak tree. Oh, how she would miss it! She must go there. Somehow she must go there! Adam! She wasn't bad! Surely she wasn't bad! She was just in love—in love with

Adam Chandler. He wasn't dirty and sinful and disrespectful. He was clean and good, educated and kind, wealthy and mannered. He was strong and brave and beautiful, and he loved her. What could be so wrong about loving a man like Adam Chandler? Yes, he was a man, not a boy like Mrs. Endicott called him. And she was a woman, not a child. She belonged with Adam. Soon the coach and Mrs. Endicott vanished from her mind. She was in Adam's arms. . . .

Reverend Jessup approached the Sanderses' farm in his buggy, his heart heavy over the story he'd heard from young Adam Chandler and his father. He felt sorry for Adam, who was a brilliant young man with a great future, if the Georgia citizenry didn't decide to move in and take everything that belonged to the Cherokee. It was difficult for any Indian to become a great and accomplished person, for he met adversity on every side. Reverend Jessup considered that a ridiculous waste, and he didn't like the rumblings in Congress and among Georgia folk against the Cherokee. The Sanderses were just one example.

He sighed and shook his head as he came closer to the Sanderses' house. Young love . . . it certainly could be complicated, mostly because young people were so passionate and impetuous. Still, he remembered his own eagerness when he'd met his own wife. But they had not had to deal with the fear of being separated by hatred for people who are different. They hadn't had to wonder if each moment together might be the last. Perhaps, if it were not for that, Adam and Andrea would have waited until marriage for what they wanted, instead of having been pushed into joining. He could not fully blame the young pair, for they'd had to deal with their problem all alone, afraid to tell anyone, afraid to make their love public knowledge so they could marry and do everything the right way. But perhaps there was still hope. Perhaps now that the Sanderses had had a little time to think about the fact that their daughter had already joined herself to Adam

Chandler, they would consent to a marriage. That certainly wouldn't be the end of the world, and it would make everything honorable and legal. It would also make their poor daughter happy.

The minister was at the house then, and he halted the carriage and climbed out, tying the horse. He stepped onto the porch and knocked on the front door of the simple frame home, looked around while he waited. This was a fine farm, a little run down, but then Sanders had not owned it for very long and there was a lot of work to do. The Chandlers were obviously much more wealthy than the Sanderses, and he didn't doubt that part of Morgan Sanders's problem was jealousy. A lot of white men were jealous of the success and progress of the Cherokee. Jessup considered that foolish. Jealousy was a wasteful emotion. Why couldn't men be happy for each other, help each other? It was all so ridiculous.

The door opened then, and a stern, dark woman looked at him. Jessup immediately wondered where Andrea Sanders had gotten her blond hair and blue eyes. He remembered seeing her in church that weekend she had stayed with Ruth Chandler. He nodded to the woman in the doorway. "Mrs. Sanders?"

"I am," she answered coldly. "Who are you?"

"I am Reverend Harold Jessup. May I come in?"

She softened a little. After all, this was a minister. She stepped aside. "Is your husband home?" he asked as he entered.

"He's out in the corn fields. He'll probably see your carriage and be along soon. What can I do for you?" She closed the door.

"Well, Mrs. Sanders, I'm here about . . . about Adam Chandler . . . and your daughter."

The woman colored and frowned. "What about them? What would you know about it?"

The tall, homely but kind man removed his hat and bowed slightly. "I preach on the other side of the ridge, Mrs. Sanders, among the Cherokee. I have a church there. The Chandlers are members of that church. Adam and his

134

father came to me last night, after their little . . . encounter . . . here at your home."

Harriet Sanders drew in her breath and eyed him narrowly. "And do you, a preacher, approve of what that Cherokee boy and our daughter have been up to?"

Jessup smiled, a twinkle in his eyes. "The only thing they have been 'up to,' Mrs. Sanders, is love. They're terribly in love. It's that simple. They're good children, and truly now they are no longer children. Surely under the circumstances, you and your husband could allow them to be married. Adam Chandler is a very wealthy young man, and sincere in wanting to care for Andrea. The poor boy is just about crazy over what happened last night, and he asked if I would inquire about Andrea's health."

"Andrea is not here!" the woman interrupted. "And if you approve of the scandalous, sinful carryings on between those two, then you can't be much of a minister, Mr. Jessup! Surely you don't approve of a good Christian white girl groveling in the dirt with a heathen! That boy ruined our daughter. His lustful, devilish heart persuaded her, in her innocence, to do bad things. She has been sent away, where that Cherokee trash can no longer influence her!"

Jessup's face reddened in repressed anger and shock. "Sent away? She was here only last night."

"And before dawn she was gone. Do you think we'd let her stay anywhere near that boy for one more second? She's too young to know what's good for her. The foolish child would probably have tried to run to that boy. We're seeing to it that she can't."

"But, where—"

"None of your business! Don't you think we know the boy would try to go after her if he knew? Her father and I are the only ones who know where she has been taken, and she will not be allowed to write any letters or contact anyone. She will be assigned hard labor and long prayers to atone for her sins, and in two or three years she will be a woman, and will understand the foolish thing she did. We hope someday she will marry a man who is proper for her, and we intend to keep this ludicrous affair a secret from our friends, Reverend Jessup. You would do well to get back to the other side of the ridge and say no more about it."

Jessup just stared at her for a moment. She was like a piece of stone. "Perhaps you think what you're doing is the Christian thing to do," he finally said, "but it's wrong, Mrs. Sanders. If you love your daughter—"

"Love has nothing to do with it! There is no room for love in such matters, Reverend Jessup. There is right and wrong, no more, no less."

He swallowed back an urge to grab her around the throat and force her to tell him where Andrea was. He was surprised at the unexpected urge, for normally there wasn't a brutal bone in his body. Immediately he said a silent prayer for forgiveness.

"Mrs. Sanders, I urge you to reconsider. Think about your daughter, her feelings, her happiness. Adam Chandler is an intelligent, progressive young man who will one day inherit his father's wealth."

"His father's wealth will be short-lived, if the Georgia citizens have their way," Harriet Sanders replied coolly. "And they will. Valuable farmland should not be owned by mere savages. It should belong to white men who know what to do with it."

Jessup glared at her then. "The Cherokee run some of the finest farms in Georgia. They don't need white men to tell them what to do with the land. And in all my travels, the Cherokee are some of the finest people I've ever met. At the moment I can honestly say that most of them know more about being Christian than you do, Mrs. Sanders! Perhaps you'd do well to reread the Bible, especially Christ's teachings in the New Testament—about love and forgiveness, and about not judging others!" He put on his hat. "You're no mother, Mrs. Sanders, and right now I'm wondering if you're even human."

He opened the door and went outside, to find Morgan Sanders was approaching the house. As he walked up to him, Sanders frowned. "Something we can do for you, mister?"

Jessup glared at him, seeing the same stern, cold look in Morgan Sanders's eyes that he'd seen in his wife's. "Probably not," he answered. He untied his horse and climbed into his buggy. "When you and your wife decide the only really important thing is your love for your daughter, your concern for her happiness, come over to New Echota and see me."

Sanders watched him with smoldering eyes as Jessup backed his horse and carriage and drove off. Then he looked toward the doorway in which his wife stood.

"It's all your fault," he grumbled at her. "You planted the bad seed in her! Now you know the meaning of passing on your sins! You sinned, and now our daughter! I told you a long time ago I'd take care of her, provide for her, pretend she was mine and cover for your sins, woman, but she has shamed me now! She'll stay at that school until she's a proper lady. After that it's up to her. I don't care if I never see her again."

He stormed off, and Harriet Sanders went back inside the house, closing the door. She had tried to love her daughter, but Andrea was the seed of one night of passion with a traveling salesman—her one night of weakness, her one moment of wondering if lying with a man could be more than just duty. That was all Morgan Sanders had ever made it, strictly a wifely duty—undress, submit to a man she did not love, then watch him turn over and go to sleep as though she were nothing more than a "thing" to be used for his pleasure. The salesman and his devilish ways had brought out new emotions in her; silly, lustful feelings that had made her wonder about sex and why some women seemed to enjoy it. And for one night she had enjoyed it—one night of sin for which she had paid for the rest of her life. Andrea had been the first payment. Blond-haired, blue-eyed Andrea, who bore no resemblance to Morgan Sanders, but a strong resemblance to the blond-haired, blue-eyed salesman. For some reason Morgan Sanders had never gotten her pregnant, but the salesman had, in one night of sinful passion.

Morgan had tried to forgive her, but first he'd given her a terrible beating after seeing the salesman hurriedly climb out of the window when he'd come home unexpectedly. Then had come the silence, and, finally, an attempt at forgiveness. But he'd used her violently after that, taking out his revenge through his use of her at night. Then the blond-haired baby came, and after that she still could not get pregnant by Morgan. That and her building resentment, and her own suffering over her sin, had driven her to take another bedroom. She wanted no more of men and sex. She had tried to warn Andrea about feelings of lust and passion, and even love, but the child had not listened. Now she would suffer, too. That Cherokee boy could not possibly have loved her, no more than the salesman had loved her mother. Andrea had surely been used. And the worst part was that it had been done by an Indian boy. A white girl was not supposed to love an Indian boy. It simply wasn't right. But then, Andrea came from bad seed. Harriet had worked hard to make her daughter a proper, Christian girl. But when a child came from bad seed, there wasn't much that could be done. Perhaps the strict Christian school to which they had sent her would help. She could only pray that it would. She hated bringing more shame to poor Morgan. She had failed him. She knew that sometimes he went to visit the wild farm girls who lived north of them. But she couldn't blame him now. A man had a weakness for the animal instincts born in him, and she had had enough of such things. She was no longer willing to satisfy those needs.

Adam walked up the ridge toward the oak tree. All around him was summer beauty; singing birds, blooming wildflowers. But he heard and saw none of it. Andrea was gone, and he didn't even know where. Andrea! If only he could kill Morgan Sanders! If only he could do something, anything! This lonely, helpless feeling was almost more than he could bear. He wanted to cry, but his anger would not let the tears come.

He winced with pain as he climbed over a fallen log. He was still sore from Morgan Sanders's cruel kick, and his lower lip was swollen. But if he could have been given free rein, he knew he would have licked the man. He was strong enough. But poor Andrea had been lying there on the floor. He'd had to go to her, to try to help her . . . and then there was the rifle.

It all flashed through his mind over and over. He'd never dreamed there was that much hatred and prejudice in Morgan Sanders's heart. If he had known, he'd have done everything differently. He'd never have tried to speak to him of marrying Andrea. He'd have stolen her away as he'd wanted to do in the first place. At least then she'd be with him now. They'd probably be waking up together and . . .

He picked up a rock and threw it, the hot tears finally starting to come. Andrea! Andrea! Where had they taken her? He hated being too young to know what to do. He hated Morgan Sanders, and all the whites who hated Indians. And he hated those who were trying to make him leave his homeland, his fine house, his oak tree. He had never been truly afraid it could happen until now. He'd already lost Andrea, and now he'd seen just how deep the whites' hatred and jealousy ran. They really were a threat. It was possible that the whites would take the Cherokee land away, just like they'd done with the Creeks and the Choctaws! Yet the only thing that really mattered was Andrea. She was more important than anything else. And she was gone. Gone! What was he to do? Where should he look for her? Reverend Jessup had said he doubted she would even be registered under her own name, so checking all the schools in the north would probably lead to nothing. And maybe she had been taken farther south, rather than north. There were any number of places she could have been taken. To try to contact them all would take a lot of time and would probably prove fruitless. He did not doubt that the Sanderses intended to keep her identity and whereabouts a secret.

When Adam reached the oak tree, it really hit him. She was not there. He would never see her standing here waiting for him again, never lie beneath the tree with her naked body in his arms, never be one with her again, hear her voice, taste her lips, be inside of her, love her in every way. Andrea! Andrea!

He burst into tears then, for he was free to cry here under his tree, where no one could see and call him a child. Why couldn't a man cry? It hurt to try to hold it back. He put his face against the gnarled old trunk and wept as he had never wept in his entire sixteen years. He wanted to curse his Cherokee blood, but nothing could convince him there was something about it that made him a lesser man or an unworthy one. His pride only grew stronger; his determination to prove he was as good as the next man would not be crushed by Sanders's cruel words, nor by the outside forces that tried to keep him down just because he was Indian.

He cried for a long time. He had to get rid of all the tears before he went back. In a sense it seemed he was allowing himself to be a little boy for the last time. He wouldn't cry after this. He'd be strong, and if he had to wait, then he would wait. For one thing he was very sure of: if he could not find Andrea Sanders, Andrea Sanders would find him, just as soon as she could. When she came back home from wherever they had taken her, she would come to him. They would not break her any more than they could break him. Nothing and no one would stop them from loving each other, nor could anything kill that love in the future.

He sank down onto the grass under the tree, curling up, wishing Andrea were there to curl up with him. All he could do was pray that she would be all right and would somehow come back to him. Adam knew Reverend Jessup would try to find her, but neither he nor the minister had any hope of success. He wanted to be angry with his father for not letting him go and steal Andrea away, but Jonas had been right to think they should try it the honorable way first. He had only been thinking of the Cherokee and of the consequences of stealing her. And his father felt bad enough over what had happened. There was no sense in making him feel worse. Anyway, it was really his own fault. He shouldn't have let it go for so long. Yet how was he to tell anyone? How was he to know what to do when he loved a forbidden girl? But love her he did, and he would never stop.

He sat up and touched the tree trunk again. She'd loved this tree. It was their tree now, not just his. And although he ached for her, he knew that Andrea's situation was worse, for she had been taken someplace strange and new. Perhaps she would be punished, and would have to work like a slave. She would be told she was bad, and she would be afraid. Oh, yes, she would be afraid. He should be with her to hold her and protect her. The frustration of not being able to be with her was painful, and the thought of living without her for months, maybe years, made his chest ache fiercely. He'd considered putting a gun to his head or hanging himself, but the hope that someday she would come back had stopped him. If she returned, he must be here for her. He must be. So he would go on living, for Andrea, and nothing more.

CHAPTER NINE

For days that turned into weeks, the coach rattled on, and through it all Andrea was kept drugged, staying nights at times at unknown locations, carried in and out by a man she didn't know, constantly watched by Mrs. Endicott. It was a drizzly, gray day when they arrived at the school, a dreary-looking brick building four stories high. Andrea had no idea where she was, but it was cool here, and quite green. The grounds were overgrown and dark, and from what she could tell, being somewhat groggy, there was nothing pretty or cheery about this building, nor was there any welcoming warmth in the cold voices of the people she heard talking when she was carried inside.

"Andrea Sanders," someone said. She caught pieces of words and sentences—"has lain in sin with a Cherokee Indian boy" . . . "should do hard labor along with her schoolwork" . . . "will take a lot of hard work to cleanse her of her sins" . . . "slut, but still young enough to be saved. It's the boy's fault. Indians have the devil in them."

She felt herself being carried up several flights of stairs, then sensed the closeness of a small room. Someone set her on a bed. "Pay attention, Andrea." Mrs. Endicott's voice. "This is Miss Darcy. She runs this school, and will be in charge of you from now on. I have to go back to Georgia and tend to my mission work there."

Andrea blinked, staring through blurred eyes at a huge woman with black hair pulled back tightly into a neat bun. She couldn't see well, but she knew the woman was giving her one of those stern, disapproving looks.

"You won't need to take the medicine anymore, Andrea," the woman declared, her voice hard and gruff. "Your room will be locked, so we needn't worry about you running away. Besides, you're four stories up and there are bars on the window."

Adam! She could think only of two things. Where was she, and what had happened to Adam? If he were here, he'd help her.

"Once your head is clear you will begin some rigorous chores, and you will be watched at all times. You have proven that you need watching, haven't you? You've been a very bad girl, Andrea, vain and slutty. You will work hard here, and we'll humble you until you understand the seriousness of what you have done and beg God's forgiveness. The first thing we do here to rid our bad girls of vanity is cut off their hair."

Someone bent close, and she saw the scissors. "No!" she screamed. "Adam! Where's Adam! What have you done with him!"

"You must not talk of this boy again, Andrea," the fat woman told her. Someone grabbed her hair tightly, and someone else held her arms. "And from now on, you are not Andrea to the outside world. We will keep your identity hidden. According to our records, you are Marie Higgins."

Andrea heard a long, loud scream as scissors chomped through her long, golden mane. Did the scream come from her own lips? She wasn't sure. "It will grow back in time," someone said. "When it has done so, you will be a reformed woman, ready to go out again into the world and live as a godly person, not as a wanton woman."

They let go of her, and a moment later the voices were gone, cut off by the sound of a door closing and the click of a lock. She looked around a tiny room hardly bigger than a closet. How she wished she could think more clearly. Why was this horrible thing happening to her? She reached up with a trembling hand to feel her hair. It ended at her neck, a short clump of nothingness. Another scream welled up in her throat, came out as a long groan, was followed by uncontrolled sobbing. She threw herself down on her bed, pulling a pillow close to herself and aching for Adam. If he knew, he'd kill them all and take her away from here! Adam! But had someone already killed him? How had she come to be here? What had happened to Adam that night he came to her? How could her parents be this cruel?

She wept bitterly, well into the night. But she was determined not to give up. She would not stop loving Adam Chandler, not ever, no matter what they did to her. They could never stop her from loving him. Someday she would get out of this place, and Adam would be waiting for her. He would never desert her, never stop loving her, and he'd probably try to find her. But the fat woman had said they were going to call her Marie! How could he find her if they didn't call her by her right name? They had thought of everything! She had been whisked away to some secret, horrible place hundreds, maybe a thousand, miles from home, where she was imprisoned and was to be called by another name. Adam could never find her this way. But she would get to him! If it took a lifetime she would get to him!

Douglas Means watched the neat, frame farmhouse burn, while the Creek family that had owned it, and the small farm it sat upon, watched in horror. Douglas only smiled. He enjoyed this job much more than he'd thought he would. Most of the Creeks were well on their way to Indian Territory, but the few holdouts like these made his job quite pleasant, for the militia had free rein with these stubborn ones, permission to roust them out of Georgia in any way they saw fit.

Douglas was a sergeant now, ruling over a motley bunch of men who were total failures in life and who had nothing better to do than ride with the Georgia Militia and have their fun at the expense of the Indians. Now some of his men ordered the husband and wife into a wagon.

The couple clung to each other, both naked and bleeding from a brutal whipping. One of the men threw them blankets to cover themselves, then he tossed in a few of their meager belongings. Most of their valuable possessions—household items and stock—would be kept by the soldiers and turned over to headquarters for "the cause," although some things would be kept by the men.

A little boy tried to run, but the men herded him down, laughed and threw him around before flinging him into the wagon. More men came from behind a shed, dragging a naked and beaten girl of about fifteen. Douglas licked his lips. Never had he had such a wonderful serving of young virgins as he had since joining the militia. This one had been especially exciting, had fought like a she-cat until four men had pinned her into helpless submission while Douglas, as always, had been the first to try her. The others were through with her now. She could get into the wagon.

A heavyset man with a five-day growth of beard rode up to Douglas then, his uniform soiled and sweat streaming down his face. "Got a letter for you from headquarters, sir," the private stated. Douglas loved it when older men had to call him sir. "They told me to bring it out to you, seeing as how you were going west from here and might not get back to headquarters for a few days. I have orders to join up."

The man handed Douglas the letter, eying the naked young girl being loaded onto the wagon.

"Thank you," Douglas told him. "What's your name, Private?"

"Wilson, sir. Greg Wilson." He kept watching the girl. "Now that's a sweet, young thing, I've got to say. Any chance of me getting something out of my system, sir, before you haul her away?"

Douglas glanced over at the girl, who sat with her head hanging. He laughed lightly. "Go ahead. It will take me a few minutes to read this anyway."

The man saluted. "Thank you, sir." He rode up to the wagon and said something to two other men, who proceeded to drag the girl back off the wagon. She screamed and protested again as they forced her battered body back behind the shed, the heavyset man following. And her little brother cried, huddled against his parents.

Douglas paid no attention to the girl's pitiful wailing, nor to the laughter of the men. He opened the letter. It was from Mary. As he read he smiled more broadly, feeling victorious.

"So," he muttered when he'd finished, "I was right about that little slut after all. Spreading her legs for a Cherokee boy." He shook his head. "What do you know about that? Little Andrea, pretending to be such a prissy thing." He wished she were there right then. He'd take her down a notch or two. He knew all about women now, and since Andrea Sanders had been bedded by an Indian boy, he could have her anytime he wanted, and she couldn't say a thing about it. It was too bad she'd been taken away. Even Mary didn't know where she was. He hoped it was to some horrible place. Maybe she'd even die there. It would serve her right.

He stuck the letter into his pocket and took out a cigar, lighting it. Things had quieted behind the shed, except for a few grunts out of the fat private. He lit the cigar, wishing he could turn his attentions to the Cherokee. The first family he'd hit would be the Chandlers. He'd cut Adam Chandler down with his sword and then cut off his privates. And he'd rape that pretty little sister of his, right under Adam Chandler's nose. That would be one pleasant experience. What would be even better would be to have Andrea with him, to strip her and have at her right in front of Adam. He laughed aloud at the thought of it. Too bad the Cherokee were so damned clever at legal things. Georgia was having one hell of a time getting rid of the pests. The federal government had declared that all land that was a part of Georgia belonged to Georgia, not to the Cherokee. But they had not offered to help Georgians get the Cherokee out, nor did they condone force. And half the country was crying out in defense of the cursed Cherokees.

"Fools!" he muttered. Why would anyone defend Indians? Those on the side of the Cherokees were making

Georgians look like heartless landmongers who would stop at nothing to get what they wanted. Georgians didn't like looking that way, so they'd backed away from attacking the Cherokee just yet. In the meantime the Cherokee continued to wage a brilliant legal battle, with men like Daniel Webster on their side, and the whole thing was at a standstill. In Douglas's estimation, what the Cherokee needed was a little "convincing," a raid now and then, a burned farm, murdered stock, raped women, whippings—all done in the night by hooded unknowns. Several men had talked about it, as a way of giving the Cherokees a little "push," and Douglas knew it would happen sooner or later. He intended to be in the middle of the action when it did.

The men finally came out from behind the shed. This time the girl was completely limp and had to be carried. They threw her onto the wagon like a sack of potatoes.

"Get them to the holding camp," Douglas ordered. "Then we'll make camp ourselves for the night. There's a farm on the other side of this valley we'll see to tomorrow."

"Any women?" one of them asked. The fat private was still buttoning his pants.

Douglas grinned. "Just the wife, I think. But then they can't all be virgins, can they?"

There was a round of laughter, and the soldier driving the wagon whipped its team into motion. Douglas waited for them all to get moving, then rode past and ahead of them, thinking of how pleasant it would be to get his hands on Andrea Sanders now. Imagine that! Andrea Sanders laying with a Cherokee boy. He laughed again, taking his place at the head of the men, feeling victorious.

Six months passed, and Adam was seventeen. He turned his hatred and frustration into energy, running every day, lifting heavy things to build his muscles more, practicing shooting with a rifle and a handgun, throwing his knife. Always his people spoke of peace, but he saw a day coming when peace would not be possible. And there was no peace in his own heart. He wanted to kill people. How much better he would feel if he could just kill Morgan Sanders!

He was in constant agony, forcing himself to eat but not really having an appetite; using mental concentration to sleep and relax; for his thoughts were so full of Andrea that such things were almost impossible. Where was she? Was she some kind of prisoner? Surely she was, or she would have tried to get a letter to him. Andrea! Time had not weakened his love for her in the least. If anything, it had grown stronger. All he had to do was wait. She would come. She was still alive, that much he knew. Reverend Jessup had visited the Sanderses again, and had got that much out of them. Adam had feared she had died and they had not bothered to tell him.

It was nearly February now, 1827, two years since the government under President Monroe had declared that all land west of the Mississippi River was Indian Territory into which no whites could enter. "Indian Territory!" he muttered, slinging some wood onto a pile. "Barren, worthless land! And at that, whites are already moving in, against the law, and no one stops them!"

Was there no end to what the whites could get away with, no end to what was denied the Indians? Peace! How could there be peace? Yet by not using any physical force, the Cherokee seemed to be winning ground. That was the secret, the only thing that kept the Georgians frustrated. They needed a damned good excuse to kick out the Cherokee, and they couldn't come up with one. Meanwhile the Cherokee continued to display in court their legal possession of the land. Over and over they were warned not to fight back physically, even if the militia should attack, yet surely the time would come when they would be deliberately provoked. Adam was not sure how he could hold himself back in such an instance. If he did, then someday, in some way, he would get his revenge.

But already some whites were moving onto Cherokee land by more clever means, by marrying Cherokee women who were stupid enough to allow such marriages. Some of the people actually thought that such unions would help keep the peace, and would insure that the woman's family stayed on their land. Adam thought otherwise. The whites were only buying time, and when the invasion came, some of those white men would hand over their Cherokee wives for removal to Indian Territory, with no guilt whatsoever. How ironic it was that no one thought a thing about those white men marrying Indian women, yet his wanting to marry Andrea had been looked upon with horror. What strange values the white man had.

He threw on the last log and wiped sweat from his brow. Even though it was supposedly winter, the weather was very mild in Georgia, and much of this wood would not be used. He wondered what it was like where Andrea was. Was it hotter? Or was it cold? Was she being properly cared for? She was fifteen now. Had she changed very much?

Again the lump came to his throat. Andrea! How would he ever get over this? When would the helpless feeling go away? Why couldn't he just go over to the Sanders farm and torture Morgan Sanders until the man told him where Andrea was? If these were the old days . . .

"The old days!" he growled. He picked up a hatchet and slammed it into an upended log, splitting the wood with one mighty blow. He had grown in the past six months, was broader, stronger, more a man. The only thing that kept him from going crazy was working with Elias Boudinot, helping interpret Greek and English books into Cherokee. It took hours, but it made the time go swiftly. Someday they would have their own newspaper, Elias said so.

Everything would be perfect, if only Andrea were with him. But she was not, and sometimes he wanted to die. Only the knowledge that she still lived and would surely come home someday made him want to keep going, as well as his own stubborn pride and his refusal to let anything make him stop loving Andrea Sanders. Let them laugh. Let them think him too young. Let them chide him for loving a white girl. He didn't care. He loved her and that was all there was to it. They could all think what they wanted.

His nights were spent dreaming of a pretty little girl with long blond hair and soft blue eyes, who whispered his name in sweet, innocent ecstasy when he touched her in magic places, who opened herself to him for sweet pleasures no other girl could bring him. Those others didn't understand that she was his wife in every way. A man didn't give up on his wife. He didn't give up loving her, hoping to hold her again, trying to find her. But all his searching had been fruitless. Now there was nothing to do but wait and pray, and it was agony for him. Andrea! He slammed the hatchet down again, pretending the log was Morgan Sanders's head.

Andrea sat at the small window of her room, looking through the glass and bars to the swirling snow outside. Everything was buried, the tree branches bare, the land dead. She had never seen such snow, had no idea it could blow so hard or get so deep.

Vermont. She had heard of it. That was where she was now, she'd finally been told. Vermont. She was a thousand miles or better from Georgia—from Adam. But her love for him had only deepened with all the hard work, the insults, the studies, the bars, the locked door. How could it not deepen, when Adam's life grew in her own belly?

She looked down at her swollen stomach, running her hand over it. She was seven months along now, and every day she made Miss Darcy tell her again that she would be allowed to keep her baby. She told them over and over that she wanted it, for it was a part of Adam. Already she planned to take the child straight to Adam as soon as she got out of this terrible place where she worked and studied eighteen hours a day.

She had scrubbed floors and walls and washrooms; she had worked in the kitchen, changed beds, washed clothes. The chores never ceased, and in between she was given rigorous studies. She was learning many things, even some French. She was learning everything, except how to stop loving a Cherokee man who, she knew, was waiting for her. But that was her secret. She would not tell them she still loved Adam. The more she told them so, the longer she would stay here. She had finally figured that out. They wanted proof that she was losing her feeling for Adam Chandler, that she was repenting her "sins" and becoming a respectable young lady. But now there was the baby. Miss Darcy had told her that she should give it up, that keeping it would be carrying around the proof of her sin. But Andrea had refused.

"The baby is not to blame," she had told the woman. "The child should be with its real mother. I owe it the kind of love only a mother can give."

"Are you sure you aren't keeping it just because it is a part of that Indian boy?"

"No," Andrea had lied. "I hate him for what he did to me. I know now what I did was wrong. But my Christian upbringing prevents me from turning out one of my own. I will keep the child, and bear the burden of raising it. Every time I see it I will remember my sin, and it will help me not to sin that way again. To raise the child alone will be my punishment."

Miss Darcy had agreed that she could keep it, but inside Andrea was filled with terror. Somehow she felt Miss Darcy didn't believe her story. The woman was shrewd and calculating, and Andrea was afraid. At first she feared they would do something terrible to her, poke her or make her drink something that would make her lose the baby. Other girls had told her it had happened to them, but for some reason she was allowed to carry her child. After hearing the stories of some of the others, however, she worried. Would they kill it after it was born? Would they truly let her keep it? Every day she asked again, and got the same answer. "Yes, you may keep the child, if that is what you wish."

Tears slipped down her face as she ran her hand over her belly, feeling the baby move. Her baby. Adam's life. Adam! Sweet, wonderful Adam. His seed had been planted inside her in those beautiful moments they'd had together, and now his life grew in her. She must keep it! She must have

Adam's baby. Oh, how she would love it!

But she was terrified of having it. Miss Darcy kept telling her she was too young, that young girls sometimes died giving birth, or their babies died. The woman never failed to remind her how painful it would be. And there was the ever-present threat that she wouldn't be allowed to keep her baby.

She put her head on the window sill and wept. This truly was a terrible place, cold and cruel and miserable. The other girls in it had been sent here for much the same reason as Andrea. All had had their hair cut short when they'd first arrived. Some of the most sinful ones had had their heads shaved. The pregnancies of many were aborted, some were whipped. Andrea had been whipped, her second night there—the first act of "cleansing" her soul. Never would she forget the pain of it, the humiliation of hanging naked while Miss Darcy and two other women witnessed her whipping, which was administered by a stern man with a huge hooked nose who called himself a minister. Andrea knew better. No minister looked at a young girl the way that man had looked at her. Did her parents know what really went on here? Did they approve? Why had her father so quickly sent her away? Life at home had never been happy, but it had not been unbearable, nor had she been cruelly treated. Why was she being so severely punished for her one mistake? And why didn't her parents even try to understand that in her mind it had not been a mistake at all, but an act of love. Surely they didn't love her. Why? How could parents not love their child?

She wept until her ribs ached. Adam was the only person in the whole world who really loved her, and now she didn't even know what had happened to him. She could only pray he was all right, pray she'd get back to him. But she didn't pray to the kind of God they talked about here at this terrible place. That couldn't be the real God. Her God was kind and loving, forgiving, and understanding. Her God would have approved of her love for Adam Chandler, would have smiled down on the union that had resulted from that love. Her God understood that she was Adam's wife in every way. These people tried to make their joining ugly and sinful. But it hadn't been. She would never believe that. They would not break her. She would not let them.

She wiped at her eyes and watched the snow again. Even if she could get away now, she'd never be able to get to Adam. She couldn't go far in the deep, icy white below, and even if she could, she wouldn't know which way to go. She had no money, not even a proper coat or boots for such weather, and the door was still kept locked, the window barred. Would she ever get out of this room, ever live through this agony and go home to Georgia—to Adam? Such a hope seemed a distant dream now. Perhaps they had no intention of ever letting her go. Perhaps they had something terrible in mind for her and the baby. Her young mind invented all kinds of awful things they might do to her. And who was there to turn to? No one. If only Adam were with her . . . How wonderful it would be to feel his strong arms around her, hear his whispered words of love and reassurance. Adam! No, they had not made her stop loving him. They could never make her stop.

She got up and went to her small cot, curled up under the heavy quilts. One blessing that came with her growing larger with the pregnancy was that they had finally lightened her chores. And for being so good, they had actually told her that tomorrow she needn't rise early. Sleep. Wonderful sleep. She would really get to lie in bed in the morning for the first time since coming here. She closed her eyes and dreamed of Adam, feeling her cropped hair with one hand, wondering what he would think of it being so much shorter. But it already fell to her shoulders, and maybe by the time she saw him again, it would be long. But that would take months. That would mean not seeing him for months. And surely it wouldn't be that much longer. Once the baby was born, they would let her go home, if she convinced them she was repentant and no longer cared for the Indian boy.

In a large room on the first floor of the school, Miss Darcy sat at her desk composing a letter to Morgan Sanders.

According to your wishes, Mr. Sanders, an abortion has not been performed on your daughter for fear of damaging her health. However, as you requested, the child will be given immediately upon birth to an orphanage of our choosing, and his or her identity and whereabouts will never be divulged to the mother or even to you, her parents. Since this child is the illegitimate offspring of your daughter's sinful union with an Indian man, I fully agree that she should not keep it, and I understand your own rejection of this grandchild. Be assured all will be taken care of. Your daughter has been told that she may keep the baby, only to keep her calm until after the birth, which could be hard on one so young. Once that is over with, she will never see the child and will be told that it died. After she has delivered the baby, I am convinced that soon thereafter she will be fully recovered of her senses and ready to return home, a repentant and humble young lady, well schooled and ready to start life anew. She has worked hard and learned well, and I see some goodness beneath the sin visited upon her by that heathen who drew her into his den of iniquity.

God bless you both in our struggle to keep the world a decent place for our little children.

> Sincerely,
> Evelyn Darcy

The woman folded the letter, put it in an envelope, and addressed it. Then, hearing the protests of a new arrival, she set the letter aside and took the scissors from her desk drawer. It was time for another haircut.

*   *   *

Adam watched the whirling skirts and smiling faces. But he stood alone, having no desire to dance with any girl there. It was spring. Last year he had escorted Andrea to this annual dance. How he had wanted her that night. But he'd gone with that wild farm girl who'd shown him all the ways there were to please a girl. He was glad he'd gone to her first, glad he'd known what to do with Andrea.

But it mattered little now. Andrea was not here. He could see her, watch her float around the floor, feel her in his arms, see her smiling face, the blush that came to it that night when he'd danced with her. They were both nervous, both falling in love. But that had been a whole year ago. How did she look now? What was happening to her? What was she thinking? His eyes stung with the tears provoked by the memory of that last dance. He took a deep breath and swallowed his pain. He must not show his emotions here. Hurriedly he joined a group of men, including Elias Boudinot and John Ross, the Cherokee leaders. The men were discussing politics, as always, and welcomed Adam into their circle.

"Lumpkin is trying to get Indian Removal brought up before Congress," Boudinot continued. "He wants to go over the President's head and stir up the public."

"We have plenty of people on our side," John Ross declared. "Many ordinary citizens, especially in the North, sympathize with us, as do some prominent men in Congress."

"Yes, but we all know who our next president is likely to be," another offered. "Andrew Jackson has announced he's in the race, and everybody knows how popular he is. All of us are aware of what that could mean to us."

Faces hardened and hearts tightened. There was a time when the Cherokee had called Andrew Jackson their friend. They had even gone to war with him against the British and against the Creeks when the Creeks had fought on the British side in 1812. They had been loyal to Old Hickory, had won many battles for him, battles for which Jackson had taken all the credit, not mentioning his

Cherokee fighters.

John Ross spoke up. "We fell for the old white man's trick of divide and conquer. We wiped out half of the Creeks at Horseshoe Bend, then Jackson turned around, took all the credit, and opened up a lot of Indian land to white settlement. It is too bad we could not all see what was happening even back then. Since the white man stepped foot on this continent he has used Indians against each other to achieve his own ends. The Indians were just too ignorant to realize it. But we aren't ignorant any longer. Andrew Jackson could become our next president, and we all know he speaks for Indian Removal. He has turned on us, so we must be careful. He will have an answer for our constitution and our request to consider ourselves a separate state. We must emphasize that the land we now own is protected under the treaty, a federal document. The state cannot interfere with a federal act."

"But it already has. Pressure has gotten the federal government to declare that all this land now belongs to Georgia," Boudinot answered. "Just to wipe the noses of indignant Georgia politicians like Lumpkin, who want us out of here, the federal government has said Georgia can claim this land. But they refuse to help its citizens to oust us only because they know a lot of people sympathize with us and it would make them look bad to come in here with federal troops to clean us out. That's why we have to concentrate on the Georgia courts. We have to do everything we can to make Georgia congressmen and others in charge look like asses if they kick us out. We have to keep the public stirred up in our favor. That's the only thing that will prevent the militia from coming in here and attacking us. We must constantly embarrass the Georgia citizenry and those in power by constant legal challenges of every move they make."

"I heartily agree," John Ross replied. "But it's a game that will keep us hopping. We must keep telling our people that they must not do anything that will give the citizens an edge against us. So far the Georgians don't have one. The federal government has left them in a fix, telling them this is their land but not helping them get it from us; and the eyes of the world are on them. The best thing we ever did was educate ourselves. We have shown the world how we can take care of ourselves and even be wealthy. Some of us have even visited other countries. Now we must demonstrate our intelligence and authority. Believe me, there is a lot of sympathy out there for our cause, and the more we keep people aroused, the better off we are."

"Well, our illustrious Congressman Lumpkin certainly won't sit back and take any of this lightly. I think he burns the oil all night, thinking of ways to trick us," Boudinot grumbled. His eyes moved to Adam. "How are things going with you, son? You've been a great help to us, you know, and I still expect you to help me with the newspaper."

Adam nodded, his eyes showing the strain of his suffering. "I will be glad to help you, sir. And I am fine, thank you."

"Well, you don't look fine. Have you heard anything about that girl?"

Adam held his gaze, feeling the others looking at him. "No, sir. Reverend Jessup has made inquiries, but he has come up with nothing. I am just hoping she will return home soon."

Boudinot frowned. "It isn't easy for a Cherokee man to love a white woman. My poor wife went through hell. The stir up at Cornwall resulted in the closing of the school. But my wife never stopped loving me, and I'll wager that whatever has happened to that little girl you love, she won't stop loving you either."

John Ross gave the boy's shoulder a squeeze. "We all hope for the best, Adam. We're damned sorry about what happened last year. But remember how careful you have to be. Don't go looking for revenge. We're walking on eggs."

Adam sighed and nodded. "Yes, sir. I think I'll go outside for some fresh air." He turned and left, and the men watched him go, some of them shaking their heads.

Adam made his way outside, where two girls stood giggling with a couple of Cherokee boys. They were the kind a young man could have an easy time with, but Adam had no desire for such things now. If he couldn't be with Andrea, he didn't want to be with anyone.

"Adam! Adam Chandler, is it you?" One of the girls left the group and sauntered up to him in the dim light of the moon. "It is you!" She giggled, her dress hung open, revealing part of a breast. Her hair was tangled. She ran a finger over the front of his shirt, unbuttoning part of it. "Don't you remember me?" She kissed his chest and he stood rigid, trying to remember. She looked familiar. "God, I love Cherokee boys," she purred. "I've learned so much the past year. I could show you a hell of a time, Adam, give you a lot more than that stupid Andrea ever—"

She gasped then, as he grasped her wrist painfully. "Mary! You're Mary Means!"

"You let go of me! You're hurting my arm!"

He planted his other hand tightly around her throat, half lifted and half dragged her by the neck around the side of the building. His grip was so tight she could barely breathe, let alone talk. He shoved her to the ground, planting a knee in her stomach. "Where is she!" he growled. "Where is Andrea!"

He released her throat slightly so that she would squeak out a reply. "I don't know! Honest to God, I don't know!"

"You do! You goddamned slut! You're the one who told, aren't you? You stinking little piece of white trash! You told on her and now they've sent her away! Where? Where did they send her?"

He drove his knee into her even harder and she started crying. "Honest, Adam. I don't know. They won't tell." She choked on a sob. "All I know is they told my folks . . . that they decided to send Andrea away to school. They never . . . said where . . . never answered when my folks asked. They didn't even mention . . . anything about you . . . or any boy . . . I swear to God! So I never said anything either. But I . . . I never thought it meant . . .

that much to you."

"That's right! You never thought! Andrea was supposed to be your best friend. She was a good girl. She never did anything to you. But you were so damned jealous of her. You aren't worth the dirt under her feet!" He squeezed her throat harder again. "Oh, how I would love to kill you! How I would love it!" He squeezed harder and harder, until suddenly someone was pulling him off her. Strong arms grabbed him away, but not without difficulty. Tears were streaming down his face, and his eyes were hard and filled with hatred. "Slut! Filthy, stinking slut!" he roared.

"Calm down, Adam." It was the Reverend Jessup's voice.

"Harm her and you'll have a white mob on us." It was John Ross's voice.

"She told. She told on Andrea. She's the reason they sent Andrea away!"

"What's done is done, Adam!" John Ross said sternly. "She isn't worth being hanged."

The other white girls were helping Mary up. She was choking and crying. "I'll . . . have you arrested!" she sputtered.

"Try it! Then try explaining what you were doing here, slut!" Adam countered. "Go ahead! Explain to your God-fearing parents why you were over here at a dance flirting with Cherokee boys!" He grinned at the fear in her eyes. "You won't tell on me. You can't! Because you'd be in a lot more trouble than I would. Go on home, white trash! Go home where you belong—and don't come back here!"

The girl ran off, and as the others ran after her, Adam jerked his arms away from the men who held him. Andrea! Seeing Mary Means, hearing her mention Andrea's name, had brought everything back to him, vividly, painfully. He wiped angrily at his eyes.

"Are you all right, Adam?" John Ross asked him.

"No! I'll never be all right—not until Andrea comes back!"

160

"Don't do something foolish, Adam," the reverend warned.

"Don't worry!" Adam sneered. He stormed off into the darkness, his body on fire for his Andrea, his heart pounding for her, his mind full of her. For a moment he'd hoped he had an answer, but he'd seen in Mary's eyes that she truly didn't know where Andrea was being kept. All hope was gone again, and for him there was no spring.

CHAPTER TEN

The pain was much worse than Andrea had ever dreamed it might be. This was a time when she should have had her mother with her, but she was without mother, father, or friends. She wanted Adam most of all, and she knew that if he knew what was happening and where she was, he would be there. She was having his child, and somehow she would get back to him with her precious baby. He would be surprised and pleased. They would marry and be happy forever. All she had to do was survive this birth and get out of this place. That thought was the only thing that kept her from going crazy with fear and loneliness. At least now, she told herself, she would have her baby to hold and love. She would not be so alone.

She lay on her little cot in the tiny room she had lived in for nearly nine months. Part of the time she was alone. No doctor had been summoned for Miss Darcy was to take care of the delivery; and she came in only occasionally to check the progress of the baby. When the gripping, black pain engulfed Andrea, she screamed and wept alone, terrified of what was happening to her, too young to understand it, unable to talk to anyone beforehand about what to expect in childbirth. Her body was still not really mature enough for this; her young muscles and narrow hips were fighting the inevitable. Over and over she cried for Adam. If only he were here! He would have brought a doctor; he would have sat by her side, would have told her how much he loved her, how proud he was of her; he would be so happy to be having a child.

Adam! Sweet Adam! Every time the pain rose again, she screamed his name. Never had she been so frightened. Would she die in this little room? Would they even bother to tell anyone if she did? If only someone she knew and loved were here . . . If only a real doctor were here . . . She didn't like Miss Darcy coming in and looking at her, poking at her. The woman was cold and unfeeling. She didn't explain anything, didn't give her any instructions on how to make the baby come easier. Andrea wondered if Miss Darcy had ever even been with a man. No wonder she didn't care about Andrea's suffering. She was a woman without feelings. Devoid of love and passion, she lived by a book of rules that left no room for emotion or human error. Already she had talked of how glad she would be when the baby was born, because then Andrea could get back to full-time duties. She treated her like a tool that had broken down.

The pain grew worse. Its claws ripped at her insides without mercy now, almost constantly. She wondered how much more she could take. The labor had gone on for nearly twenty hours. Finally Miss Darcy returned, this time announcing that the baby was coming and she would stay. From then on, Andrea had no control over what happened. Her body took over. She could not stop the baby from coming, in spite of her terror of that happening. The child had decided it was time to enter the world, no matter how painful that entrance might be for its young mother. And Andrea had no choice but to let the horrible Miss Darcy help her, for a blackness swept over her and she felt that her insides were suddenly being expelled. Surely she was dying.

The worst pain suddenly ended, and she lay limp and exhausted, nearly unconscious. She heard someone say something about "cleaning him up." A boy! She'd had a boy! Adam had a son! She groaned his name, but she couldn't move or open her eyes. Someone was pushing hard on her stomach then, making her scream. She heard talk about heavy bleeding, felt something being packed against her. Whatever was happening, she would live, for she had a son now. She would rest and get well, become healthy. Soon they would bring her baby back to her and she would put it to her full, young breasts and nourish it. She smiled at the secret wonder of what Adam would think of her breasts now. They weren't small anymore. They were heavy with milk for his son.

But then she felt something being wrapped tightly around her breasts. Why were they doing this? So tight! Something tight around her chest, squeezing her painfully full breasts so that it was hard to breathe. She wanted to object but was too weak. Why was everything so black?

"They'll be painful for a while," someone said. "But eventually the milk will dry up. Are they here for the boy yet?"

"Yes, ma'am. They're downstairs."

No! What was happening? She tried to speak, but nothing would come out.

"Is it a healthy boy?" someone asked quietly.

"Very healthy, a beautiful child."

"Well, for the record he's dead. Remember that."

A door closed. Andrea wanted to scream, to get up and run downstairs and find her son. Where was he? He should be lying next to her now. She had gone through hell to deliver him—Adam's son. She had dreamed of nothing these last few months but having her baby and having something to love, something that was a part of Adam. Where was her baby? What did the voices mean? *Are they here for the boy yet?* What boy? Hers? *For the record, he's dead.*

She tried again to scream for Miss Darcy, but only a pitiful whimper actually exited her lips. A heavy loss of blood had brought her near to death, though she didn't realize it.

Adam stirred awake, shivering and drenched in perspiration. Something had awakened him, a strange cry. In his first sleepy thoughts it seemed he heard Andrea's voice, calling to him. He'd fallen asleep late, after restless thoughts of Andrea; for seeing the slut Mary Means had made him desperate to find his love.

He got out of bed, leaving sheets wet with sweat. As he did so, there came a cry, from an animal in the surrounding mountains. He went to a window and threw it open, breathing in the sweet spring air. The cry came again, and his heart tightened, for somehow he knew that somewhere Andrea cried out for him.

He went to his knees, resting his arms on the windowsill and looking out at the stars in the black sky. Where was she? How long must he wait and wonder? He wanted to pray, but he felt forgotten by his God and his faith was fast dwindling.

The strange cry echoed hauntingly through the mountains. "Andrea," he whispered. "I love you, Andrea. Wherever you are, I love you, and I will wait for you, forever if I have to."

Thunder rolled beyond a distant hill, as though to emphasize the storm in his own soul. Was it some kind of black omen? He watched the shadows of the trees, sniffed the spring air, listened for the sounds of the night and the woods. He felt an ancient yearning to be out there, living with the animals and the trees, roaming free, hunting for his food. Out there was where he belonged, where they all belonged, not in brick houses cared for by servants. This was a good life; the natural intelligence of his people had brought them wealth. But what good did that do the Cherokee? The way the whites treated them, they might as well still be running around in the hills, half-naked and living in huts. What use was it to struggle for education and riches, when at any time the whites might decide to swoop in and take everything from them. In the minds of the white men, the Cherokee had not progressed at all. They were still Indians. Why that should matter so much baffled the young man. Why was he any different from anyone else? He'd had a great deal to offer Andrea. Her parents should have been pleased. In the beginning he had liked them, trusted them, but he had learned a hard lesson about trusting people, about prejudice. And so had Andrea. Poor Andrea.

He closed his eyes and thought hard, hoping in some way she would sense he was with her in spirit. "Hang on, Andrea," he whispered. "Wherever you are, hang on, and come home to me. Come home to Adam."

The thunder rolled again, mixed with the sad wail of the unknown animal. Or was it Andrea, crying in the wind?

Andrea awoke to pain and weakness. Miss Darcy was bent over her, trying to make her drink some kind of liquid.

"You've lost a lot of blood," the woman told her. "But the bleeding has finally stopped. You'll need to drink lots of liquids now to get your strength back. But you'll be fine in a couple of weeks." She set the cup aside after Andrea took a couple of swallows. "It's all over now, Andrea. No more pain, no more fat stomach. You can return to your old self, go back to your studies."

"My . . . baby. Where's my baby?"

Miss Darcy sat down on the edge of the cot and took her hand. "I'm afraid the baby died, Andrea. We did all we could, but you were simply too young to be having a child. He took too long in coming, and he wasn't breathing by the time he entered this world. I'm sorry, dear."

Andrea just stared at her a moment, a terrible panic building in her soul. "You're lying!" she whimpered. "My baby isn't dead! What did you do with my baby!"

The woman's eyes hardened. "I told you he died. When you're well enough, I'll take you out to see his grave. I know it's hard to take, child, but—"

"It's a lie! I heard you! I heard you . . . talking about a boy . . . healthy and beautiful . . . about someone being here to take him!"

The woman rose. "Nonsense! You were in a lot of pain, Andrea, and nearly died from loss of blood. Your mind must have been affected, dear. That can happen when a person is so far gone. I'm sorry, but it's true. It was a boy. He died and we buried him. I know it hurts, but you must remember that he was a bastard and half-Indian. I'm sure God knew what He was doing when He chose not to let the child live. It would have been a burden to you, a constant reminder of your sins. What happened was best for you and the child. There will be more children for you someday, when you are married to a proper man and can have your children legally—that is, if a decent man will have you."

Andrea's breathing came in desperate gasps. She struggled to get up, but Miss Darcy pushed her back down.

"You must lie still, Andrea, or the bleeding will start all over again."

"I don't care! If I can't have my baby, I don't care if I die. What did you do with my baby! I have to take him to Adam! Please give me my baby! He's all I have!"

"Your son is dead, Andrea!" Miss Darcy said sternly. She called for an aide. "Bring the medicine!" she said. With her large frame and powerful arms, she had no trouble holding down the weak and crying Andrea.

"My baby! I want my baby, you fat, ugly . . . witch!" Andrea screamed. "You took my baby! You killed him, didn't you? You killed my baby!"

"I did not kill him. He died the moment he came out of your womb, young lady, and you'd better watch your tongue!"

"I hate you! You're a witch! A witch!" Andrea struggled, but to no avail. Someone came in with the brown bottle of medicine that always made her sleep. She didn't want to sleep. She fought, keeping her mouth closed, until the aide squeezed her nose so that she was forced to open her mouth to breathe. Some of the bitter liquid was poured down her throat then, and she had no choice but to swallow it.

"You'll understand when you're well enough to visit the grave, Andrea," Miss Darcy was telling her. "You're just weak and confused right now. I'm sorry about your baby, but God knows what is best. It would not have been a happy life for him. Believe me, we do not go around killing little babies. The child died, and that is that."

"Witch . . ." Andrea groaned. "Witch . . . somebody took him . . . you did something with my son . . . Adam's son."

"She still has that Indian boy on her mind," Andrea heard Miss Darcy telling someone. "Apparently she will have to be here a good while longer before we can rid her soul of her sinful thoughts. If she hadn't gotten pregnant, it would have been much easier. The baby only kept reminding her of that evil boy. Perhaps now, with the baby gone, she can begin to forget. Write to her father and explain that the deed is done. Tell him she'll have to stay, perhaps another year. We must be very sure before she leaves here that she is truly repentant, and that she has rid her soul of any feelings for the Indian boy. She must be completely cleansed of her sins and of all sinful thoughts and feelings before returning home."

"Yes, ma'am. I'll write him right away."

Miss Darcy urged the woman out into the hallway and then closed the door. "Be sure he is never told where the boy was sent. The child's identity must be kept secret, and the girl must come to believe that he truly did die. You understand, Lillian."

The woman nodded. "Like the others."

Miss Darcy nodded. "Like the others."

Morgan Sanders set the letter aside. "The child has been given away to the orphanage," he told his wife. "They didn't say if it was a boy or a girl, but it matters little. It was a bastard, either way."

"Is Andrea all right?" the girl's mother asked.

"She'll be fine. There was some trouble with loss of blood, but she survived."

Harriet Sanders closed her eyes and sighed deeply. "It's over then. I'm glad. Maybe she can come home now. Maybe the pain of childbirth has taught her a good lesson."

Her husband ran a hand through his hair. "I don't think so. Miss Darcy says she's pretty distraught over the loss of the baby. She was told it died, but Miss Darcy says she's been very obstinate about it—won't believe them—very stubborn and sassy. She still talks about Adam. She'll have to stay a while longer." He shook his head. "That boy surely did ruin our daughter, Harriet. We can only pray she'll come to her senses. I never should have let her stay over with that Indian girl."

"It isn't your fault, Morgan."

He gave her a contemptuous look. "We both know that well, don't we?"

She looked down at her lap. "I've paid for my lapse long ago, and she was raised in a Christian home. Sometimes a child just has to learn by his or her mistakes."

He grunted, rising from the table. "She's got the seed of the lustful man who came here and filled you with it, and the seed of her mother's curiosity about lust. I see little hope for her, for she was born out of a sinful act. What you did can be forgiven, I suppose, but she cannot help what she is because of it. It will take a lot longer at that school, a lot more hard work and learning and a few more whippings to get all that evil out of her for once and for all."

He walked out, slamming the door behind him. Harriet Sanders put her head in her hands and wept. She had hoped her one lustful act would not be revisited upon her, but it had, through her daughter.

Adam threw himself into his work and his schooling. The waiting was too much, the familiar places, the old oak tree. He decided to go away again after all, using his wealth and impressive scholarly record to enroll at Harvard. He knew of no other way to bear the waiting, and his father and those in charge of the Cherokee Nation agreed that young ones like Adam should pursue an education. He was sorely needed at home to help with the legal battles constantly plaguing his people, yet the

Cherokee knew that the best way to fight was to learn even more, and an opportunity to go to Harvard should not be overlooked.

Jonas Chandler's heart was heavy the day his son left. He was aware of the boy's constant mourning for Andrea, the awful helplessness Adam felt at not knowing where she was. It would be good for him to go away again, to make new friends and keep his mind occupied with further education. And Jonas had no doubt that his brilliant son would come home with a law degree, for he was certain that Adam intended to plunge wholeheartedly into his schooling for the next two years, or until he received word that Andrea Sanders had come home.

The months wore on, until the cold snows of the winter of 1827–28. Adam Chandler studied to the point of exhaustion, little realizing that only a few hundred miles away in Vermont, Andrea lived, and that for those first several months after the baby was born her mind and heart were broken. She spoke to no one, accepted her whippings silently. She spent her free time, of which there was little, staring out her window, dreaming of an Indian boy, and an old oak tree. But she had learned she must never speak his name, or talk of those beautiful times. She had learned that her only hope of ever getting out of the cold, brick prison was to pretend total submission and repentance; to work hard and study hard. To show defiance or to speak of her lover or her baby brought another whipping and avowals that she would never go home again.

So close! They were so close to each other and didn't even know it. Adam also spent his free time dreaming, staring out at the cold snow and thinking of Georgia, of warmth and sunshine, of green mountains and colorful wildflowers; of the oak tree and the soft grass beneath it on which he used to lie with Andrea Sanders. Had she ever really existed? Did she still exist, or was she dead? Did she still love him?

In the summer of 1828 Adam went home for only one month, just long enough to feed some of his ideas to Elias Boudinot, for use in the brand-new newspaper, the

Cherokee Phoenix, printed in both English and Cherokee. Adam agreed to send home articles about life for an Indian among the elite whites at Harvard, stories about the importance of education, as well as advice that might help his people in legal matters.

There could not be a visit home without going to the old tree, but when he saw it again, all the pain returned. He was sure after almost two years away from Andrea that he could start forgetting her, for perhaps he must. But he could not. If only he knew for certain what had happened to her it would be easier. Yet whether she was dead or in some place where she was being cruelly treated, his heaviest burden was realizing it was his fault. Did she hate him now? Was he bad for having enticed her into letting him make love to her? Others probably saw it that way, but not Adam. He still considered her his wife, and since that was so, how could he forget her or give up on her? How could he stop loving her, when she was surely alive . . . somewhere. Andrea! Nothing had changed. He could still hear her voice, still see her hugging the tree that first day he met her, still hear her whisper his name while he invaded her, claimed his woman, his wife.

Now his father and others were after him to see other girls, to prepare himself for the possibility of never seeing Andrea again, or perhaps for the distinct possibility that if and when he did, she would no longer be in love with him. Perhaps she would even be married to someone else. Her parents might have arranged such a thing, for it was common among her people. Adam tried to look at other girls with interest, but there were none like Andrea. Many Cherokee girls were interested in the maturing young man called Adam Chandler, so handsome, so intelligent and educated, filling out so provocatively, growing so tall and beautiful. But he was not even around most of the time, and when at Harvard, he dove into his books as though to close one was to end his life. He would not, and could not, give up hope that Andrea would someday come home; nor did Andrea give up hoping she would return.

* * *

In the fall of 1828 Andrew Jackson was elected president, following a bitter and scandalous campaign. Enemies had been made among those in Congress, a bad omen for the Cherokee; for personal and political interests were sure to outweigh fairness when it came to the handling of Indians. And worse than that, Andrew Jackson was an advocate of Indian Removal. Their fight was getting harder, and rumors of the Georgia Militia possibly raiding and harassing the Cherokee grew stronger, making people afraid to step outside at night. The cloud over Cherokee land was growing ever darker. Whites surrounded it, hungry to have that land for themselves. Georgia citizens cried out for help from the federal government to get the Indians out, but there were too many Indian sympathizers among the voting constituents in the North for the federal government to act too quickly, in spite of Jackson's own support of Indian Removal.

Bitter fighting ensued in Congress. It began to split the North and the South. Southerners claimed that it was easy for Northerners to point their fingers at the South and to say that Southerners were being cruel to the Indians who still occupied their land. After all, most of the Indians in the North had already been exterminated or pushed westward. The South felt the North had no right to stick its nose into Southern affairs. Since large numbers of Indians still lived in the Southern states, Southerners felt it was time they left.

Cherokee leaders like John Ross, Elias Boudinot, and John Ridge had their hands full fighting constant legal battles, traveling back and forth to Washington with petitions and arguments. The future looked most unpromising for the Cherokee when Adam came home with his degree in the summer of 1829. He went right to work for the *Cherokee Phoenix:* editing, writing articles, and delivering copies of the paper to Cherokee villages in the mountains.

In the autumn of that year he turned nineteen but looked even older, for he was broad and tall and well built. A lingering memory of his first love still ached in his heart, and although he had begun to socialize, he was unable to take any real interest in another girl. He had had only one sexual encounter in three years since Andrea had gone away, that night, when in a drunken agony over her, he had violently bedded an accommodating farm girl while on a short visit home. But even then in his mind it was Andrea he wanted.

Now his hope was fading; her face becoming harder to remember. He knew that somehow he must go on with life, must tend to his manly needs and find a new love. He couldn't go through his whole life waiting for someone who might never come. At least that was what his father kept telling him, and what others suggested out of sincere concern for his health and happiness. Sometimes he was almost grateful for the growing political problems and the constant legal battles. They kept him working long into the night, to the point of exhaustion, so that he fell asleep with little effort. As soon as he awoke, he refused to let himself lie about and think of Andrea. He was immediately up and back to work. His parents and friends worried about him, and Reverend Jessup had talked to him several times. Adam had tried to take their advice. He knew they were right. He must face reality and think about the future.

But the past haunted him constantly. He was certain that Andrea was out there . . . somewhere . . . that she might come home. He had truly loved her. That was what none of them understood. They equated his feelings with puppy love, young love that could easily be forgotten. But it wasn't that way at all, and he couldn't believe it was that way for Andrea. Surely if she was alive she still loved him, wherever she was. And wrong as he knew it was, he still visited the oak tree, as often as possible. Each time he went to it, he hoped that by some miracle he would find her there, and each time he was again disappointed.

The leaves were turning. Andrea knew that if they didn't let her go home this time, she would spend her fourth winter in this cold and ugly place. She was seventeen now, a woman, old enough to know her own mind. Yet she had never once stopped loving Adam Chandler, although she had long ago stopped talking about him, stopped asking about her baby. Yes, she had learned her lesson, but not in the way Miss Darcy and the others smugly thought. She had learned how to fool them, learned that to fight them only prolonged her stay and made things harder for her. She would play their game now. She would be humble and submissive, show shame and repentance for her past "sins," but never would she truly believe them to be sins, not in her own heart. She worked like a slave, and she demonstrated a gift for learning, quickly absorbing French and Spanish, learning proper etiquette, practically memorizing the entire Bible.

Her hair had been cut short again not long after the baby was born, for she had been full of sinful thoughts and words, or so Miss Darcy said. She had called Miss Darcy a liar, and she had continued to pine away for Adam. But the clipped hair and several whippings had soon made her understand what she must do. Her only goal became to get out, to get back to Adam. She had decided to go to the Cherokee, knowing that even if Adam no longer wanted her, he would help her find a way to go to a place where she could start over. She was determined not to go home. She never wanted to see her parents again. They had done this to her.

And so she had become a model student. She had stopped talking about Adam. She had pretended to accept her baby's death. But she had not. She never would. And not seeing the child that she had carried in her womb for nine months, the child she had suffered so terribly to de-liver—Adam Chandler's son—would leave a bitter, painful void in her soul for the rest of her life. She would never hold him, never see him, touch him, nurture him. It would have been wonderful to take a son home to Adam, hard at first, but Adam would have understood. He would have loved the boy and been proud of him. How sad he would be if he knew. Her baby! Her heart cried out for her baby!

But she sat silent now, in Miss Darcy's office. Again she had come up for review. She had been industrious. She had been obedient. She had passed all her courses, and was a fully educated young lady, ready to go out into the world. Miss Darcy came into the room then, carrying an envelope. She sat down across the desk from Andrea, a gold cross hanging around her neck. Andrea wanted to laugh at the cross, for in her eyes there was nothing Christian about Miss Darcy.

"Well, Andrea, you have been here a little over three years now," the woman stated. "I must say, you were a difficult one in the beginning. Still, if it were not for the baby, it might have been easier for you. And for the past two years you have been a model student. I'm very proud of your progress."

"Thank you, Miss Darcy," the girl replied quietly. "I guess I just needed to grow up a little, to understand what a foolish child I was. For the rest of my life I will regret what I did. But I will try to overcome my shame, and lead a Christian life. I think perhaps I will never marry, Miss Darcy. I'd like to work in the missionary field. Then one day I may help other young girls as you do here."

The woman beamed. "Why, thank you, Andrea! I consider that quite a compliment. And with all that you have learned, your languages and all—and with what you have learned about the consequences of sin—I think you would make a wonderful contribution to the missionary field. Is there any church or missionary school to which you would like to be referred?"

Andrea tried not to reveal her building excitement. Were they really letting her go? Her heart pounded wildly.

"I'd like to go home and think about it, Miss Darcy. I have so many things to consider. And I miss my parents. Perhaps in January I could enroll in a school. I would like to serve in a country overseas, if possible."

"Wonderful! Your parents will be very proud, I'm sure." She leaned back and studied Andrea as though the young woman were her own personal creation. "You're an exceedingly beautiful girl, Andrea. Remember that.

Devilish boys and young men will be eyeing you. You must be strong and always remember what you've already been through because of your moment of weakness. Remember that the work of the Lord is much more glorious than marriage and children. But if you should weaken, you must marry, and then be a devoted wife and mother. Marry a good, Christian man, Andrea, an honorable man of good family, one who commands respect."

"If I marry, I will do just that," she answered, smiling inwardly, for Adam Chandler was all of those things. Yes, if Adam still wanted her, she would be a devoted wife to him.

Miss Darcy rose. "Andrea, I'm letting you go because I've seen wondrous changes in you. I'll send a messenger to notify your parents that you are coming, and—"

"Oh, please don't tell them, Miss Darcy! I want to surprise them. Please!" She did not want her parents looking for her, waiting for her, expecting her; for she had no intention of going home. And this way, by the time they knew she had been let go, it would be too late.

Miss Darcy nodded. "All right. I think that's a fine idea. I have some papers you should take with you, and a letter of recommendation for the school you might choose, or you might present it to a minister or an employer should you seek work." She handed the girl the envelope. "There is also a diploma in here, certifying that you have received a Christian education. You may pack your things today, and in the morning we will have a coach ready for you. Your fare will be covered by the fee your parents have been paying."

"Thank you, Miss Darcy. I . . . I'll miss you." The words almost stuck in Andrea's throat. The woman had wanted complete surrender. She had given it to her, on the surface. But never would she surrender her heart, her love for Adam Chandler. She would hold onto that forever, whatever happened to her, whether Adam still wanted her or not.

"We'll miss you, too, Andrea. Hurry up to your room now and pack your things."

"Thank you, ma'am." She actually went up to the woman and hugged her. It was the most difficult thing she had ever done. She turned then, and hurried up to her room, wanting to laugh, scream. She was climbing these cold marble stairs for the last time. How many times had she mopped and polished them? She would sleep in the horrible little barred room for one more night. But she wouldn't sleep well, for tomorrow she was going home! Home! She was certain that she would lie awake all night, watching, waiting, afraid something would go wrong or Miss Darcy would change her mind. Was it really true?

Adam! Her heart pounded so hard her chest hurt. Would he still be at New Echota? Would he still love and want her? How much had he changed? What would he say when she told him she'd had his baby? Adam! She was afraid to even think of him, afraid Miss Darcy would sense her thoughts and make her stay. Adam! She was not going home at all. She would go to New Echota, and no one would stop her! And if Adam Chandler still wanted her, she would never leave him again. She would live among the Cherokee, suffer whatever might come to them, learn their ways, have Adam's children.

A lump rose in her throat. What had happened to her little son? He would be two years old now, wherever he was. But she didn't dare ask about him, at least not until she was safely away from this place. All she could do in the meantime was pray for him, and hope that, wherever he was, he was safe and well. All was in God's hands now, and only by some miracle would she ever see or hold her little boy. At present she could do nothing except remain quiet and get out of this horrible place, then go home—to New Echota and to Adam!

CHAPTER ELEVEN

The weather grew slightly warmer, the terrain more familiar as they moved through Virginia, then North Carolina. Everything was greener here, for in the North the colors began to turn earlier than they did in this land. With every mile Andrea's chest tightened with anticipation and a little fear. What would she find? What would Adam be like? Perhaps he would be angry if she showed up. What if he'd found someone else? The thought provoked painful jealousy, yet she told herself she must not blame him if he had found another. After all, she had been gone three years, and that was a long time for a young boy to wait, especially when he probably didn't even know if she would ever come back.

Adam! Every green hill, every cedar, hickory, oak, and pine tree, every wildflower and every inch of red earth reminded her of him—of those sweet stolen moments that seemed to have occurred a century ago. Had she ever really lain with him beneath the great oak? Was it still there? She touched her stomach, painful memories shooting through her. The baby. Yes, she had lain with Adam Chandler. She had borne his son. It was all so unreal, except for the miserable ache she felt inside every time she thought of the baby, wondered what had happened to her son. Those first few weeks after the birth had been such agony, both physically and emotionally. Would she ever get completely over it? No, that was impossible. But if she could find Adam, and if he still wanted her, she would be stronger, she would make it.

The land became more familiar. Andrea's problem now was to get away from the woman who had been sent along to escort her home. Every proper young lady must have an escort, according to Miss Darcy. But Andrea knew it was this woman's duty to make sure she went directly home and did not end up where she was not supposed to be—Indian country.

Every night they had stayed at a proper inn, and the woman with her never left Andrea's side, except when Andrea was in the bath. Somehow Andrea had to get away from her, and the driver. She would not go home! She was determined to go to New Echota, even if she had to leave her belongings behind and flee on foot. She had considered bribing the driver. Surely Adam's family would gladly pay the man well if he helped her. But how could she trust him? He might betray her. She could trust no one anymore—no one but herself and Adam.

She must ask how long it would be before she was home. She could tell by the terrain that she was very close, but the road from the north was unfamiliar to her. She had never been farther north than her own farm, except the night she'd been whisked away, and then she had been unconscious for many days. She had not seen the route they had taken. And if she had, it was three years ago. She would never remember. As they took a break to stretch from their long day's ride, she approached the driver, pretending girlish curiosity and eagerness.

"Oh, I must be so close to my home!" she said excitedly. "This all looks so familiar, but I've never been this far north. Are we close, Mr. West?"

He dug a stone from a horse's hoof. "That we are, little lady. Just another day's ride. There's a fork in the road near the inn where we'll stay tonight. One way goes south, right past your farm. The other goes to the west—into New Echota, Indian country. There's a high ridge between the two. It's the only thing that separates the whites from the Indians, I hear. They even say the Indians want to have their own state. I don't doubt there's a lot going to be happening down here mighty quick. The papers up North say as how you Southerners want the Indians out altogether, but the Cherokee have got themselves some good land and a real nice town and all. I'm glad I'm from up North. I wouldn't want to get mixed up in any of that mess."

Andrea put a hand to her chest. "Oh, it frightens me, Mr. West. I'll be glad to get to my folks and make sure they're all right. It's been so long since I've seen them."

Mrs. Drew spoke up. "I'm sure they're fine." The tall, stern woman walked up beside Andrea. "Isn't it good to be back to normal, Andrea?"

"Oh, yes, it's wonderful," the girl told her, assuming a smile. "I feel like a new person."

The older woman smiled proudly in return. "Well, you are! And won't your parents be surprised!"

Andrea looked to the western mountains, toward New Echota. "Yes. They'll be very surprised." She had no feeling for her parents. She would never forget the past three cruel years, the loss of her precious baby and of her precious Adam, the whippings and the hard work. Nor would she forget that her parents had never once visited her, that they had written to her only twice. She didn't care if she never saw them again. Only Adam mattered. She would find him. She would leave tonight, while Mrs. Drew and the driver slept. She would sneak to the stables behind the inn where they were to stay, and she would take one of the carriage horses, bridle it, and ride it bareback along the western road—the road to New Echota. Surely God was with her this time! Surely he had not brought her this far only to let something go wrong! She would head for New Echota, and by midday tomorrow she would be there, in the shelter of Adam's arms—at least sheltered by him out of respect, if that was all he had left for her. Perhaps she would not find the love she expected to find, the happiness in his eyes that would be in hers when she saw him again. Perhaps he wouldn't even be there. If so, she would have to count on his family to help her. But she would go, no matter what. She would not return home.

The night was cold, so cold and dark! But the autumn moon was full and the road ahead easy to see. Still, what lay behind the shadows? The trees along the sides of the road were thick and shadowy. Evil men or vicious beasts could be lurking behind them. Was it at night that wolves and bears and all sorts of creatures prowled? And didn't men with evil intentions hide in the shadows waiting to attack?

Andrea breathed deeply to stay in control. She must not let fear overtake her. She pictured the same road in daylight. Surely it was beautiful and sunny, free of frightening things. She would not let the dark frighten her. She would remain calm so that the horse would do the same. She pushed the animal on. She had to get as much ground between herself and the town behind her as she could. She had to get close to New Echota before Mrs. Drew awoke to find her gone! Once the woman realized her charge was missing, she would know right away where Andrea had gone. She and the coachman would take the western road and they would find her. Andrea decided to hide among the trees, perhaps let the horse loose and go on by foot, as soon as the sun was up.

The night air was filled with the sounds of singing insects, hooting owls; and an occasional rustling in the nearby woods brought terror to Andrea's heart. She wanted to scream, was even tempted to go back to the warm, safe room at the inn. But she had no choice now. The next day they would take her home, and she didn't want to go there, for she was certain that if she did she would never see Adam again.

Adam! She must think only of Adam. She must be strong and brave for him. He was all that mattered. She could not let her childish fears of the dark woods make her turn back. She had been through so many hardships in these last three years, so much pain and loneliness. She couldn't give up now. Not now! She talked soothingly to the horse, urging it on and on, terrified that in the dim moonlight the animal would take a wrong step and falter, throwing her and leaving her injured and helpless in the dark night. And then, in the morning they would come. They would come and find her. If only Adam would come and find her . . . How wonderful that would be! Again she concentrated on him. Adam. She must think of nothing else.

Deep into the night, for over four hours, she urged the horse on, giving thanks to God for every minute the animal kept going. She kept her cloak wrapped snugly about her shoulders, the hood up over her head. Somehow it seemed the garment might protect her from evil demons. She rode hunched over. She felt safer that way. If she sat up straight, someone could more easily sink a knife into her back. And this was Indian country. Perhaps the Cherokee were not all as civilized as Adam and the Indians she had met through him. Perhaps evil Cherokees lurked in the trees and bushes. But no. She would not believe that. The Indians she had met were nice and kind, and peaceful. They would not harm her.

She came upon a steep downward grade in the road just then, and far in the distance she could see lighted windows, a sign of civilization, a town! Was it New Echota? How many hours had she been on the road, feeling her way bravely through the darkness? Adam would be proud of her when she showed up at his door in the night!

She urged the horse forward. She would have to slow down now. This was a dangerous grade. She continued to talk quietly to the animal, heading it toward the lights. If only they were a little closer! If only it wasn't such a long way yet! If only it were not so dark and frightening! She shivered in spite of her cloak. She had brought along only the clothes she wore, nothing extra. She hadn't wanted to have to worry about baggage, for she would be riding bareback. If she made it to New Echota, Adam would see that she was provided with everything she needed. And then there would be no more loneliness, no more worry, no more fear. She would be safe and warm, and she would be loved forever. All she had to do was make it to the lights by morning.

She pictured Mrs. Drew and the driver still sleeping, unaware of her absence. She smiled at that thought. How clever she was! How brave and clever to have fooled the hateful Miss Darcy and all the others, to have made Mrs. Drew think she was anxious to get home, to have sneaked away and braved the dark night road. Yes, she had fooled them all! She had not stopped loving Adam Chandler for one moment. If anything, she loved him even more, for he had fathered her little baby. She had given birth to a life, even though that baby had been taken from her. She wasn't sorry for joining with Adam, being his wife. That was what she was, after all. He had told her so. And if he thought of her as his wife, then he would wait for her. Young love ran deep and strong, did it not? Yes, he would be waiting. She had only to get to the lights.

At that moment a fluttering sound came from a nearby tree, and something large flew in front of the horse. Andrea didn't have time to wonder what it was—a hawk, an owl, a demon. Its movement was enough to startle her mount, to make it suddenly rear in terror. Without a saddle Andrea could not hang on. She screamed as she slid off the horse's back, and as she landed hard on the rough ground, one hoof came down on her ribs. She let out a grunt and tried to get out of the way, but slipped on loose gravel and fell again, rolling down and down. She could hear the horse somewhere, whinnying and running off.

"No!" she screamed. "Come back! Don't go!" All the while she slid and rolled until she landed, with a jolt, against a rock. Panicked, she tried to rise, but pain gripped her, and she collapsed, gasping. Her every attempt to breathe suddenly provoked excruciating pain, and she knew she dare not try to rise again, for it was suddenly dangerous just to breathe.

"Adam!" she whimpered. "God, no! Don't let them find

me! Help me!" She struggled against tears, for to breathe in quick, hard sobs would be unbearable. How long would she have to lie in pain this way, in the cold night with no help? She could hear a running horse, far away now. So far away! She pulled her cloak over herself, a painful effort, then huddled beside the rock, praying she had landed someplace where she would not be found by the wrong people. She could not stop the tears of panic and despair now, in spite of the unbearable pain they brought on. Why? Why had this happened? She'd been doing so well. Surely something was broken inside her. Perhaps she would die here. How ironic to die in this place, after all these years, so close to him, so close to Adam. How cruel and unfair! How could God have done this to her? But if she was going to be found by Mrs. Drew, she would rather die. She hoped the woman would find her dead, for if she did not, surely she would take her right back to that horrible school. No! She could never go back! If she could not get to Adam now, she wanted only to die.

She curled up under the cloak, resting her head against leaves, wondering if a wolf or some other creature would come along and eat her. But soon her eyes drooped and she fell into an exhausted sleep, her body slipping into unconsciousness due to her injuries. Yet her mind floated . . . to Adam . . . to the oak tree . . . to nothingness. She was sure she must be dying. She would simply let it happen.

Andrea awoke to an awareness of slight movement and bright sun in her face. Her heart pounded wildly when she saw two figures standing over her. The glare behind them was so bright she couldn't make them out. One of them had turned her onto her back. He was running his hands over her.

"No!" she whimpered. "Don't touch me!"

"It's all right, little one," a man said kindly. "We only want to help you. Who are you? Where should we take you?"

She struggled to gather her thoughts. This was not Mrs. Drew . . . or Mr. West. Who was this? She must be careful. The pain! It was so bad, so hard to breathe! The man was moving his hands over her again, and she cried out.

"I think a rib is broken, perhaps more than one. She must have been thrown from a horse or something."

"Who . . . are you?" she gasped. "Please don't hurt me!"

"We are not here to hurt you. We are from New Echota. I am Sam Williams, and this is my brother, Robert. We were on our way home when we saw you lying here. Who are you? Where are you from?"

"New Echota?" Her breathing quickened. "Take me there! Please . . . please . . . take me there . . . to Adam . . . Adam Chandler. I'm . . . Andrea. He knows me. I was . . . trying to get to him."

Sam turned to look at his brother. "It's her—the one Adam brought to the dance a long time ago, the one he wanted to marry before she disappeared. Remember? Everyone talked about it for a long time."

Robert frowned. "It could make much trouble to take her to New Echota."

"Please take me," she whimpered. "Please! Don't . . . take me home. I've been through . . . so much . . . to get here. Please take me to Adam!"

The one called Sam sighed. "The boy Adam will be very upset if we do not take her to him. I say this is the boy's problem—Jonas Chandler's problem. It is not up to us to decide. I say we take her to Chandler's house."

"Then let us do so quickly. She is badly hurt, and she will be sick from lying here all night in the damp cold."

Tears of joy and relief ran from Andrea's eyes. She tried hard to hold them back, but she could not. She kept slipping in and out of consciousness as someone wrapped another blanket around her and picked her up. She cried out with pain then, but there was no choice but to move her. They laid her in a wagon full of straw, on which they had transported eggs the day before. Sam sat in the back with her, and Robert carefully drove the team down the steep road into the valley.

Andrea smiled in spite of her pain, lying back and allowing the sun to warm her face and body. God was being good to her after all! Adam! She was going to Adam! The people who had found her were Cherokee, not from the school! She fought the unconsciousness that kept trying to overtake her, though it sometimes succeeded momentarily. She had to be awake. What did she look like? She had planned on looking her finest when seeing Adam again, to have her hair pretty. She'd worn her best dress when she'd left the inn, hoping nothing would happen to it. Now it was surely torn and dirty, and she was in so much pain she could not even stand up to show him how much she had grown. He wouldn't be able to tell how she had changed and filled out. But maybe it wouldn't matter to him. Maybe he would be so glad to see her it wouldn't matter.

Was this really happening? She drifted in and out of a strange, painful sleep. How long did the wagon bounce over the rough road before she felt it stop, heard voices?

"Andrea! My God, it's Andrea Sanders!" a man exclaimed. The voice was familiar, but it was not Adam's. "Someone go and get my son right away—and a doctor! Adam is at the newspaper office. Get the girl inside. Take her to the guest room. She looks badly hurt."

She was being moved as gently as possible.

The voice came again. "Where did you find her?"

"Up the road, Jonas. Looks like she was thrown from a horse or something. She begged us to bring her here, not to take her home. We didn't know what else to do."

"I am glad you brought her here. It is dangerous, but my son will be so happy."

Happy? Adam! Then he was still waiting! He still loved her! The voices faded again, and then a woman spoke, and a young girl. Her clothes were being removed and she cried out with pain.

"The doctor will come soon," the woman told her. "And Adam will be here quickly, I am sure. Try to relax, Andrea. You are badly hurt."

Cool sheets came over her, then a blanket, wonderfully warm and soft. And a warm, wet rag moved over her face, washing it clean. "Poor child," the woman soothed. "Where have you been, dear girl? How did you come to be lying hurt along the road?"

"She must have been running away from someone, Mother." The younger voice.

"Yes. I wonder what she has been through. God only knows. Perhaps her parents do not know she is here. We will not tell them, not until we find out from Andrea what has happened. We must be prepared for unwanted visitors who might follow her here. If strangers come, tell them nothing."

"Yes, Mother."

"Adam will be so happy . . . so happy."

"Adam!" Andrea whimpered the name half-consciously.

"He will be here soon, Andrea dear. You just hang on. Adam is coming."

The doctor came out into the hall where Adam paced anxiously, reluctantly obeying his mother's instructions not to go inside until the doctor had seen Andrea. All four Chandlers looked at the doctor as he exited. He was a white missionary, a man who had worked with the Cherokee for years, and he considered them friends and family, his own wife being a Cherokee woman. He knew the story of Adam and Andrea, and there was sorrow in his eyes now as they met Adam's. He now had to look up at the tall, well-built young man. Adam was handsome. It was easy to see how Andrea, how any girl, could love him.

"What is it?" Adam stepped closer, looking as if he were ready to explode. "Is she badly hurt?"

"It isn't that, Adam. She has a couple of broken ribs. I wrapped them good, and the rest of her wounds are superficial. But she's just plain exhausted. From what I can glean the past three years have been rough on her, very rough. And you'd better watch out for pneumonia. She lay out in the cold for hours last night."

"Rough . . . in what way! Where has she been?"

"I don't even know. She never knew, except that it was some special school in the North for . . . wayward girls."

Adam let out a hissing sound, his eyes black with rage. "Wayward! She is the best—" He turned to go into the room, but the doctor grabbed his arm.

"Wait, Adam. You should know something."

The young man turned back. "What is it? I want to see Andrea!"

"She had a baby, Adam."

In spite of his dark skin, the doctor could see the color drain from Adam's face. Mrs. Chandler let out a small gasp. "Dear God!" his father muttered, and Ruth just stared at her brother.

Adam's eyes teared and he swallowed. "Mine?"

The doctor nodded. "Of course it was yours. I saw tiny stretch marks on her hips. For a girl that skinny I could think of no other reason for stretch marks. When I asked her where her baby was, she started crying. She said 'they' took it away from her. She said she wanted to bring your son home to you, but she never even got to see him. She said they told her he'd died, but she grew almost hysterical when she insisted the boy is still alive somewhere. I gave her a light sedative."

Adam turned away. "They" took his son away. Who were "they"? If only he knew! A son! Somewhere he had a son! And poor Andrea, having her baby at such a young age, and all alone in some hellish place.

"There are a few marks on her that look like the remnants of a whipping, maybe more than one," the doctor told him gently. "I'm sorry, Adam."

The young man covered his eyes and wept quietly. "This is all my fault," he whispered.

The doctor put a hand on his shoulder. "No. It isn't your fault, son. It's the fault of hatred and misunderstanding. The two of you didn't do anything wrong. The sin does not lie with you. It lies with those around you who tried to stop you from loving each other, those who don't even understand real love. Go and see her. Right now all she needs is to know you still care for her. I can tell by her mutterings that the thought of you kept her going. You were her only reason for hanging on, the reason she risked her life riding in the dark last night.'' The man turned to Jonas and Rose Chandler. "From her mumblings I gather she fled from someone back in Blairsville. They were probably bringing her home and she was afraid to go there. So be prepared for company today or tomorrow. They're bound to come here.''

"Then marry us!" Adam said determinedly.

The man's eyebrows arched in surprise. "Today?"

"Yes. Right now. Today. When they come she will be my wife—legally, the Christian way, with papers and everything. They cannot take her then. Marry us, please. You are also a preacher. You can do it. I will go and see Andrea. If she agrees, you can come in and marry us.''

"But . . . you haven't even had a chance to talk. It's been three years, Adam.''

"I don't care! You have seen what she went through for my sake. Still, she loves me and has come back here. What more could a man ask for than that kind of sacrifice? I am not going to let anything take her away from me again, not after waiting this long. Marry us today, please.''

The boy's eyes were red with tears. The doctor looked at his parents questioningly, and Jonas Chandler rubbed at his eyes and sighed.

"Marry them, Doctor Cunningham. God knows they deserve to be together,'' he said.

Adam looked at his father gratefully, then back at the doctor. "Wait for me.''

He quietly opened the door, and stepped into the lovely room to which Andrea had been taken. The rugs on the floor were pink, the flowered wallpaper was pink, the canopied bed was draped in pink. He moved quietly to the edge of the bed and looked down at her. She wore a white flannel gown now, and the covers were drawn up to her waist. Even though she lay on her back, he could see that her breasts were full and mature, and her face was even more beautiful than he had remembered. The freckles were gone, as were the traces of girlish fat. She was a woman, indeed. Her hair was shorter, falling just past her shoulders rather than nearly to her waist. He wondered why she had cut it.

His heart pounded with joy and love, pleasure at seeing how much more beautiful she had become. Andrea! She was here, right here in his very own house! Andrea! He turned away, wiping at tears and breathing deeply to get control of himself. Then he turned back and gently leaned over her, bending down and kissing her cheek lightly.

"Andrea," he whispered.

Her eyes opened slowly, her senses dulled by the sedative. She looked up at a dark, handsome face, a face that could be Adam's. But he was so much broader, so much more manly looking, and so much more handsome. Did she dare to believe it was he, or was she foolishly dreaming again! Perhaps she was back at the school! Panic suddenly filled her, and she looked around the room and started to rise. Strong but gentle hands grasped her shoulders and held her down.

"It's all right, Andrea. You're safe now. It's me— Adam."

She stared up into the handsome face again, tears beginning to spill from her eyes. "Adam?" she gasped out. "Is it . . . really you?"

He smiled, the beautiful smile. "Have I changed that much? For the better, I hope. You certainly have."

She broke into painful, gasping sobs, muttered his name. And he sat down on the bed and leaned over her, wrapping his arms about her as gently as possible so that she could press her face against his neck and know that he was real.

"Try not to cry, Andrea. It only makes everything hurt more."

"Adam! I thought . . . I'd never see you. . . . Adam, I had . . . a baby . . . your baby. . . . They took him away! They took him away . . . my baby!"

"Be still, Andrea. The doctor told me. We'll talk about it

191

when you're better. I just thank God you're here and . . ." His own tears fell into her hair. "My God, Andrea, can you ever forgive me? If only I hadn't been so anxious! If only I hadn't come to your house that night—"

"Nothing to . . . forgive. I . . . loved you. I still love you, Adam. It took so long . . . to finally get away from that . . . horrible place. Please tell me . . . you still love me, Adam. It's been . . . a long time. Tell me you . . . don't love somebody else."

"Somebody else? Don't be silly, Andrea. I've waited and waited. I knew you'd come back. I knew it. I searched and searched for you, but had no success. I'm never letting you out of my sight again. We're going to be married—right now. The doctor is also a preacher. He'll marry us before anybody can get here and try to take you. You'll be my wife, and there's nothing anyone can do about it." He raised up and looked down at her. Neither could see the other well, for both looked through eyes blurred with tears. "Will you marry me, Andrea? I'll have to get a ring later. But I'm scared to wait. Marry me right now. I won't touch you. I won't expect you to be my wife right away. We've been apart a long time. I just want you to be my wife so they can't take you away. And I want to sleep beside you tonight and keep reminding myself you're really here. I won't ever let you out of my sight again."

She didn't have to see clearly to realize that he was more handsome than any Cherokee man in the mountains, or to convince herself that his dark eyes were sincere. It was like meeting him all over again, and the thought of truly being his wife, of lying with Adam Chandler again, made her feel like the virgin child he had first taken under the oak tree.

"You know . . . I'll marry you," she said in a near whisper, the pain building in her midsection again. "We . . . have to get to know each other . . . all over again . . . don't we, Adam? Are you sure? It's . . . been so long."

"Of course I'm sure. I've never stopped loving you, Andrea." He put a big hand to her face. "My poor Andrea.

How awful it must have been, being so young and having a baby all alone. My God, I'm so sorry."

"I didn't mind. It was . . . your son. I wanted to bring him home . . . to you. But they said . . . he died. I don't believe them, Adam . . . I heard them talking . . . about how healthy he was . . . and someone said something about people . . . being there to take him. He's alive, Adam! I know he is! . . . My baby is alive. He'd be two years old now . . . my little son!"

He could see her hysteria building again and he grasped her hands. "Stop it, Andrea. Not now. You can't think of everything all at once. First you must get well, and we will be husband and wife. We'll be together, Andrea. Then we will decide what to do. Just get well first. And don't be afraid anymore. I am with you. You don't have to make these decisions all alone, and nobody will ever hurt you again."

The feel of his strong hands squeezing her own was like a blessing from heaven. Adam! How safe and loved she felt. What could be bad about this? Where had she sinned? He took out a handkerchief and gently wiped her eyes and nose. "Are you well enough to say the marriage vows? Are you awake enough? The doctor gave you a sedative."

She managed a smile. "After all I've been through . . . I think I can fight a sedative . . . to marry Adam Chandler."

He smiled in return, already knowing he wanted her as much as ever. It would be even better now. They were older, eighteen and twenty now, more mature, man and woman. And they had been through so much in order to stay together. Surely that could only enhance their lovemaking.

"Adam, when we . . . our first time . . . when I'm well . . ." She reddened then, closing her eyes and putting his hand to her face, kissing his palm. "I want it to be . . . at the oak tree. It's still warm enough . . . and the leaves will be all golden and beautiful . . . and that's where we . . . fell in love and where we first . . ."

He bent down and kissed her eyes, then her lips, gently, sweetly. "I'll take you there. You tell me when you're ready, and we'll go to the oak tree . . . and only when you're ready, not before. You take as long as you need. I am satisfied just to know you are my wife, just to look at you and know you are really here, just to hold you next to me in the night. That is enough for now."

He squeezed her hand and rose. "I will get the doctor and my parents. We will be married right now."

She watched him walk to the door, tall, beautiful, handsome, kind Adam Chandler. How could Miss Darcy and the others call him evil and full of the devil, a heathen, a dirty savage? He was the most wonderful man in the whole world. He had never once wronged her, or stopped loving her. Within moments all the Chandlers and the doctor were in the room, and Adam sat down beside her on the bed, taking her hand.

"We are ready," he told the doctor.

The man took the Bible Ruth Chandler handed to him, and soon Andrea was sleepily saying her marriage vows. Was this real or had she fallen into some kind of insane state? Was her mind playing tricks on her? At any moment she imagined she would wake up to find she was in the tiny room, its door locked, the window barred. She clung to Adam's hand with amazing strength considering her condition, desperately afraid to let go of it. Was she really saying these words, making these promises? Was Adam really making the same promises in return?

A voice pronounced them man and wife: "What God has joined together, let no man put asunder." Those words had a painful meaning for Adam and Andrea Chandler.

Someone touched her lips lightly, with a sweet, warm kiss. "I love you, Mrs. Chandler," Adam's voice was gentle.

Mrs. Chandler? Was it true? If only they could have had this in the first place. They would have their baby with them, their son. She would not have had to go to that terrible place. But she was safe now. She was with Adam. She was his wife.

She heard distant voices and then the room quieted.

Someone slipped into bed beside her. An arm slid under her neck and she was cradled against a strong shoulder, snuggled under the warm covers. A strong hand gently stroked back her hair.

"Sleep now, Mrs. Chandler," Adam told her. "No one can ever again take you away from me. You'll never be afraid and alone again."

And they slept there together, two young people in love, while in Washington debates raged over Indian Removal. The days of peace and prosperity for the Cherokee were growing short.

CHAPTER TWELVE

"I've come for my daughter!" Morgan Sanders roared. Behind him stood Douglas and Wilson Means, Douglas wearing his militia uniform and assuming an authoritative air.

Jonas Chandler swallowed back a fear of the uniform. He would not let this rabble interfere with his son's happiness. "Your daughter is not here," he answered calmly. "I thought you sent her away someplace, Mr. Sanders."

Sanders barged through the door without permission, and Douglas followed, his hand on his saber, his eyes resting hungrily on Ruth Chandler. The girl cringed closer to her mother, who looked back defiantly at Douglas Means.

"You know damned good and well she was sent home and that she ran off only a few miles from here!" Sanders growled, looking around the grand entranceway. "I've tried to hide what the sinful girl was doing, but I can't hide it any longer. The whole world can know what a slut she is, but I want her back! She'll go back to that school and spend the rest of her life there if need be! But she'll not live here in sin!"

"She is not here," Jonas repeated. "If she ran off, it wasn't to us. Perhaps you should search your own conscience about why she would run from you, Mr. Sanders. And where, by the way, did you send the girl?"

Douglas kept staring at Ruth. He'd had plenty of young Indian virgins by now. But to take Ruth Chandler would be the ultimate prize, the ultimate revenge against the girl's brother, who had been the first to have Andrea Sanders. Andrea belonged to Douglas Means! And someday he would have the permission of the State of Georgia to ride into Cherokee land and raid and rape and burn. His first target would be the Chandler house, and Ruth Chandler. And Andrea Sanders would also feel the weight of his power. He wondered how long it took to rape a woman to death. It would be interesting to find out, with both of them.

Sanders started to answer Jonas but caught himself. If Andrea had come here, she would have told the Chandlers about the baby. That was something Douglas and the others still did not know, and never would, if he could keep it from them. And if Jonas Chandler knew where Andrea had been taken, he might have a way of finding the baby. If he could do no more, Sanders decided he could punish his daughter and Adam Chandler by making sure they never found their bastard son.

"Where she went is none of your business, Chandler! The point is, she was pronounced well. She was sent home to us, to surprise us. But instead a man and woman showed up without her, carrying on and saying that she had run off in the night. We all know where she would go! Now you get her for me!"

"I'm telling you again she is not here. Search the house if you wish, Mr. Sanders. But do not destroy anything. You are in my territory now, and slightly outnumbered."

Sanders looked at Douglas, then back to Chandler. "This young man belongs to the Georgia Militia, Chandler. I'd be careful what I say."

"So far the militia has no power here, and no right to be here, I might add. Many of my people have seen you ride in. Do you think we are stupid enough not to keep watch now, with everything that is going on around us? Take a look outside. Then decide whether you will abuse us."

Wilson Means walked back out. Cherokee men were

gathering in a circle around the Chandler house. Where they had come from, he could not imagine. Not one of them had been visible when he'd ridden in. He came back inside and eyed his son. "He's right. There are a lot of men out there, and they don't look happy."

Douglas turned cold gray eyes on Jonas Chandler. "Do what you will for now, Chandler. But the day will come when the militia will ride in here and take whatever they wish, including your wives and daughters."

Jonas stiffened. "And the whole world will see the kind of scum Georgia uses for its greedy, unlawful takeover of Cherokee land! It will be to your shame! Men like yourself will make the State of Georgia hang its head in sin and embarrassment."

Douglas reddened. "Our only embarrassment is that there are still so many Indians in Georgia! We will soon rectify that! The Creeks and Choctaws are already gone, Chandler. You're next!" He turned his eyes on Ruth. "I anxiously await the day."

"So do I," Jonas replied. "It will give us an excuse to kill the likes of you."

Their eyes held in a hard challenge.

"Leave it be for now, Douglas," his father told him. "Let's help Morgan search the house."

Douglas backed away, his jaw flexing from his desire to kill. He turned then, and followed Sanders and his father up the stairs. Jonas went up behind them.

"Be careful, Jonas!" his wife whispered, terror in her eyes.

He gave her a smile. "Do not worry."

Sanders and the other two went through every room, opening closet doors, looking under beds. They stormed into the pink guest room, but the bed was empty and neatly made. Finding no sign of anything amiss, they stormed out of the house after searching every nook and corner, and tried not to look afraid as they went through every outbuilding, then stabbed around carefully in the haystacks. For better than an hour they searched, coming up with nothing. When they returned to the Chandler doorstep, Jonas stood in the doorway.

"Now are you satisfied?"

"No! Where is your son?" Sanders asked.

"Adam is gone. He has ridden to some of the other villages with a delivery of the *Cherokee Phoenix*, as he does every week. And I assure you, if he knew Andrea had been anywhere about, he would not be off delivering papers. He would also be searching for her." He folded his arms smugly. "If you would like to search the entire city of New Echota, every house and church and place of business, the school, you may do so, Mr. Sanders. But first you had better go and get some kind of legal permission from the state to do so. Even then, I assure you, you will find nothing. I am sorry about your daughter. If she should show up, we will send someone to tell you. I do hope she has not come to any harm."

Sanders's face was black with rage, but there was nothing he could do but leave. It was obvious that the men who stood around them now—all holding pitchforks, hatchets, and whips—did not intend any more searching to take place without legal permission. Until something was done by the federal government or the Georgia legislature, this was still Cherokee land. The Indians' cleverness thus far in hanging onto it fed the fury in many a white Georgia citizen's heart, and exacerbated the frustrating dilemma causing heated debates in Congress.

Sanders turned and mounted up, ordering the Meanses to do the same. "I'll be back, Chandler!" the man warned.

"It would be useless," Jonas replied. "But perhaps you and yours could come for Sunday dinner sometime. By the way, did you plant any of those peanuts I gave you? They're quite tasty, you know."

Sanders looked as though he might pass out from rage. "You . . . Cherokee slime!" he hissed. "That heathen son of yours had better stay away from my daughter, or—"

"Or what, Mr. Sanders? Even if you can legally come and take our land, there is no law against a marriage between a white and a Cherokee, not if both are consenting adults. There would be nothing you could do about it. However, it matters little in this case. The girl is simply not here, and my son long ago lost his interest in her. He is promised now to a Cherokee girl."

Sanders breathed deeply, striving for control. Chandler seemed to be telling the truth, but where else could Andrea have gone? "Someday all this land will be mine, Jonas Chandler," he growled. "You'll see!"

"At the moment I would be more concerned with finding my daughter, Mr. Sanders. She has apparently run away from you, perhaps headed north, perhaps farther south. It seems she does not want to see you again. Perhaps you should just let it be. She is grown and apparently well educated now. You can no longer stop her from whatever it is she wants. But if you are intent on finding her, then you had better concentrate on other places. She is not here in New Echota."

Sanders whirled his horse. "Come on," he ordered Douglas and Wilson Means. Wilson turned his horse to follow, but Douglas stared at Jonas Chandler a while longer.

"Andrea Sanders was mine," he glowered. "We were going to get married. Someday I'll kill Adam Chandler for making a slut out of her!" He whirled his horse then and rode off, and Jonas breathed a sigh of relief. He waved his thanks to the men who had come to help before he turned to Rose and Ruth.

"I'll send a messenger over to Reverend Jessup's to let Adam and Andrea know her father was here looking for her and that he left. I hope I have bought them a little more time. By the time the search leads them back here again, Adam and Andrea will have been married for some time. Then we'll make the Sanderses harassment public if we have to, embarrass him before the world if he gives Adam and Andrea any trouble. I don't think under such circumstances he will persist."

Rose blinked back tears, hugged Ruth tightly. She was haunted by the look in Douglas Means's eyes. "I hope you're right, Jonas," she said.

Andrea looked up from her bed. She had been moved to a

spare room at the Reverend Jessup's home during the night, a necessary precaution. As Adam entered, the afternoon sun cast its light on his handsome face.

"Adam! Where have you been? I get scared when you go away," she said.

"I had some things to tend to at the newspaper office." He came to her side, looking worried. Then he bent down and kissed her lightly, and her eyes teared again. Would she ever stop crying with happiness?

"I still can't believe I'm really here, that I'm really your wife."

"Well you really are both." Their eyes held, old urges and desires stirring deep inside them, but their bashfulness at having been apart so long was stronger. He kissed her again, a little harder this time, and the lovely warmth that had left her so long ago surged through her. "I'll be glad when you're well enough to be taken to the oak tree," he told her, his voice husky now with desire. "I want you truly to be my wife again, Andrea. And now it's very important." He sat up and sighed deeply. "Your father came to see my father this morning."

Her heart tightened. "They didn't tell him anything, did they?"

He held her hand tightly. "No. They apparently convinced your father that you never showed up here. That gives us a little more time. When they find out the truth, we will be long married."

She studied him, his wonderful build, his dark handsomeness. Was this beautiful man really her husband? Would she really lie naked with him again, giving him pleasure and taking her own? The thought of it made her shiver with love and anticipation, as though they had never been together that way at all.

"My father tried to find out where you had been, but your father would not tell. From you, we know you were in Vermont. The reverend is checking with all the schools there. It will take some time." He met her eyes again, anger in his own. "That Douglas Means was with your father, militia uniform and all! My parents said he had bad eyes for Ruth, and that he threatened my sister and my mother. And he said that you belonged to him, that someday he would get you back." His grip on her hand tightened. "I will kill him first!"

"Adam, don't let him make you do something foolish," she pleaded. "You have to be so careful."

He let go of her hand, and stood up to pace. "I am tired of being careful! I want to fight with my hands, not just on paper!"

"But you can't. That's what they're all waiting for, Adam. Isn't that what John Ross says?"

He nodded. "It will not be easy. Not if the militia gets into it. I know what they are capable of doing."

"We can only take a day at a time, Adam. I'm just so glad to be here right now. That place . . ." She turned her head. "They whipped me, Adam, for my sins. And they . . . they cut off my hair to rid me of my sinful vanity. Then they cut it off again when I cried out for you when the baby was born, when I screamed at them that they were lying about his being dead. He isn't, Adam. I just know he isn't dead."

His heart ached for her. He came to her side, bent over her and ran a hand over her forehead and cheek, smoothing back her hair. "What can I do, Andrea? How can I ever make it up to you?"

Her eyes teared and she took his hand. "You already have. I was so afraid that when I got back you'd be in love with someone else, or that you would have forgotten me."

"Never! I would never forget my Andrea. I never gave up on you. We searched and searched with what little we knew. I never stopped loving you, Andrea, and sometimes I felt you were calling me. So many nights I could not sleep. And now here you are, more beautiful than I imagined you would be, and still mine." He sat down again, rubbed her shoulders. "At first it all seemed so strange, as if we had just met. But in this short time, after lying beside you the last two nights, talking with you, it seems like . . . like it was only yesterday that you left. You are still my Andrea, only more beautiful."

Again his dark eyes held her own. He bent closer,

meeting her lips. So handsome. He was so handsome. And so kind and gentle . . . still her Adam. One hand moved gently over a breast, lightly caressing it through her soft flannel gown, and both whimpered with renewed passion. Nothing had changed! Not one thing! He was still her Adam, and as soon as she was healed a little more, he would make love to her again and she would be his woman, forever this time. Nothing would ever again keep them from being together.

His lips strayed to her neck. He was breathing deeply, and his hand still moved over her breast in gentle, massaging strokes. "My God, Andrea," he whispered. "I thought I'd go crazy when they took you away!"

She reached up and buried her fingers in his thick, dark hair, so shiny and wavy. He was so much a man now. There was nothing of the boy left in him. And he had a law degree, was an accomplished, brilliant young man; yet he belonged to her, to Andrea Sanders—no, no more Sanders. Andrea Chandler. Andrea Chandler! She was this beautiful man's wife! She would be the best wife she could be. They would build a home of their own, a grand house over which she would rule. And with her education, she could help him in whatever he chose to do in life. Adam Chandler would go far, that was sure. And she would be right by his side. She would give him more sons, and— More sons. But what of the one that had been taken from her? What would happen to her little boy? Perhaps she would never know. It was the one black spot in her life that might never be erased, the one painful hurt that even Adam Chandler could not make better. There would be one empty spot in her heart for the rest of her life.

"Hold me, Adam. Hold me and never let me go!"

He moved onto the bed beside her, cradling her in his arms.

They rode slowly, Adam not wanting her horse to falter, for she was not yet totally healed. The day was a splendid one, unusually warm for early November, the colors of the mountainsides magnificent. He had looked forward to this moment for over two weeks, yet now he felt almost as nervous as the first time he had ever touched Andrea Sanders. He smiled. He must start thinking of her as Andrea Chandler. And since she bore his name, he could now claim her by right, and no one could tell them it was wrong.

Somehow he had to make it up to her—all the hurt, all the horror of the past three years. He would treat her like a queen. He would build her a fine home, and she would have servants and slaves. Andrea Chandler would want for nothing. She would never again be alone or afraid. He would see to it.

He looked over at her. So beautiful! Her golden hair hung in thick waves. Her waist was tiny, her breasts were full and firm, her hips firm and rounded. Her face was exquisite. His body burned for her, even more than when they had had their affair three years earlier, for now he was older. He was a man with a man's needs and a man's appreciation for a good woman. And this woman had been through hell for him. He would never forget it, nor would he ever again let her out of his sight.

"Are you all right?"

She turned and smiled, blushing a little. "I'm fine. My side is a little sore, but I'll be all right."

"We're almost there. You rest when we get there, and I'll set up our tent and tend to the horses. We have enough food for the rest of today and part of tomorrow."

He moved in front of her, carefully leading the way up the steep ridge and choosing the safest route. She watched the broad shoulders of the man she called husband, noted his firm hip and leg muscles, slim waist, and lustrous, dark hair. She still wondered sometimes if all of this was real. They would spend the night here, only this time she would not be afraid of the dark woods. She would be with Adam.

Minutes later she saw it—the oak! The splendid oak! Her heart seemed to catch in her throat. How many nights had she lain awake thinking of this tree, this beautiful tree, and of Adam? She could not speak as they drew closer to it, and his heart ached for her when he saw how she looked at the tree. He dismounted and went to her, gently lifting her down and walking, his arm around her, up to the gnarled old trunk.

When she rested her head against the tree and wept, he touched her hair. "Please don't cry, Andrea. This should be a happy time."

She ran her hand lovingly over the rough bark. "I didn't think I'd see it again ever," she declared.

He hurried to his horse and removed a blanket, spreading it out for her. "Here. Sit down, Andrea, and rest. Go to sleep if you like. I'll tend to everything else."

She looked at him and forced a smile. "How I love you, Adam!"

He bent down and kissed her cheek. "And I love you. Now do as I say and rest."

He left her then, to prepare wood for a campfire, pitch a tent on the soft grass, unsaddle the horses and stake them nearby to graze. At last when he started to take their bedrolls inside the tent, she spoke.

"No."

His eyes met hers, and she reddened.

"I . . . I want it to be like then . . . out here under the tree, where I can look up at the branches and the sky. Maybe later . . . when it's dark, we can move the bedrolls into the tent to sleep." She looked down at her lap, and he smiled, opening one bedroll and spreading it out on the soft grass beneath the oak.

"Whatever you wish, my love," he said, bowing like a prince. He met her eyes and gave her an understanding smile. "Would you like a little wine?"

She nodded, and he retrieved a bottle from his parfleche, along with the two glasses he had brought. Then he sat down beside her, removed the cork, poured, handed her a glass. "To Mrs. Adam Chandler, the most beautiful, most elegant, most wonderful woman who ever walked—and she's all mine."

She smiled, wiping away tears, and touched her glass to

his. "To the most handsome, most wonderful man in all of Georgia."

They each took a sip, their eyes holding. They had been together two weeks. They had talked. It now seemed that nothing was different. They were still Adam and Andrea, still in love. She was his wife now, legally. She did not have to feel there was anything wrong in uniting her body with his. She knew how much he needed this, just as she needed it. For two weeks she had been his legal wife, but he had not touched her that way, except sometimes to move his strong hands lovingly over her in the night. How gentle and considerate he was. She swallowed a little more wine, looked at her lap then.

"Adam, I'm . . . scared. I feel like a stupid little girl again."

He took the glass from her hand and set it aside with his own. Then he put two strong hands on either side of her face, making her look at him. "I took away that fear once, and I was just a boy then."

"But . . . maybe I've changed. I mean . . . maybe it will be different . . . the baby and all. I might not satisfy you. What if—"

A kiss cut off her words. He pressed his mouth firmly to hers until he felt her relaxing; then he gently laid her back, being careful not to put his weight on her because of her ribs. When his lips left hers, he raised himself slightly and looked down at her. "How in God's name do you think one baby or ten babies would make any difference? The way I want you, Andrea, something like that can't change anything. It's the heart that matters, the love that makes it beautiful and satisfying. Do you think that someday when you're old and lose your firmness I will stop loving you? A man sees far beyond those things. How do you think some women end up having eight and ten children, h'm?"

She reddened deeply then, her eyes tearing. "I want so much to satisfy you . . . not to disappoint you," she whispered.

He studied her lovingly. "There is no way, my beautiful Andrea, that you could fail to please me."

His lips covered hers again, searching, tasting, his hand moving gently over her body until it didn't matter anymore what happened. She needed him as much as he needed her. She was soon lost in him, for this kiss was not like the others he had given her up until now. This kiss was demanding, probing, pleading. This time he would have his woman, and the thought of being one with this beautiful man brought out all her passion and helped her ignore the pain in her side.

The magic had begun. She was lost in him. And all the beautiful ways Adam the boy had possessed her were magnified now. Every movement was more exciting, every touch brought more ecstasy. She shivered with fear and anticipation as he began to take off her clothes, finally closing her eyes as he sat up to undress her completely. Carefully, he moved her onto the bedroll where it was softer. Then he removed his own clothes, and she watched him, her body on fire at the sight of his magnificent physique. She had not yet seen him completely naked since her return. Her breathing quickened, and her body ached for his as he knelt by her.

Holding her gaze, he took hold of her ankle and raised her leg to kiss the top of her foot and run his hands over her calf. Gently and slowly his hands moved up her thigh, and he leaned farther forward, teasing her as his fingers traced her inner thighs and around that special place he had only dreamed about during the past three years. She shuddered, closing her eyes in a mixture of bashfulness and utter abandon.

He was beside her then, his lips searching hers wildly as his fingers sought that which belonged only to Adam Chandler, bringing out its warm moistness as a groan of ecstasy came from her lips. The gentle circular movements of his fingers made her wonder if flames would appear on her skin at any moment, and her ecstasy grew almost painful as his lips moved down to taste her full nipples. Soon she was gasping his name, offering herself to him in total abandon, allowing him whatever pleasure he chose, letting him touch and explore and renew his memory of the secret places he had claimed, allowing him to do some of the things he had only hinted at doing when they were younger.

He took her to realms unknown to her before this moment, caressed her until the great branches of the oak tree were only a blur of gold above her head, his touches milky soft. She felt as though she were floating on a kind of cloud, being given the ultimate pleasure by some god of love. Gentle hands and warm lips were everywhere, loving, giving, taking, claiming, and it didn't matter. This was Adam. He sought her mouth again, and she ran her hands over his hard muscles, then down to his most manly part, suddenly grasping at him in hot desire, wanting him . . . wanting him.

He moved over her, careful not to put his weight on her. Within a moment he had carefully guided himself inside her, bringing a little cry to her lips. At last! At last he was one with Andrea again! He felt like a conquering warrior upon seeing the look of ecstasy on her face, upon hearing the gasps of pleasure. She arched up to him despite the pain that must have brought to her ribs. Nothing had changed. He was so full with the want of her that their coming together was just as glorious and pleasing as it had been that first time.

He raised up to watch her, to study her beautiful body—the flat stomach, the slender hips, the way she moved rhythmically with him. Andrea! She was really here, under the oak tree with him, one with him again. Nothing in his whole life had ever been, or could ever be, as wonderful as this very moment. Forever he would remember this, his Andrea, open to him, her face beautiful and full of rapture, her golden hair spilling around her shoulders. Andrea!

He groaned then, spilling his life into her in surging, uncontrollable pulses, grasping her hips and pushing deep. He felt victorious, almost as though he had conquered an enemy. In a way he had, for he had conquered the enemies who had tried to keep them apart. Let them come now! Let them try to take away his Andrea!

He pulled away from her then, to lie down beside her and pull a light blanket over them both. When she curled up next to him, he held her close.

"I did not intend to . . . I didn't mean to do it that quickly," he told her. "Are you all right? Did I hurt you?"

She broke into tears against his chest and he held her closer, alarmed. "Andrea? Did I hurt you? God, I'm sorry."

"No! I'm just . . . so happy. I still can't believe we're here . . . together."

He breathed a sigh of relief and kissed her hair. "Nor can I."

"Tell me it was good, Adam," she whispered. "Did I please you?"

He laughed lightly then, rubbed at her back. "What do you think, you silly thing? I let go of myself almost right away, like a young boy who doesn't know what he's about. There is only one thing that makes a man so quick."

When she smiled through her tears, sniffed and wiped at her eyes, he sat up on one elbow, gently running a hand across the gauze over her ribs. "Are you in pain?"

"Some. But it was worth it."

Their eyes held and he kissed her gently. "You rest," he told her. "I will help you wash and I will make us something to eat. Then we will just sit here under the tree and talk, and later we will do this again, only not so quickly next time." His eyes were glassy with desire and passion. "I want to enjoy every beautiful inch of you. I can't get enough of you. And this is our time, no matter what happens afterward, to us, to the People. This is our time, Andrea Chandler, our tree, our private moment. Nothing can ever take this from us."

Their eyes held in promised love. "Nothing," she whispered in reply.

It was a golden time, a day and night of splendor, during which it seemed no one else in the whole world existed. It was their true wedding night, a night of discovery and joy, a night of reunion, a night of giving and taking with pure abandon. They were husband and wife, friends and lovers. Both knew many problems lay ahead, but they would weather them together. Time and distance had not made their love die. If anything, it was stronger than ever. The golden oak spread its protective branches over them, hiding their naked bodies, shrouding their whispers and groans of passion, sheltering them from all dangers with its golden splendor. They would have this moment. There would be time enough to go back and face the problems that lay ahead, and they would face them together. Let the storm develop around them. They lay beneath the sheltering arms of the old oak tree, in their own little heaven.

PART II

". . . situated as they are now, and where they are, there can be no rest for the sole of an Indian foot. . . ."

—Wilson Lumpkin, Georgia Congressman

"I informed the Indians inhabiting parts of Georgia and Alabama that their attempt to establish an independent government would not be countenanced by the Executive of the United States, and advised them to emigrate beyond the Mississippi or submit to the laws of those States. . . ."

—Andrew Jackson, President

CHAPTER THIRTEEN

They rode side by side, the Reverend Jessup behind them, as well as Adam's father and several more Cherokee men. It must be done. Andrea's parents must be told. Adam and Andrea had been married for a month now. They would be told and that would be that.

Andrea sat, rigid and afraid, on her horse, preferring always to ride rather than use a carriage. She did not want to see her parents, and would not have come at all were it not for her desire to see the looks on their faces. She wanted to hurt them, for they had hurt her in the cruelest way. Because of them her baby son was probably forever lost to her.

Adam watched her with concern. She was holding the reins so tightly that her knuckles were white. "Andrea, one of the men can take you back if you prefer."

She stared straight ahead. "No. I want to be there."

He sighed, concerned. Perhaps it was too soon. She'd been through so much. He hated to think of her being hurt. She was still too thin, but she looked ravishing in her blue velvet riding skirt and jacket, a matching feathered hat perched seductively atop blond curls. His wife was beautiful and elegant, a full woman now, compared to the near child he had taken so long ago.

As they approached the farm, Andrea's stomach hurt. Her parents had always been stern, but she had felt loved. Never would she understand why they had sent her away for so long. Surely they had known what was happening to her. They must even know about the baby, their own grandchild! Yet they had let the school send the child away. She would not forgive them for that.

She saw her father then, running from the barn, ordering two hired hands to stay put. Her mother came to the front door then, curious about the sound of so many horses. The woman's eyes widened in surprise, and she walked onto the porch and grasped a post.

"Andrea! We've been looking everywhere for you! What in God's name—"

"And have you spent any time searching for your grandson?" Andrea interrupted, swallowing back an urge to scream at this woman and then beg her to love her. She detected a hint of remorse and a spark of love in the woman's eyes, but then her father was there, pushing her mother back.

"What is this!" he roared.

"We've come to tell you that we are married," Adam declared. "Andrea has been with me for a month now. I married her the very day she returned."

Harriet Sanders pressed her lips together in an effort to keep still, and her husband turned red with anger.

"Your effort to make me forget Adam didn't work, Father," Andrea stated coldly. "If anything, it made me love him more. Do you know what they do to girls up there, Father?" She turned her eyes on her mother. "They cut off their hair. They whip them. They nearly work them to death, and they keep them imprisoned. And they"—she choked up—"they take away their babies!"

"Andrea . . ." Her mother started to go to her, but Morgan Sanders shoved her back.

"Shut up!" he roared. "Look at her! They lied to us! They all lied! All the while we were searching for our daughter, she was right there with them, living in sin with this heathen man, sleeping with an Indian like a common harlot!"

Adam started to dismount at the remark, his dark eyes on fire and murder in his heart.

"No, Adam!" the reverend put in. "It would be your worst mistake!"

Adam's breath came in quick, angry gasps. "What kind of a man are you!" He glowered at Sanders. "You turn your own daughter over to a place like that! You turn out your own grandson! Where is he! Where is my son!"

Sanders haughtily put his hands on his hips. "Even if I knew I wouldn't tell you. But I don't know. Not even the school knows what happens to them after they're taken."

"Then tell us the name of the place where Andrea was kept. My God, man, she's your daughter! She wants her son!"

Morgan Sanders looked Andrea over as though she were dirt. "She's not my daughter. I owe her nothing! I've done enough for her by raising her and pretending to be her father!"

Silence hung in the air then, and Andrea felt her blood turn cold. She met her mother's eyes, but Harriet quickly hung her head. Then, breaking into tears, she ran into the house. Andrea turned terrified eyes on her father.

"What are you talking about?" she asked in a near whisper.

"Look at you, girl! Then look at me and your mother. How could we have birthed a child with light hair and blue eyes?" He smiled then, seeing the hurt in her eyes. "You look much more like a salesman who came by our old farm about eighteen years ago, while I was in town late on business!" His smile widened at the stricken look on her face. "Now do you understand? Your mother laid in sin, girl, and now you've laid in sin, too. Like mother, like daughter! We thought there might be hope for you, but you've got the wild seed of your worthless father in you. You're a bastard child who bore a bastard child, and now that I see how hopeless you are, I want nothing more to do with you! Go on with you! Go back home and spread your legs for your Indian boy, slut!"

Adam was off his horse then. Not heeding the reverend's shouts, he lit into Morgan Sanders, no longer a boy trying to hit a man, but a strong, hard-muscled man in his own

217

right, and much younger than Morgan Sanders. He knocked Sanders to the ground and hit him twice in the face with a hard fist before some of the other Cherokee men could drag him off the man.

Adam resisted furiously. It took four men to hold him back. "Let me go!" he roared. "I'll kill the son of a bitch!"

The unexpected and horrible news she'd received had brought a sick feeling to Andrea's stomach. She barely saw the fight, and suddenly wanted nothing more than to get away. She whirled her horse and rode off. While Adam continued to struggle against those who held him, and Morgan Sanders rolled to his knees, coughing and choking, his lips and nose bleeding profusely.

"Let me go!" Adam growled again as Andrea rode away. "Andrea! Let me go after her, damn you!"

"Not until you promise not to hit her father again," one of the men yelled.

"I won't!" Adam gritted his teeth, sneered at Morgan Sanders. "But I might come back!" The men slowly let go of him, and he stood, towering over Morgan Sanders, fists clenched. "The only bastard here is you," he hissed. "A bastard and a hypocrite! How dare a son of a bitch like you speak of being a Christian! You're more full of the devil than any man standing here! I'm glad Andrea isn't of your blood! If she had your stinking blood in her, she wouldn't be half the woman she is now, and she most certainly would be ugly, now wouldn't she?"

Morgan Sanders looked up, then dove for him, but Adam skipped out of the way and Sanders fell to the ground.

"Stay there in the dirt where you belong," Adam growled. He quickly mounted up then. "I'll find my son!" he roared then, nearly in tears himself. "Somehow I'll find my son!" And he rode off after Andrea, who was riding hard and fast. It would not be easy to catch up with her, and suddenly he was afraid for her, for he realized what must be going through her mind. Andrea! She wasn't even well yet, and she was riding wildly and blindly. He dug his heels into his own mount, a fast, sleek Thoroughbred, faster, he was sure, than the gentle mare Andrea had ridden. He must catch up with her!

Behind him the other men mounted up, turned to follow. Reverend Jessup was the last to leave. He looked down at Andrea's father sadly. "I'm sorry for you, Mr. Sanders. You have turned away a beautiful daughter and a wonderful young man. You've turned away love and happiness, an innocent child who would have loved you as any child would love a father, if you would have let her."

Sanders stood up, shaking dirt from his hair. "Get off my property, preacher! We're tired of your kind coming down here from the North and pampering the goddamned savages! Go back to your precious Cherokees! But you just remember that when we come in and take over, you'll suffer the same punishment and banishment as they, white skin or not!"

Jessup's eyes saddened. "Then I will suffer it gladly before I would desert them," he answered. "And I and my Cherokee friends will some day be watching from heaven's gates while they drag you into the fiery pits of hell, Mr. Sanders." He tipped his hat and rode off, feeling guilty for the remark but unable to stop himself from making it.

Far ahead of them all, Adam rode hard, his horse getting lathered but gaining on Andrea's. Her hat had flown off and her hair was coming unpinned. He managed to come up beside her, and noted that her face looked oddly cold and wild. Tears streamed down her cheeks, and her hair was tumbling every which way.

"Andrea, slow down! You'll get hurt!"

She acted as though she didn't even hear him. He urged his horse in closer then, risking the danger of their legs tangling and causing a bad spill. Then he reached out with a powerful arm, quickly grasping her about the waist. Tugging hard, he yanked her off her own mount, and hanging on with all his might while she fought to get away, he struggled to keep his own horse under control. A man of lesser riding skills would never have held in his mount, but Adam managed to do so, bringing the animal to a stop while Andrea wriggled, struggling to make him let go of her.

"Stop it!" he yelled, almost falling off his horse, but refusing to let go of her as he dismounted to the right. Her tears were coming harder now, and she made little kittenlike sounds as she beat at him with her fists like a crazy woman.

"Let me go!" she screamed. "Don't look at me! Don't look at me!"

"Why! Because of what your father said? I'm glad, Andrea! I'm glad you don't have that man's damned blood in you!" He grasped her arms and shook her. "Stop it! You're my woman and I'm ordering you to stop carrying on this way!"

She put her hands over her face and half crumpled to the ground. Now she understood why her mother had felt she had to warn her against feelings of passion and love. For one night her mother had allowed such feelings free rein, and Andrea was the result, a child born of sin and lust.

"How can you love me now?" Her tone was bitter. "How can you respect me!"

She tried to rise to her knees, but he would not let her. He hung on, wrapping his arms tightly around her so that she could barely move. "Don't talk stupidly," he answered. "The woman I married is too intelligent to take the blame for something someone else did. You're just Andrea—my Andrea. A sweet, beautiful, wonderful woman who loves me and who went through hell to come back to me. How could I not love and respect the woman you are? Who cares how you came to be? God saw fit to put you on this earth, Andrea, maybe for no other reason than to be the wife of Adam Chandler, for you're the perfect woman for him. Your parents are the guilty ones. You are innocent."

She wept bitterly, shaken by deep, wrenching sobs of shock and shame. When the other men caught up to them, Adam motioned for them to keep going. He held her quietly, letting her cry, knowing she needed that much. Reverend Jessup caught up to them then, halted his horse and dismounted. He met Adam's eyes with his own sad ones.

"I'm sorry. She probably shouldn't even have gone."

Adam kissed her hair. "She wanted to go." He blinked back tears. "I guess she didn't get to enjoy her revenge the way she'd planned."

"I'm bad! It must be true," Andrea declared. "I'm bad! That's why God took away my baby!"

"Stop it!" Adam said sternly.

Jessup sighed and touched her shoulder. "Andrea, the bad ones are those who have deliberately brought you this unhappiness. The bad ones are those who hurt and punished you for loving someone innocently and devotedly. God didn't take away your baby. They took him away. God let you come back to Adam, and he will give you more children. God loves you, Andrea, and He loves your little boy. And there is no law that says children born out of a questionable situation can't be good, godly people." He squeezed her shoulder. "Andrea, I'll tell you both something." He took a deep breath. "I never knew my father. My mother worked the streets of New York. She drank heavily and had different men in her bed every night. That's how she made her living. Only God knows who fathered me."

Adam looked at him in surprise, and Andrea quieted. She wiped at her eyes, pulled away from Adam slightly. Taking a handkerchief from Adam's shirt pocket, she blew her nose and wiped her eyes. Finally she looked into the reverend's sad eyes. The man nodded.

"Yes. I am a bastard in the true sense of the word, Andrea, for I can't even name my father. Does that make me less capable of bringing God's word to others, less capable of loving, less deserving of the lovely wife and children I have? Does the manner in which I was conceived mean I must always suffer, live a life of sin and unhappiness? God loves all of us, Andrea, no matter what our origins. It is for that reason I work among the Cherokee. They are no less important in God's eyes than anyone else, and those who look down on them just because they are Indian will one day have to answer to God for it."

"But it makes me feel so . . . so undeserving," she choked out. "Adam is special and good and brilliant. He comes from good family, and—"

"That's foolish talk, Andrea," Adam told her almost angrily. He would not let her out of his arms completely, and he tightened his hold on her again. "I fell in love with Andrea Sanders because of the person she was, the goodness in her soul. I didn't care who your parents were. I only knew you were sweet and beautiful and that I loved you. And in our hearts we were married that first time I made you mine. We did nothing bad, Andrea, and no one will ever convince me that we did. You gave yourself to me out of love, nothing more; and didn't we make a vow that nothing would interfere with that love, that no man would come between us in any way? Don't let your father's cruel words put wrong thoughts in your head. Remember your vows, and remember our love. That is all that is important."

"But surely you're disappointed—"

"Disappointed? I am relieved! It is over now. We have told them we are married and now we are going home. Don't you see? It doesn't matter if your father wants to disown you! It is better for us! Because you are not his real daughter, he will not try to come after you. It is finished. He thinks you are lost to evil, and he is letting you go." He grasped her face and made her look up at him. "He does not know you are simply lost to love, and that he is letting you go to happiness. You have won, Andrea. And he knows it. That's why he's so mad. That's why he wanted to hurt you. Don't let him win by making you run from me, by making you hang your head as though you need to be ashamed of something. Don't ever hang your head around me, Andrea, or I will think it is me you are ashamed of, not yourself. If you think you are bad, then that means marrying a Cherokee man makes you a bad woman. And how does that make me feel?"

Her eyes widened with love. "Oh, no, Adam, it isn't that

at all! Surely you know that! You're the most beautiful, honorable, wonderful . . . you're so much more than I deserve. I feel almost unworthy of you."

"Don't ever say that, Andrea. Not ever again, or I will truly be angry with you. I mean it. You are a woman of honor and beauty and goodness. We will never look at each other as Cherokee and bad white girl. Our love takes us above such foolish thoughts. We are both better than that. I am proud to be Cherokee, and you are proud to be my wife. Is that not so?"

Her eyes teared again. "You know it is."

"Then that is all we need to remember. I will not have my wife going around with her head hanging, not for any reason! I mean it, Andrea!" His hands gripped her face firmly. For the first time he was truly giving her an order. "Do you understand me?"

Their eyes held. "I understand," she said quietly. "Don't be mad at me, Adam. I can't stand for you to be mad at me. I love you so."

He loosened his grip slightly, bending down and kissing her forehead. "I am mad at your father, not you. But I will be angry with you if you ever again say that you are bad or hang your head in shame. You are the beautiful and honorable Mrs. Adam Chandler."

She smiled through her tears, and he hugged her close. Adam then met the reverend's eyes, thankfully. "I know you did not have to tell us what you did. I thank you, Reverend Jessup."

The man sighed. "Just remember you are the only ones who know, besides my lovely wife. Not that I think I'm unworthy myself, but there are some who would pull me out of the pulpit if they knew, and I want to preach. So I don't tell them."

"I understand. You are a good man, Reverend Jessup."

The reverend donned his hat. "Well, I just wish I could find your little boy. But I'm afraid we're going to find nothing but dead ends. Something tells me that even if we find the school where Andrea was taken, they'll not even acknowledge she was ever there, even if we use the name

Marie which they used on her records. They are apparently a very careful outfit, and my guess is Andrea's father was telling the truth when he said even the school doesn't know where the babies are taken. I think the two of you should prepare to face the fact that you will probably never find your son, Adam. My advice is to have more children, as soon as possible. It will help fill the void in your wife's heart. And we can all pray very hard for the son that was taken from her—pray that God will watch over him and keep him safe."

Andrea cried harder at these words, and Adam held her tightly.

Then the reverend mounted up. "I'll leave you two alone. But you'd better hurry up and get over to the other side, Adam."

Adam nodded. Andrea's horse was ambling back toward them as the reverend rode off.

"Andrea, we have to head back. Come on, honey. It's all over now. We'll be okay." He hugged her tightly. "Let's go home. If we're to have more babies, we can't do it standing here, can we?"

She looked up at him, held back a sob. "Oh, Adam, I love you! Don't ever leave me!"

He grinned. "And why would I do that?" He kissed her eyes, tasting salty tears. "Andrea, Andrea, I am my own man. I have chosen you. What else is there to ask or to worry about? I am so happy you have come back. Every day I fear something will take you from me. Why on earth would I leave the woman I love?"

"I . . . don't know. I just get scared."

He smoothed back her hair, one arm still firmly around her. "You told me once you would never be afraid as long as you were in my arms, remember? Were you fibbing?"

She managed a smile then. "No."

"Then why are you afraid now? Am I not holding you? Don't you sleep in my arms every night?" He took the handkerchief and wiped her eyes. "Stop being afraid." He kissed her lightly. "And I think the reverend is right. I think it is important that you have another baby as soon as

I can get my life to grow in your belly. I think we should go home and work on it. What do you think?"

She stared up into the handsome face and teasing eyes, feeling a rush of love and desire. "There is nothing I want more in the whole world than to have your children. I would like another baby, Adam. But I'll always love the one I never saw."

He sobered then, his own eyes tearing. "Of course you will. And so will I. But right now he's in God's hands, and we must trust God to take care of him, pray every day that somehow, someday, we will find our son." He reached out and pulled her horse forward. "Come on now. We should get away from here. We can't ride them too hard now. The poor things are worn out and will need a good rubdown when we get them home."

She mounted up, patting her mare apologetically. "I hope I didn't hurt them, Adam," she said with concern, noticing that his horse was still panting and was lathered.

"They'll be all right if we walk them the rest of the way. Besides, it's a pretty day, and on the way back our hearts will be a little more relieved than when we came. Right?"

She glanced back at the farm, far in the distance now. She would never go back. She truly was free now. But what of her mother? Her mother would never be free. She looked back at Adam.

"I'm so glad I found you, Adam Chandler. Some women are forced to marry men they don't really love. I feel so lucky."

His eyes ran over her lovingly. "I am the one who is lucky."

There followed a time of peace, of calm before the storm. The black clouds of debate over Indian Removal remained on the horizon and still did not move in as Adam and Andrea Chandler had their own home built, smaller than the elder Chandler's brick estate, but just as elegant. Those first few months Andrea was so afraid of being apart from Adam, he did little more than help on his father's farm, sharing the profits, so that he could be close to his wife. And their heated nights of lovemaking, which seemed to grow ever sweeter, brought the pregnancy Andrea so wished for.

But by the spring of 1830 the clouds had rolled in a little closer, and now the thunder could be heard all the way from Washington. Copies of Congressional debates were reprinted in the *Cherokee Phoenix*. Theodore Frelinghuysen of New Jersey, who would one day be called the Christian Statesman, sympathized with the Cherokee. "I ask in what code of the law of nations . . . their (Indian) rights have been extinguished?" he said. "Where is the decree or ordinance that has stripped these early and first lords of the soil? . . . Who is the injured, and who is the aggressor? . . . Do the obligations of justice change with the color of the skin? . . . We . . . (are) about to turn traitors to our principles and our fame, (are) about to become the oppressors of the feeble. . . ."

But those in favor of Indian Removal spoke the most frequently, the loudest, and the longest; men like John Forsyth of Georgia. "We will not take the trouble to interfere with such questions," he declared. "The United States obtained, by treaty, the power to legislate over the Cherokees, and transferred it to Georgia. . . . Georgia stands justified in her course; I shall proceed. . . ."

Congressman Wilson Lumpkin, soon to become governor of Georgia, declared that his state stood "charged before the House, before the nation, and before the whole world, with cruelty and oppression towards the Indians. I deny the charge . . . our political opponents have availed themselves of the aid of enthusiastic religionists, to pull down the administration of President Jackson . . . the undefiled religion of the Cross is a separate and distinct thing, in its nature and principles, from the noisy cant of these pretenders. . . . The inhumanity of Georgia . . . is nothing more nor less than the extension of her laws and jurisdiction over this mingled and misguided population who are found within her acknowledged limits . . . if the heads of these pretended mourners were waters, and their eyes were a fountain of tears, and they were to spend days and years in weeping over the departure of the Cherokees from Georgia, yet they will go!"

This last and most threatening speech made everyone uneasy. Adam lowered the paper and looked across the table at his wife, heavy with child and due in two more months. He had been reading the speeches to her. Now he noticed that she knitted the baby blanket she'd been working on with more vigor. Her face was flushed and her breathing shallow.

"Andrea?"

She finally met his eyes, her own red with tears that wanted to come. "It's preposterous!" she said in a desperate, angry whisper. "They can't just come here and make all of us leave. What in God's name have you done! Name one thing the Cherokees have done wrong, besides become educated and successful! They're jealous! That's all it amounts to! You were supposed to remain un-civilized. You're supposed to be living in tipis, running around half-naked and eating human flesh! That's what they want, Adam. But the Cherokee fooled them! They proved they were intelligent people who learn quickly and who could be as successful as the white man, perhaps more successful. Now you live on soil that is becoming more and more valuable, and they want it!" A tear slipped down her cheek. "It makes me sick! And it frightens me." Her voice broke. "What . . . will happen to us? What will happen to our baby?"

Adam came around the table, pulled the knitting from her hands. "Nothing will happen to our baby, or to you and me. I won't let it." He sighed deeply. "Andrea, I want to go to Washington for the vote. There is still time. I want to be there. John Ross is going, and Elias and—"

"No! Don't leave!"

"You can go and stay at Reverend Jessup's. You'll be safe there. Even if they vote for removal, Andrea, nothing is going to happen right away. Anyhow, I'd get home faster than the news could get to the rest of Georgia. And believe me, the last thing the government wants is to look bad. They will emphasize that forced removal is to be avoided at all costs. Even if they vote the bill in, it will take years to make it work, and we'll fight it all the way. We won't let them win, Andrea. There are a lot of people in this country, even around the world, on our side. Washington does not want to be embarrassed."

"They'll get out of it by handing it all over to Georgia, and I don't think Georgia cares about being embarrassed! They'll find a way to make it look right."

He wiped at her tears and ran a hand over her swollen stomach. "Either way, nothing is going to happen in the next couple of months. I'll be back in less than three weeks, and certainly in time for the birth of our baby. I wouldn't miss that for anything."

She flung her arms around his neck. "Promise me! It was terrible the first time, so painful! I was so afraid, Adam, and I called and called for you."

He rose, picking her up as he did so. "It won't be like that for you this time." He kissed her hair, then leaned over to blow out the lamp. "Come on. It's getting late." After carrying her down the hallway and into their bedroom, he placed her gently on the bed, then lay down beside her, pulling her into his arms. "I don't have much longer to make love to you," he told her, running his hand over her stomach again. "Pretty soon we'll have to quit. I don't want to do anything that will interfere with having a nice healthy baby, and at the right time." He kissed her several times over, moving his hand to a full breast. "Is it still all right, Andrea?"

She could not forestall the blush that came to her cheeks, in spite of all the times he had been one with her, all the places he had seen and touched and tasted and invaded.

"The doctor said it would be for a couple of weeks." She buried her face in his shoulder. "Adam, I'm so big. How can you possibly want me this way?"

"What did I tell you about that once?" He unbuttoned the front of the dress, leaving the lamp lit so he could see her better. "It's the love that counts. Besides, that's my child in your belly, and as far as I'm concerned, you're prettier than you've ever been. I've never loved you more."

He pushed her dress open and, placing his lips on her shoulder, raised up slightly to pull it down to her waist. He then kissed each full nipple; her breasts were getting larger now, in preparation for nourishing an infant. Unbuttoning her dress past the waistline, he helped her ease out of it. Andrea wore a specially made dress to accommodate her full belly, and she wished she were slender and shapely for him, though she saw the love in his eyes when he ran his strong, dark hands over her stomach, holding them still for a moment to feel the movement. He smiled then, his eyes shining.

She loved him so much that it almost hurt, for she knew that he was trying to keep her from worrying, while deep inside he was himself torn with agony over the Indian issue. Surely his heart screamed at the thought of leaving his beloved and sacred Georgia mountains. This was the land of his ancestors. His blood was in this land. To leave it would be to cut out his heart. He had said so more than once. Now that threat was getting worse. He leaned down and kissed her belly, then rose to remove his own clothes.

"This might be our last time for quite a while. By the time I get back we won't be able to do this anymore."

"You won't go to one of those wild girls while you're waiting?" she teased.

He laughed lightly, tossed his clothing aside. And as Andrea drank in his masculine beauty, she knew a fiery jealousy at the thought of any other woman touching him.

"No, I will not go to one of those wild girls." He thought for a moment about Mary Means and how she had turned out. He had never mentioned it to Andrea, and he would not do so now.

"It will be as hard for me as for you," she told him, reaching up for him.

He gave her a seductive look as he lowered himself beside her to devour her lips, groaning lightly and catching her hair in his fingers. Her locks were getting longer and longer now. "And how shall we compare?" he teased, moving hungry lips over her breasts—kissing, tasting, moving his hand to secret places and making her gasp.

"I . . . don't know," she whispered. She reached up and touched his face. "You're so beautiful, Adam. It's so easy for women to want you."

"And am I married to a woman that men would not want? I think perhaps it is I who need to be wary."

Her eyes teared. "Never. I will never want anyone but you."

He met her lips again, parting them in his hunger while his fingers moved magically to make her forget her swollen belly. So strong he was, yet so gentle; and so handsome, yet he wanted only his Andrea. The kiss grew hot and hard, their breathing heavy; and the familiar, wonderful explosion rippled through her, telling him she was ready for her man. He moved his lips back down over her breasts. To him she was beautiful, perhaps even more beautiful now. He moved between her legs. Parting them gently and raising himself because of her stomach, he grasped her hips firmly to support her as he planted himself deeply within her. He did not want her straining when she arched up to him, so he pulled her up himself with strong hands and arms, making her cry out with the pleasure of it.

He would never tire of her. He was very sure of that. There were some things that made a woman so beautiful that each union with her was special and new. Andrea was like that. She had suffered for him. Now she carried his child. A man did not lose his appreciation or desire for such a woman.

They moved in gentle rhythm, accustomed to one another now, knowing how to move, how to please, how to satisfy and take pleasure in return. She would not think about tomorrow, about his going away. He would not think about the important vote on the bill to remove Indians from Georgia. They would both try in these

230

moments not to wonder what had happened to their first child. The boy was in God's hands. Still, they would keep searching. They would not give up.

He forced himself to hold out. He wanted this to last, for such sweet pleasure would not be his again for perhaps three months. How would he bear being near her for that long without touching her? But her health came first, and the baby's. In that light, he could wait.

His love for her was finally released in passion, and with whispered Cherokee words of love. He pulled the covers over them then, lying down beside her and holding her close, enjoying the feel of her breasts against his bare chest.

"Promise me you will not worry, Andrea. I will be fine. And you will be safe with Reverend Jessup. You do get along well with his wife, and perhaps she can help you know how to make this birth easier. She has had four children. Don't be afraid to ask her about it. Let her help you. She is a kind woman. Promise me you'll talk to her about it."

"I promise."

"My mother can help, too."

"Why don't I just go and stay with her and Ruth?"

"Because my father is going with us. Mother and Ruth will stay with Elias Boudinot's wife, as will Mrs. Ross."

She pulled away from him, studying his eyes. "They're afraid, aren't they? The women are afraid."

He held her eyes, reaching out and caressing her hair. "These are bad times, Andrea. It is true what I told you, about there being no real trouble for a long time yet. But neither can we be too careful. The citizens of Georgia cannot be trusted, and certainly the militia can't. They are straining at the bit. It does not hurt to be a little more careful than usual, in case they decide to harass us. They cannot yet come in and make us go, but they can try to make us want to go."

She closed her eyes and grasped his wrist, suddenly thinking of Douglas Means. He would gladly come if he had the legal right, and he was full of jealousy and hate. She had always been afraid of him, now that was even more the case. She snuggled against her husband then. Such fears vanished when she lay here like this, his strong arms around her, his life in her belly. Nothing could harm her when she was with Adam Chandler.

CHAPTER FOURTEEN

Adam stared down at this gathering of the most important men in the United States. These men governed the America he lived in, the America his people had occupied since long before any of the white men below or their ancestors had set foot on its soil. The words still rang in his ears, the long, agonizing roll call, the yeas and nays. So close! It had been so close! One hundred and two in favor of Indian Removal, ninety-seven against. It had passed.

The Cherokee delegation around him was already busy talking and planning, deciding what their next step must be. Adam only stared at the men who had so casually decided that eventually he must leave his home, his mountains, his beloved oak tree. Surely this was not really happening. How could he go home to Andrea with such news? And what if things got as bad for the Cherokee as they had become for the Creeks? The Choctaws were already gone, as were many of the Creeks. The Chickasaws would soon go, he was sure. They were confident that their long record of friendliness to the United States would save them, but Adam knew better now. Many of the Creeks and Choctaws who had already left had been harassed into going. Now that the bill had been voted through, it would be much worse, and the Cherokees could no longer be confident that horrors would not be visited upon them, even though Congress had constantly emphasized that no force was to be used. At least not yet.

His heart literally pained him. He wanted to kill. Just kill and kill—every man on the floor below, every Georgia Militiaman. Someone put a hand on his shoulder then, and he turned to face John Ross, the man who was more and more becoming their leader in the fight to stay in Georgia.

"Hang on, son. We have a lot of fight left in us yet. All this does is turn us over to Georgia, so now we'll fight the state instead of the Federal Government. All we have to do is keep our noses clean and keep this all before the public so that anything they do illegally embarrasses the hell out of them."

Adam swallowed. "I want to kill them all."

Ross squeezed his shoulder. "I know. So do I sometimes. But one wrong move like that is all they need to put us away, Adam. And no matter what happens, the last thing we'll give up is our pride. Even if they drive us into the mountain caves, we'll keep fighting." He glanced at Elias Boudinot, then back to Adam. "There are some who speak of getting out right now. They say it's best for the Cherokee, and the only way to save our possessions. What do you think of that, Adam?"

The boy's eyes teared and his jaw flexed in anger. "Never! It is the principle that is important! Let them strip me to nothing! I will not leave!"

John Ross smiled. "There are plenty who feel that way, so take hope, son." He sighed deeply then. "But I see some bad days ahead for us, Adam. Not just from the outside, but from the inside. This thing is going to split us. I hate to think of it, but I see it coming, and when that happens, when some of us give up and leave, it will be that much harder on those who stay behind. United we can win. Divided, we'll fall, Adam, and if we do, there will be some who pay a dear price. There will be a lot of hatred and bitterness in our own people."

"Then we must make sure we all stand together in this."

John Ross nodded. "I agree. But I am sorry to say that some of our people have lived so long like the white man, and have enjoyed so much wealth, that they think a little too much like white men. They worry about their possessions and wealth, and don't want to risk losing those things. What about you? Your father is wealthy, and as his heir, so are you."

Adam glanced at the talking, laughing men below, shaking hands, relieved that the vote was over—a vote the Cherokee had no say in. He looked back at John Ross. "Once we lived off the land. If we have to do so again to win our cause, I am ready. If I lose all I have, I will just work harder to get it back again. I am young. I have an education."

John Ross nodded. "There are some who are not so young, who don't have enough years to gain it all back, to start all over someplace new. They're the ones to watch. They'll give up first."

"Not my father. He is not like that."

Ross sighed deeply. "And what about that new young wife of yours? Is she strong enough to face losing everything, to face losing all that you have, to face running and hiding? It could come to that."

Adam straightened more. "Andrea will do whatever she has to do, as long as we can be together. That is all she cares about. She has chosen a Cherokee man and she will take whatever that brings. She has already suffered for me. And now she carries my child. She will fight every step of the way, right by my side."

Ross smiled. "Good. We can do it, Adam. You just watch."

John Ridge approached them then, motioning all to gather around him. "I have been talking to the secretary of war, General Eaton," he told them. "He said to tell all of you that President Jackson is going to his home in Tennessee for a vacation. Eaton and General Coffee, a relative of Jackson's, are going along. The President wants delegations from the Southern Indian tribes to meet at Eaton's home in Franklin to discuss this bill and its implications. He has invited the Creeks, Chickasaws, Choctaws, and Cherokees. What do you think?"

John Ross frowned. "No. We have too much planning to do. We're going to fight this thing, and if we go right away to such a meeting it will look as though we're giving in and have decided to go along with it."

Boudinot looked worried. "We can't turn down an invitation from the President, John!"

"Can't we? We must, to show our strength and our intention to continue to fight this thing. We'll not give up that easily. They take a casual vote, we smile and say it's all right. We go to the meeting, where they tell us when to leave and where to go, as though it is nothing at all. I say no! We go home and start planning our next move!"

Boudinot sighed, looking upset. "What are we fighting for? A little more time perhaps. We all know how it will end, whether it be tomorrow or six years from now."

"Six years is six years! A lot of things can change by then," Ross argued.

"Yes—for the worse!" Boudinot shot back.

"Are you a Cherokee or not? Do you love our sacred land or not?"

Boudinot sucked in his breath, his face red. "Of course I am Cherokee! Of course I love the land! It is my home!"

"Then fight for it! My God, man, you run the newspaper. You're educated. You have all the necessary tools. Most of us here today do. We just have to keep planning, stay a step ahead. We can't give up this soon! We're going to fight the whole State of Georgia!"

"And who runs Georgia," Boudinot reminded him. "A pack of Indian haters, hungry for our land! What kind of a chance do we have!"

"We have a hell of a lot of people on our side, and practically all of the North, except for the damned Democrats. We have some great and prominent men on our side, and the whole world is watching to see what Georgia will do. We have plenty to fight with!"

Adam's father stepped forward. "I will fight to the end. Let them take my home and my cattle and anything else. But they will not take those things easily, and they will take me last!"

John Ross nodded proudly and looked at the others. "Well?"

Boudinot scowled but nodded. "All right. We keep fighting. And we send no one to the meeting."

Ross reached out and they shook hands. "Good. Let's go home, Elias. Our women wait for us."

Andrea lumbered out onto the porch, great with child. She had heard his horse, had heard him call out to one of the farmhands. She watched him coming now, his face grave. He rode close to the house and just looked at her for a moment, his eyes dropping to her huge belly. He wondered what he had to offer her now. What kind of hell would she go through for marrying a Cherokee? He swallowed, tense with the agony of having to tell her, seeing the hope in her blue eyes.

"The bill passed," he said quietly. He dismounted then. "What are you doing here, anyway? You're supposed to be at the reverend's."

"I . . . I asked the reverend to bring me over. I wanted to check the plants, and I needed some different clothes—"

"Do as you're told when I'm gone!" he barked, tying the horse.

A chill swept through her, and her eyes teared. "It was only for a little while, Adam. I don't like being away from home. I feel closer to you here."

He came up the steps, his angry eyes suddenly softening. He grabbed her and held her close, breathing in the scent of her hair. "I'm sorry, Andrea. I just don't want anything to happen to you because you married me. I never should have gone after you. I should have left you to your own kind."

"Oh, Adam, don't talk silly." Her eyes teared, and she kissed his neck, his cheek, and in the next moment their lips met, not so much in sexual desire as sheer love mixed with the fear of losing each other to outside forces. He kissed her over and over—her lips, her eyes, her cheeks, her hair—struggling not to break down. How could he not wonder about and worry over what the passage of the bill would mean to them, to her?

He kept a supportive arm around her then and helped her inside. "You're so big you can hardly walk. Are you sure you have another month to go?"

"That's what the doctor thinks. But he said being the second child and all, it could come a little early, and should be easier this time."

Their eyes met. Again the first and missing child haunted them both. He was as real and alive to Andrea as though she'd held him and nursed him. Months of searching had been fruitless. This one torment he could never make up to her. Adam sighed and kissed her cheek, helped her sit down. "Did you talk to Mrs. Jessup?"

"Yes. She's going to be with me when the baby is born."

"Good." He sat down wearily, running a hand through his hair and then leaning back, closing his eyes. "I have to go away again, just for a week or so. I have to deliver the news to the other villages, and get some votes as to whether or not they want to continue to fight this through the Georgia courts."

She wanted to protest his leaving. He'd just gotten home. She was afraid when he was gone. But she had married a Cherokee and they were in trouble. She had to think of the People, the cause. She must not be a child and whimper and beg.

She put on a smile for him. "It's all right. I think the baby can wait that long."

He opened his eyes then and looked at her lovingly. "I'll make the trip as quickly as possible. I'll get an extra man to cover the eastern farms so I don't have to ride the whole circuit."

She nodded, forcing back tears. "Are you hungry? I'll fix you something." She started to get up, but it was a real effort. He rose and pushed her back into the chair.

"You stay put. You have servants, remember? And even so, I can get myself something. You don't have to do it. How about me getting something for you?"

She sighed and rubbed a hand over her belly. "I'm not

hungry." She looked up at him then. "I'm sorry you couldn't come home to a slender energetic wife who could welcome you to her bed after your long trip."

He laughed lightly and put his own hand on her stomach. "I can't imagine anything nicer to come home to than this." He leaned down and kissed her lips. "I waited three years for you, woman. I think I can manage a few weeks, especially for such a nice cause." He rose then, to walk to the kitchen.

"Adam?"

He turned, still smiling. "What?"

"Is it dangerous . . . riding to the villages? I mean . . . now that the bill has passed, I don't like you out riding alone."

He gave her a wink. "Don't worry about me, Mrs. Chandler. You just worry about having a nice healthy baby. I'll be in Cherokee country. I'll be all right."

She waited until he'd disappeared around the corner, then covered her face with her hands, trembling, not wanting him to know how frightened she was by the latest events. She had to be strong, for his sake.

"God, don't let anything happen to him," she prayed quietly.

Adam moved through the thick, green forests of the northern Georgia mountains he so loved. It was a lovely June day, and his heart was happy in spite of the grave news he'd carried to the villages, the long sheets of signatures he had to procure for new petitions to the state. At least today was lovely, and things were peaceful. And Andrea would have his baby at any time now. He'd been to most of the villages he was to cover. There was only one left, and then home. He'd be there tomorrow, and he'd not leave again until the baby was born.

He urged his sturdy Thoroughbred slowly along a rocky path, listening to the calls of birds, studying the colors of the flowers that sprouted among the rocks. He guided the horse forward to a small clearing in the midst of oaks and cedars, where he often made camp during his trips. Halting his horse, he dismounted, picked up a few sticks, and carried them to the little pit he'd dug out on another trip for a campfire. He gathered up a few leaves and dropped them into the small hole, put the sticks on top of the leaves.

Then something heavy fell onto him from above, knocking him to the ground, making him grunt and temporarily knocking the breath out of him. "You'll not eat lunch today, Cherokee!" someone growled. Before he could understand what was happening two men jerked him up, each holding an arm, while a third came up to him and drove a big fist into his gut, provoking black pain and another loud grunt. Someone grabbed his hair then, and jerked his head back. "What's your mission, Cherokee? You riding to the villages to tell your people to fight?"

Adam, struggling to get his breath, stared into the face of a Creek man. He had not expected trouble from any Creeks. "I don't . . . understand."

"No, you don't." The man sneered. "Has your mother or your wife been raped yet, Cherokee? Have they burned your home yet? You'll understand when that happens!"

"You are . . . Creek. We are all fighting . . . for the same cause."

The Creek man backed up a little, but Adam was still too stunned by the sudden attack to wrench himself away from the two who held him.

"Why is it the Creeks are already suffering, and they still have not touched the Cherokee, huh?" he asked. "Are you special? Are you smarter than the Creeks?" He spit at Adam. "All your fighting with the government is doing is making it worse for the rest of us! You Cherokees fought on Jackson's side at Horseshoe Bend, killing many Creeks. We did not fight for the same cause then. Are you Jackson's pets now? Is that why you still live high and free, Cherokee man?"

Adam swallowed, his anger rising. "It was different then," he answered, his breath coming in gasps. "Then we were all foolish enough . . . to let the white man divide us. We must not . . . let that happen now. Our cause . . . is the same as yours. Anything the Cherokee win, the Creek win also. We are in . . . as much danger as you. We have only . . . held them off longer."

The Creek man grinned. "You will find out how bad it can be, Cherokee! Your wife and loved ones will find out! You make the rest of us look bad when you keep fighting. You stay, so we stay—yet we are the only ones who suffer! You still have your fine homes, your land—"

"They're doing it again, don't you see?" Adam shot back. "They're dividing us! They know the Cherokee will hold out to the last legal fight! They are only using you as examples, and by doing so they turn you against us, to weaken us! It is the same thing they did at Horseshoe Bend! You fall right into their plan!"

The Creek stepped closer. "I no longer have eyes to see clearly, Cherokee! My eyes only see my wife and daughter raped repeatedly while I am held back. That is what my eyes see—nothing more!" He landed another hard fist into Adam's stomach, but Adam saw it coming and hardened his muscles against it as best he could, warding off the worst of the blow. He could see now that they intended to beat him almost to death, to use him as an example to the other Cherokees, a warning to stop fighting and get out. A fist came up into his face then, and Adam kicked up hard, landing a booted foot into the Creek's privates.

He struggled, furious at their stupidity, wrenching himself free from one of those who held him and landing a big fist in the other man's face, knocking him backward. He whirled then, and the third man landed a blow to the side of his head. It was made with a fist-size stone, and it was so hard it knocked Adam to the ground. His head reeled with pain and blackness, but he struggled to his knees. When someone knocked him back down, he growled with manly pride and anger, then reared up and literally threw the Creek off. He was bigger and stronger than any of them, but he was outnumbered.

The man he had kicked was struggling to get up, still

holding himself. He whirled on the third man and landed several hard punches then, feeling pain in his hand but ignoring it. He saw the man's lips split open, and the last blow knocked his nose sideways. That Creek went down screaming and lay writhing on the ground. The second man had recovered from Adam's first blow and he came at him again, landing into his side. Adam grasped his hair and pulled hard, yanking the man off him. Then he scrambled to his feet and kicked hard, landing a foot in the man's middle and then on his head.

As Adam whirled about, he saw the man he had kicked in the groin stumbling to his feet. The Creek pulled a handgun from his belt and pointed it at Adam. Before Adam could react he saw the flash from the end of the barrel, felt a searing, hot pain go through his right thigh. It knocked him backward, but he knew he had to move quickly and could not succumb to the pain and shock. He scrambled for his horse, to retrieve his rifle.

"Let's go!" someone yelled. "Come on! Come on! I shot him, but he's alive enough to go back and tell them how the Creeks feel! Now they'll know!"

Adam crawled and scratched his way to his horse, grasped the stirrup and pulled himself up. He reached over the animal, pulled out his rifle, and turned with it in hand, forcing his injured leg to hold him up.

"Stupid, ignorant bastards!" he roared. He fired wildly, the pain in his leg making it impossible to aim properly. The first man fired back, the bullet narrowly missing Adam's arm, while the other two scrambled off into the woods, one still screaming and holding his nose. The first man turned and rode toward him, firing at the ground in front of Adam while Adam tried desperately to reload.

"You tell your Cherokee friends to start getting out now!" he shouted. "Jackson's pets will get theirs just like we did! You make it harder for all of us, Cherokee, so get out now. Or are you wealthy bastards paying somebody off to let you stay? Huh? Is that it?"

By the time Adam got his rifle reloaded, the man had disappeared into the trees. A moment later he heard horses riding off. Adam bent over, panting. Everything hurt. His head reeled, and the ground kept trying to come up and meet him. His leg felt on fire, and a great thirst began to build in him. He grasped his saddlehorn, managed to get his left foot into the stirrup. He clung to his rifle and groaned as he swung the wounded leg over the saddle. He leaned down then, his face against the horse's neck, panting with pain and near unconsciousness. After a moment's rest he raised up, sliding the rifle back into place and daring to look at his leg.

His pants were already soaked with blood. He took a bandana from around his neck and tied it around his leg just above the wound. Praying he could reach home before loss of blood made him pass out, he urged his horse into motion, glad it was a dependable mount who knew the way. He had to get back as fast as possible . . . home, home to Andrea. He couldn't die without seeing Andrea again.

Andrea heard his horse and waited for the familiar footsteps on the porch. It was after dark. Adam had never been this late before, but she had forced herself not to worry, for the baby's sake. She breathed a sigh of relief, certain Adam was coming, but after a moment she looked at the entrance to the parlor. No one had come in. She rose from her chair with much effort, lumbering to the hallway and calling to the kitchen to Adam's father. His parents had come to stay with her at night while Adam was gone, Andrea preferring to stay in her own house. Jonas came from the kitchen, where he had been drinking coffee and studying further petitions.

"What is it?"

"Someone rode up. But no one came to the door."

Jonas frowned, hurried back to the kitchen, and returned with a rifle in his hand. Andrea's heart pounded.

"Get back in the parlor," he told her as he went to the door.

Andrea listened. She did not move.

"Who's out there?" Jonas called out.

There was only a faint reply, but Andrea recognized the voice.

"Adam! It's Adam!" She hurried back out into the hall, but Jonas put his arm out and pushed her against the wall.

"Stay back!" He opened the door cautiously. In the light of the oil lamp outside the door he could see his son, still on his horse, leaning over and struggling to get down.

"Help me . . . Father."

"Good God!" Jonas set the rifle aside and hurried out, followed by Andrea, who screamed her husband's name as he slumped off the horse into his father's arms. Adam was much bigger than Jonas, and the older man could not hang on to his son.

"Adam!" Andrea screamed again. She hurried down the steps and went to his side, hardly able to bend over to him due to her size. "No! No!"

Rose Chandler, who had come running at the screams, gasped when she saw her son.

"We've got to get him inside," Jonas told her. "Stay here by him. I'll go get some help—the doctor." He quickly mounted Adam's horse and rode off, and Rose hurried back inside to get a pillow and blanket.

Andrea bent over him, saying his name over and over, running her hands over his torn and dirty clothes. His face was bruised, and he was covered with dirt and scrapes. It was too dark to see very well, and she gasped when her hand touched a warm wetness on his pantleg. She held up her hand and saw the red blood. "My God!" she whispered. Her hand started to shake, and she stared wide-eyed at Rose, who had returned and was placing a pillow under Adam's head. The older woman looked at Andrea's hand and saw the terror in the girl's eyes. She grasped Andrea's wrist firmly.

"Don't you let go, Andrea. Don't break apart. Remember the baby. He'll be all right, and the most important thing you can do for him now is have a nice healthy baby."

Andrea continued to shake as she stared at the blood, but Rose jerked her arm and the girl finally met her eyes.

"Stay calm, Andrea. If you love him, stay calm, and

remember that baby.''

A sob convulsed Andrea as she looked down at Adam. ''His leg . . . it's covered with blood. His pants . . . they're soaked with it.''

Her mother-in-law felt along the leg, forcing herself not to gasp or panic. Then she put a blanket over her son and hurried back inside, while Andrea leaned down and kissed her husband's forehead, smoothing back his hair, gently kissing his facial bruises.

''Adam, don't die. I couldn't live . . . not without you.''

He opened his mouth and she leaned close. ''Creeks,'' he whispered. His body shuddered. ''Shot me . . . got to get . . . to Andrea.''

''You have, darling. You're with me. You'll be all right. Don't die, Adam! Promise me. Remember the baby!''

''An . . . drea,'' he whispered. He tried to reach for her, but was simply too weak. His mother returned with scissors and gauze, as well as an oil lamp.

''Hold the lamp, Andrea, while I cut off the pantleg and wrap the wound. We've got to slow the bleeding.''

The girl's heart pounded, and she felt sick when she held up the lamp. She had never seen so much blood. To know it was Adam's was even more terrifying.

But again she forced herself to be strong. The baby! Rose was right. She must remember the baby, for Adam's sake. The woman worked quickly, cutting off the pantleg and wincing as she pulled away the part that was sticking due to dried blood. ''I just pray that the bone wasn't damaged. It looks like this could have happened early this morning, maybe even yesterday. I pray to God the wound doesn't get infected.'' She handed Andrea the gauze. ''I'll go get some whiskey to pour over it. The men should be back soon.''

She hurried away again, and Andrea stared at Adam's leg. Her beautiful, muscular Adam, wounded. He was not the type to give up a fight. What more would happen to him if he lived through this? His mother returned with whiskey and a glass of water, knelt down. She set the whiskey aside and held the water to his lips.

''Adam. Son. Try to drink this. You need water, Adam,''

she said softly. She raised his head slightly and he groaned, seeming to rouse a little again, taking a sip. He coughed then.

"Andrea."

"She's right here, Adam. She's all right, and so will you be."

Andrea held the lamp in one hand; with the other she reached out and took Adam's hand. "It's all right, Adam. You'll be all right," she told him, trying hard to sound strong.

Rose opened the whiskey, and poured it gingerly over his leg. As he moaned and his body jerked, Andrea fought back tears. Her husband was in such pain. As Rose began to wrap gauze around the leg, Adam called for Andrea again. She squeezed his hand.

"I'm right here, Adam."

"The . . . baby . . ."

"The baby is still in my belly. I didn't have the baby yet, Adam. I'm all right, and so is the baby."

His mother applied pressure to slow the bleeding, and he cried out from the pain just as several men rode up, among them Dr. Cunningham. He immediately went to Adam's side, replacing Rose.

"His leg, Dr. Cunningham," Andrea said. "He's been shot! He's lost so much blood!"

The doctor quickly checked Adam over, saw no sign of other bullet wounds. "Get him inside right away," he told the men. Four of them hurriedly lifted Adam, and as they did so he groaned and called out Andrea's name. She set the lamp down, and Jonas helped her get to her feet. He felt her tremble.

"You, young lady, get to a bed and lie down," the doctor told her.

"No! I want to be with Adam!"

"You're better off waiting until I'm through with him."

"No! I want to be with him! Please! I'll feel better if I'm with him. He might need me."

The doctor could see that her panic was building. "All right. But you'll sit at the head of the bed, and do nothing more than hold his hand and comfort him. I may have to cut that leg open, and I don't need you passing out on me or going into labor. This isn't good for you. Not good at all."

"I'll be all right," she assured him. "I can be strong for Adam."

The doctor smiled and patted Andrea's shoulder. She looked at Jonas then, and at the men who had come along. "He told me . . . it was Creeks that did it," she told them.

"Creeks!" The small group of men muttered the word, and John Ross stepped forward. "Are you sure?"

She nodded. "Maybe he was just delirious. But that's what he said."

Ross's face darkened. "Some are wondering why our homes and farms haven't been attacked yet," he said. He looked at Jonas. "The white man is very clever at knowing how to keep the Indians divided, isn't he?"

Jonas's eyes saddened. "He always has been." He put an arm around Andrea, and helped her inside, leading her to the bedroom where Adam now lay, already stripped. His mother was bathing him while the doctor laid out instruments. Andrea breathed deeply and rested a hand on her belly. There he lay, maybe dying, in the very bed where he had planted his life in her belly during those beautiful moments when they were one. She forced herself to walk to the bed, took a washcloth from her mother-in-law, and sat down at the head. Then she gently washed his face.

"You'll be all right, darling," she told him softly.

His eyes opened, and he actually managed a half-smile. "You're . . . fatter every time . . . I come back home."

Her eyes teared and she smiled back. "You have no one but yourself to blame."

His eyes drooped shut again, and the doctor leaned over him, forced a brown medicine down Adam's throat. "You just let this stuff put you into a nice deep sleep, young man. Then you won't feel a thing till I'm all done with you." He glanced at Andrea. "You sure you want to stay?"

She kept smoothing back Adam's hair. "I'm sure."

The next hour and a half was spent in near silence,

except for occasional groans from Adam, the clink of the doctor's instruments, and the few quiet orders he gave to Rose and Jonas. Andrea didn't watch. She just kept stroking her husband's hair, talking to him now and again. When the doctor probed for the wicked piece of shot still in Adam's leg, Adam went rigid and cried out, in spite of the heavy painkiller he'd been given. But his ordeal was soon over, the wounded leg drenched in alcohol and stitched and tightly wrapped. The doctor quickly examined the rest of Adam's body. It was covered with bruises—large purple ones over the ribs and stomach muscles—but no broken bones.

"Must have got into quite a tussle before he was shot," Cunningham muttered. "I wonder how many there were and what condition they're in. Adam doesn't go down easy."

Andrea kept smoothing his hair. "I hope they're all dead," she said coolly.

"You shouldn't hope for that. With all the trouble going on around here, we don't need another war with the Creeks." He patted her arm. "Come away now. We'll cover him up and let him sleep." Only then did he notice the perspiration on her face, the ashen gray color of her skin. "Andrea? My God, girl, are you in labor?"

"It takes a long time. I . . . wanted to stay with him . . . until I knew he was all right."

The doctor looked at Rose in alarm. "Have someone go and get Mrs. Jessup. Where should I take her?"

"Across the hall—the spare bedroom." Rose quickly went to send someone for Margaret Jessup, while the doctor helped Andrea to a bed.

"But Adam—"

"He'll be fine now. The flesh was torn badly, but the bone is intact. If he lies still and we get plenty of liquids down him, he'll be all right, Andrea. His biggest problem is loss of blood, but now that the bleeding is stopped, he'll be all right. Don't let him come around just to find out you lost a baby because you wouldn't do what you're supposed to do. Now come to the other room. It's time you presented

Adam with a fine new son or daughter, isn't it? How long have you been having pains?"

She finally met his eyes. "Since he first got here."

The doctor shook his head. "Come on, young lady."

She grasped his arm and walked with him, bending over once with pain before she got to the other room. "Adam," she whispered. She'd wanted him with her. Now she had to be strong and brave, and do this without him. At least he was home, alive. "You must . . . be so tired, Doctor," she muttered. "Everything . . . is happening at once."

"Don't worry about me. It's you and that young man who matter, and your baby."

Adam stirred, fighting whatever it was that kept him so groggy. Something was wrong with Andrea. Someone said something about being in labor. Andrea? Was she having the baby? He opened his mouth to call her name, but nothing came out. When he tried to move, pain shot through him like a knife. In his sedated state he was sure Andrea was screaming for him. Suddenly he felt men beating on him, felt the hot pain in his leg, saw a gun flashing. Andrea! Had something happened to Andrea? Was it the militia? "My wife and daughter raped repeatedly . . ." someone had said. Whose wife and daughter? Would that happen to Andrea? No. Never! Again he struggled, certain he'd heard her scream again. He must get to her. He must save her from the militia. Wake up. He must wake up!

CHAPTER FIFTEEN

Adam stirred, sure he'd heard his name called. Pain shot through his leg and he winced, then rubbed his eyes, trying to remember everything. Men. Men beating on him. A gun firing. Again he felt pain and his breathing quickened. He opened his eyes, ready to fight, but soon realized he was in his own bedroom. He sat up slightly, looking around in confusion. The sky was colored a brilliant pink by the awakening sun.

Then he heard it again, this time for certain, his name being cried out. Andrea! Was it the baby? He threw off the covers and saw that he was naked, his right thigh heavily wrapped and slightly bloodstained. The gunshot. Yes, he remembered now! He'd been shot in the leg. Creeks had attacked him and he'd fought back. He felt pain in his right hand. It was black and swollen, and apparently sprained.

Andrea cried out again. "The baby!" he muttered. Surely he had turned up here in a bad state. The shock of it must have brought on her labor. He should be with her. He'd promised.

He sat up, gritting his teeth against the pain as he swung his legs over the side of the bed. The room seemed to spin then, and he grasped a bedpost. "Mother! Father! Who's out there? Where is Andrea?" he shouted. No sooner did he get out the words than his father came into the room.

"Adam! Lie back down, son. You've lost much blood!"

"Get me some pants."

"Adam, the doctor said—"

"Goddamn it, find me some pants, Father! I have to go to Andrea! I promised her! I'll go in there naked if I have to!"

Jonas sighed and went to a closet. Taking out a pair of his son's trousers, he brought them to him. "Where do you keep your underwear?"

"Forget the underwear. Help me get these on. Please!"

The man slid the pants over Adam's feet. "You should not be doing this, Adam."

"It doesn't matter. How the hell long has she been in labor?" He gritted his teeth and grasped the bedpost, standing up on his good leg. Jonas slid the pants up and buttoned them.

"All night," he answered. "The doctor says the baby is not positioned right. He will have to turn it. It will be very painful for her, but if he does not do it and get the baby born, it will die, and Andrea could die, too."

"My God! And no one came to get me?"

"Adam, you have been unconscious or in a deep sleep this whole time. It was you we'd first thought might die. Even now you should not be up. It will only upset her more to see you up when you shouldn't be. She has been very strong and brave. She is determined to give you a child."

The man put an arm around his son's waist. "Lean on me."

"She wants one, too, Father," Adam said. "She needs this baby very badly. God can't let anything happen to it."

Jonas helped his son cross the hall; then knocked on the door of the spare bedroom. Adam was met with "You shouldn't be up" and "You must lie down. You've lost too much blood." But he insisted that Jonas help him to the bed, where Andrea lay covered for the moment. The doctor was washing his hands. Rose stood nearby ready to help, and Mrs. Jessup was bending over, wiping Andrea's brow.

"Adam, this is very bad for you," the doctor grumbled.

"You'll open up that leg again."

"I don't care! I promised her I would be with her."

Andrea stirred, her face as white as the sheets, her eyes dark and hollow-looking. Was it really Adam's voice she'd heard? He had not died?

"Andrea." He spoke softly, close to her ear, and she felt a gentle kiss. "I'm here, Andrea. You'll be all right."

She opened her eyes, to look up through blurred vision at his dark face. She did not have to see clearly to know it was him. "Adam. Your . . . leg . . ." She could not finish; another pain tore mercilessly at her insides. She took quick deep breaths, then cried out, this time muffling her cry in his shoulder.

He took the wet cloth from Mrs. Jessup then, and gently wiped the sweat from her face. "Don't think about me, Andrea. Just think about the baby. I promised you I would be here, and I am."

It didn't matter to her now what the doctor did. She had been terrified when he'd spoken of turning the baby. But Adam had come to her, and she would give him a child no matter how much suffering it took. Still, moments later she suffered an agony she was sure was worse than any torture ever suffered. Her screams tore at Adam's heart, her nails dug into his arms until they drew blood. He fought his own urge to scream, to weep, to tell the doctor to stop. But Cunningham had no choice in the matter. He must turn the baby or lose both mother and child.

When it was over Andrea collapsed against the pillow, seemingly lifeless. Adam clung to her hands as, finally, the deep pains of birth began to consume her, her muscles working of their own accord. She was suddenly too weak to cry out, and she was so white he was filled with terror. Would she die after all? The baby came almost too quickly then, and Andrea lay quiet, responding to nothing, not even her husband's voice.

Adam heard and saw nothing but his wife's colorless face. Around him the women busily cleaned up a baby that was beginning to cry, while the doctor worked with Andrea, forcing out the afterbirth, mumbling something about her losing a lot of blood. She was washed and packed and covered. Then the doctor waved something under her nose, and she stirred.

"Come on now, Andrea girl, don't you go slipping away on me," Dr. Cunningham said in a loud voice. "Wake up. I'm the one who should be sleeping. Between you and your husband, I've been up all night. You two are young enough to take it. I'm getting too old."

She stirred more. "Baby . . . don't take my baby away," she whimpered.

"Nobody is going to take this one away," Adam told her. He bent down and kissed her lips, but she didn't seem to be aware of the present.

"No! Don't take him away! Where's my baby?"

Adam grasped her shoulders. "Andrea, the baby is right here. Calm down and lie still."

She opened her eyes, confused. "Adam?"

"It's all over."

"I want you to try to stay awake awhile, Andrea," the doctor told her. "Don't be slipping off on me. Drink some water now, please. We'll get you all settled and then this husband of yours can go back to his own bed where he belongs."

She gazed at Adam, seeming to realize fully, for the first time, that he was there. She reached up and touched his bruised chin. Then Rose brought the baby over, a smile on her face.

"I have a fine grandson, Adam. Thank you." She leaned down and kissed her son's cheek before gently placing the baby beside Andrea. Adam stared in amazement at the wrinkled, red bundle with the sparse black hair. His son looked out of place lying next to his blond, blue-eyed mother. The contrast brought a smile to Adam's lips, and seeing a son brought tears to his eyes. He reached down and, with a big finger, touched a tiny, soft cheek.

"A son," he whispered. "Andrea, we have a son."

She reached over and ran a hand over the tiny body, opening the blanket to see that her baby had all his fingers and toes. Then she looked up at Adam, who was speechless. Tears on his cheeks, he smiled, bent down, and hugged them both.

"Thank you, Andrea," he whispered.

"Nobody can take this one away, can they?" she pleaded. "I can keep my baby."

He held back a sob. "Yes, you can keep this one."

It was called the Treaty of Dancing Rabbit Creek. Signed by only a minority of the Choctaws, it was deemed valid by the government. The State of Mississippi could now expect the Choctaws to leave, and as soon as the treaty was signed whites began to make their appearance, swarming onto Indian farms, declaring ownership, looting homes. Federal Indian agents did nothing to stop the white pilferers, and the Choctaws fell into utter chaos and confusion, many turning to the alcohol that white traders brought them. To be drunk was the only consolation, and the whites didn't mind. A drunken Indian was easier to swindle.

The Cherokee were now beginning to get their own taste of the effects of the Indian Removal Bill. Gold was discovered near Dahlonega, in the heart of Cherokee country. Nothing could have been worse for the Cherokees, for the word *gold* meant a literal white stampede. Georgia had to get legislation into gear to arrange for the removal of the Cherokee. But the Cherokee continued to fight their legal battle, in spite of the Removal Bill. There was still widespread sympathy for the Indians, and the Cherokee were politically well organized and disciplined. Meetings were held almost daily. At these Cherokee leaders urged unity and coherence. Over and over again, as the threat of white atrocities came ever closer, the Cherokee were urged to remain nonviolent, despite provocation, to suffer whatever indignities, insults, deprivations, and outrages were visited on them. Only by not fighting physically could they have any hope of winning any legal battles. The moment a sword was raised, the government would declare war, and with more numbers and weapons, the whites would gladly ride down on the Cherokee and exterminate them all. John Ross was the most ardent in urging unity and nonviolence. He became president of the Cherokee Nation and the leader of the Cherokee fight.

It seemed, during this time, that Adam was gone almost constantly. But Andrea had the baby now, little Jonas Adam, named for his grandfather and father. The baby was fat and healthy, dark and handsome like his father, and a great joy to Andrea, helping to ease the pain she felt because of the child she had never seen. She watched him like a hawk, keeping him by her side at all times, holding him so much that Adam declared she would spoil him. But he understood, for the deep terror in her own heart was also in his. All around them danger lurked and chaos prevailed. Yet the Cherokee stayed together in their desperate fight, while in Mississippi the government proceeded to root out the Choctaws; and the Georgia Legislature handed down a new set of laws to the Cherokee, hoping that just the threat of this new legislation would frighten the Indians into running. A few did, for the words of the new act, passed immediately after the Indian Removal Bill was approved by the Federal Government, provided for the confiscation by the state of all Cherokee land. A lottery was planned, in which whites could buy chances to have their names drawn. The winners were awarded sections of Indian land. That precious, sacred land that had belonged to the Cherokee for hundreds of years was to be gambled away to whites. Other threatening provisions of the new act were the abolition of the authority of the Cherokee government and nullification of all Cherokee laws; prohibition of meetings of the Cherokee Council and of all other Cherokee gatherings, even religious ones; punishment by imprisonment of any Cherokee who urged others not to migrate; denial of the right of any Cherokee to testify in court against any white man; denial of the right of the Cherokee to dig for gold on their land.

The Georgia Militia moved into the gold fields, seizing

and destroying all tools and machinery, burning all buildings and homes that surrounded the immediate area of the gold fields.

Every time Adam went out the door, Andrea lived in fear until he returned. Her own health was making a slow return, but worry about her husband's well-being was keeping her spirit down. She was sure he'd returned to his busy schedule too quickly after his attack; after nearly two months he still limped. And she'd had to leave her precious home. Since there was more safety in numbers, Adam had insisted she stay at his father's house. In her heart she grieved for her own home. They had been allowed to live in it such a short time. Everything was happening too fast now, too fast! She couldn't even live in her own house. The Cherokee dwellings around the gold fields had been burned. Torched! She feared a visit from the Militia, and she feared Douglas Means. Worse yet, she could not help but wonder if her own father was among those prepared to buy a chance to win Cherokee land.

It seemed impossible that any of this was happening. How could a government simply create laws to suit its fancy, laws that in so many words said that a certain people no longer had the right to exist, that all they loved and had worked for could no longer be theirs, that they must simply uproot themselves and move to a land so different from their own that many of them would die just from the change in climate? How could Georgia and the nation do this to such a good, proud, intelligent people, a people who had been there for hundreds and hundreds of years; a people who were educated, civilized, settled; who were good Christians. What was the crime in being an Indian? Yet with all its bills and acts, the government had declared it a federal offense to be an American Indian.

It was late October, 1830, when Adam returned from another journey to Washington with John Ross. Andrea looked up at him from the bed, where she sat nursing Jonas.

"Thank God, you're back," she said quietly. "You look so tired."

He closed the door, removing his jacket. "I am tired— tired of constant arguments, and of digging at my brains to come up with the right words to stall off the inevitable."

She swallowed back a lump in her throat. "You can't give up, Adam."

He smiled almost bitterly. "Now you sound like John Ross. Are you sure you don't have any Cherokee blood in you?"

She smiled. "Come and see your son. He's growing up and you're missing it."

He stared at her a moment, then came and sat down on the edge of the bed. Reaching out, he touched the boy's soft, black hair; studied the little dark fist curled against his mother's milky white breast. Then he smiled and traced a finger over the full, white skin himself. He met her eyes.

"I couldn't make love to you for a long time. You had so much healing to do," he said quietly. "And my leg and all . . . then all of this traveling."

"Adam, I'm all right now. It's been three months. We're letting too much get in the way. I don't want what's happening to stop us from loving each other—or from making love. And every time you walk out the door I die a little bit inside. Let's not talk any more tonight about Washington or the militia or John Ross. Tell me in the morning. I want my husband to make love to me. That's where I get my strength. I'll get stronger a lot faster if I can draw my strength from you."

He smiled, his eyes tearing. "I'm sorry. I've had so much to think about."

When he choked up, she put a hand to his face. "I know that. My God, Adam, you have to worry about losing everything that you love. But you won't lose me, or little Jonas. Whatever happens, we'll be with you, whether we stay here or have to go to a new land."

A tear slipped down his cheek, and he took her hand and kissed it.

"You get undressed, Adam. Let me put the baby in his cradle." She got up then, pulling the sleeping infant away from her breast and gently placing him in a large wooden cradle, hand-made for him by his grandfather. That done she turned, to study her husband lovingly and with desire as he removed his shirt. Their eyes held, and she could see a near-violent passion building in him. It had been a very long time, and his heart was torn inside. He undressed very deliberately, almost provocatively, a demanding look in his eyes.

She watched, her own passion building as she took in his magnificent physique. Her heart ached at the sight of the long scar on his right thigh, so white against his dark skin. Yet how beautiful he was! She opened her robe then. She'd worn nothing beneath it, hoping he would come home this night, hoping they could finally be one again. As she let it fall to the floor, she reddened slightly and then ran a hand over her belly, now flat again.

"I . . . hope I haven't changed too much . . . from having the baby and all."

He walked close to her, grasping her face in his hands. "And why would it matter to me if you had?" He bent down and met her lips, at first tenderly, then with a sudden, gripping passion. He pulled her close, embracing her so tightly she could barely get her breath. She felt his hardness against her stomach, and her own hunger was keen and urgent. Each time they did this could be the last, or so it seemed to them, for all around them was fear and sorrow.

Suddenly they could not get enough of each other. They kissed and groaned and touched and cried. He carried her to the bed, and as soon as he laid her upon it, he was on top of her, pressing, kissing, feeling, tasting, moving over her in hard, demanding urgency, trembling with the want of her and the fear of what could happen to her. He spent very little time in preparing her. He simply had to have her and that was that. He pushed her knees apart with his own legs, devouring her mouth as he guided himself into her in hungry fury, making her cry out; for the first time joining after giving birth is sometimes painful. But it didn't matter. She had to have him. Adam! Her sweet, beautiful

Adam! He was here, safe in her arms; she safe in his. They surged in desperate rhythm and he raised up, grasping her hips and pulling her up to him. She felt like a rag doll in his hands, totally at his mercy, letting him use her as he wished; for he needed her this way, and she liked nothing more than to please her Cherokee man.

He uttered something in the old tongue as his life surged into her belly. Then he stayed rigid for a moment before practically collapsing beside her and pulling her into his arms.

"My God," he whispered. "I took you as if I were raping you."

She kissed his chest. "It's all right. We'll do it again, a little more gently perhaps."

He tangled his fingers in her golden hair. "I'm sorry, Andrea."

"For what? I wanted you as much as you wanted me."

"Not just that. The rest. Not being able to be with you and Jonas—all the danger. I planned on being with you all the time when I married you. I was going to just stay here and farm, maybe do some legal work on the side. We'd all be together."

"We will all be together. Somehow it will work out." She had to be strong. There were times when it was he who needed her strength, rather than the other way around. She sensed this was one of those times. He was going through hell. He lived with insults and abuse, whenever he set foot off Cherokee land and went to Washington, or whenever he encountered the militia. "Remember what John Ross tells you and keep following him, Adam."

He swallowed. "Most of the time I can handle it. I get so mad—" He gripped her hair. "We can't fight back. I want to kill them all, but I can't, and it's tearing at my guts!"

"I know, darling," she whispered.

"I'll have to fight, Andrea. If they ever . . . touch you or Jonas . . . I won't be able to stop myself."

Alarm went through her, and she pulled away and met his eyes. "Don't talk that way. If you harm one white man, you know what will happen to you. It isn't worth it, Adam. I can bear whatever might come, as long as you don't do something that will mean we can never be together again. Promise me you won't do something stupid and get yourself hung!"

His eyes teared and he touched her face with a shaking hand. "I can't make a promise like that. I won't let anyone hurt you, Andrea, not ever!"

Their eyes held. There was no arguing with him tonight. More tears slipped down his face. "Oh, Adam," she whispered, her own throat aching now. She reached out and touched the tears. "My poor Adam."

"I can't help it, Andrea," he hissed, struggling against the tears. "Sometimes . . . I just can't hold it in any longer."

She moved up, pulling his face against her breast, stroking his hair. "Then don't. Don't hold it in, or you'll lose your mind. You're here in the privacy of our room with your wife. If you can't cry to me, then what good am I."

He shook quietly, and she felt wetness against her skin as she rocked him gently, kissing his hair, her own tears falling quietly. If anyone had reason to weep, it was Adam Chandler. Her heart saddened even more when she suddenly thought of the oak tree, his tree—the place where he prayed and got his strength. They couldn't even go there anymore, up on the ridge where everything was quiet and beautiful. It was too dangerous now. It would always be theirs, standing on the ridge, tall and silent—the oak tree, where Adam Chandler first made a woman of her. Others could come and take the land, but they couldn't take away their memories.

In the wee hours of the morning when little Jonas stirred and cried, Andrea awakened, aching and tired from strenuous lovemaking with her husband. Quietly, she slipped out of the bed and pulled on her robe, then went into an adjoining washroom, to sponge off her body, so recently touched and tasted by her husband. Then she quickly changed the baby, picked him up, and sat down in a rocker to feed him. She studied her beautiful little son, who, it was evident, would be as strong and handsome as his father. And she closed her eyes then, and prayed—for Adam and for the courage and wisdom they would both need in the days ahead.

Never once had she regretted marrying her Cherokee man, no matter what horrors lay ahead for them. She would have it no other way. She knew he felt guilty about putting her in this situation, and smiled at what a foolish thing it was for him to feel that way. How she loved Adam Chandler! Her heart ached not for her own danger, but for the Cherokee, for Adam. Such a good man he was, so intelligent, so kind; normally a peace-loving, Christian man. The whites were bringing out a side of him that would ordinarily have remained dormant. She could see anger building in him, desperation and hatred and a need for vengeance. That worried her more than anything. She knew he'd meant it when he'd said he'd never allow anyone to hurt her. She couldn't allow herself to think about what that could mean. She forced back the thought of Douglas Means, the worry over where that man was at this moment. She wondered sometimes what had ever happened to Mary, but that didn't matter anymore. It was Mary who had caused Andrea's exile to the north. She would never forgive Mary Means for that.

Jonas finished feeding, and she placed him in the cradle, covered him. Then she removed her robe and crawled back into bed, wanting to feel her naked body against Adam's. As she snuggled close to him he stirred, then turned over, more asleep than awake as he pulled her against him.

His hands began to move over her, his eyes still closed. He whispered her name and kissed her hair, slowly awakening, enjoying the soft warmth and sweet comfort of being suspended between sleep and wakefulness in a warm bed in the early morning, his woman beside him. It had been so long since he'd had her this way. For the moment he had depleted his worry and rage in that one fit of weeping against his wife's breast, and somehow he felt stronger, more at peace. How would he have borne any of this without his Andrea? he wondered.

He gently moved over her, vaguely remembering taking her in one hard, nearly violent intercourse hours before. Poor Andrea. She put up with so much. His lips moved over her neck and shoulder, down to her breasts, which he sucked gently, tasting some of the milk meant for his son. The thought of the sweet mother that she was only made him want her more. Sensing no protest from her as his lips moved back to her throat, he gently massaged her secret places with his hand, exploring, bringing out the sweet juices of love and building her passion as he should have done that first time. He'd hardly given her a moment to breathe then. This time would be for her. He could show her he was sorry, let her be a woman, do all the things that satisfied a woman.

She whispered his name, and he met her lips, tenderly now, parting them gently, drawing out her passions and needs. Her breathing came in long, deep sighs of pleasure, and he felt her relax totally, knew she wanted whatever he could give her. She lay limp and willing as he caressed her intimately, arousing her passion. No man but Adam could make her feel this way, yet she sensed an apology in his movements, a desire to somehow make up to her for all the absences, all the worry, and for taking her so quickly and cruelly that first time after the birth. But if what he'd done had led to the way he was touching her now, it was worth it as far as she was concerned.

Now no danger existed. There was no heartache, no militia; there were no new laws designed to strangle the Cherokee into death or migration. There was only this— this quiet morning, birds singing, her baby fed and sleeping, her husband making love to her. Yes, she lived in luxury and comfort. But that was not why she had married Adam Chandler, and if she had to give up everything to stay with him, she would do so. She would go out to Indian Territory with him, live in a tipi if she had to. But she would not abandon him. How could she live without

Adam, without moments like this? They were still young and in love, and they would not allow outside problems to keep them from enjoying these moments. She knew that even in their aging years, they would see one another with young eyes, feel this same passion, know this same joy.

He was inside her then, gently joining with her in slow, rhythmic movements that made her arch up to him, her inner muscles pulling at him, taking him in in sweet abandon. He hung on this time, forcing himself to give her all the pleasure he could before exploding into his own desires.

It was all done quietly, gently, with not a word spoken, and then it was over and they were both asleep again. When she awoke later in the morning, Andrea found herself wondering if it had really happened. Surely it was just a beautiful dream. But she lay naked beside him, still in his arms, one leg still wrapped around him. She pulled the covers up over them, and lay there a long time just watching him sleep.

"John Ross still believes it's possible to reverse the Congressional decision on the Indian Removal Bill," Adam told her at breakfast. He held Jonas in his arms, toying with the child's tiny fist. "There's a hell of a lot of sympathy out there for us, Andrea, a lot of people willing to help. Church groups and missionaries all over the North are speaking in our behalf. We're planning to make a tour of the North, to speak at churches and explain what is happening to the Indians down here."

She turned from the stove to pour him some coffee. His father was already outside working on the harvest, and his mother had not yet come downstairs.

"Let me go with you, Adam, when you go North. I hate it when you're gone, and if you go on some kind of tour, it will be for weeks and weeks." She met his eyes pleadingly. "Please let me go with you. I'd be safer in the North with you than I would be down here anyway. Wouldn't that make you feel better?"

He sighed and looked her over, wanting her already. It had been so long. One night was not enough. He would want her every night for a while. He looked down at the baby. "Why not?" he answered. "Maybe having a white wife along, and a little baby son, would just build up sympathy." He looked into her happy eyes. "Besides, I miss you so damned much when I'm gone I can hardly stand it."

"Oh, Adam!" She bent down and hugged him. "Oh, it will be so much better than sitting here worrying about you, waiting, lonely, worrying about the militia and Doug—" She stopped herself, kissed his cheek, and turned away. "Do you want some pancakes? I told the cook to do what she wanted. I wanted to make your breakfast this morning."

"Andrea."

She turned to face him.

"I've not seen Douglas Means anyplace on Cherokee land. I think he's over in Mississippi helping herd up the Choctaws. Georgia sent some men over there to help, if you can call it that."

She turned away and began to mix some batter. "He'll be back. When he finds out Georgia has given permission to overrun this land—"

"Don't think about it, Andrea. Pretty soon we'll take a trip together and get out of here."

She sighed deeply. "That means more meetings first. Georgia has forbidden you to meet, or even go to church together. Soon they'll send the militia to New Echota to make sure you're obeying those laws."

"We'll meet all we want. They won't do anything about it right away. They're waiting to see if the new laws will scare us out. But they'll soon discover that it takes more than a threat to get rid of us. And it will take more than sending in the militia and burning our homes."

She beat the batter vigorously, swallowed a lump in her throat. "I miss being in our own little house. We lived together there such a short time."

He bent down and kissed his son, then set him in the

cradle they kept in the kitchen. "Someday this will all be over and we'll live like normal married people again. I promise."

She smiled lovingly at him. "I know." She sighed deeply. "I'm so glad you're home, Adam. And thank you for letting me go along next time."

He stretched, then sipped some coffee. "It will be good, having you along. I think John Ross would agree."

His father came in then, and walked directly to Adam, who rose. The two men hugged. "Thank God you are back, son. I was asleep when you came in last night."

"I'm sorry I didn't get up early to help with chores, Father. I was pretty exhausted."

"Ah, and not just from your trip, I'll bet," the man answered, with a wink and a nod to Andrea. Andrea blushed deeply and Adam laughed lightly. Then the two men sat down and Jonas sobered. "How did it go?"

Adam shrugged. "Like always. Some of the Congressmen would speak to us and read our petitions. Some wouldn't. And, of course, President Jackson won't even consider our arguments. He can't do one damned thing without Georgia screaming that the federal government is infringing on state's rights—not that Jackson would do anything to help anyway. If someone were president who sympathized with our cause, we'd be in a lot better shape. But Jackson cuts us down on every front."

Jonas nodded. "It is bad. I am told that the effort to get the Choctaws underway is one big, confused mess, just a mess. Whites have swarmed in like bees over honey, taking over some homes before the Indians are even completely moved out of them. Everything is unorganized. There are not enough supplies. I fear there will be a lot of hunger and death for the Choctaws on their journey, Adam. It will be bad."

Their eyes held, both men realizing the same fate could come to the Cherokee, but not without a fight. Adam rubbed at his eyes. "John says there are rumors that Georgia is setting up a secret fund with which to bribe some of us to leave, Father. They will pay extra money to any Cherokee who promises to go now, and give him a nice, soft journey."

Jonas noticed his son glance at his wife, and knew the torture he was suffering. The man reached out and touched Adam's hand. "When we think of our loved ones, it is tempting. But what would happen to our pride? And how much would our families love us if we took the easy way and deserted those who choose to fight?"

Andrea turned and looked at Adam. "I would never allow you to leave that way, Adam. It isn't in your heart or in mine. I love this land as much as you do, and I love you. Don't ever speak of leaving under such circumstances." She knew he was only tired, remembered how he had wept the night before.

Adam looked back at his father, sighed deeply. "I just think about it sometimes, only because of Andrea and my son."

"Do you think I don't think about it? Some of us have already been secretly approached, Adam. I will have none of it. I intended to talk to John today and tell him what is happening when he is gone. We must be careful even among our own now, Adam. There are some who are taking these bribes, and some who will spy for the militia, in return for money and a promise of a safe and comfortable trip west. Georgia will want to know everything that is happening here, what goes on at our meetings, our next move—everything. There is only one way for them to find out, and that is for our own kind to tell them."

Adam's eyes widened. "Traitors? Among our own?"

"Some have lived too long in comfort. When this is over, Adam, there will be much bitterness among our own people. I see it coming. And there is one more thing. The Georgia legislature has passed yet another law designed to stop the missionaries from helping us."

Andrea turned away from the stove, her first thought being of the kind Reverend Jessup and his family. "How can they stop them?" she asked in surprise. "They aren't even Cherokee. They're white."

Jonas looked at her. "Indian haters also hate any whites who are our friends, even good ones like missionaries. A new act has been proposed, stating that after next March no whites are permitted to reside in Cherokee country without a special license from the governor; to get that license, they must swear an oath of allegiance to Georgia, meaning they must swear to uphold Georgia's Removal and promise not to aid the Cherokee in their fight. They must agree to preach Removal and to urge us to leave."

The room fell silent. Andrea turned away then. Reverend Jessup! And the doctor! Dr. Cunningham was white, a missionary as well as a doctor. Who would tend to their sick if he left? What about their own son? What if she had another baby?

"Devils!" Adam banged his fist on the table. "Devils, all of them! They think of everything!"

"What worries me is that some missionaries, like Reverend Jessup, are very loyal friends. It would be like them to face imprisonment before they'd succumb and take such an oath. And Georgians are ready to use them as examples! They are using everything possible to break us, Adam. We must be ever alert now for raids. I think that soon we will have to move in closer to town and abandon the farm all together."

"Abandon the farm!" Adam rose and walked to the doorway. "If we leave here, they will come. They will loot the house, burn it and the outbuildings. We must stay and guard it."

"You are gone half the time, Adam. I am thinking of your mother, and of Ruth."

Adam nodded. "I know," he said, his voice husky with emotion. He took a deep breath and sniffed, and Andrea knew he was struggling with his emotions. "I . . . uh . . . I'm going on a tour in the North with some of the others. We'll travel to churches and Northern towns to raise funds and support for our cause. I'm taking Andrea and Jonas with me this time. I'm tired of always being away from them."

"Fine. That is a good idea. And we need any funds we can come up with. Our income is dangerously low, Adam. We cannot sell our land outright because Georgia says it is already theirs, and we have no access to the gold that has been discovered on our land. The money we had coming in from treaties has been cut off, yet we are forbidden to tax our own citizens. Suddenly no one on the outside will buy our crops or our cattle, and—"

"Stop it!" Adam hissed. "I don't want to hear anymore!" He charged outside. "I am going riding."

"Adam!" Andrea rushed to the door.

"Let him go," Jonas told her. "It will be good for him to go riding. He has always liked riding alone. There are many things weighing him down." He blinked back tears. "For me it is not so bad. But he has his whole life ahead of him, and he sees all his plans being destroyed." He rose and went to Andrea. "He is strong, much stronger than he knows. Someday this will be all over, Andrea. And when it is, wherever you two end up, you will still be together and in love. You'll make it. Adam is a very intelligent young man. He'll find a way to rebuild and be successful."

"I just want him to be happy," she replied in a near whisper.

"Of course you do. And as long as he has you and Jonas, he'll be all right." He sniffed. "Do I smell something good, like pancakes?"

"Oh!" She hurried to the stove and removed the pancakes from it. Putting some on a plate for her father-in-law, she set them on the table before him, then glanced at Adam's empty chair. Their moments of happiness and laughter were becoming rare. She wondered how soon the day would come when there would be no laughter at all. She glanced through the door to see him riding off, a young man who was as much a part of this land as the trees and the very soil. When a tree was uprooted, it died. When soil was turned up, it blew away. What would happen to Adam Chandler and the others if they had to leave their beloved Cherokee country?

CHAPTER SIXTEEN

The winter of 1830 was one of calamity for the Choctaws. Suddenly torn from their homes and put under guard, they were hurried and shoved by agents and contractors, herded along like cattle to their new, desolate destination. To move thousands of people out of their homes and into a new land quickly was a monumental task, one which neither the state nor the federal government was prepared to undertake with any kind of order and discipline. Federal soldiers were sent to help, but not many. Yet their aid was the only sign of sympathy for the Indians, for the young men who were sent, many from the North, cried out against the way the Choctaws were being treated. Some even risked their careers by protesting to their superiors about how the movement was being handled, and a few used their own money to help some of the Indians who had lost everything. Such a gigantic undertaking was a round-the-clock project, and many of the Choctaws had to walk their way westward. Since there were not nearly enough wagons and horses for everyone, the wagons were reserved for the feeble and for children. And hunger was rampant. No one in charge had thought to store up food, and the Indians had been caught unprepared. Corruption was also rampant. Private contractors were hired to help with transportation and food, but they overcharged the government and provided less than satisfactory services to the Indians. The government, responsible for providing food through the contractors, withheld the food appropriation until the Indians had spent nearly every last cent of their own money on the open market to keep from going hungry. This served two purposes. The Indians were bled of their savings, making them more helpless; and the government spent less money on feeding its charges.

The migration was monumental, both in size and in bad organization. Steamboats were taken, were overcrowded, which caused many accidents. Indeed, a great number of Choctaws died for a variety of reasons as they worked their way through swamps and forests and rivers toward the arid West, leaving behind the warm, green climate to which they were accustomed. En route, the weather turned colder, and the Choctaws, not used to raw winters, had an insufficient supply of blankets and clothing. Some froze. Others lost limbs to frostbite, and great numbers died of lung diseases and from a cholera epidemic. The entire venture was a horror, and was deemed a disgrace to the federal government; and in the North, the cries of sympathy for the Indians grew louder.

The wind howled outside the hotel window, and snow blew in every direction. Andrea watched, remembering another time in the North, when she watched the snow through a tiny, barred window, wondering if she would ever see Adam Chandler again. It made her think of that first baby. He'd be over three years old now. Poor baby! Poor, poor baby! Where was he? How was he? She shivered and walked to the bed, where Adam lay sleeping, little six-month-old Jonas beside him.

Never would she tire of such a sight—Adam, her beautiful, tender, loving Adam, sleeping beside her equally beautiful son. Was their first son as handsome? Surely he was. She studied her husband, so driven, so dedicated. But he was tired, and she sometimes wondered how long he could keep going. She, too, felt tired, but he carried the extra burden of being Indian, of knowing his life's blood was threatened, of leaving his beloved mountains. Sometimes she wanted to scream and scream, and then weep until she died. She never dreamed her own government could be so unfair and callous. Every day they heard tales of the horrors of the Choctaw removal, and every day the fear grew that the Cherokees would suffer the same hideous fate, the same unnecessary suffering. Envisioning whites crawling over Adam's beautiful land, taking over their home and farm, invading New Echota, she shuddered. What hope did they have if this journey through the North to win support for their cause did not work?

It had to work. Day after day they preached and begged at town halls and churches and schools. Their own delegation of five was matched by other delegations traveling other Northern areas, collecting signatures, money, pledges of letters to Congress—anything that could be used to reverse the vote for Indian Removal. Andrea herself had spoken many times, impressing people with her beauty and her beautiful baby, convincing them with her own testimony of the civilized, advanced, peaceful state of the Cherokee Nation; stressing the intelligence of her husband's people, their determination to remain nonviolent, their utterly amazing progress over the past fifty years.

Would it work? It had to. Adam's leather business case was packed with petitions and signatures, letters and money—money he would not touch because it belonged to the People. It would be taken back to Georgia and used to pay white attorneys to fight for their cause.

The wind rattled the window, making her jump. Again the black memory of her years at the hated school rushed over her, and she quickly crawled back into bed. She had just fed some wood into the pot-bellied stove in the room, but the fire in it didn't seem able to match the bitter cold outside. She snuggled next to Adam, needing to remind herself that he really was there. He sighed deeply and pulled her close.

"Good morning, *agiya*."

She kissed his nose. "It isn't really morning yet. And it's too cold to get up, so you might as well go back to sleep."

He snuggled his face against her neck. "I am warm and very hungry for my wife," he said in a sleepy voice. "Wouldn't you like to get warmed up?"

She laughed lightly. "We'll wake Jonas."

He stretched and snuggled down more, pulling the quilts up over their heads. "He sleeps like a log, and you know it. We've been running so fast we've been too tired to enjoy each other." He nuzzled his face between her full breasts, kissing them through her flannel gown. "We can be lazy this morning. They say there will be a blizzard today and we won't be able to go on for a day or two. Might as well enjoy it."

He ran his hand up under her gown, and she felt herself weakening. "Adam, Jonas is right there beside you!"

He ran a big hand over her bare hips, moving it around and between her legs. "So what? Even if he wakes, he won't know what we're doing. He is six months old, Andrea. He hardly knows his toes from his fingers. You still have enough white woman in you to keep you from relaxing, don't you?"

She grinned and tousled his thick hair as he nuzzled at her breasts again. "You don't play fair."

"Why should I, when there's something beautiful and warm waiting to give me extreme pleasure?"

He seemed more relaxed and happy this morning than she had seen him in a long time. So far their tour had been very successful. It was good to have him more like the old, teasing Adam she had married. She unbuttoned her gown. "Shouldn't I take this thing off first?"

He raised up slightly, already naked himself. "By all means."

She reddened slightly and pulled the gown to her waist, then sat up and pulled it over her head. Shivering at the touch of the cold air on her shoulders, she threw the gown to the floor, and they both snuggled back under the quilts, laughing quietly.

"We can't move too much or make too much noise," she

chided as his lips nibbled around her own.

"That might not be easy," he answered. His mouth covered hers then, in a sweet, warm, provocative kiss that brought her body alive and made her blood run warmer. Her breasts pushed against his bare chest, warm skin against warm skin, the marvelous, shivering sensations that their nakedness brought them making them both tingle with anticipation and desire.

As his lips traveled over her breasts and ever downward, over her flat belly, his touch filled her with ecstasy and she knew he would do something wonderful again, something different and special. To him the act of love was almost sacred, for it was the ultimate invasion of his woman's privacy, something reserved for Adam Chandler alone.

It was never easy for Andrea at first, but once he touched her the right way, she lost all inhibition and moments of lost enchantment followed. Then nothing existed but Adam and the way he touched her. She was pleasing him, giving to him in the most intimate way, taking trembling pleasure in return until she could no longer hold back the explosion he brought forth from her depths. She cried out his name in glorious abandon, aching for the final and grand invasion, and he moved back up over her belly, his body on fire, full of her sweetness. How proud and masculine he felt at his ability to invade his woman's most private places and bring forth her wildest passions. He was quickly inside her then, with a groaning hunger, pushing hard, their lovemaking heightened by morning's sweet warmth and sleepiness. He trembled with the want of her, his own breathing labored, his body on fire now, their skin covered with the moistness of hot desire.

The wind and snow didn't frighten her anymore. All bad memories were temporarily wiped out as she lay beneath her beautiful man and gave him pleasure. His dark, broad shoulders hovered over her, and his hard-muscled body moved rhythmically so that she felt almost insane with pleasure.

It was one of the special moments she would always

remember in the days to come. She knew somewhere deep in her heart that perhaps this could not always be. Every day she prayed ardently that she would never have to be apart from her husband and her baby. And moments like these were precious. She gloried in every touch, every movement, determined to remember . . . remember . . . remember. Adam, sweet Adam. Their beautiful son lying near them. Warm and making love beneath the soft covers, huddled against the winter storm in each other's arms, where no harm could come to them. The wind howled and groaned outside, and the snow buried the little town in Ohio where they had stayed the night.

The night was still, and warmer than usual for January in Georgia, although even at this time of year it was seldom extremely cold. Jonas and Rose Chandler slept soundly. They did not hear the approaching horses, ridden at a walk so as to keep down the noise, nor did they hear the whispered orders. They heard nothing, until with a loud crash their front door was bashed open.

"Everybody up and out!" a voice shouted.

Jonas jumped awake, and Rose sat up, her eyes wide with fear. Before either could think what to do, a man slammed open their bedroom door and waved a rifle at them. "Outside!" he barked. Both rose, trembling with fear, and Rose reached for her housecoat. "Leave it!" the man ordered. "You won't be wearing anything when we're through with you."

The woman stared at him in horror, frozen in place.

"What is the meaning of this!" Jonas growled.

"You'll soon find out," the man sneered.

They heard the screams then—Ruth! Men dragged her past their bedroom door and down the stairs. Rose and Jonas both moved then, Jonas reaching for the militia man's rifle. But the man swung the butt hard, smashing it across Jonas's face with a shattering blow that left Chandler reeling in blackness. Rose screamed his name and bent down to him, but more men came, pulled her away from him and carried her downstairs, dragging Jonas behind her. Within moments they were all outside. Jonas was held up by two men, and a third man approached him. To little Ruth's horror it was the man who had invaded their house looking for Andrea nearly two years earlier. She cringed, terror engulfing her. The man grasped Jonas's hair and yanked his head back.

"Are you Jonas Chandler?" he asked, speaking loudly.

Jonas spit blood, hardly able to see. "I . . . am. What is that . . . to you?"

"Did you speak at a meeting earlier this evening? And did you not preach to the Cherokee that they must stand and fight and must not willingly leave Georgia?"

"We will . . . never leave!" Jonas spit out.

Douglas Means slammed a big fist into Jonas's stomach and Jonas buckled. "It is against Georgia law for the Cherokee to hold meetings!" Means roared. "It is against Georgia laws for any man to speak against Indian Removal! You have disobeyed our laws, Jonas Chandler, and you will pay! Your people will learn from the example we set for them this night!"

He turned steely gray eyes to the women then. Smiling hungrily, he walked up to Ruth, ran a hand over her breast. She was eighteen now, soon to wed a Cherokee boy. She jerked away from Douglas Means's vile touch, but he only grinned wider, his eyes glittering. "You've filled out since last I was here, little one." He grasped her gown then, ripping it open at the bodice and exposing her breasts. "You Indian girls are so pretty, and most of you fight, but I know down deep inside you enjoy every minute of it!"

Ruth's terror knew no bounds as he ripped the rest of her gown away and she stood exposed to all of the men. "Take this one back upstairs," he ordered. "When I'm through with her, I'll bring her back outside and then we'll burn the houses." He glanced regretfully at the smaller house nearby. He'd learned from his informant that Andrea Chandler was not on the premises right now. He'd have delighted in ravaging her until she was dead from his abuse. That would be a fitting punishment!

"What about the woman?" one of them asked.

Douglas met the defiant eyes of Ruth Chandler, and his gaze then ran over her body. "A nice-looking piece of woman . . . for her age." He looked at the men who held her. "Do what you want with her. But when you're through I want her whipped. And make sure her husband sees it all." He motioned to those who held Ruth, and they dragged the screaming, kicking girl into the house.

What followed was beyond Jonas Chandler's endurance. His aged body slumped to the ground, overcome by horror and helpless rage. The last things he remembered were the screams of his wife and daughter, followed by the acrid smell of smoke and the sounds of timbers falling.

It was April, 1831, when Adam and Andrea returned. They were refreshed and inspired from the trip, excited over the wonderful support they had found among the religious and business communities in the North. Little Jonas was fat and smiling, his brown eyes always looking for something to get into, preferably something forbidden. His strong legs now held him up as long as he had something to hang on to. And Andrea suspected she was pregnant again, although she had not yet told Adam.

They guided their buggies and coaches into New Echota, the entire group laughing and happy, glad to be back in Georgia, in their beloved homeland for which they had fought by touring and preaching all winter in the North. Their belief that things would change for the Cherokee was boosted by rumors that the North was outraged at the treatment of the Choctaws that winter, that the President and Congress were red in the face over the terrible mishandling of Choctaw removal. The journey was labeled as nothing but literal abuse, unforgivable and deliberate, scandalous. Surely this gave the Cherokees of Georgia more fuel for their battle to stay in that state.

Their first stop was the newspaper office, and Adam

noticed an odd, grim look on Elias Boudinot's face when he shook Adam's hand vigorously and welcomed their small party home.

"It went well, very well!" Adam told him. "And it helped to have Andrea along. I am glad I took her."

"That's good, Adam. Did you bring plenty of petitions and letters!"

"My case is bulging with them!" Adam laughed, then turned to shake the hand of John Ross, who had just come from a back room. But he noticed that Ross looked at Boudinot strangely. His heart tightened with a vague warning, and his smile faded. "I expected you two to be a little more excited than this," he joked.

John put a hand on his shoulder. "We are excited, Adam. But it seems that for every step forward, we take two steps back."

Adam and the others frowned, and Andrea held a sleeping Jonas closer to her breast. "What has happened?" Adam asked.

The two men looked at each other again. "Why don't you take Adam and Andrea in the back," Boudinot told Ross. "I will talk with the others."

Ross nodded and extended an arm to Adam. "Come on, Adam. Come in the back and sit down. I have coffee. How long have you been on the road?"

"Close to eight hours straight," Adam replied, his voice seeming distant now. He felt as though the blood was draining from his body. Whatever was wrong, it had to involve his family. Why else would he be singled out? He looked at Andrea, and saw that she was struggling to be strong. Putting an arm around her, he followed John Ross into the back room.

Ross closed the door, rubbed at tired eyes, and then sighed deeply. Adam and Andrea sat down on an old, stuffed loveseat, and Andrea set Jonas on her lap. Ross poured two cups of coffee and brought them over.

"Drink some of this, both of you. Relax for a minute."

Adam's eyes hardened, and he shook his head. "I don't want it. I want to know right now what is going on."

Andrea accepted a cup with shaking hands and took a swallow. Ross set Adam's aside. He held Adam's eyes, and Adam could see the man was visibly trembling. "I want you to remember our vow to remain nonviolent, Adam. If you don't keep that vow, then anything your family has suffered will be for nothing. Don't let it be. Your father stuck to his vow, and now you must do the same, or you will ruin the chances of the rest of the People. We all have our sacrifices to make."

Andrea set her own cup aside, feeling sick inside. Perspiration appeared on Adam's forehead. "What is it?" His voice was husky, his fists were clenched.

John Ross swallowed. "Your father is dead, Adam. We think it was a heart attack."

"Oh, no!" Andrea whispered, covering her mouth. Adam just continued to stare at John Ross, his eyes teared.

He rose then, his whole body bristling. "My father was a strong and healthy man for his age. Something caused the heart attack! Tell me the rest!"

John Ross tensed, as though ready to pounce on Adam if he should run off. "It was brought on by a raid—the militia." He took a deep breath, his heart tightening as a tiny groan came from Andrea. "They . . ." The man closed his eyes. How could he tell this young man such news? Yet he must. "They raped your mother and sister—several times. Your mother was whipped, your father beaten. They burned both houses."

Adam stood frozen, his body beginning to shake violently, his eyes smoldering. "My . . . mother and sister . . . are alive?"

John Ross nodded. "They're with Margaret Jessup. I think your mother will recover, but I don't know about Ruth. I think your mother is trying to be strong for her sake. The girl is half-crazy—keeps talking about her china dolls. She doesn't even mention the rapes, just the dolls."

Adam turned and headed for the door. "Adam, wait! Where are you going?"

"They are out there somewhere! The stinking Militia is out there and some of them will die!" He opened the door and John Ross lunged at him. Andrea screamed his name, and set little Jonas on the loveseat. Ross had tackled Adam to the floor, but Adam was bigger and stronger and he quickly threw him off, but he was barely on his feet before five more Cherokees, Boudinot among them, wrestled him back down. Due to Adam's state of mind, it was almost impossible for the five men to restrain him, so John Ross straddled the struggling, cursing, weeping young man, sitting on his legs.

"Adam, you can't do it! I told you it's the worst thing you could do. It was deliberate! Your mother said you knew one of them, a young man who had an eye for your wife once. It was deliberate, don't you see? He knows you'll want to come for him! Think of your wife, Adam! If you go after them and are arrested and hung, she'll be left alone and unprotected!"

Andrea stood staring, terrified. One of the militia men knew her. It could only be Douglas Means! How much longer would it be before he came for her! How could she bear to have his filthy hands touch her, to be humiliated by his men! Ruth! Poor, sweet Ruth! And Rose, such a lovely, gentle woman. And Jonas! She loved him like a father. He couldn't be dead! No man so kind and good should die that way, seeing his wife and daughter being brutalized.

"I should have been here! I should have been here!" Adam screamed the words, but his struggle was weakening now and unwanted tears were choking him.

"And what if you were," Ross shouted back at him. "That means Andrea would also have been here. The same thing would have happened to her! Maybe your son would have been killed! Use your head, Adam. It was probably God's blessing that you were *not* here!"

Adam's resistance lessened even more, his body and face bruised from the fierce struggle on the hard floor. "We're not letting go of you, Adam, until you promise to stay right here and talk this thing out. Right now your mother and sister need you, and so does your wife."

Little Jonas suddenly started to cry. He had climbed off the loveseat and was crawling toward his father, sure the men were hurting him. Andrea hurriedly picked him up, held him tightly, thanking God that at least her husband and son were all right, and she had been gone when the vile Douglas Means had come to call. She fell to her knees beside Adam.

"Adam, please don't! Don't go after them. It's what they want," she said pleadingly. "Nothing would make them happier . . . and they're expecting you. You wouldn't have a chance! They'd hang you, and they'd declare war on the Cherokee! Please, Adam!"

He knew she was right. They were all right. But a man had his pride; to have a mother and sister wronged called for vengeance. And his father! His father was his strength, his wisdom. He had always been there to turn to for advice. But he could hear his father warning him that whatever happened, he must never resort to violence. His body jerked in grieving sobs then, as he muttered the word *father* in the Cherokee tongue. Andrea clung to a crying Jonas, trying to soothe the boy and the father at the same time, one hand on her husband's shoulder. Two men let go of Adam and he didn't move. Two more let go then, and John Ross moved to sit beside him, Elias Boudinot did the same.

"I'm damned sorry that after such a good trip you had to come home to this, Adam," Ross told the young man. "I don't know what else to say."

Boudinot looked up at one of the men. "Go get Doc Cunningham. Maybe he can give Adam something to calm him down."

"I don't need anything!" Adam growled. He got to his knees, his body shaking, his face red and bruised, his whole body drenched in sweat. He turned to look at Andrea with wild eyes, reaching out and touching her hair. Then he looked at Ross. "I will keep my stinking vow," he hissed, sobs breaking his words. "But if they ever . . . touch my wife . . . they will die! Do you understand? They will die a slow . . . and cruel death . . . even if that means war on the Cherokee Nation!"

Andrea hung her head, rocking little Jonas who clung

to her as he shed frightened tears. He had never seen his father this way.

"When your grief settles you'll see things differently, Adam," Ross answered.

"I will never see things differently! Never! They will not take this land—and they will not touch my wife!" He got to his feet, stumbling to the door jamb and leaning on to it, hanging his head, and breathing deeply as he attempted to get his thoughts under control. Ruth! Mother! Father! Their homes were gone, burned! He couldn't even go home! He threw his head back, feeling sick. "There had to be a legal reason," he groaned. "They couldn't have done it just for spite, even Douglas Means couldn't have." He turned to John Ross, his eyes wild and bloodshot. "It was Douglas Means, wasn't it?"

Ross nodded carefully. "According to your mother."

"But even the militia has to have some legal reason, no matter how flimsy. What was his trumped-up excuse for burning my home and raping my mother and my sister!"

John Ross held his eyes. "He claimed your father had been to a meeting and meetings are illegal, which is true. He claimed your father preached against removal, which is also true. He said he had to set an example for the rest of us to stop meeting and to stop advising others to fight removal."

Adam looked around the room, slowly scrutinizing every man there, his eyes resting on Boudinot for a moment, then turning back to John Ross. "And how did the militia know about the meeting, and what my father said? They haven't camped in our town. Someone informed them of what is happening—one of our own!"

Ross looked at Boudinot, then at Adam. "We've already thought of that. We just don't know who it might be."

Adam's eyes hardened even more. "Then I will find out my own way. I will find out, and when I do, he will be a sorry man!"

Boudinot started to speak. "Adam—"

"No! I do not want to hear it! I may not be able to take my vengeance on the militia, but there is no law that says

283

one Cherokee cannot go after another! Whoever sent the militia is just as guilty as the men who attacked my family! When is our next meeting? I trust you have not let this stop you from getting together. I'll find the son of a bitch who sent the militia after my father!"

"We're laying low for a few days, but we will meet again. Now that everyone is back from the North, we have no choice. We must get things settled before making another trip to Washington."

Adam looked at Andrea, who was being helped to her feet. He suddenly realized what a horror this was for her, and how afraid she must be that Douglas Means would come after her. He walked over to her and embraced her, holding her tightly. "When did it happen?" he asked, as he cradled his wife and son in his arms.

"About four days ago. And that isn't the only bad news. About a month ago several missionaries in other villages were hauled out of their homes in the middle of the night. They were beaten and arrested for preaching against removal. We got them released on the grounds that their work is partially funded by the federal government, but believe it or not local representatives of the federal government declared that they were not protected under federal laws, as they were not considered federal employees unless they worked directly for a federal establishment, such as a post office. We got them released, but only after a stiff warning that they had better leave Cherokee country or face being arrested again by the militia and confined for a good long time. Most of them refuse to leave. Our own Reverend Jessup is ready to stand up to anything they throw at him, and I suspect it won't be anything good. They roughed up the first ones pretty badly, and they'll do a worse job the next time. They're out to set examples. Margaret Jessup is scared to death for her husband."

"My God!" Andrea whispered. Adam turned then, keeping an arm around her. "They would actually beat missionaries? Their prejudice runs that deep?"

Ross ran a hand through his hair, as others muttered among themselves. "I'm afraid so, Andrea. From now on no one is safe and nothing is sacred. I think you and Adam should stay right here in town, and we should all team up, two families to a home, if possible. It will be strenuous, but it's necessary. I think Margaret Jessup would want you to stay there. God only knows how long it will be before her husband gets hauled away in the middle of the night, and then there will be no man with her."

"You'll have to find someone else," Adam quickly declared. "If there is danger they will come for the reverend, and it will probably be Douglas Means who comes. I don't want him to find my wife there. It would be too dangerous for her. We must stay with someone more obscure, someone who draws no attention. If they come for the reverend, then we can move in with his wife and children. They would already have what they want, and Andrea would no longer be in danger. My mother and sister should also be taken out of there."

John Ross nodded. "I understand. You're right. There are plenty of frightened families who would be glad to move in with the Jessups. I'll find someone else. How about if the two of you stay a couple of doors down, with Martha Bluecrow, the widow."

Adam ran a hand through his hair, confused, his insides screaming with grief. "I guess for now. I don't know. I have to think." He sniffed and swallowed. "Where is my father buried?"

"We took him to the foothills beyond the house. It's a nice place."

"I want to go there."

"You'd better take plenty of men with you. We never know where the militia will roam next."

"Let them come! I intend to see my father's grave."

"I want to go, too," Andrea sobbed.

"No! It would be too dangerous," Adam said quickly. "You will stay here in town."

Their eyes held. "But I loved him."

She could feel his trembling. "Do you think I don't know that? But he would understand, Andrea. And I have enough to think about now. Just do what I say."

She hung her head, then wept against his shoulder. He looked at John Ross. "Just send the doctor to the reverend's house. She will need him more than I do. We will go there now. I should see my mother and sister right away."

"And you won't do something foolish, like ride into a militia camp?" Ross asked. Never had he seen more hatred than he saw in Adam's eyes now.

"I won't . . . for now."

"Staying put and not fighting is just as much a defense as going after them, Adam, perhaps our strongest defense. I told you once they will do everything they can to make us retaliate. Your father told you the same. Out of respect for his wishes, don't try to take revenge."

Adam scanned the room. "I will not take my revenge— this time. But there are traitors among us, informers, stinking bastards who would sell out their own mothers! I will find out who they are, and I think we all have a duty to let them know what we think of them! They are lower than snakes!" He urged Andrea along then, heading for the outside door. John Ross looked at Elias Boudinot, and he realized that more and more Boudinot was contemplating heading west while he could still get out with his belongings and family in one piece.

"Don't look at me that way!" Boudinot told Ross. "You have seen Ruth and Rose Chandler, the burned homes! We must think seriously of what is truly best for our people. I would not be a traitor, and that you well know. I have fought as hard as you. But it is a losing battle, John. Perhaps we should just go."

"It is because of Ruth and Rose Chandler and others like them that I will fight to my last breath, in every court in the land if necessary!" Ross retaliated. "We must stand together. We must! That boy just came back from a long tour, bringing many signatures, many letters, money to help our cause. He has paid the supreme sacrifice. I will not let him down, nor any of the others who love this land that is sacred to our hearts! You have lived with wealth too long, Elias; you are growing too much like the white man.''

He stormed out behind Adam and Andrea, and the others mumbled in confusion. Their two greatest leaders had quarreled. Which way should they go? Surely John Ross's way, for he was their President and a man of iron strength, a clever man who knew the law and how to use it advantageously. He was their greatest leader. They would follow John Ross.

Adam and Andrea walked on weak, shaking legs toward the Jessup house, dreading what they would find. A black bruise was swelling on Adam's right cheek. Their happy, relaxing trip was over, and Andrea could not help but wonder if things could ever be sweet and happy between them again.

CHAPTER SEVENTEEN

Andrea looked up to see her mother-in-law coming into the small kitchen of Martha Bluecrow's house. The home was small but comfortable, and it had four bedrooms on the upper floor, though they were not large. Until the raiding had begun, Mrs. Bluecrow had lived there alone, her children grown and gone. Now Rose and Ruth occupied one room, Mrs. Bluecrow her own; and Adam and Andrea occupied a third. The fourth was reserved for little Jonas. Martha Bluecrow was a patient, generous woman who enjoyed their company, but she was unhappy about the reason the Chandlers had come to stay with her. She fussed and fumed about the whole tragic event, and worried over more raids. Now she was outside watering her flowers. Andrea sat in the kitchen alone, wondering what to do about poor Ruth, who sat just staring most of the time, her eyes lifeless, her face and arms still badly bruised. Thinking about what had happened to the girl gave Andrea the shivers, and it made her worry about what could happen to herself and her family. Being abused by strange men would be bad enough, but to her it was more horrible because one of them was Douglas Means. She hated him even more than she hated the militia.

"You shouldn't be up," she told Rose, her heart breaking for the woman. Rose had lost weight, and her eyes were hollow and dark from too much crying, too much worry, and too much grief. She fussed with her robe, walking slowly, the cuts from her whipping still raw and painful.

"How does one sleep?" she answered quietly, going to the coffee. She picked up the kettle with a shaking hand and poured a cup, then set it back down on the iron stove. She picked up the cup, but her hands shook badly so Andrea got up and took it from her.

"Let me carry it for you." She set it on the table, and Rose just stared at it a moment.

"I keep telling myself . . . out of respect for Jonas's wishes . . . I must be strong," she said in a shaking voice. "I am trying. But I'm not sure I can do it."

Andrea took her arm and led her to a chair. "Of course you can. I'll never be as strong as you are. All of you are so strong, so brave."

The woman smiled bitterly, easing herself into the chair. "That is only on the outside, child. Inside I feel the whip . . . see those men . . . hear my daughter—"

"Rose, don't," Andrea interrupted, taking the woman's hand. "Ruth will get well. She has to. James has been coming to see her every day. He still loves her, still wants to marry her. She just has to learn that what happened was not her fault, that she paid a martyr's price but she can still hold her head up and be a wife and a mother."

"First she must face what has happened, and she has not done that. She sits . . . in her own child's world now . . . worrying about those dolls. She has not faced reality, Andrea. I am afraid of what she will do when her mind allows her to remember."

Rose choked, and for all of Andrea's words of encouragement, she wondered herself how she would react to such horror. She would want to die, she thought. How could she bear such humiliation, bear to be so cruelly abused.

"I wish I knew the answer," she told Rose. "Sometimes I feel like Adam. I just want to go out and kill every white man beyond our borders. I want to . . . scream and—" Her eyes teared and Rose squeezed her hand.

"As women we are even more helpless than our men

who are struggling to remain peaceful. Even if we could fight we are not strong enough. And the militia will use us again, for it is their clever way of urging our men into fighting. Nothing stirs a man's desire to fight more than offending his woman. It is worse than taking his land or his money." She pulled her hand away from Andrea's and sipped some coffee. "They are smart people, those men who plan our removal. They think of everything, every law and every atrocity they can design to force us to leave." She met Andrea's eyes then. "Adam understands this now. Realizing what they are trying to do makes it easier for him not to go out and kill. Remaining peaceful and fighting this through the courts is just as painful a blow to them as physical fighting. They are so sure we will give up." She sighed deeply, wincing slightly. "But we will not. We embarrass and harass them politically just as they harass us physically. But we shall beat them."

Andrea blinked back tears. She was prepared to make her own sacrifices if necessary, for she no longer felt white. Her heart was Cherokee. Her son was Cherokee. She had already suffered for loving a Cherokee, and she would do so again if need be. Adam had calmed somewhat, although beneath his façade she knew a volcano was boiling. He was constantly tense and angry, and most of all determined to find the informant who had sent the militia after his family. The happy, gentle boy she had met under the oak tree was turning into a bitter, vengeful man. Yet she could not blame him, and she loved him as much or more than ever. Someday, somehow, he would be her sweet Adam again. They would find peace, find the happy, carefree love they had known as mere children before her father had sent her away, the love that was reawakened when she'd returned and married Adam.

She glanced at her mother-in-law, the proud, once-beautiful woman now haggard and older looking. How could she bear losing her husband? That was probably harder on her than anything else. To Andrea, that would be the most unbearable loss of all. She couldn't survive without Adam Chandler. Perhaps that was why God sent children, to give a man or a woman something to live for when the mate was lost. Yes, she would have little Jonas, sweet, precious Jonas. And now there was another child on the way. Another child! Yes, that might help bring Adam back to normal. She hadn't yet told him that she thought she was pregnant. She would save the news for just the right moment. Perhaps tonight would be a good time. He'd be gone all day, mostly at the newspaper office, and he'd welcome some good news when he returned. He needed to hear something positive. His heart was so shattered and full of grief.

"Mother, have you seen my china dolls?"

Andrea and Rose both looked up to see Ruth in the doorway, still in her nightgown.

"I've looked all over for them," she continued in a voice that sounded like a little girl's. "I saw them sitting along my window ledge not long ago. Can't we go home and get them?"

Rose swallowed. "No, dear. We . . . we have to leave them there for now. We have to stay here with Mrs. Bluecrow, and we couldn't bring any of the dolls with us."

Ruth scowled. "I don't see why I couldn't bring just one. I thought they were here. I've looked everywhere."

"They are not here, Ruth. Now go upstairs and get dressed. James is coming to see you again."

The girl sighed, pouting like a child. "He comes every day. Why does he come so much? I don't like playing with boys or even talking to them."

Rose got up from her chair, and walked over to her daughter, she took hold of her shoulders. "James loves you, Ruth. He wants to marry you. Don't you remember?"

The girl blinked. "I can't get married. I'm too young. I just want my dolls."

Rose pulled her into her arms, patted her shoulder. "You're eighteen, Ruth. You're not too young. And stop thinking about the dolls. Think about . . . about here and now, Ruth . . . about Adam and Andrea and their baby . . . about pride and love . . . about James."

The girl pulled away. "Where is Father? He'll go get my dolls if I ask him."

Her mother took her hands. "Your father won't be back for a long time, Ruth. Now go upstairs and dress."

The girl sighed deeply and turned away, muttering that she did not like it where she was and wanted to go home. Rose turned to Andrea, who was wiping at tears.

"I feel like it's my fault," Andrea declared. "If Adam hadn't married me Douglas Means wouldn't have—"

"Nonsense!" Rose said sharply. "They would have come, Douglas Means or no Douglas Means. He just happened to be the one in charge that night. But any others would have done the same thing, Andrea. That's the way they are. This same thing has happened all over Indian country. Douglas Means does not lead every expedition. We were singled out as an example. It wouldn't have mattered which men came that night."

Andrea burst into tears, covering her face with her hands. In the next moment Rose was beside her, grasping her wrists. "Andrea, I need you to be strong for me. Please don't do this. I love you like a daughter, and none of this is your fault. You are my son's wife, the woman he loves, the mother of my first grandson. I don't want you blaming yourself. It does no good to blame anyone. There is no single person to blame. It's destiny, Andrea, the destiny of the Indian. But we will not go down in shame and tears. We will go down proud."

Andrea hugged her then, and wished they could all just go and live under the arms of the great oak tree, where no one could harm them, where Ruth would be happy again and Jonas would come back to life. And she would lie with Adam. Happy and laughing again, they would share bodies and hearts and love.

Upstairs Ruth began to dress, staring at the bruises on her face and wondering where they came from, not understanding why her stomach and everything down below hurt so much it was hard to walk. She wondered if she should go back to their house by herself and get her dolls since no one else seemed willing to do it.

Again they came. Adam barged into the house, ordering

all the women to the cellar. Two months had passed, and Ruth had stopped talking about her dolls. silent now, she occasionally was awakened by bad dreams, but she never remembered what they were when fully awake. She let herself be hustled to the cellar, oblivious of the reason.

"Adam, what is it?"

"The militia! They're riding right into town. Stay down here and keep quiet. Try not to let Jonas make any noise."

When they reached the foot of the steps, Adam turned to go back up. "Adam, no!" Andrea begged. "Maybe they're coming after you!"

"I don't think so. Either way I'll not let John Ross and the others face them alone." He started up, but she grabbed him.

"Adam!"

Their eyes held. They had not had much time together since returning to find their house burned and Jonas dead. The lovely peaceful time they had had in the North was over, and he was so full of hatred and worked so diligently at fighting for the cause that he was seldom home. He had not even made love to her since their return, and she still had not told him about the baby. In that moment he suddenly seemed to realize how much he had neglected his wife. He bent down and quickly kissed her cheek.

"I'll be back." He put a hand to her cheek, then suddenly kissed her again, this time on the lips, a quick, hard kiss of passion. "Stay here," he told her, suddenly reluctant to leave her. "I'll put a rug over the door. I'll go out the back way so they don't see which house I've come from."

He was gone then, and Rose huddled into a dark corner with Ruth, horrible memories engulfing her. She struggled to be strong for the others, struggled not to scream. Martha Bluecrow held Jonas, who was wriggling in her arms, and Andrea hurried over to the boy and took him, trying to invent a game that would keep him quiet. Outside they could hear muffled shouts, and the ground shook with the passing of several horses.

Upwards of an hour passed, during which they heard

more distant shouting. Jonas fell asleep, finally, in Mrs. Bluecrow's lap, and Andrea scrambled to the one and only window of the cellar, a single glass pane that was so dirty she could barely see through it. She quickly wiped away one spot with her bare fingers, just enough to peek through. She saw nothing at first, and she struggled against her desire to scream, praying heatedly for Adam's safety.

She could feel horses returning then, coming closer and closer. She watched with terrified eyes, wondering if they were coming here for her and the others. Gradually the animals came into view, but they kept moving, horse after horse going on past. She began to feel relieved until she saw what followed the horses.

"Oh, dear God!" she whimpered.

"What is it!" Rose asked quickly in a near whisper.

Andrea just stared a moment longer. Hurrying behind the horses, trying to keep up so they would not fall, were Reverend Jessup and Dr. Cunningham, both hooked to the horses' harnesses with heavy chains, their wrists cuffed. More chains were hung around their shoulders to weigh them down, making it next to impossible for them to remain upright for long. But both men walked proudly, trying to keep their shoulders straight. Minutes later Margaret Jessup could be seen running after her husband, her children all following, until some Cherokee men grabbed her and tried to console her.

Andrea climbed down and looked at Rose and Martha. "The reverend and Dr. Cunningham. They just took them away . . . in chains."

"No!" Martha gasped. "They're . . . they're good men . . . men of God! What kind of animals are these people, to drag away men of God, men who preach the gospel and help God's children?"

Andrea turned away, grasping her stomach. "They aren't animals, Martha. Animals are kinder, worth much more than those men." She thought of Douglas Means and his depraved mind. She didn't know if he'd been among today's riders. She hadn't been able to see them well.

"They're the devil's helpers," she declared. "They're evil demons. The devil is hard at work here, Martha."

"You're white, Andrea," Martha returned. "You could go north now and get away from all this. Perhaps you shouldn't even stay, child."

Andrea turned back to meet the woman's dark eyes. "No. I am no longer white, Martha. And I won't take the easy way out. I love Adam. I love the Cherokee. I won't desert them now."

The woman shook her head. "You're a good girl, Andrea. But you've seen what they've done with their own kind, good Christian men at that, men of the Cross. No one is exempt now, Andrea. Your white skin won't save you."

Andrea walked over and picked up Jonas. "I'm well aware of that, Martha. I never expected it to save me. Besides, I don't need saving. I am right where I want to be."

They heard footsteps overhead then, and the cellar door opened. Andrea cringed into the shadows until she heard Adam's voice. "Everybody okay down there?"

"Adam!" She hurried to the stairway and climbed up, and in the next moment she was in his arms. "Thank God, you're all right!"

He held her tightly as the others came upstairs, Ruth helping the now-wakened Jonas climb up step by step. "They were after the missionaries," Adam said quietly then, his voice heavy with sorrow. "Jessup and the others have been arrested for advising us to fight removal, and for refusing to take the oath of allegiance to the state in order to have permission to reside among us. I have a feeling it will be bad for them. They will be used as examples." He met his mother's eyes. "We all know what that means. Several people are with Mrs. Jessup now, trying to console her."

"I'll go over there myself," Rose stated, walking over and taking down her shawl from a hook.

"Oh, Adam, where will it end?" Andrea sobbed. "Poor Reverend Jessup . . . and Dr. Cunningham. Who will deliver my baby!"

He pulled back then, to wipe tears from her cheek. "Hold on there. What baby?" He pushed some hair back from her face and their eyes held.

"Our baby," she answered, holding back a sob. "Around Christmas, I think. I . . . I wanted to find a good time to tell you, but so much has been happening that I haven't . . . had the chance."

His eyes teared. "I've neglected you, haven't I?"

"No, Adam. You didn't mean to. I know how hard it is."

He bent down and kissed her tears. "I'm sorry, Andrea. And I'm happy about the baby. I just wish . . ." He sighed deeply. "I wish I knew what kind of future he or she will have." He hugged her tightly. "Listen, you calm down and stay here. Start some supper. I'm going to see what needs to be done to get Jessup and Cunningham and the others out of prison. I'll be back in time for supper." He kissed her hair. "We've got to try to keep some kind of order in our lives, to keep some kind of family life going, for Jonas's sake. I hardly know my son." He kissed her eyes then. "And lately I hardly know my wife. Here you are four months' pregnant and you've kept it from me. My poor, sweet Andrea. You must get so scared. But I won't let anything happen to you. Not ever."

He kissed her quickly and, in one quick gesture, brushed his lips past her ear. "Tonight," he whispered, as though he thought she needed to hear it, needed to hope, and she did. She knew he'd decided he had to stop letting the tragedies around them interfere with their own sweet love, for each moment was precious. They both knew the day could come when something would tear them apart in spite of all his efforts to stop it, and the realization that their love was so threatened created a sudden hunger in both of them, a sudden desperation that told them they must not waste one moment. Men had been dragged away from their loved ones this day. Who would be next?

Adam turned on his side to face her as she came to bed

after soothing Jonas to sleep. He would not tell her the terrible news that outriders had brought that evening—that the reverend and all the missionaries who had been rounded up that day were going to be forced to walk all the way to the county jail at Lawrenceville, chained to the backs of wagons. The trip would take several days, and Adam did not doubt that the militia would see that they made at least twenty to thirty miles a day. By that first evening some missionaries had already been beaten and spat upon. Adam knew it would only get worse, but despite the atrocities around him, and because of them, he felt a sudden need to remember that there were beautiful things left in the world, that there was still love and gentleness. He had played with Jonas until past the boy's bedtime, and now his beautiful wife was crawling into bed beside him. She reached to blow out the lamp.

"Don't," he told her quietly. "I want to look at you."

She met his dark eyes, more full of tenderness and passion than they had been for quite some time. She knew the torture he suffered over his mother and sister, the grief he still felt for his father, and the worry that plagued him over this latest event. She reached out and touched his face.

"I didn't mean to sound like a spoiled little girl, complaining that I'd felt neglected lately. God knows neither one of us—"

He put his fingers to her lips. "I'll not let them keep me from enjoying my wife and family. I'll not let them destroy our marriage, Andrea. And lately every time I look at you and Jonas, I find myself wondering if the next day you'll be gone, somehow stolen away from me."

She studied his handsome face as he bent closer to kiss her neck. Breathing in his masculine scent, she ran her hands over the hard muscles of his arms and shoulders, realizing that it was torture for him not to seek vengeance for the atrocities committed upon his mother and sister. He was more than capable of handling himself. He was strong and skilled and unafraid, and he often lamented that it was not the "old days" when he could have sought Cherokee justice. She could not help but imagine what a fine warrior he would have been. But the white man fought a different kind of war, a war of words and laws and tricks, the kind of war few understood. But the Cherokee, highly intelligent, were the first Indians to give the government an almost insurmountable challenge. Now the government was getting desperate, and so was Georgia's government. The militia was fighting mean and dirty, fighting the physical side of the war that the Cherokee were not allowed to fight. They could only sit and watch, and Andrea knew that on the inside that was killing Adam Chandler.

His kisses grew more urgent then. He had something to prove to himself, and she knew it. He must prove she was really there, that no one had stolen her away or hurt her again. And in his heart, he was grateful for her pregnancy, although he worried about what kind of future he could give two children.

"*Asgaya,*" she said softly as he pushed aside the front of her gown and kissed at a breast. Yes, he was her beloved man, no matter what happened to them. He always would be. He had been her love since she was fourteen. Now she was nearly twenty, though all they had been through made her feel much older. She had been forced to mature, to be strong, to deny fear and to stand by her husband no matter what dangers that might bring.

He moved up and devoured her lips. It had been a long time—too long. On their journey north they had nourished their sweet love, had found peace and happiness. She had even gotten pregnant again. That was a good time. And they could both go there again, live there if they wanted, even though he would have to start all over again. But they would not. There was a point to make by staying, a battle to be won. Yet what would be the toll on their love? That was the question that haunted them, that made them hunger for one another, their intense desire suddenly emerging in writhing bodies and heated kisses. Her gown was soon off, and they enjoyed the glory of skin against skin, enjoyed the teasing nakedness, searched each other hungrily. So long! Too long! Why did so many things keep bringing so much sorrow that they could not enjoy this? Why did all these things have to happen now, when they had found each other again and were married and so much in love. This should be their happiest time. They were so young, so in love, so healthy. It wasn't fair that so many things should happen to destroy their love. They would not let them. They must not!

He whispered her name in a husky rasp, his whole body alive for her now, his eyes enjoying her beauty, his heart loving her, his skin tingling at her touch, his manly needs suddenly keen and almost painful. Then he kissed her rapidly, almost desperately, her face, her neck, her taut nipples, her belly, her thighs, and that secret place that he'd sworn no other man would see or touch.

Andrea allowed herself to forget the horrors she had known, to stop wondering what had happened to her first baby, to forget the awful events of this day, to let go of her fear and sorrow—just for these moments. How else was one to go on living, to find strength, to keep alive a marriage and the sweet love that had brought it into being. He moved back up her body, whispering loving words in the Cherokee tongue, its soft flow always exciting her. Let the government and the militia do what they would, they would not destroy this, not even if she and Adam were forced to be apart. Nothing could stop her from loving this man forever, her Adam, the Cherokee boy who'd so gently stolen her virginity under the oak tree. This handsome, virile man belonged to Andrea, every inch of him, every hard muscle, every dark hair. The lips that moved over her now were gentle and teasing, and little flicks of his tongue made her breathing quicken. She was limp in his hands. She always had been. Those strong hands knew just what to do with her. He could be brutal if he chose, and she could not stop him. But when he was with his woman Adam was a tender man.

He was soon inside her, his hard thrusts reminding her that her man had not had his woman in a long time. His movements were urgent and somewhat demanding, and she found herself arching up to him in a needy response, wanting all of him, pulling him in so that she might enjoy every last bit of him, even though that sometimes brought some pain, for Adam Chandler was well built. She enveloped his manhood in a moist warmth, inviting him into her depths and offering the ultimate pleasure as they surged toward each other in rhythmic motion, each lost in the other, each feeding on the other and drawing strength. When they were one this way, their courage grew, their determination became stronger, their love unconquerable.

She raised her head and kissed his shoulder, running delicate fingers over his nipples and making him feel on fire. He studied the blue eyes that glittered with ecstasy and knew how much he pleased her. Then she gasped and dug her fingers into his arms, and he could feel the pulsations of her most female parts as they tightened and pulled; and he knew he had brought her the ultimate ecstasy. He surged harder then, holding out, wanting to give her the enjoyment she deserved, wanting to love her in every way. But soon he could no longer control his own ecstasy, and he spilled his life deep inside her, thrusting several times more until the glorious throbbing eased.

He seemed to go limp all at once then, and rolled off her slightly but pulled her immediately into his arms.

They lay there quietly for a few moments while he toyed with her golden hair. "I won't let it go so long next time, Andrea. I promise."

"I thought maybe . . . I don't know . . . maybe you were a little bit angry with me."

"For what?"

"I don't know." She blinked back tears and kissed his chest. "For being white, I guess. Right now I wish I weren't."

He smiled and squeezed her close. "Reverend Jessup and the other missionaries are white. It isn't the skin, Andrea. It's the heart. There are bad hearts among the Cherokee, too, you know. Some talk now of leaving, and some are out-and-out traitors. I think I know who might have told the militia to single out my family. I'll know at next meeting."

She pulled back, her eyes wide with concern. "Adam! You won't make trouble?"

"I don't know yet. It depends on what happens. But I'll not let my father's death and what happened to my mother and sister just be forgotten. Someone turned my father in, Andrea, and he's got to be made public. All I have to do is figure out how I'll keep from killing him with my own two hands."

"Adam, please be careful!"

He sighed deeply. "I'm tired of being careful. But I will, for your sake and for Jonas's . . ." He ran a hand over her belly. "And for the sake of the next one. Are you sure, Andrea?"

She nodded. "I just wish Dr. Cunningham could be here."

He kissed her forehead. "Maybe he will be, if we can get him out of prison. But I'll be with you, no matter what, and there are plenty of women who know what to do." He rolled onto his back, rubbing at his eyes. "I just wish I could give you the kind of home you deserve. I'd rebuild the house if I thought it was safe, but we can't go back there. My father's land is too close to the white border. I had quite a bit of money hidden in a root cellar. I managed to find that. And I found one sympathetic white man on the other side who agreed to buy what cattle we had left. I have enough to keep us going for a while, but I don't know for how long. I can't farm the place, and right now I can't go into anything else, like teaching or business. The government stops us on all sides, forbids everything." He took her hand and raised it to his lips, kissing it. "Hang on, Andrea. Someday I'll make a good life for you again. That's a promise. I swear it."

She snuggled into his shoulder. "All I need is you and Jonas, and the baby. I don't care how we live, Adam, as long as it's together."

She thought about the first baby. He was four now, four years old. Did he look like Adam? Was he happy and loved? All their searching had turned up nothing. More and more she realized she would have to accept his absence, accept the fact that she would probably never see or know her first child. But he was in God's hands, and this was not the time to bring that up to Adam.

"Adam."

"Hmmm?"

"Was . . . was he with them . . . Douglas Means?"

He sighed deeply, tensing at the name. "No."

She breathed a sigh of relief and snuggled against him. "I thought of something today, Adam, something that frightened me."

He toyed with her golden hair. "What's that?"

"All that work we did in the North, all the talking and collecting money, getting petitions signed, and greeting people who wished us well—it all seemed so wonderful, so nice to have so much support there. Yet despite all that we got from them, there was one thing they did not offer."

He kissed her hair. "What are you talking about?"

"Refuge." She kissed his chest, her heart heavy. "They never offered us refuge. No one said that if we absolutely cannot stay in Georgia, we're welcome to come north to some nice place rather than go to Indian Territory. And nearly all of their Indians are gone now. They've either died off or are living in the West. In the end, if we must leave, I wonder how much the North will back us then. If we have to move west, I'm afraid they'll just stand and watch like all the others."

He didn't answer right away, but she could feel him trembling. "I've already thought of that," he said, his voice sounding strained. "But for now we'll take what we can get from them and hope that's enough. Now go to sleep. We must deal with one day at a time, and I just want to hold you in my arms and not think about it."

She said nothing more, and he was soon asleep.

CHAPTER EIGHTEEN

The meeting place was packed; the Georgia Militia would not stop them. They met late at night inside an old barn. Adam sat at a front table with Elias Boudinot, John Ross, and others, but his eyes were on Luke Cloud, a man he had watched carefully throughout several meetings. He had been told that his father had argued with this man at the meeting held just before the Chandler farm was raided; and Cloud often spoke in favor of Removal, and reminded the others of the benefits to be gained from the government if they left now and stopped fighting. There were few who spoke in favor of Removal, and antagonism against them was growing. However, the People were being torn apart by differing attitudes, and Adam, like John Ross, feared a split that would destroy all their efforts.

Now Luke Cloud sat listening, his dark eyes sly. Adam had already decided it was time to dispense with those who worked against the cause and fomented doubt and fear. The men present were talking among themselves now about the reverend and the doctor, for the news was not good. All talked in low voices, fearing a raid. Women had ceased coming to the meetings, for they all knew that at any time the militia could ride in to break them up. If women were present, they would be arrested along with the others, and all knew what would happen to them. He worried about Andrea and the strain she was under from being in constant danger. It was early October, and her stomach had suddenly mushroomed so that she seemed almost too big to be only six months along.

John Ross banged a gavel to bring the meeting to order, and the men quieted. Then Ross stood up, slowly scanning the crowd of faces, some sad, some angry, all afraid.

"You've all heard the rumor," he announced. "I can tell you now that it is true. Reverend Jessup, Dr. Cunningham, and the other missionaries arrested last July have been tried and sentenced to four years at hard labor." There was a general mumbling, and Ross fought to control his own feelings. It was difficult for him to speak, for tears kept threatening to come. He held up his hand for more silence. "They have been sent to the penitentiary at Milledgeville, and our sources tell me that they are being treated badly, often abused and fed very little. They have also been denied any visitors, so there is no use in any of us going there to see them."

The murmuring became louder, and there were angry whispers, clenched fists. "They can't do that!" one man argued, standing up from the bench where he sat. "Surely the federal government can step in for them."

"We've tried that before, Charles," Ross replied. "We can see more and more that the federal government is not about to go against anything Georgia does. All they say in reply to any of our petitions is that they cannot interfere with state affairs. We all know it's a farce, but Andrew Jackson is still president, and as long as he is in office, every avenue we take will be blocked. The American Board of Commissioners for Foreign Missions has been in contact with us and plans to petition the President themselves, but I have little hope that they will get any farther than we have. We're getting strong support from the North, and even a few people in Georgia are repulsed by what has happened, but Georgia won't bend, and the federal government won't interfere."

"So what do we do now? We live every day in fear of raids, of our homes being burned, our women being abused. Is there any use to keep fighting?"

"We must keep fighting," Adam replied. "For our Cherokee pride, if nothing more. I have lost my father, my home; my mother and sister were brutalized by the militia, but I am still here, and here I will stay. This is our land! It is beloved and sacred. It belonged to us long before the white man ever stepped foot on this continent."

"We still have a lot of support," John Ross assured them. "We are putting the federal and state governments to every test, embarrassing them in every way possible, because they know we are right. Our constant battle, our refusal to give up, and our commitment to nonviolence has them puzzled and grasping for anything they can use to make them look right. So far they've come up with nothing truly convincing, but I have some top men advising me on their every move—men like Jeremiah Evarts and Daniel Webster. And we have found a sympathetic law firm willing to represent us right here in Georgia—Underwood and Harris. They're very good, and we continue to get support money from the North to help defray expenses. If and when our case is carried to the Supreme Court of the United States, we will be represented by William Wirt. You can't ask for much better. Wirt served as attorney general under Monroe and Adams, and he was special prosecutor at the treason trial of Aaron Burr. I am also happy to say that an attorney from Pennsylvania has volunteered his services for free—a John Sergeant. He is a great speaker. I assure all of you that we still have a mighty sword to wield. We have involved the President, Congress, the church, educators, writers, the Supreme Court, lecturers, practically every political entity one can name. There are many great and influential people fighting for us. We cannot—we must not—allow the random attacks of the militia to make us give up now. We must hang on, for we will win in the end. They won't stop with the militia. They'll invent yet more laws to crush us. They will try to bribe us, they will do anything and everything they can to make us just leave quietly and make no more fuss. But they are finding out just how intelligent, educated and strong the Cherokee people can be. United we can win this battle."

There was a general feeling of relief and new hope among the gathering of men. Elias Boudinot rose then to speak. "We all know that right now there is a battle going on between Governor Lumpkin and Chief Justice John Marshall. This can only be good for us. Georgia is fighting with the Supreme Court over the court's right to tell the state what to do. Lumpkin has brazenly disobeyed court orders in the past, but this only makes Georgia look bad, and it fuels the determination of the Supreme Court to demonstrate their power, making them more likely to rule in our behalf. We seem to have a friend in John Marshall, who presides over the highest court in the land. We can only take great hope in this."

He sat down and Adam rose and the crowd quieted as his eyes moved over them. They respected Adam Chandler, in spite of his youth. He was a well-spoken young man who worked hard for the cause. He was highly educated and very intelligent. He would some day be a great leader. Finally the young man's eyes rested on Luke Cloud, who scowled back at him.

"Our only hope, in spite of all the help we receive from men in power, is to stay together," he told those gathered, his eyes still on Luke. "We cannot afford dissension, and we cannot afford to have . . . traitors . . . among us."

A silence hung in the air, while Luke Cloud's face darkened.

"I am calling you a traitor, Luke Cloud," Adam said calmly.

Cloud jumped to his feet while others mumbled. John Ross rose and grasped Adam's arm, but Adam jerked it away.

"Prove your words, Adam Chandler!" Cloud growled.

The crowd quieted again, waiting for Adam to speak. Now Adam's calm was fading, fury was building in his hot blood. "I have watched you for many weeks, ever since I heard that the night my family was brutalized you and my father argued heatedly about Indian Removal. Three times I have seen you ride off after a meeting, to disappear into the night, over the ridge! Where do you go, Luke Cloud? To the militia? What other reason is there for a Cherokee man to go riding off into the night after a meeting?''

There was a clamor of voices then, and everyone stared at Luke Cloud, who suddenly could not think of a thing to say.

"Tell us, Luke Cloud, how it was that the militia knew exactly where Reverend Jessup and Dr. Cunningham lived, how they could so quickly invade their homes and take them away? They did not stop to ask where they could be found. They already knew! How did they know, Luke? Maybe you told them!''

Adam was over the table then. He knew by the man's eyes that he was right, and his furious need for vengeance knew no bounds. He charged into Luke Cloud before the others realized what was happening, and although Cloud was a huge man, known for his strength, he was no match for the angry Adam Chandler who had lost his father and had lived with the shattered remains of his mother and sister.

Men moved out of the way as Adam and Luke tumbled into the benches. Adam paid little heed to the pain of landing against the hard wood. He felt nothing but hatred as he jerked Luke Cloud up and landed a big fist on the man's face. Cloud flew backward and started to get to his feet, but Adam kicked him hard in the middle and then in the face. Blood flew from Cloud's mouth and nose, and Adam bent down and picked him up as though he were a small child. The men watching were circled now, cheering for Adam, their young hero; for many others had wondered about Luke Cloud's loyalty, and it seemed, through Adam, they were satisfying some of their own need for vengeance.

Over and over Adam dealt shattering blows to the stunned Luke Cloud, who had never even had a chance to hit back. Adam picked him up again, shoved him against a wall. Cloud grunted from the jolt, and reached inside his jacket. Adam did not see the move. He made ready to, again smash his fist into the bloody mass he had made of Luke Cloud's face, when suddenly he felt a piercing pain in his side. His eyes widened and he stumbled backward, blood pouring from his lower left side. Men gasped and quieted, while Luke Cloud waved a knife at all of them.

"You . . . stay away . . . from me!" he grunted. He backed toward the door while others just stared. Then he disappeared into the dark. John Ross was immediately at Adam's side, supporting the young man as his legs began to go out from under him.

"Help me get him to Martha Bluecrow's house," he ordered the others. "We have no doctor now. We'll have to do the best we can."

Adam felt himself being lifted. He didn't care that he'd been stabbed, didn't mind the pain. He'd hurt Luke Cloud badly, he would have killed him with his bare hands if it weren't for the knife. At least now everyone knew the man was a traitor.

Andrea watched in quiet terror as Martha Bluecrow cleaned her husband's wound and sewed it up. She had wanted to do it herself, but no one would let her, afraid the strain would be too much. Adam lay abed, drunk from whiskey given him for the pain. He laughed off and on, talking over and over again about how he'd given Luke Cloud what he had coming, expressing a wish that he had killed the man and a determination to do so. Andrea could only hope she could talk some sense to him when he was sober, for if he killed Luke Cloud, the Georgia Militia would arrest him. The Cherokees were no longer living under their own laws, but the laws of the state. One Cherokee who had killed another earlier in the year had already been arrested and hung.

He called for her then, and when she rose from her chair and leaned over him, he grasped her hand and kissed it. "I did it . . . I found him!" he mumbled, his words slurred. "I found the traitor, Andrea . . . I beat him good. It was the next best thing to . . . getting my hands on Douglas

Means. But I will Andrea . . . someday . . . I'll kill that bastard."

"Adam, don't talk that way," she said quietly. "You know you can't do that. In the meetings you speak for nonviolence, just like the others. You know that to kill a militia man would only ruin the Cherokee cause and destroy all our efforts."

"A man . . . has to stand up . . . for his loved ones."

"Of course he does, darling." She bent down and kissed his forehead. "God knows you have the strength and skill to do it. But the bigger fight has to be fought with words, Adam, not fists and knives."

"He . . . deserved it," he moaned, suddenly saddening. His eyes teared. "The . . . son of a bitch . . . deserved it! I should have . . . killed him! Because of him . . . they singled out my father." He choked on a sob then. "I . . . miss him, Andrea."

"I know you do. We all miss him. But just think—he won't suffer anymore. He's free of all this worry and warring. He's at peace, Adam."

He met her eyes then and reached up for her. "Don't go away from me, Andrea," he begged. "Don't ever . . . go away. We have to . . . go sit under the oak tree. You . . . remember the oak tree . . . don't you, Andrea?"

She smiled and smoothed back his hair. "Of course I remember the oak tree. How could I forget?"

Their eyes held and he smiled through his tears. "I loved you . . . that first day . . . when you hugged the tree," he told her. "I knew you loved it . . . as much as I did . . . and I loved you."

"You can help me wrap him, Andrea." Martha Bluecrow touched her shoulder. "If he doesn't get an infection, he'll be all right. We'll have to keep an eye on that wound. He's darned lucky the blade went in far enough to the side to miss his vital organs. And you're lucky your man is alive. That Luke Cloud ought to be hung."

Andrea gently kissed Adam's swollen hand. Then Rose watched, her arm around a still quiet and withdrawn

Ruth, while Martha and John Ross lifted Adam slightly so that Andrea could wrap his middle with gauze. By the time she'd finished, Adam had drifted off into a drunken sleep.

Luke Cloud quickly packed his immediate belongings onto two mules and then saddled the horses. He and his wife and daughter would leave that night, to head west with the substantial sum of money given them by Douglas Means. He could no longer act as an informant now. He must get out and get himself to Indian Territory. He could barely see because of his swollen eyes, and his pain was almost unbearable. But he had to ignore it and get away, for fear a mob of angry Cherokees would come after him and beat him some more. He smiled to himself as he slunk away in the wee hours of the morning. By the time the rest of them came staggering west after losing their ridiculous battle with the government, they would be poor and broken. He, on the other hand, would be rich and well established in Indian Territory. Maybe Adam Chandler would even have to beg him for help. It would serve him right.

The little troop of small boys was marched into the strange man's office. Outside was the noise of machinery, so loud it hurt the ears sometimes. Little Indian turned his wide, dark eyes to the window, to look out at boys not much older than he running machinery. They stood like silent statues, moved automatically; their eyes were hollow and tired-looking, and their bodies were frail. Little Indian, the only name he'd ever been called, wondered why on earth he had been brought here with the others. Life was hard at the strange, cold place where he'd been raised, but that was home to him now and he didn't like being brought out of it to this strange, new place.

Big Father, as the man who'd brought them here was called, was now talking to the man behind the desk, a frail-looking fellow with a hard look to his dark eyes, and glasses on his long, thin nose.

"Some are still a little young," Big Father was saying. "But you can see already why I brought them. You might wish to pay something down on them now. When they're old enough, I'll bring them back—sturdy, fresh young boys to run your machines."

The thin man with the thin nose walked around his desk, eying each boy, pinching their arms to see how much meat was on them, looking into their eyes to see that they were clear, turning them around and around to make sure they were whole and healthy.

"This one has very strong legs," Big Father said of one. "That one is quick to learn." "This one here is very intelligent, already reads and writes." They came to Little Indian, and the thin man looked him over with a scowl. "This one is a Cherokee Indian," Big Father told the man. "He is very strong for four and a half, one I don't think you'll want to let go. He's a bit too young, but in a couple of years you can put him to work. I think you'll be pleased. He's a mixed breed, has the intelligence that usually comes with the mixed ones."

"Which one was white?" the thin man asked.

"The mother."

The thin man pinched and poked and then turned Little Indian around. "How did you get him?"

"Come now, Stuart, you know I'm not authorized to divulge such information. The origin of these children is kept strictly confidential. Most of them are given up willingly anyway."

The two men continued talking, but Little Indian again became lost in the wonder of where he came from. Did he drop from the sky? Come from the walls, like the mushroom he'd seen growing once in the cellar of the old house where he'd been raised with the other boys? None of them seemed to know exactly where he had come from. And none of them knew the meaning of mother and father, home and hearth. They had grown up knowing only regimented days of work and very little play, of specific times to do everything, of rigid teaching by stern-faced men and women who showed no sign of warmth. And so none of the little boys there even understood affection or the meaning of love. But there was a strange longing in Little Indian's heart, a flicker of wonder and curiosity that he could not yet understand or act upon. He only knew that down deep inside him there was an odd longing to know something, and a tiny softness that made him want to cry sometimes, especially at night when he was afraid and alone. And what was a mother? Big Father had told the thin man that his mother was white. That was the first time the boy had heard any mention of something that had to do with where he came from.

He looked down at his hand. White? Did he mean like the white people who watched over him at the house where he lived? He'd been told several times he was an Indian, whatever that was, and that because he was Indian, he was born from evil, and he could never live out in the rest of the world like others. He had to stay in that house, and someday he would work in big factories. He must prove his worth by working very hard, and then someday he would be free to go out into the world. He wondered if there were more Indians out there. Were they all born from evil, as he had been? What did being born mean, and how was he born? All he knew about evil was that it was a very bad thing, so he must be very bad, too. He reasoned that therefore he must do all that they told him, for he'd been told that disobeying would mean being thrown into a terrible pit, where he would burn and burn but never die. He was afraid of the pit. He would be good. But maybe someday he would find out if there were other Indians. And maybe he would even find out about the white mother Big Father had said he had, although he wasn't quite sure what a mother was. Perhaps she was bad, too.

"I'll pay something on the Indian now," the thin man was saying. "He looks good and sturdy."

"Fine," Big Father answered. "Miss Williams will be pleased. She picked that one up the moment he was born."

The thin man studied Little Indian again, shaking his head. "Imagine, a white woman mixing with an Indian.

314

Makes you feel kind of sick."

"Well, it takes all kinds. But she paid her price."

"Too bad you didn't bring her along. I know what I'd do with the little hussie."

Both men laughed and Little Indian frowned. Were they talking about his mother again? He wasn't completely sure who or what she was, yet to hear the men laughing about her made him strangely angry. He scowled at them, wishing he were bigger, for suddenly he didn't like either of them.

He was herded out then, through the noisy factory to a back alley, where he and the others were hustled into a windowless coach. The door was closed and locked, and they waited, huddled together and cold, while Big Father and the thin man finished their business. Little Indian turned to an older companion, unable to see his face in the darkness but knowing who it was.

"Johnny, what's a mother?" he asked.

"A mother? You don't know?"

"No. They said my mother was white."

"A white woman? By damn, Little Indian, if your ma was white, that makes you a half-breed. You sure look all Indian for being a half-breed."

"A half-breed?"

"Yeah. Half-Indian, half-white, dummy. Hey, you know that cat that hangs around our place?"

"Yeah."

"Well, remember a couple of weeks ago, when she had those baby kittens?"

"I remember," came the little voice, the boy's heart racing with curiosity.

"Well, that made the cat a mother. The kittens are her kids. That's what a mother is. You came out of a white woman's belly, and an Indian man planted you there."

Little Indian frowned in total confusion. Did the Indian man cut open the white woman and put a seed in her that turned into a baby? And if he came from inside a woman, where was she? Was she bad? Was the Indian man bad?

"You don't really know, Johnny," he pouted. "You

don't know about babies and mothers."

"Sure I do. I heard Miss Andrews tell the big cat to be a good mother. That big cat is the kittens' mother. And if we have mothers, then they must be people mothers."

Little Indian scratched his head. "Would Big Father know where my mother is?"

Johnny shrugged. "I don't know. I suppose somebody does."

The coach suddenly lurched, and Little Indian fell forward. Hands shoved him away and he settled down between two boys. His mind whirled with wonder. A mother. A white woman had carried him in her belly like the cat had carried the kittens. But the cat had taken care of her kittens. Why hadn't his mother stayed and taken care of him? What was it like having a mother who licked you clean and gave you milk? He would find out. Someday when he was bigger, he would find out where he came from. He would find this strange mother and ask her why she went away. And he would find the Indian man who had given him his dark skin and hair, and who had deserted him.

The coach rattled on, toward what he'd heard some call an orphanage. He wondered if he would be returned to the noisy factory, and when. He hoped never. He didn't like the noise, and he didn't like the thin man or the way the boys who worked there looked. They looked sad and hungry.

Adam looked up from his desk at the newspaper office to see James Bird standing there, his face ashen.

"She's gone, Adam. I went to see her today, and she's gone," he said. James had remained faithful to Ruth since her brutal attack, patiently waiting for the day when she would be well again and they could be married.

Adam frowned. He rose from his desk, rubbing at his still-painful side, although it was nearly healed now. "What do you mean? Did you check the cellar?"

"We checked everywhere. Your mother is beside herself,

and Andrea is fretting and blaming herself for not noticing the girl leave the house. Your mother said to come and get you, to ride out to the old place. She's afraid Ruth went there to find her dolls. If she sees the burned-out houses, Adam . . ."

Adam was already around the desk and putting on his hat and jacket. "Come on! Did you bring me a horse?"

"Yes. I figured you'd want to go right away. Are you sure you can ride?"

"I can ride, considering the circumstances."

Both young men rushed outside and mounted up, Adam wincing as he did so. He didn't really look forward to riding yet, but the sooner they got to Ruth the better.

"All morning your mother and Andrea thought she was in her room," James told him on the way. "They didn't realize she was gone until I came and they went to get her. You know how she usually just sits in her room sometimes and won't come out. They didn't think anything about it."

"It isn't their fault," Adam answered. "I've been noticing a change in her lately. I think she was starting to come out of it. I've been a little worried about her."

It seemed they couldn't ride fast enough, and Adam was surprised that if Ruth had headed for home, she could have gotten so far on foot. But after twenty minutes of riding he saw a horse in the distance. It looked to him like one that belonged to a neighbor of Martha Bluecrow. In her crazy quest to get home, Ruth must have stolen it. His heart pounded with fear and dread as they approached the blackened ruins of the once-beautiful homes. He hated to look at them and avoided doing so as much as possible.

"Good God!" he suddenly shouted, seeing Ruth stumbling through the ruins, tearing at blackened boards and bricks. He kicked his horse into a faster gallop. Dismounting before it stopped completely, he ran to his sister. "Ruth, get out of there! You'll get hurt!"

"No!" she screamed. "I want my dolls. Where are my dolls! And where is Father? The house is burned. Didn't anybody tell him? Find my dolls!"

Adam grabbed her from behind. She kicked wildly, elbowing his side and bringing momentary blackness and pain. But he held on. James was with them then, grasping her legs. As Ruth struggled wildly, they forced her away from the rubble. "No! No! No!" she screamed at the top of her lungs. "Don't touch me! Please! Please! Father, make him stop! Make him stop hurting me!"

Adam's heart was torn. They pushed her to the ground, and he laid on her to hold her down with his weight. James held her arms, and she screamed even louder. Both realized she was reliving the nightmare. Adam grasped her face between strong hands, yelling her name over and over.

"Ruth, it's me! It's Adam, your brother! It's all right, Ruth! It's over and nobody is going to hurt you!"

They struggled for a good ten minutes until she wearied and he could talk to her without provoking her to shout. Then she broke into deep, heaving sobs, wrenching gasps of humiliation and shame. "You cry, Ruth," Adam told her, his own eyes tearing. "You cry. You've needed to cry for a long time. And when you get up, you show us how strong a Cherokee woman can be. You hear me, Ruth? You didn't do anything wrong and you've nothing to be ashamed of. James is right here, and he loves you. He's never stopped loving you. He's come to see you every single day since your attack, and that was six months ago!"

She stared at him, quieting more. "Six . . . months?"

He nodded. "Your mind left you, Ruth. We've been waiting for you to come back to us. Mother will be so happy to have you back."

She stared up at her beloved brother, her breathing quickening again. "Mother! They did terrible things to her, too . . . didn't they?"

"It's over, Ruth. Watching the effect on you was hardest on her. You have to get well, Ruth. For her. She needs you. We . . . we don't have Father anymore."

Her tears came again, this time accompanied by pitiful sobs of grief. He sat up then, cradling her in his arms, rocking her. "We'll make it, Ruth. You'll see. We're still fighting. Andrea and I are back, and Andrea is pregnant again. We're living with the widow, Martha Bluecrow. You've got to be strong now, Ruth, for Mother's sake. It's what Father would want. We won't let them beat us. If you stand up strong and lead a normal life now, then you've won, don't you see?"

She clung to his shirt, weeping. "You . . . don't know!" she sobbed. "He said . . . terrible things . . . about Andrea."

His grip on her tightened. "He'll never touch Andrea. If he does, he'll die. I wanted to go after him when I found out about you and Mother, but they stopped me. They won't stop me the next time."

"No! Don't go after them! I don't want to lose you, Adam!"

He kissed her hair. "It isn't me you should rely on so much anymore, Ruth. It's James. He still loves you. He's standing right here, and I think you two should be alone."

He got up, pulling her up with him. As she clung to him, hanging her head, James reached out with a shaking hand and touched her hair. "Don't do that, Ruth," he said, his voice full of grief. "Don't hang your head like that. Look at me."

Adam carefully let go of her, pushing her toward James. As that young man put his arms around her, Adam turned away. "We'd better get in closer to town before you do too much talking," he told them, mounting up. "It's too dangerous out here." He picked up the reins of Ruth's horse. "You ride with Ruth in front of you, James. She should be close to you." He rode forward, walking his horse several yards before looking back to see James lift Ruth onto his mount. Then the young man climbed up behind her and reached around her to pick up the reins. Adam turned away again, wiping at tears. He liked James. Ruth would be all right now, with a little more healing time. And James Bird would show her the gentle side of man, make it all brand-new for her. If anything could erase horror, it was love, and he vowed that no horror that ever came between him and Andrea would destroy their love. All they had to do was cling to that love . . . and remember the oak tree and those first sweet days of happiness and discovery.

He felt a chill at Ruth's words—*He said terrible things about Andrea*—and he longed to seek out Douglas Means and slaughter the man. Perhaps someday he would have to do that after all.

December came, a month of relative peace when a few things brought some happiness to the Chandlers. Early in the month Ruth married James Bird, and on December twentieth, John Ross Chandler was born to Andrea and Adam. With only Martha Bluecrow and Rose to aid in the birth, Adam had stayed by Andrea's side. Without his presence, she would have been terrified, but this birth had gone well. The baby had come quickly, a strong boy with lighter coloring than his older brother, a grand mixture that resulted in a tawny brown skin and sandy hair. The boy had his mother's blue eyes, and his hair was curly. His birth again brought on the old longing to know where their first son might be. He was going on five years old, and Andrea had insisted that they give him a name and stop referring to him as the first baby. She'd named him Nathan Peter, and had declared that they would call him Nathan and speak of him as though he were a part of the family, for in their hearts he was, wherever he might be. She would not allow anyone to forget him, nor would she ever stop hoping that someday she would see her first son.

Christmas was as happy as could be expected under the circumstances. Special services were held for the reverend and the doctor and the other missionaries who were suffering in prison. At the widow Bluecrow's house, gifts were exchanged, mostly hand-knitted items or toys made by Adam. There was not a lot of money for such things now, but it mattered little. What mattered was that they were together and well. Little John Ross was only five days old, and eighteen-month-old Jonas toddled everywhere now, getting into mischief whenever he could, the cause of much laughter and commotion during the opening of presents.

That winter was mild, the nights cold, and most days requiring little more than a sweater. And all of the Cherokee Nation waited for a Supreme Court decision that could affect their entire future. Georgia's right to rule over the Cherokees was being tested in the highest court of the land, due to the plight of the missionaries who had been arrested and condemned to hard labor. Attorney Wirt carried the case to an appeal in the Supreme Court, declaring that the Constitutional rights of the missionaries had been violated, since they were citizens of the United States, invited to the Cherokee Nation by the Cherokees under a valid treaty with the United States and therefore exempt from Georgia law. If there was any wrongdoing, it should have been handled by the federal courts, which have jurisdiction over the Indians. The argument was a delicate one, as the President had declared all Indians within Georgia's borders to be under Georgia's rule. But the clever Cherokees had the Supreme Court, the federal government and the state government all arguing among themselves as to who truly had control over the Cherokees, and whether or not early treaties with the United States were still valid.

One missionary was chosen to represent all, in a case that was to become famous as *Worcester v. The State of Georgia*. John Ross, Adam, and the entire Cherokee Nation waited through that long and tense winter for the outcome, the final decision of the United States Supreme Court, which would decide not only the fate of the missionaries, but the fate of the entire Cherokee Nation by determining whether Georgia had the power to enforce their removal. For if the court declared in favor of Worcester and the missionaries, the Cherokees would be under the control of the federal government and not the State of Georgia.

CHAPTER NINETEEN

The decision was handed down on February 28, 1832, but the news did not reach New Echota until two weeks later. Adam had wanted to go with John Ross and be present during those final days of deliberation, but he was afraid to leave Andrea, who was constantly haunted by the threat of the militia. It was mid-March when he came barging into the house half stumbling from too much whiskey. He rarely allowed himself to drink, for already many of his friends had fallen into almost constant drunkenness, seeing no hope for the future. White traders roamed the perimeter of Cherokee land, selling firewater to now listless Cherokees, glad to take the dwindling Indian money, for the sooner they broke the Cherokees financially, the sooner the Indians would have to go.

But the news from the United States Supreme Court gave even the most destitute new hope. Adam grinned, holding up his bottle. "It is time to celebrate!" he told Andrea and his mother. "James is going to his home to get Ruth, and tonight we will dance—all night long!"

Andrea smiled. She could not be angry that he was drinking, for to see him so happy warmed her heart. It had been a long time since she had seen her husband so elated.

"What happened, Adam?"

He laughed and took another drink. "I don't think I'll tell you. I'll make you wait."

"Adam Chandler!" Andrea rose from her chair and

walked over to hug him. "You tell me right now, or I'll—"

He took her lips, making a moaning sound like a man in ecstasy; suddenly wanting her, his joy making all his other senses come alive. She was slim and shapely again, and he decided his beautiful wife seemed to get more beautiful with each child. "You will what," he answered, crushing her tight against him. "Let's go upstairs."

"Adam!" She reddened deeply. "Your mother is sitting right in front of us!" She shoved him away playfully. "Now tell us what you're so happy about."

He bowed low to them both. "Chief Justice John Marshall and his esteemed colleagues, have declared that Georgia's prosecution of the missionaries was unconstitutional, and has reversed the state's judgment. Reverend Jessup and the others must be set free."

Rose's eyes teared with relief, and Andrea hugged him again. "Oh, Adam, is it true? I can't believe it! Finally a decision for our side!"

He laughed and whirled her around. "It is the same as declaring that the Cherokee are not under Georgia's control," he told them. "This gives us a strong defense for staying on our beloved land." He picked her up in his strong arms. "Watch the boys, Mother. I am taking Andrea upstairs."

"Adam! It's the middle of the day!"

"So? Is there a law against a man making love to his wife in the middle of the day?"

"Adam Chandler! James and Ruth might be here at any minute."

"I have a feeling James is going to do the same thing I am doing, Mrs. Chandler. He has had his own share of whiskey, and there is much to celebrate." As he whisked her up the stairs, Rose smiled and shook her head. It was good to see her son so happy, good to know Ruth was healing, good to have her grandsons at her feet. Jonas toddled to the stairs and tried to follow, but his grandmother ordered him to stay put.

*   *   *

"Tonight we will dance all night, and I will get so drunk I will not be able to make love to you at all," Adam told his wife with a laugh as he carried her through the doorway. "So we'd better do this now, woman." He threw her on the bed, and she screamed lightly. Then he laughed and quickly removed his shirt, kicking the door shut before coming over and falling onto the bed beside her. Grabbing her close, he kissed her hungrily, and she felt more passion and desire than she had for a long time, for fear and tension did not haunt her. She was with her beautiful man, and he needed her; that was all that mattered. His kisses were hard, his movements deliberate and demanding, the whiskey heightening his need of her. Clothes came off amid kisses and suggestive words and laughter, and soon they lay naked, hands and lips exploring and tasting and enjoying. He was full of love for her, glorying in her beauty and loyalty and devotion, proud of her for giving him two sons and for having to live with the loss of a third just because she had loved a Cherokee man.

Andrea responded with an explosion of desire, and he rolled onto his back, pulling her on top of him. To her it was an act of reckless abandon, making love to him this way, and in the light of day she could not help but redden as he drove into her, then ran his hands along her slender thighs, over her stomach and up to her full breasts.

"Adam, I can't—"

"Yes you can. I love to look at you this way. Do not feel ashamed, *agiya*. You are my beautiful wife, and it is right that I enjoy you however I choose."

He rocked himself in a gentle rhythm, sending shivers through her, and she closed her eyes and threw her head back, feeling a certain power over her man—a strange, wonderful feeling—for he was the powerful one, so manly, so strong. Yet he whispered that she made him feel weak, that sometimes he was the conquered one. Teasing suggestive Cherokee words came from his lips as he gently urged her to enjoy him and throw off her inhibitions. Seeing her this way brought forth his wildest desires. He knew every inch of her, every curve, every vein, every dimple, every crease. He had explored her, invaded her, and he loved her to the marrow of his bones.

He rolled her over then, now the conquerer, his broad shoulders hovering over her and making her feel lost and weak, his teasing kisses bringing out the fire that her shyness always fought. How wonderful to be so possessed by one man—her husband. He had every right to enjoy her however he chose, and she had the same right to enjoy him. It was give and take, erotic pleasure the reward for both.

She was rising now, rising to the mountains, where all was sweet and beautiful, and where a golden oak tree stood waiting. And she was under it, in her husband's embrace and under the protection of the great limbs of the oak. She was fourteen again, and he was sixteen, and there were no laws, no militia, no bigotry and hatred. There was only their sweet love.

They danced through the night. Never had there been such celebrating among the Cherokee. And it had been a long time since laughter had been heard among them. Some who had been prepared to head westward called a halt to their plans and unpacked their belongings. They could stay! There was still some political wrangling to be done, but surely after such a Supreme Court decision, there was no argument left over their right to stay in Georgia; the missionaries would be released any day now. They danced until Andrea's feet ached so badly that she took off her shoes. Many had wanted to join in the celebrating so two barns were used, for they couldn't possibly all fit into one, and even then the crowd spilled outside, where people danced on the grass or lay passed out in drunken glory.

But before the night was over the first warning came, in the form of a troop of militia. Inside Andrea and Adam were dancing when they heard shouts and a couple of screams outside. The music tapered off and everyone sobered as several soldiers rode right into the barn amid the Cherokees, led by none other than Douglas Means.

Andrea felt the blood drain from her face, and she recognized that whimpering sound nearby was coming from Ruth, who hurriedly pushed her way through the crowd to hide behind a haystack at the back of the barn. James quickly followed her, and Douglas watched them, a smile on his face. Then his eyes moved to Rose, who stood beside Andrea, both women looking boldly back at him, as did Adam Chandler, who stepped in front of them. The crowd was hushed, and John Ross and some of the other important leaders moved to the front of it, watching Adam carefully.

"So, the Indian boy still has his white woman," Douglas sneered. His gaze ran over Andrea as though she were naked.

"Get out of here, you slimy white bastard!" Adam growled. "You have no right to be here now!"

Douglas fingered a whip and Rose cringed. "Don't I? You Cherokees think you have won some kind of landmark case. You think you're out of Georgia's hands now." His steely gray eyes moved over the rest of the crowd. "Think again, Cherokees. Georgia has no intention of obeying any Supreme Court ruling. Those judges can stick their ruling up their pompous asses!"

"And who are you to speak for Georgia?" Adam sneered. "I should think Georgia would have more pride than to let trash like you represent her!"

Douglas glared down at him. "You are as smart-mouthed and stubborn as your father—and as ignorant. I am surprised that with your glorious education, Chandler, you're stupid enough to slander a militia man."

Adam moved closer to him, and Andrea's heart pounded with fear. How she hated Douglas Means! It had been many years since she'd last seen him, that awful day he had pushed her down in the barn and threatened her. She felt sickened by the sight of him.

"Man?" Adam shot back. "I see no man before me! I see a stinking coward, who is so repulsive that he cannot get a woman without tying her down and forcing her!"

John Ross stepped closer to Adam, amid gasps at Adam's daring, and Douglas reddened, his jaw flexing in anger. "I thought perhaps you had learned your lesson when you came home to find your homes burned, Chandler, and your women . . . defiled. I found your sister quite enjoyable, I must say. And my men claim that for her age your mother was surprisingly pleasing. I shall have to try your wife next."

Adam lunged toward him, but Douglas threw out the whip, catching Adam around the neck, its biting end cutting into his face and drawing blood. Men gasped, several women screamed, and Andrea cried out Adam's name, but amidst all the commotion, and to Douglas's surprise, Adam grabbed the whip and yanked, rather than trying to get out of it. And in the next second Douglas found himself landing hard on the dirt floor. He was temporarily stunned, just long enough for Adam to push a knee into his breastbone so hard that he could not get his breath. In seconds he was too weak to do anything but lie there. His men moved closer, some pulling guns, but none knew quite what to do without orders.

Adam grasped Douglas's hair tightly, while the crowd backed away, and Andrea was speechless with fear for her husband, who hovered over Douglas Means, his eyes wild with rage.

"Perhaps I cannot kill you here and now, Means," he growled. He pushed harder on the man's chest. "But the right time will come! You see already how easily I could do it! And I warn you, white scum, if you ever touch one of my loved ones again, you will not die quickly, but you will surely die! You will want to scream for mercy, but you will not be able to scream, because your balls will be stuffed into your mouth, and you will choke on your own bloody privates! This I swear, no matter what would happen to me when I finish with you. There is no torture too great to keep me from killing you! Remember that, Douglas Means!"

"Adam! Get off him. He can't breathe. Don't do this,

Adam!" John Ross's voice brought Adam back to reality, for his fury had momentarily dispelled rationality. He reluctantly let go of Douglas Means, wondering if it might be the biggest mistake he'd ever made not to kill him then and there. He spit in Douglas's face and then got up, and Douglas rolled over, gasping for breath, bent over, and holding his chest. Adam unwound the whip from his neck, took a knife from his belt, and whisked it through the whip several times, cutting it into pieces.

Douglas struggled to his feet, grasping his saddle, while his men watched and waited for direction. When he turned to Adam, his breath was coming in panting gasps. "You'll . . . pay, Chandler! You'll pay!"

"Touch my woman and we'll see who pays!" Adam hissed.

Douglas glanced at Andrea, who faced him boldly, proud of her husband's strength. Then he looked back at Adam. "I'll have you arrested."

"Try it! Take it to the Supreme Court, white scum! I killed no one. I did not even hurt you. Once you get your stinking breath back, you will realize you cannot arrest me. There are no charges. I was defending myself, against a militia man who does not even belong here, a man who threatened my woman, who is white. You must be physically harmed before you can bring any charges. That is what you want, isn't it? That is why you harass us. Georgia thinks we will retaliate and start a war, and you're all pissed off because we haven't done a thing! But you look like the bunch of fools, and the whole world is laughing at you! Now get out of here, trash!"

The rest of the crowd closed in threateningly then, spirited by Adam's words and by the sight of blood running from the deep cut along Adam's jawbone. It dripped onto his white shirt, but he hardly seemed to notice the wound. Douglas Means mounted up, still breathing hard, perspiration on his face. He glared down at Adam.

"There are some dark days coming for you, Adam Chandler. Mark my words!" He turned his horse and motioned for his men to leave. Everyone started talking then, some coming up and shaking Adam's hand, thanking him for standing up to the man. Andrea dabbed at the cut with a handkerchief, and when he finally met her eyes, he saw terror in them.

"I meant what I said and he knows it!" Adam told her. "Do not be afraid."

She blinked back tears, and he encircled her in his arms. The crowd was sober, their spirits dampened now, and the talk turned to the possibility that Georgia would not heed the Supreme Court decision. If not, what were they to do?

The time for celebration was brief, as day after day the missionaries remained imprisoned. It became more apparent that Georgia did, indeed, intend to fight the decision by ignoring it. Senator George Troupe spoke through an open letter printed in a widely distributed Georgia newspaper, telling citizens that they must not give up on the question of Indian Removal; that allowing the federal courts to win placed the slavery issue in danger also. Little did the Cherokee know that their battle to stay in Georgia would become the source of future issues over slavery, resulting in a Civil War. Lines were drawn for battle between State and Union, even though in this particular case the President stood behind Georgia. Not only would Georgians defy the Supreme Court, but the President himself would not chastise them for doing so; he, too, was for Indian Removal. And more than that, holding the Union together was the most vital issue. If that meant getting rid of Georgia's Indians, then so be it.

Months passed; the missionaries remained imprisoned; Cherokee hopes dwindled. The missionaries were offered a pardon, more than once. But they refused, for to accept a pardon would mean they had committed a crime, and they had not.

Georgia, in open defiance of the Supreme Court ruling, set up a land lottery. Whites could take over Cherokee land by buying chances, and soon new settlers were swarming into the border lands of Cherokee country. The full force of what was happening did not hit Adam and Andrea until the day Adam came home from his farm. He'd gone there to get some tools. His face was grim, and in his hand he held a large branch covered with golden oak leaves. Jonas ran up to him, hugging his leg, and little John Ross crawled over to his daddy, but Adam saw only Andrea. He held out the branch. "From our tree," he said in a choked voice.

She set aside her sewing and walked over to take the branch, while the widow Bluecrow and Rose looked on. "What is it, Adam?" Andrea asked.

He looked at his mother then. "The farm." He swallowed and looked back at Andrea. "White men live there now. They're . . . they're building a new house. I couldn't even take my father's tools. They said everything there belonged to them."

Andrea turned away and covered her face, clinging to the branch with one hand. Adam looked at his mother.

"We don't get a cent for it. Not a cent. All that land, the buildings, the tools—and not a cent. They won it . . . in a lottery!"

He stood there looking dumbfounded. He still could not grasp the unfairness of what had happened, and worse, the irony. He looked at Andrea again. "Your father. It's your father and that Means fellow and his wife. They pooled their money for the lottery, and it's our land they took."

Andrea turned to him, wide-eyed, shaking her head. "It can't be!"

Their eyes held, and she knew that was not all. He reached out and took the hand that held the branch. "Your mother is dead, Andrea. In a few blunt words your father informed that she . . . she killed herself."

She stared at him in disbelief. As Rose hurried over to get the boys away from their father and mother, Andrea's eyes teared and she began to tremble. "It's my fault!"

"No," he said gently, drawing her to him. "It is not your fault, Andrea. If it's anyone's fault, it's your father's, if you

331

want to call him that."

She hugged him around the middle and wept, still holding the branch. He kissed her hair and held her tightly. "I'm so sorry, Andrea. If you're going to blame yourself, then blame me, too, for stealing away their daughter."

"No, never. You did nothing wrong," she sobbed.

"And neither did you."

"Oh, Adam, it's as though the whole world is against us! Ever since we fell in love everything around us has crumbled!"

The boys stared at their mother, afraid of the mysterious thing that was making her cry. It was several minutes before she finally pulled away from Adam, took a handkerchief from her apron pocket, and wiped her eyes. "The worst part is that the Means are living on our farm," she said in a shaky voice. "That means Douglas will be close whenever he's home ... and with the militia keeping quarters on Cherokee land all the time now, he'll probably try to get as much duty here as he can, just to harass us."

"I've thought of that." He sighed deeply as he reached out and patted her hair. "I think we should move farther up into the hills northwest of New Echota. More and more Cherokees are withdrawing from the border lands, and gathering together for safety. We expect the militia to come through town at any time and destroy the newspaper office. We aren't supposed to be printing the *Phoenix*, but we have continued to do so. It's our only way of getting the latest news to the people. But if we can't have a paper, we'll get word through some other way."

"I don't want you riding alone anymore, Adam," Andrea answered quickly. "You promised you wouldn't. You've made enough sacrifices, and I'm afraid when you're gone."

"I won't go. Now we have to fortify ourselves against militia raids. And in our case we have to be extra careful. We know Douglas Means will single you out if he can."

She cringed, and he reached out and pulled her close

again. "Several of the men are building log cabins right now, Andrea, in the hills north of town. Some will be quite large with several rooms so that more than one family can be together. There seems to be safety in numbers. But the cabins will have to be almost windowless—perhaps they'll have only one small window up high on each end—so that they cannot be broken into. We're devising escape tunnels to be used in case the militia should try to burn us out."

"Adam!" His mother rose, her eyes wide. "Is it truly that bad?"

"I can see it coming, Mother. We're still fighting this, but we've got to do something to protect ourselves against raids and harassment by the militia."

His heart tightened at the look of terror in her eyes. She reached down and picked up John, held him close. "How soon must we go?"

"We'll go within a week. They're working night and day, and already have one started for us and for Ruth and James and James's family."

"Oh, Adam, I can't believe any of this is happening," Andrea groaned, feeling suddenly weak. "When I remember coming to visit you . . . your beautiful home . . . your happy family—"

"Don't, Andrea. Don't look back, not right now. It hurts too much." He turned her slightly and took the branch from her hand. "I rode to the tree, not caring if anyone tried to stop me. But no one did. I went to our tree. It's still there, beautiful and golden, shedding its leaves for winter. That tree will go on for a long time, Andrea, and so will we. And no matter what happens to this land, it is Cherokee land and always will be. And I make you a promise this day. One day I will be a rich man again, much richer than my father ever was. And I will come back here and buy my land out from under them. I will get my land back, Andrea, as God is my witness! And someday you and I will sit under our tree, and make love under it again. I swear it."

She looked up at him with tear-filled eyes. "Even if

something should happen to me?"

Their eyes held, and he took a leaf from the branch and touched it to her cheek. "Even if something should happen to you. If I do it merely in honor of your memory, I will do it. This is Cherokee land, Andrea, and that piece of land is mine. Mine! Someday Adam Chandler will own it again—outright! And no one will ever take it away from me again!"

She reached up and touched the hand that held the leaf. He squeezed her hand, and she kissed his fingers. "Remember that promise, Adam. No matter what happens, or how long it takes, or what we suffer—even if we are no longer together. Remember it, and keep it." She looked up at him, and he bent down and kissed her lightly.

"I will remember."

She turned away then, her heart heavy, not only for the loss of the land, but for more, much more . . . her mother . . . her poor, unhappy mother who had never known the kind of love she had with Adam. She slumped wearily onto a chair, and Adam laid the branch in her lap. She touched it, feeling somehow comforted by the little reminder of the happiness they had once shared beneath the oak. She would keep it, forever and ever, even after the leaves crumbled away. She wondered how much her mother had really loved her, and wished they could have been friends.

Realizing that their refusal to accept a pardon was adding fuel to Georgians' hatred of the Cherokee, and was disrupting the Union and bringing increased harassment to the Indians, reluctantly, the missionaries signed the hated Georgia oath, and in January of 1833 they were released. By then their stubborn insistence on refusing a pardon had only highlighted Georgia's successful defiance of the ruling in favor of the missionaries and the Cherokee, and the pompous leaders of that state were satisfied that Georgia looked like the ultimate conqueror.

Still, the harassment did not end. Georgians, confident

and victorious, now felt they had full rights to badger the Cherokees out of their remaining land. Two nights of raiding left homes burned, women stripped and whipped and raped. Schools were closed, and white men set up shop in churches, selling liquor to those Cherokee who saw no reason to do anything in life but drink. Militia men were posted all over Cherokee country now, making sure there were no meetings and that there was no resistance. Brutality was rampant, as Georgia pumped up its efforts to make the Cherokees give up and leave. It was more and more difficult for the Cherokees to get word to the rest of the world now, and in some areas people began to forget, unaware of the horrible injustices being inflicted on the Indians in Georgia. But a handful of brave and stubborn men still managed to find ways to meet, men like John Ross and John Ridge, Elias Boudinot and Adam Chandler.

In spite of the difficulty of communicating, word did leak out now and then about what was happening to the Cherokees. There was still considerable sympathy in the North, where the freed missionaries spoke in behalf of the Indians. Margaret Jessup and her children, as well as other missionary families, had long since left Cherokee country, to wait in the North for their husbands' release. There were no whites left on Cherokee land now, other than spouses of the Indians, but many in the North continued to fight in their behalf. People complained that Andrew Jackson's government protected only the white race, and that Indians and slaves had no protection at all. The meaning of a free America was questioned, the very core of government was questioned; and Georgia became even more angry when the question of slavery kept being brought up along with the Indian problem. Fear of the North making an issue of slavery, possibly trying to abolish it, made Georgia's citizens even more anxious to get the Indians out so that things would calm down, and they became more determined to prove they were right on both the Indian and the slavery issues. With slavery being brought into the picture, other Southern states began to

335

rally behind Georgia.

During the entire year of 1832, while the missionaries were still imprisoned, the militia had brutalized the Cherokees, yet there was a faint hope for the Indians. It was an election year, and Jackson's opponent was Henry Clay, a National Republican and a strong advocate of Indian rights. Clay's running mate was John Sergeant, the attorney from Pennsylvania who had fought for the Cherokees. A third party, called the Anti-Masonic party and composed primarily of the religious persons in the North, also ran against Jackson, led by William Wirt, the attorney who had taken the Cherokee missionaries' case to the Supreme Court. But with two Indian sympathizers running, it was thought that the votes for Jackson would be split up enough to keep him from winning.

But many who were in sympathy with the Indians voted for Andrew Jackson, afraid that with so much shouting pro and con, the country's unity would suffer without the firm hand of Andrew Jackson. More and more Cherokees withdrew to the hills, some of them living in caves. Indians still hanging on in other states were also suffering. More Choctaws were shipped out. The Seminoles retreated into the Florida swamps. The Creeks were rooted out of their strongholds and sent west, the men in chains. More and more Southern states felt they must get rid of the Indians and quiet down public outcry so as to draw attention away from the slavery issue.

Andrea fretted because her sons were not getting enough sunshine and fresh air, for she was terrified of letting them play alone outside, and terrified of being outside herself. She feared Douglas Means might find their cabin and drag her off. Adam's heart ached for his family. He felt badly about his inability to provide a good home for them, and about his sad neglect of his sons. He wanted to play with them, ride with them, teach them so many things. But it was impossible. His days and nights were spent at meetings, while Andrea taught them their letters and numbers as best she could. She tried to keep their family life as calm and normal as possible, while Adam fretted over newspaper articles and petitions. And still they fought. They printed the *Cherokee Phoenix*, refusing to halt the newspaper unless the militia came through New Echota and destroyed it, and John Ross and others ran back and forth to Washington to cope with more legal snags and to make personal pleas for help.

But a dangerous split was beginning to come about, the split John Ross had feared would come. The poorest Cherokees left their little farms and fled to the hills where they lived in huts and caves. The wealthier ones who chose to fight also abandoned their homes, took to the hills, and built themselves reasonably comfortable cabins. But it was becoming more and more obvious that among the wealthy only certain men were singled out for harassment and beatings and confiscation of property—those who fought Removal. The others were left alone, and all knew that informants and traitors were becoming more numerous. Some of the wealthier Cherokees, afraid of losing everything, were now speaking in favor of Removal, insisting it would be best after all, for the safety and health of the people. In some respects they were right, for fighting it was surely a losing battle. But in the heat of love and passion for one's land and one's rights, common sense does not always prevail. Anyone speaking for Removal was considered a traitor, and both factions were gaining a following. The very split Georgians had hoped for was coming to the Cherokees, the split that would weaken them.

Leaders of the pro-Removal group emerged—John Ridge and Elias Boudinot among them. During the heated controversy, whether they were right or wrong did not seem to matter. Hatred was building, a hatred that Adam could see would last for years, and in his own heart he knew he could never forgive those who were giving up, nor would he ever forgive Luke Cloud.

Passions and loyalties came to a head in late 1834, when Adam gathered everyone in front of the fireplace after three-and-a-half-year-old Jonas and two-year-old John were asleep. Andrea watched her husband. He was twenty-four now, but had the countenance and air of someone much older, as well he should. He had been through a lifetime in the past four or five years, or so it seemed. At twenty-two she looked even younger than her years, but felt much older. Their happy days under the oak tree seemed to have occurred a hundred years ago, but their lovemaking, though less frequent because of their situation, remained sweet and beautiful, and was made more precious by the transient condition of their day-to-day life. They were man and woman now, yet young enough to be enjoying life to the fullest. But hatred and greed had deprived them of the peace and happiness they deserved.

"There is a bad split among the people," Adam told them, lighting a pipe. "John Ridge and Boudinot are furious because John Ross came back from Washington to tell us he refused an offer of three million dollars from President Jackson to get out."

"Three million!" James whistled. "That is a lot of money, Adam."

"Not when you divide it among thousands of families." He puffed on the pipe. "Besides, it's the principle of the thing. But I figured you should know. We all have to decide. It's getting down to the worst now, and I want to take a vote right here and now among all of you. From here on we'll get pushed back into the hills. I no longer hold any high hopes of winning this thing, but John Ross still thinks it's possible, and what we've come down to is a matter of pride and a belief in what is right. I'll stay and fight until they put a bayonet in my belly and force me to go. I need to know what the rest of you want to do."

James took Ruth's hand. "We're staying, no matter what, even though Ruth is pregnant." Ruth put a hand to her swollen stomach. She considered her baby a gift from God to help her forget the horrors of the past. She still lived in fear of the future, but she would have her baby. And she had her brother's stubborn will. "I want to stay," she told Adam.

Their eyes held and he nodded, then shifted his eyes to his mother. She held up her chin defiantly. "I stay, in honor of your father's memory. I will not run, not after he died fighting to stay."

"I'm too old to care what happens to me," Martha Bluecrow declared, scratching at a wrinkled cheek. "I'll stay and fight the bastards!"

Everyone grinned a little. "We will stay to the end, too," James's father stated. "We have come too far to give up now."

Adam's eyes moved to Andrea, and she smiled for him. "You know my answer." He saw the fear in her eyes, and loved her all the more. "Wherever you go, I go. Just remember your promise. Someday that land will be yours again, and we will sit under the oak tree."

He blinked back tears and puffed on the pipe again. "It's settled then. We all stand behind John Ross. And I intend to make sure plenty of others do the same. If Elias Boudinot and John Ridge want to run off just to protect their riches, let them. I hope they can live with themselves later. In their hearts I suppose they think they're right, that it's best for the People. But right now I cannot make myself believe it's anything but an effort to save their precious wealth. They'll end up taking money from the government to get out, and they'll no doubt have a nice safe, comfortable journey, but I would rather sleep with snakes than take something from the government and run at this point. Still, if any of you changes his or her mind, I will understand. We have nothing left now. You wouldn't be leaving just to protect possessions. Ruth, you and my mother have already suffered too much. You needn't take any more risks. It's your choice, and I will love you whether you stay or go."

"You know we won't go, Adam," Ruth told him. "Save your speeches for the others. They aren't needed here with your family. We love you, and are proud of everything you have done. And we have our Cherokee pride to think of."

Adam sighed and rubbed at tired eyes. "And I love all of you." He tamped out his pipe and set it on the mantel. Everyone quietly watched him, but he said nothing more. He hurried out of the room, going to his bedroom and closing the door.

"Three million dollars!" James murmured. "Ol' Jackson must be getting desperate, huh? We're sure giving them a run for it!"

Andrea stared at the bedroom door, but she did not go to her husband. She knew he needed to be alone for now, knew the terrible weight that he carried. If she could lighten it, she would gladly do so. But there was nothing she could do, other than stand at his side through whatever was to come.

CHAPTER TWENTY

Government payoffs and promises of safety became more and more evident, as the homes and property of the wealthier Cherokees who had fought Removal were seized by the militia. John Ross soon found himself and his family homeless, and he joined those who had moved farther into the hills. Yet the land of the wealthy Cherokee who preached Removal remained untouched. All avenues to education were closed. All gatherings ended. The office of the *Phoenix* was ransacked and the paper was put out of business. The militia moved into Cherokee country, setting up headquarters in taverns and stables, in former mission buildings, in schools and council houses.

During 1834 seven hundred Cherokees gave up the struggle and journeyed westward, and tragedy followed as it had followed the others who had undertaken the trip to a new land. Eighty-one of them died of measles and cholera, forty-five of them under the age of ten, and half of those who survived the trip died from yet another cholera epidemic in Indian Territory. Then a further blow came to John Ross's dream of winning his battle when the American Mission Board decided it would no longer continue its work among the Cherokees remaining in Georgia, considering the brutal treatment of the missionaries who had already worked among them. Missionaries were sent instead to aid the Cherokees heading west and to help them once they'd arrived at their destination.

Still, those who believed in John Ross remained totally devoted to their leader. Most of them lived in the woods and hills now, obeying the order that they must not retaliate against those who came to brutalize and harass them. All firmly believed that by remaining nonviolent the injustices committed against them would rally the hearts of the American people and bring pressure against the government to let the Cherokees stay.

While they were attacked from the outside, the Cherokees were splitting apart from within. Pro-Removal Indians called for a vote, declaring that John Ridge should be their leader rather than John Ross, but the majority of the remaining Cherokees overwhelmingly chose John Ross to continue to represent them. Upon Ross's arrival in Washington, however, he was surprised to find that John Ridge and some of his supporters had come by another route, to appear in Washington and declare that many Cherokees were now in favor of Removal. John Ross's efforts in Congress to win anti-Removal favor were overshadowed by the appearance of the Ridge men, who made it impossible for him to get enough support against Removal.

The divison was becoming even greater. The President declared he would deal only with John Ridge and his men, but since John Ross was the elected president of the Cherokees, Ridge could not truly speak for the People. A new offer of five million dollars was made, but Ross again turned it down, causing hot arguments among the Cherokee leaders once they got home.

Adam walked behind the cabin with Andrea. The morning was quiet, and they had awakened early, had quietly come together and shared bodies, fearing that today could be their last day of peace for a long time to come. Removal seemed to be inevitable now, yet Adam would not give up on John Ross. He would not desert the man, nor would he leave his homeland without one last struggle.

They walked together, enjoying the beautiful early summer morning. Dew still blanketed grass and leaves, and the forest was alive with birds and spring wildflowers.

"In moments like this, everything is peaceful and beautiful," Andrea said quietly, looking up at the tall cedars and oaks, the pine and walnut trees. "It seems there is no militia, no Indian Removal, no hatred and greed. Why can't men just leave each other alone? What's so terrible about the Cherokee living here in their own land? Sometimes I just can't grasp it all, Adam."

He led her to a wooden bench, on which they sat down. He kept an arm around her, and she rested her head on his strong shoulder. His dark eyes drank in the rays of sun piercing the canopy of leaves in a splendid display. A squirrel dashed in front of them, chattering as it rustled through fallen leaves from last autumn, then scampering up a walnut tree. Adam's throat was tight at the thought of leaving this beautiful land. He missed his farm, the happy days there, his home, the old oak tree. How could he leave these hills? He loved the land as much as he loved the woman who sat beside him now. He kissed her hair.

"I don't understand it either, Andrea. Never once did we commit one wrong against the people of Georgia. Every argument we have presented in the Georgia courts and to the Supreme Court has been valid and undeniable. It's like pointing to the sun and having someone say it isn't there. They take the bold truth and throw it to the wind, and for only one reason. They want this land. It is valuable, fertile, beautiful—and gold lies beneath it in some places. It's jealousy, Andrea. Plain jealousy. Jealousy can be a mean, vengeful, ugly thing. It can destroy." He sighed and took his arm away, taking a pipe from his pocket and packing it with tobacco from a pouch he carried at his waist.

Andrea watched him. He was twenty-five now, an extremely handsome man with dark, moving eyes and a very masculine build. He was strong, not just physically, but emotionally; intelligent, determined. Her heart ached for him, for what he was going through, yet she knew that if he was forced to leave his country, he would do so with head held high, with the knowledge that at least he had fought for his rights and gone down fighting. The Cherokee had thrown the state and federal governments off their course over and over again, stumping them with truth and fact, slowing them because of the overwhelming support of the religious communities of the North, as well as the support of many Southern citizens. Their fight had delayed Removal for years, but now things were fast coming to a head. Andrea worried as much about the strife from within as she did about the attacks from without.

Adam lit his pipe and puffed on it for a moment. When Andrea watched him, she sometimes shivered at the pleasant realization that this handsome man she was looking at had bedded her, had planted his seed in her, touched and explored her, owned her. Her love for him bordered on worship. She would follow him into the pits of hell if necessary, just to be with Adam Chandler. He turned and met her blue eyes, grinning as she reddened.

"All right, woman, what were you just thinking?"

She laughed lightly and looked away. "Just about you . . . about this morning . . . how beautiful you are . . . how much I love you."

His eyes ran over her slender form. She seemed to get more beautiful every year, and she was exquisite and charming—a strong woman who had held up well under adversity. She had given him two beautiful sons, and lived with the ache of wondering about the third. Sometimes, to him, she was still the little Andrea he had teased and cajoled into lying naked with him under the oak tree, the girl who had let him claim her virginity in that first beautiful and exciting union.

"I love you, Andrea," he said softly. "Do I tell you enough?"

She met his eyes then, drinking in his manly handsomeness. "You tell me all the time. Do I tell you enough?"

He grinned. "You don't have to say it in words. Just being here, hidden away in the forest risking all kinds of abuse to stay at my side, that says it more than words." He turned away then, resting his elbows on his knees and puffing at the pipe again. "There is a lot of hatred amongst our own people now. It worries me. Some talk about chasing off John Ridge and Elias Boudinot. Some even talk of killing them."

She studied him closely, put a hand on his arm. "And you?"

He kept puffing the pipe and staring at the cabin. "I've thought of it," he finally replied. "I think they're totally wrong, yet I can't bring myself to do them harm because I think in their minds they believe they're right. They really believe it would be best for us to go peacefully, and in the end perhaps they will be right. But I can't do it, Andrea. I just can't do it. I'm sorry, because it will probably mean great danger for us all, a lot of hardship and abuse. There are missionaries in the North who would gladly take in you and the boys. Or maybe you have relatives farther south—"

"No! I won't leave you. Don't make me leave you, Adam!"

"You could always join me later, after all this hell is over with."

"No! I'm as much Cherokee now as you are. Your sons are Cherokee. I won't leave you to face this alone. Together, we'll protect and care for the boys. We'll be all right, Adam. It's my decision. I'm ready for whatever is to come."

He turned to face her then, his eyes full of pain. "Are you ready to face Douglas Means if it should come to that?"

Some of the color drained from her face, but she held his eyes boldly, refusing to look shaken. Nonetheless, he could see her fear and revulsion as she swallowed before answering. "I am. Let him come! Even if he were to . . ." She swallowed again. "Your mother told me . . . a woman can be touched . . . without being touched at all. In her mind, your father is the only man she ever loved and the only man who ever touched her as a woman. No man can take away what I have known in your arms, Adam Chandler. I belong to you, and nothing can change that."

His dark eyes began to smolder. "That part is true. Always remember it. But I'll not let harm come to you if I can help it, and if he touches you, I will have to break my vow of nonviolence. Somehow, someday, I will kill that man anyway, even if he doesn't harm you. I will kill him for what he did to Ruth and my mother. I will find a way, Andrea. That's just between you and me, but it must be done and I will do it."

Her eyes teared. "Don't talk that way, Adam. It frightens me. You'd be hung!"

He puffed at the pipe again and shook his head. "I'll think of a way to do it so I don't get caught. But I'll do it, as God is my witness."

"Adam, please don't. It's such a beautiful morning, and we've just made love. We have so few peaceful, pretty moments like this. Don't talk about him."

He reached over and took her hand, removing his pipe with his other hand and throwing back his head to breathe deeply of the morning air.

"You're right. Let's walk. The boys will be up soon and you know what that means—no more time alone."

She smiled and rose, her heart warmed by the thought of little Jonas, nearly five now and very bright, already spelling words and speaking in both English and Cherokee. Little John Ross was three and a half, a wild, impish boy with blond curls and blue eyes, extremely handsome because of the contrast of blond hair and dark skin. Both boys were sturdy and healthy, and Andrea prayed constantly for their safety in the days ahead.

She and Adam walked to the next cabin, in which three families lived, and then went on to a third, where John Ross now dwelled. Ross was outside chopping wood, and he smiled and waved at Adam and Andrea, grateful for Adam's devotion to the cause and for the help he had provided over the years. Adam approached him, but his overture at conversation was interrupted when an open carriage clattered up the narrow dirt road that led into the mountains where they now lived, away from New Echota.

Both men sobered, and Adam pushed Andrea behind

him. "Don't try to get back to our place. Go inside John's cabin," he told her quietly. "Hurry up!"

She dashed inside and closed the door, telling the Ross family not to go out. She latched the door, but stayed near it, listening, her heart pounding. Everyone in the house quieted, waiting.

The approaching carriage carried two men, both white and both wearing well-tailored suits. They stopped in front of the Ross cabin and stared at John and Adam.

"Might one of you be John Ross?" one of them asked. He was a heavyset man and wore a gold watch on his vest.

"I'm John Ross." He stepped forward. "What do you want?"

The heavyset man climbed down, several long sheets of paper in his hand. "I'm representing John F. Schermerhorn, United States Commissioner. Have you heard of him?"

Ross slammed his ax into a log. "I've heard of him. He's the man who deceived the Seminole into signing a document they didn't understand, and it is now being used to claim the Seminole agreed to move West. But they are not budging, nor are we."

The robust man with the papers reddened, then eyed Ross and Adam closely. "Mr. Schermerhorn is not a deceitful man," he retorted. "He is a United States representative who has the best interest of our Indian population in mind. Believe me, Mr. Ross, it is for your own good that we urge you to leave for Indian Territory without further resistance. To hold out until the end can only bring disaster."

Ross folded his arms, and Adam walked closer beside him. "Just why are you here, mister?" he asked.

"Mr. Schermerhorn wants to meet with all the Cherokees to explain this." The man held out the papers, and John took them with reservation. "That is a new treaty proposed by the government. Mr. Schermerhorn will explain it in every detail to your people, and a vote will be taken in October, at Red Clay. Make sure your people are there. We'll have a more specific date when you meet with

Mr. Schermerhorn in New Echota one week from today. In the meantime, you would be wise to look this over and talk to your people about it. Get them to come to the meeting, Mr. Ross."

"And if we don't show up?"

The fat man's eyes narrowed. "It could be bad for you if you don't cooperate, Mr. Ross. I suggest that you do."

Ross folded the papers, then reached out and stuffed them into the surprised man's vest. "I'd rather stuff these someplace else," he said calmly. "You take these papers to Schermerhorn and tell him the only meeting we'll come to is the final voting, so that the Cherokee people can show him just what they think of a treaty. The treaties we have already made with the government have all been broken. The food and supplies that we are supposed to receive are not being issued to us. Many of our people are starving. But we'll make it through the summer and we'll crawl to the voting place in October and vote your treaty into hell! Good day, sir."

The fat man was furious. "You're a fool, John Ross!"

"And you are on my property, sir. I suggest you get off it right away." Ross put his hand on the ax and the government man's eyes widened, for he was certain that every Indian was a savage. He hurried back to the coach and it was driven off.

Ross turned to Adam and they shook hands. But both knew the gravity of the situation. "I might as well tell you, Adam, that I'm going across the border into Tennessee. I have no doubt that if I stay here I will be arrested, and I can't continue the fight if I'm in prison. Some people in Tennessee have offered me refuge. The Georgia Militia can't touch me there. It will only be for a while, until this voting nonsense is over. And a man who wants to write a book about Cherokee history is meeting me there. I think that is very important. His name is John Howard Payne. Have you heard of him?"

Adam's eyebrows arched. "He is very famous. Of course I have heard of him. He is a fine choice to do a book about the Cherokee. And such a book can only help our cause."

"Yes. I hope you understand why I have to go. And I want you to lie low for a while and stay out of the picture, understand? Things are going to get very bad. Just hang on and trust that I will return."

"I'll do whatever you say."

Ross's eyes teared. "I know. You're a brilliant young man, Adam. Whatever happens, I think you'll be very successful, even if you have to leave Georgia. I appreciate your loyalty and all your hard work. These are times when a man finds out who his friends really are."

Adam nodded. "This is true. I am afraid that many who once called themselves friends are becoming enemies."

Ross pulled the ax from the log. "I am afraid you're right, Adam. If we are forced to go to Indian Territory, I am afraid much blood will be spilled among the Cherokee once we get there, and the hatred will run deep for a long time to come."

During the summer of 1835 Georgia's efforts to "encourage" the Cherokees to vote for the treaty were intensified. There were surprise raids by the militia, and the poorer Indians who lived in open huts and caves were subjected to beatings and rapes. Their huts were burned, and their meat and other food stuffs were destroyed. Adam and Andrea and their family now spent many nights in the secret caverns beneath their cabin. More than once Douglas Means broke down the door to their cabin, certain this particular house belonged to Adam Chandler. But there was never anyone inside. Faithful friends told the militia that Adam Chandler no longer lived there, that he had fled to Tennessee with John Ross, but Adam and Andrea were forced to live in the caverns below the cabin a good part of the time, entering and exiting through heavy wooden planks that, when put in place, looked like any normal floor. The widow, Martha Bluecrow occupied the cabin now, along with two other families invited to stay there so that the cabin was used and would not draw too much attention. Even Douglas Means finally stopped harassing them, convinced that Adam must really have gone to Tennessee, for even after beatings the people inside insisted he was not around. His anguish over what people were doing for his protection was almost more than Adam could bear. More than once he had come close to charging out of his hiding place and landing into Douglas Means. His desire to kill the man was becoming an obsession, and their current situation worried Andrea, for now there was no time at all for lovely, peaceful things, for beauty, or even for making love. Adam began to drink whiskey more often than was his habit, and she could see a growing restlessness in her husband that could only spell disaster for him.

The vote was taken in October. The harassment had ceased temporarily, and many Cherokees, including Adam, showed up for the vote, held at a neutral spot on the Georgia-Tennessee border. The Cherokees overwhelmingly voted down the treaty. Even Elias Boudinot and John Ridge voted against it, for fear of being assassinated by their own people.

It was then announced that another vote would be taken at New Echota at a later date. Schermerhorn knew that the Cherokees would be afraid to go there, for New Echota, and most Cherokee land, was completely overrun now by white settlers and the militia. He informed them that any who did not show up would be considered as voting for the treaty. But from his stronghold in Tennessee John Ross managed to get letters to his people, urging them to hold out against all attack and urging them not to go to New Echota, for it would be too dangerous. The people's continued support of John Ross angered the Georgia leaders into raiding his hideaway in Tennessee and arresting both Ross and John Howard Payne.

It was a wrong move. John Howard Payne was a famous and highly respected author. His treatment, and that of John Ross, brought new outcries from Cherokee sympathizers. The two men were held at Spring Place, locked in a log outhouse. At one point the rotted and decaying body of

350

a dead Cherokee prisoner was hung over their heads. Ross's records and papers were confiscated and searched, as were Payne's notes, and Payne was labeled an abolitionist, a tag that often meant death to a man during those times. But Georgia authorities had gone too far; sympathy for the Cherokees was renewed. And after nearly two weeks of imprisonment Ross and Payne were let go.

Not only had their treatment instigated a new nation-wide protest, the Georgia Militia had deeply angered the State of Tennessee by crossing into that state without permission. The governor of Georgia was forced to submit a written apology to the governor of Tennessee, for Tennesseeans had threatened to cross Georgia's borders. Furthermore Ross's arrest had increased the Cherokees desire to fight, and had enhanced their spirit of rebellion.

Ross again went to Washington, armed with tales of the latest atrocities committed against him and with a new wave of sympathy and support that again put Georgia and the federal government at odds. His continued fight encouraged the Cherokees and they refused to take part in a government census in late 1835. The enraged Georgia officials gave the militia full permission to "convince" the Indians to cooperate, and many were dragged out of their homes and stripped and beaten. Still, less than five hundred of the over seventeen thousand Cherokees remaining in Georgia appeared for the new treaty vote in New Echota in December. A few hundred of the most destitute signed the treaty, and to everyone's surprise, the more prominent Cherokees like John Ridge, Elias Boudinot, and Stand Watie also signed, declaring they did so in the best interest of their people. The final bitter division of the Cherokee people had come about.

Although the treaty could not possibly be considered to represent the majority of the Cherokee, John Ross knew that the government would have it declared valid. The document was presented to Congress, and again, perhaps for a last and final time, the fate of the Cherokee lay in the hands of Congress and the people of the United States. If this treaty was ratified, the long fight would be over. The Cherokee would be forced to leave their homeland.

The wheels of power and politics were in motion and would not be stopped, in spite of considerable Congressional sympathy and of the eloquent speeches made in Congress on behalf of the Indians by such compelling men as Daniel Webster and Henry Clay. This was an election year, and Jackson's Democrats were strong. To be sure his party remained in power, and thinking his strongest support was in the South, Jackson chose Martin Van Buren to run as his successor, a Northerner. The majority of the people voted for the still-popular Democratic party, meaning another administration that backed Indian Removal. And this administration's Congress would vote on the ratification of the Cherokee treaty. Still, many congressmen who declared the treaty an act of unforgivable injustice to the Indians could, or should, be counted on to vote down the treaty. There was a last remnant of hope for John Ross and the others. If nothing more, guilt over the wrongs committed against the Indians should be enough to force some congressmen to act on conscience alone and declare the treaty invalid. Half the country and many prominent, well-spoken men had rallied behind the Cherokee and had delivered moving and convincing speeches on behalf of the Indian.

Yet in the midst of the turmoil over the Indian issue, Andrew Jackson himself, before stepping down from presidency, addressed a letter to the Cherokee Nation, warning them that for their own well-being they should no longer deceive themselves into thinking they could stay in Georgia. He urged them to leave as early as possible, signing the letter "Your friend, Andrew Jackson."

To further endanger the Cherokee cause, the Seminoles, no longer able to bear the abuses rained upon them by whites in Florida, began to retaliate. Raids were conducted. Settlers were murdered and their homes and crops burned. The government recognized the Seminoles as being officially at war. Troops were sent to Florida, and fear of Indian wars spread like wildfire. People began to reason that if the Seminoles were making war, the Creeks, Choctaws, and Cherokees were sure to follow. Rumors were used to plant distrust in the hearts of those who had spoken in defense of the Cherokee. It seemed that at every turn something happened to threaten any hopes of a Cherokee victory. Congress began to rally in support of Indian Removal, to eliminate further danger to white settlers who lived near or on Indian lands. Yet many Northern Congressmen, pressured by the Indian sympathizers among their constituents, continued to support their promise to vote down the treaty. John Ross waited with an aching heart for the final vote, as did the men who were formerly his friends but were now adversaires—Elias Boudinot and John Ridge. Both Cherokee factions were represented in Washington, and John Ross knew that no matter how the vote went, hatreds conceived because of the split would be long in healing.

The rumor quickly spread that the treaty would be voted down by one precarious vote—one congressman would make it a majority decision. John Ross took hope. But unknown to him, that one senator mysteriously changed his mind overnight. No one would ever know just who he was, or what had changed his decision, but the power of politics had again reared its ugly head, steering someone from what was morally right to what was most beneficial to himself. However, the rumor that this man's vote had changed, which would make the treaty valid by a one-vote majority, gave those Northern Congressmen who had held out against the ratification more incentive to vote according to their party's direction, rather than expressing the wishes of the people of their states, who were in sympathy with the Indians. Therefore, instead of the treaty being ratified by only one vote, it was ratified by a vote of thirty-one to fifteen.

The final blow had been delivered. The North had turned against the Indians in the final test, even once-supportive states like Maine, New Hampshire, New York,

Pennsylvania, Indiana, and Illinois. All the traveling and preaching in the North—the trips to Washington, the petitions and letters, the struggle to remain nonviolent—were to no avail.

John Ross was stunned. Daniel Webster would later declare the treaty a "base fraud on the Cherokee Indians." There was hardly a person involved in the conflict who did not recognize that everything that had been done to the Cherokees, and to all Indians, was against everything the United States government was supposed to stand for, and for a long time to come the men in power during those troubled times would suffer pangs of guilt and wonder if there was not something more they could have done.

John Ross headed for Georgia to deliver the final blow to his people. They had trusted him, believed in him. They had turned down all offers of money for their land. Now there would be nothing. If they could get away with their very lives, they would be lucky. The ratified treaty was all Georgia needed to move in and herd the Cherokees into migration.

The Cherokees were told that they would be given two years to migrate to Indian Territory. But Georgians were anxious. Again harassment and abuse was used by the militia to "convince" the Indians to go sooner. Terror spread among the Cherokees, who began to fight amongst themselves, and Andrea lived in fear every moment Adam was gone. Finally federal troops were sent in, under Brigadier General John Ellis Wool, who assumed command of Cherokee country and ousted all militia personnel. To the Cherokees the move was a godsend, eliminating some of the fear and terror under which they lived. But the troops had been told to expect retaliation by Cherokee "warriors," and stockades were quickly built to house the "rebellious Indians." To Wool's surprise, however, the Cherokee remained nonviolent to outsiders, preferring dignity and one staunch last stand to bloodshed. In spite of all that had been done to them, the

Cherokee refused to bend to Georgia's efforts to make them go to war, which was all Georgia needed to ride in and wipe them out to the last woman and child. Wool soon found himself in sympathy with the Cherokee, and he regretted the pitiful condition to which the once-proud and wealthy Cherokee had been lowered. Sickness and hunger was rampant among them, but none hung their heads.

Pro-treaty Cherokees like John Ridge and Elias Boudinot began to regret their actions, for in the end they realized they had only been used and fooled by the government. Once the treaty was ratified, their own land and possessions were taken by the militia, and only the presence of federal troops finally quieted the ruckus. Tennessee troops were also sent in, for they were not as anti-Indian as were the Georgia men.

There was a lull in militia violence during the presence of the federal troops. Andrea could take the children outside to play and enjoy sunshine and fresh air. Adam was gone almost constantly, but he knew that she was safe for the time being. He and John Ross and others helped the sick and the destitute, and guided the People in how to prepare for Removal; yet both still believed that somehow the good people of America would rally behind them and somehow stop the terrible thing that was happening.

Wilson Lumpkin, now governor of Georgia and the appointed U.S. Commissioner in charge of effecting Removal under the new treaty, was enraged by the interference of federal troops. He whipped out letters to everyone involved, protesting the infringement of Georgia's right to conduct Removal in its own way. He was furious at the bad name that his state now had, insistent that Georgia did not deserve it, and determined that Indian Removal would take place promptly. Lumpkin men managed to convince a few Cherokees to head west, and in January and March of 1837, small migrations took place. Those first to leave were allowed to take with them their possessions—horses, cattle, furniture, and ample provisions. The thousands who held out and refused to recognize the treaty knew that they would not be granted such privileges if and when they had to go. Still they refused to budge. Because of Wool's increasing sympathy for the Indians, he was replaced by a Colonel William Lindsay in July of 1837, and John Ross was warned that if he continued to urge his people to disobey the treaty, he faced arrest.

In January of 1838 Ross made one final trip to Washington, taking with him a petition signed by over fifteen thousand Cherokees. It declared that the treaty had never been recognized by the majority of the Cherokee, and was therefore invalid. Again Ross appealed to the reason and honesty of those in power. But Congress was now unwilling to reopen the issue, especially in the face of war with the Seminoles. Ross was warned that to delay any longer in moving his people to Indian Territory would bring them only disaster and calamity. In one last impassioned speech on behalf of the Cherokees, the honored Ralph Waldo Emerson himself addressed the new President, Van Buren, in April of 1838, stating among other things that "the last howl and wailing of these tormented villagers and tribes shall afflict the ears of the world."

When Adam brought home the news that Ross's last appeal had failed, Andrea knew she had never seen more sorrow in anyone's eyes. The loss of a child could not have brought any worse pain to her husband's face. "We'd better . . . get a few things ready," he said quietly. His fighting spirit was gone. Andrea could see him withering like a vine without water. He walked to the cupboard and took out a bottle of whiskey. "At least the federal troops are still in charge. We're safe if we just do what they say."

Andrea watched him slug down some of the whiskey. She wanted to tell him to stop. She was afraid for him to drink, fearing he would fall into the state of drunken despair as had so many others. No! Not her Adam! He'd always been so proud and strong.

"Are you sure—about the federal troops?" Ruth asked in a shaking voice.

Adam lowered the bottle. He looked first at her, then at Andrea. "I'm sure. If they do not remain, and if anyone is harmed, this is one Cherokee who will not remain nonviolent!" He threw the bottle against a wall and stormed out of the cabin. Andrea stared at the shattered bottle, struggling to hold back tears, feeling that her happy life with her husband was just as shattered. She walked blindly into their bedroom and began to pack their clothing, in no particular order. Meanwhile, unknown to them, the man now in charge of the federal troops was deciding who would oversee the gathering in of the Cherokees, for he did not have enough men to cover the wide area of heavily wooded land in which the Cherokees were hiding. Major General Scott decided that to effect a rapid gathering of Indians into the holding camps, the Georgia Militia would have to be utilized. They knew the hills, and they had had experience with the Cherokee. Preparations got underway. In the spring, the Cherokees must go.

CHAPTER TWENTY-ONE

Eleven-year-old Indian walked on thin legs to his bed. He was tall for his age, and the other boys and the overseers of the orphanage where he lived had dropped Little from his name. Now he was just Indian. But more and more he wondered about himself, about the mysterious white mother he was supposed to have, and the Indian father, though both apparently had abandoned him. He wanted to know why they had left him to this life. Somewhere he had something others called a family. But whenever he asked Big Father or Miss Williams about it, they told him he must never think about his mother and father, that he would never know them, that he must be good and work hard until he was eighteen. Then he could leave the orphanage and make a life for himself.

But where would he go? What would he do? The only work he knew how to do was in the factories, where he ran machines fourteen hours a day, every day. He rose early, ate bread and butter, got into the enclosed coach and went to the factory, where he worked seven hours straight with no break; then he was allowed a half-hour for the little sack lunch Miss Williams gave him each day. After eating he worked six and a half more hours, then went home. It was already dark. He ate soup, and on rare occasions some meat, sometimes even some fruit, but that was a rare treat. It was the same for all the boys at the orphanage. There was no time to play, and often one of his friends would disappear. Miss Williams always told him the boy had "gone away," nothing more. It frightened him. Some of the older boys said those who disappeared had actually died from working too hard. They simply were not strong enough to be good factory workers. Indian was not sure what dying meant, except that there was something frighteningly final about it.

He rubbed at aching muscles and curled up against his pillow, wondering if he would someday "go away" because of all the hard work. He wondered about the people he saw when he walked from the dark coach to the hot factory. Under blue skies, they walked around on the streets, some smiling and laughing, big women with little children at their sides. Surely they were mothers. It seemed to him it must be a nice thing to have a mother, and to walk about in that world he did not know; to be free to run, to touch grass and watch the sun.

He shivered and pulled the blankets around him. He could not forget the horrible accident that had occurred that day. Another boy's arm had been severed. So much blood! Why had the boss man waited so long to get the boy help? Had that boy "gone away" too? He had not come back to the orphanage that night. Indian swallowed back fear and a desire to cry. Every day he wondered if it was his turn to get hurt. He was as careful as he could be with the big machinery. He never complained, and he made no trouble. Those who were very, very good and had no accidents, those who were smarter than the others, sometimes got to work at the orphanage instead of the factories. They were allowed to do odd jobs for Miss Williams, to clean her many books and serve her her meals. Indian intended to get such a job someday. If he did, he would look at all those books. Somehow he would learn how to read and write, as he'd seen Miss Williams do many times. He had asked her about it, but she'd told him Indians must not be taught to read and write, that it was not good for them. He could not imagine what could be wrong with looking at little figures and figuring out how they spelled words. His mind was alert and bright, and he wanted to know more, about books and writing, about the outside world, the sky, and other people. And he especially wanted to know about his mother and father. Maybe Miss Williams had some papers hidden away that told all about him. If he could find them, and then find out what they said, he might find his mother and father.

Charles Adam Bird was born in the spring of 1838. But the joy of his birth was marred by the disaster about to befall the Cherokees. Ruth and James knew their little son would not grow up in the beloved homeland. It was only a matter of time before the federal troops came to take them away. There was no place left to hide, nowhere to run. There were only those last weeks of agonizing waiting.

The waiting ended in horror, in the wee hours of morning just before the sun was full up, when they slept hard, unaware that outside the cabin men had gathered for the roundup of Cherokees. But these were not federals.

It wasn't even daylight yet when Adam and Andrea awoke to the sound of the cabin door being chopped open with axes. In their sleepy state there was little time to react to the unexpected intrusion. Adam quickly pulled on a pair of pants, cursing the fact that just days earlier federal troops had confiscated all his weapons. He had expected them to come soon to take him and his family away, but they had not been abusive, and he had not expected them to come at such an early hour and to crash into his home unannounced.

Andrea groped for her robe, her heart pounding with terror. "Adam, the boys!" Already men could be heard storming around the outer room, ordering everyone up. Their own bedroom door burst open then, and even though lighted lamps were behind the soldier so that she could not see his face in the dark room, instinct told her who it was. Andrea backed away.

"What the hell is going on!" Adam roared.

"Outside," came a voice. "Get out here where we can see your faces."

"Is this the way the federal government conducts our removal? Plenty of people will hear about this!"

"We aren't Federals, Indian. We're Georgia Militia. Now get out of this room!"

Andrea choked back a whimper, and Adam was immediately across the bed and at her side. He held her close. "The militia isn't supposed to be a part of this," he said coldly, gripping her tightly.

"Well, plans changed."

Another soldier came into the room, while in the main room Andrea and Adam could hear crying.

"Let me go to my children!" Andrea whimpered.

The second soldier held up a lamp, and she paled at the realization that her suspicion was true. The voice of the man who had ordered them up was too familiar. Douglas Means grinned when he saw his captives.

"Well, well. I knew you two lived here. My timing was right this time."

Adam moved quickly. It would be better to die and know Andrea would not be harmed than to go peacefully. Andrea screamed his name as he charged into Means so fast that Douglas could not fire his gun. The two men went crashing into the outer room, and there was no doubt Douglas Means would have died at Adam Chandler's hands at that moment. But there were too many soldiers. Andrea ran after him but was pushed away, and forced to watch in horror as heavily booted feet kicked at her husband and gun butts smashed into him until he was unable to fight back. Douglas Means had easily scrambled away, and he only grinned at Andrea's screams while her husband was beaten. She was pushed back by more soldiers, until she stood against a wall alongside the rest of the family. Eight-year-old Jonas ran to kick at the men who were hurting his father, but he was struck by another soldier and pushed back to Andrea. She clung to the struggling boy.

"No, Jonas. They'll hurt you!"

"They're hurting Father!" the boy raged, tears on his face. Six-and-a-half-year-old John clung to his mother's housecoat and cried, and Ruth cringed behind her husband, her horrified eyes on Douglas Means.

It had all happened in seconds, with no time to think or fight back or hide. Everyone was gathered now, standing in nightgowns and underwear. The room seemed filled with yelling and screaming and crying. Adam had fought like a madman until a barrage of feet and fists and gun butts had silenced him. Then Douglas had finally ordered the men to stop pummeling him.

"I want him to live," he said with cold bitterness. "I want him to know I have his wife." He turned cool gray eyes to Andrea, and she felt vomit rise in her throat. "I no longer need to worry about spoiling an innocent virgin, do I, Andrea?" His eyes moved over her as the room quieted, except for the sounds of whimpering women. "It's been a lot of years since that little slut Andrea Sanders tried to fight me off in a barn. Now I shall finish what I started there. I'll let your stinking Indian man live so he can know you're in my hands. He'll regret putting his own hands on a white girl, especially one that belonged to me."

Andrea clung to her sons, her heart pounding so hard she could barely breathe, terror engulfing her, her eyes on Adam now as the other soldiers cuffed his wrists. Heavy chains were attached to the cuffs.

"Keep him separate from the others," Douglas ordered. "Chain him behind a wagon, but leave it empty. When you get him to the holding camp, keep him chained outside the walls of the camp. He's one of the leaders and he'll keep them stirred if they see him, especially if they see he's been beaten. It's important he be kept away from the others." His eyes came back to Andrea and her sons. "Are these the only half-breed bastards you have?" he sneered.

"Don't hurt my sons," she answered, suddenly calming in the face of danger to her children.

"Come along quietly and I won't, dear Andrea."

How she managed to make herself walk, she wasn't sure. She only knew that to resist could bring harm to her boys and more harm to Adam. "Please let the others gather some of their belongings and . . . some of ours."

Douglas grinned. Reaching out and placing a hand under her robe, he groped at a breast. "You've matured, dear Andrea. And I must say, you are much prettier. How sad that you wasted your gifts on an Indian man."

She jerked away but he grabbed her hair and yanked her back, pinning her against him. "I think it's about time you found out what a white man is like, don't you?"

He shoved her over to two other men. "Take her back to my tent and hold her there. And don't let anybody touch her. She's mine." His eyes moved over her coldly. "Every last little intimate part of her."

The two men pulled her out the door, amid cries of "Mommy, Mommy" from her sons. James Bird's parents and Rose hurriedly grasped the boys as they tried to run after their mother, and Adam struggled through black pain and near unconsciousness, wanting to go to her. He mumbled her name, but men were dragging him somewhere. Soon he was outside in the early morning dew. The sky was just beginning to get light, and he could hear horses riding off, hear more orders being given, hear his sons crying. Were they being hurt? Someone yanked at his wrists. He was chained to something.

"You'd better find your senses and walk, Indian, or you'll be dragged," a voice told him. He struggled to get to his feet. Andrea! Where was Andrea! She'd been taken away. Douglas Means had taken her away! No! No! He had to kill! He had to kill Douglas Means and save Andrea!

He began to pull wildly at his chains, but they were hooked to something. He pulled and pulled, ignoring the raw pain at his wrists.

"Adam, please stay calm!" He heard his mother's voice then. "You're badly hurt, and they'll hurt you more if you fight them!"

"Shut up, woman, and go get in the other wagon!" a man bellowed.

He could hear Jonas screaming then, knew the boy was kicking and fighting as he kept shouting at the soldiers, calling them names, telling them to let him go to his father and to bring back his mother. "My father will kill all of you if you hurt my mother!" the boy yelled, and he then let out a string of insults.

There was a loud slap and a sort of thud then, and Adam didn't hear his son's voice again. Rage and sorrow overwhelmed him, and he tugged at the chains again, gritting his teeth against tears. "Jonas!" he groaned. "Bastards!" he shouted louder then. "Sons of bitches! Stinking white cowards! Cowards! You're all cowards! There is not a man among you!"

Over and over he tugged at the chains like a wild animal. But minutes later he had to stop tugging and start walking, for the wagon had jolted into movement. He threw back his head and breathed deeply of the morning air, thinking that perhaps if he breathed deeply enough, he could get enough of his beloved mountain air into his lungs to keep it there forever and take it with him to the barren, unfamiliar land where they would be taken.

His mind reeled with a horrible mixture of emotions. Douglas Means had his wife, perhaps his sons were hurt, and he was being taken from his homeland. It was really happening. The very thing they had fought against for so many years was now happening. The mountains! The valleys! The green trees and running waters. The animals and the sweet red earth. The old farm, and the giant golden oak under which he and Andrea had known so much happiness. The oak! Andrea! No! He could not bear this horrible loss—not everything all at once. He could not leave this place where the earth was his true mother, the mountains his true father, the trees and flowers his strength, the running waters his blood. His ancestors' remains rested here, his own spirit lived here. To leave this place was to leave his spirit behind and to take only a shell of a man to new places. But worse than the gripping ache of leaving his homeland was the fierce need to find

Douglas Means. This could not be happening! Federal troops were supposed to come for them, not Georgia Militia.

The morning came, sunshiny and beautiful, and Adam's senses cleared somewhat, but his body was badly battered and bruised. The skin of his face was split open in several places, and blood had formed scabs on it. He knew he was badly injured, yet somehow he didn't feel the pain. His legs kept moving as he was forced to walk behind the wagon. He turned away and groaned as they passed a small cabin outside which women stood, stripped and being whipped. This could not be happening! How had the government let this happen? Didn't anyone know what was being done to the Cherokees?

He strained to see in front of him, to see if his boys were there, if his mother and sister were all right. He hoped by some miracle Andrea was with them, but he knew deep inside she was not. The choking dust from the wagons ahead prevented him from seeing anything, and the wagon to which he was attached was empty. His wrists were cuffed, and heavy chains attached the cuffs to an iron latch embedded into the tailgate of the wagon. Horror and anger engulfed him anew, and he began to tug again, not caring that his wrists were bleeding and raw now, one cut nearly to the bone. Rage at the thought of Andrea with Douglas Means consumed him, and he growled like an animal, tugging, tugging, his powerful muscles made stronger by sheer determination. Over and over he yanked, until he saw the tailgate weakening. The driver looked back once and yelled at him to stop making so much ruckus, but minutes later the wood of the tailgate splintered. Adam fell backward, but was immediately back on his feet and running, dragging the chains and tailgate board with him. Andrea! He must get to Andrea and he must kill Douglas Means. He could not go on living if he didn't kill Douglas Means. His mother and Ruth had been bad enough, but Andrea!

It seemed he was running very fast, but in reality, because of his injuries and the heavy chains and board he was dragging, he was only moving at a rapid walk, and half stumbling at that. It was only moments before a net came over him.

"Chain the bastard back up!" someone shouted. "Throw him in the wagon and chain his arms and legs!"

"I can't believe it!" Someone else laughed. "This one's as strong as a grizzly!"

Adam fought wildly. No! He'd gotten free! He had to go to Andrea! He had to kill Douglas Means! He growled like a bear, kicking and fighting the net while he felt himself being dragged over the ground. He was picked up then, and landed hard in a wagon bed, where strong hands grabbed his wrists and ankles. Cuffs went around them, and a moment later he found himself chained by both arms and both legs. He cried out his anguish, still fighting to get loose.

"I never saw anything like it," someone commented.

"This one's got a white woman. I guess they fight harder for their white women than for their Indian women."

More laughter.

"Well, if the bastard got himself inside a white woman, there's only one way to quiet him."

The next instant a grueling blow struck Adam's privates, sending him into spiraling blackness. His cries of agony echoed against rock walls, and in another wagon farther ahead Rose grasped her two grandsons close and wept. Adam could not even curl up against the pain, which made it even worse for him.

"That will quiet him for a while." Someone laughed. "Let's get them to the holding camp. The Federals can take over then. They'll have a high time handling this one."

The wagon started moving again, and a bright morning sun shone down into Adam's face. He fought the horrible, black pain now, determined to draw on that deep, inner spirit rarely found in any man not of Indian blood. He would overcome anything and everything. He would let nothing stop him. He had lost everything. But there was one thing he must do before he left this earth. He must kill Douglas Means. He began to pray for strength, only now he did not pray to the white man's God. He prayed to Esaugetuh Emissee, Maker of Breath.

The wagons rolled in, along with hundreds of others from all directions, while thousands of Cherokees walked beside and behind them, the last holdouts, now forced at gun and bayonet point to walk to the prison camps where they would be held until preparations were completed for moving them westward. Other than some crying, the thousands of Cherokees were relatively quiet. Even during these last acts of brutality they remained nonviolent.

Adam felt his cuffs coming off. He remained calm for the moment, telling himself that to fight would only mean constant chains. How was he to get away and kill Douglas Means if he was chained? Someone jerked him out of the wagon.

"This one is to be kept chained to a post outside the camp," someone ordered. "He's one of the leaders, and he's a troublemaker. You'll have a time on your hands with the others if he's allowed to mix with them."

"What the hell happened to him?"

The voice caused Adam to look up into the eyes of a federal lieutenant. The man was middle-aged, his brown eyes had a sympathetic look to them, and he had an air of intelligence and breeding. He was a far cry from the sort of man who made up the Georgia Militia.

"I told you, Lieutenant. He's a troublemaker. Some of them take a little more 'convincing' than others."

The lieutenant looked Adam over. "This man is a mess." He turned his eyes to the militia man. "I'm tired of you men bringing in whipped and battered people, especially women. I intend to report this to my superior. I think the militia should be removed from this project."

The Georgia man shrugged. "Do what you want,

Lieutenant. We know the Cherokee better than you. If you don't treat them rough, they'll burrow into these hills like worms and we'll never get them all out. You gotta know how to handle them. Besides"—the man spit out a wad of tobacco juice—"Georgia stands behind us. Our governor don't like you guys havin' any part of this affair, so if you speak up too much, it might be you that's kicked off the job rather than us." As the man laughed lightly and walked away, the lieutenant turned to a couple of his own men. "Get some medical aid for this man. Chain him to that post over there and rig up something so he gets a little shade. Chain him by one wrist only. I can't see him having every limb in manacles."

"My wife!" Adam groaned, swallowing back the pain. "They've got . . . my wife!"

The lieutenant frowned. "I'm sure your wife is fine, and is among those in the other wagons that came in with you."

"No! You don't understand! One of the militia men has her! He took her away. He'll rape her! Good God, man, he'll rape her and whip her! Somebody has to go and get her!"

Someone clamped a cuff on his wrist then, and several men pulled Adam over to a post, where they wrapped and secured his chain. But Adam had caught a glint of sympathy in the eyes of the lieutenant, and he would not give up. Again he began to tug at his chain, gritting his teeth, unable to control his anger as he had planned.

"Please help me!" he shouted to the lieutenant. "Send some men to get my wife! Douglas Means! She's with Douglas Means. He's an officer in the Georgia Militia. He took her away when they raided our house!" The lieutenant started to turn away. "Damn you, help her! She's white. My wife is white! Andrea! Andrea Chandler. I'm Adam Chandler. If you won't help an Indian woman, then for God's sake help one of your own kind!"

The lieutenant turned and studied Adam a moment. He'd heard of Adam Chandler. The man was right up there in the ranks of John Ross. Some of these Cherokee men were amazingly intelligent. He'd heard John Ross give a talk once, and he highly respected the man. He'd come on this mission out of sympathy for the Cherokee, although he had been careful not to let it show. He had a job to do, and he truly believed that in the long run it was best for the Indians to go west. But he regretted their fate. He walked back to Adam and knelt down near him.

"Are you sure?"

"Go and see for yourself! My wife is not with the others." Tears came to Adam's eyes then. "She is with Douglas Means. I cannot . . . explain it all now . . . but he has been after my wife for a long time . . . because he knew her once and hated her . . . for marrying an Indian. He attacked my family years ago . . . raped my younger sister when she was still a virgin . . . and let his men rape my mother and whip her. My father . . . died that night. Now he has Andrea! Please help her!"

The lieutenant frowned. "Good God, man, do such things really go on?"

Adam breathed a sigh of frustration. "Of course! If more people had known, had seen . . ." His chest heaved in a sob. "What if it was your mother, or your sister . . . your wife? Wouldn't you want to scream and kill? Wouldn't you want to go after them, even if it meant losing your life? Please . . . get her away from them!"

The lieutenant studied him, seeing the agony in Adam Chandler's eyes. The young man's body was badly beaten and bleeding. His wrists were raw, nearly to the bone. He had fought to help his family, as any man would and should do. He was not a troublemaker. He had only reacted the way any man would react when his family was threatened. The lieutenant had seen too many broken bodies and hopeless faces today. He sighed and removed his hat, ran a hand through his hair.

"I'll see what I can do. I think Means and his men are supposed to camp not far from here tonight. We move everyone out in two days to bigger prison camps."

"Soon! Make it soon, or it will be too late!" Adam jerked at his chain. "Let me loose! Let me go to my sons and the rest of my family."

The lieutenant eyed him warily. "I have orders to keep you separate, Chandler. You're a leader. Besides, I have a suspicion you want to be loose for another reason than going to your sons. I'll see about your wife." The man rose. "I'll send a man to tend to your wounds and bring you some water."

"My sons! I want to see them, to know they are all right. Please, go and find them. Jonas and John are their names. They are only eight and six. Please find them and walk them out here where I can see them!"

"I'll see what I can do."

The man turned away, and Adam slumped against the post, his body screaming from physical and mental agony. His mouth was parched, his lips cracked. Everything hurt, but he could not let anything stop him from somehow getting his revenge if Douglas Means had violated his wife. His nerves cried out for action. The lieutenant was moving too slowly! Something must be done now! Again he tugged at his chain. Perhaps if he broke his wrist or found a way to cut off his hand . . . He cursed the fact that he had no knife or any kind of weapon. His helplessness made him crazed.

A medic came over and gave him water, then washed his wounds as best he could. Adam sat quietly and let the man work. If he was to kill Douglas Means, he had to rest and let his body heal as best as possible. The medic decided he had one cracked rib, and he wrapped Adam's middle. He left with a promise to find Adam's family and to get him a clean shirt and something for his feet, which were bloody and raw from walking behind the wagon without being allowed to put on shoes.

Hours passed. Meanwhile Adam sat in the broiling sun. It was midsummer, 1838, and it was an especially hot summer in Georgia. He had no doubt that the bigger holding camps would not be on Georgia soil. He prayed they would be in Tennessee rather than Alabama. There was more sympathy for the Cherokee in Tennessee. Either way, it was doubtful the camps would be better than bearable. The comfortable life they had once known was gone, and would not be found again for a long time to come. Now they would all have to draw on a deep inner strength to overcome what lay ahead. How many would die? What about his own children?

Finally some soldiers put up a canvas strip that shaded him from the hot sun. But even the camps afforded little shade, from what he could see of the fenced-in compounds. Where were his precious sons? What was happening to Andrea? And what about his mother, and Ruth?

It was late afternoon before the lieutenant finally came walking toward Adam, holding the hands of two young boys.

"Father!" Both broke loose and ran when they saw him. They were barefoot and wore only pants and shirts. Adam reached out with his free arm and hugged them tightly, unable to control his own tears. At least his sons were all right.

"Where's Mommy?" John asked.

"She'll be along," Adam reassured the boy. "We'll find her and get her back. Mommy will be fine."

"Father, why are you chained?" Jonas asked, wiping at tears. "We want you with us." He reached out and touched his father's battered face. "Why did they hurt you so much?"

"I guess they just think I'm a troublemaker, Jonas. I helped John Ross fight to let us stay . . . in Georgia. They think I'll make everything worse if they unchain me and let me be with you."

"Please make them let you go," Jonas answered, his eyes tearing over again. "We're scared without you."

Adam hugged them again. "I'll get loose eventually." He kissed both of them, and wiped at his own tears. The lieutenant stood aside, unable to help but moved by the sight. Something was very wrong about how all of this was being done, and he wondered how he would feel if someone barged into his home and beat him and dragged off his wife and children. "How is Grandma, and Aunt

Ruth?" Adam was asking them.

"Grandma is okay, but she's pretty tired," Jonas answered. "Aunt Ruth looks real scared all the time and won't talk to us. She just hangs on to Cousin Charlie and won't let go of him."

Adam looked up at the lieutenant. "Thank you for bringing them."

"I'm afraid I have to take them right back. I was not supposed to do this at all. It isn't wise to show any sympathy. However, I will go after your wife. I have two men ready and we're leaving shortly."

Adam's eyes lit up with hope. "Boys, you go back now. The sooner you go back the sooner the lieutenant can go after your mother. He's going to get her. Don't you be afraid of anything from now on. Everything will be all right."

The two boys stood up, their round, angelic faces tearing at his heart. "I tried to help you, Father, but they kept pushing me back."

"I know, son. It's all right." He noticed a small bruise on the boy's right cheek. "Did they hit you?"

The boy held up his chin. "I'm okay. They can't hurt Jonas Chandler!"

Adam looked at the lieutenant. "Look at his cheek and then ask me why I tug at these chains until my skin is gone!" His anger was building all over again at the thought of grown men hitting his son. The lieutenant sighed and gently pushed the boys aside. He knelt down near Adam.

"I'm sorry, Chandler. I can't prevent every act of brutality."

"But you could let me go!" Adam growled in a husky voice. "Please! Let me go so that I can avenge my wife!"

"You know I can't do a thing like that, Chandler. And what would it get you? You have to be with your sons and your family. Such a revenge would only get you hung. And you don't even know yet if it's necessary. Your wife might be perfectly fine."

Adam grinned bitterly. "Don't be such a fool, Lieutenant! You should have gone right away." His eyes teared. "It is too late now." He jerked at his chain again. "Just think how you would feel in my shoes. You think about it! And then you will find a way to let me escape!"

The lieutenant frowned and rose. "You are a prisoner, Adam Chandler, and you shall stay a prisoner. It's that kind of talk that will keep you chained to that post. I totally disagree with this entire movement, yet there is no stopping it, and I will do my part to the best of my ability. I said I would see about your wife. That's the best I can do."

He turned and took the boys' hands to lead them back to the camp. They kept turning to look back at their father, their dirty faces stained with tears. Adam's heart went out to them. He knew the terror they must be feeling. Yes, he needed to be with them, but he also needed to kill Douglas Means. He rested against the post again, praying for Andrea. The lieutenant disappeared into the holding camp, and Adam realized he didn't even know the man's name. Everything was strange and confusing now, their lives turned upside down. He wondered if anything could ever be normal for them again. Andrea! Andrea!

CHAPTER TWENTY-TWO

Dusk was heavy in the air when the lieutenant returned. Adam saw the makeshift travois being drawn behind the horse of one of his men. Why would they need a travois, unless Andrea was dead or badly wounded. "Andrea!" He screamed her name, yanking on the chain like a wild animal. The lieutenant looked his way and urged his horse out of formation. Ordering his men to take the travois into the fenced prison camp, he headed his mount toward Adam.

Over and over again Adam yanked. "Let me go to her! Let me loose!"

"Quiet down or you'll be shot!" The lieutenant seemed to be talking louder than necessary. He rode up to Adam and dismounted. "Shut your goddamned mouth! Your wife is fine." He landed a booted foot into Adam's side, making him cry out, but Adam yanked even harder, cursing him and begging him to let him go to Andrea. The lieutenant then took a second cuff from his saddlebag. When Adam kicked out wildly, the lieutenant landed a chain across his shoulder, stunning him just long enough to permit him to clamp the cuff around Adam's free wrist and then attach its chain to the pin that held the first chain. Now both of Adam's arms were stretched up, chained to the post. The lieutenant grasped his hair and jerked him close. "Play along with me, Chandler, and you'll get your wish," he said quietly.

Adam stopped struggling, eyed the man warily. "What do you mean?"

"I mean I don't dare show you one ounce of sympathy if we're to pull this thing off."

Adam's heart lifted, and his eyes became wild with excitement. "You will let me go?"

"Your wife was badly abused," the lieutenant said quickly. "I'm sorry to tell you so quickly, but I can't sit here talking to you all day. Douglas Means raped her, then hung her outside for all the men to see while he whipped her. He was going to turn her over to the other men, but I got there first. I had them cut her down, and I brought her back with me. She's with your mother now, and my medic will tend to her." He shoved Adam hard then and stood up. Adam curled up, tears of rage engulfing him. Andrea!

"You can go to her . . . tomorrow, perhaps. For tonight, you'd best keep cursing and making trouble so I can keep you chained. I'll send a man to watch you; then I'll come back after dark and tell him I'm taking over."

Adam breathed deeply for control before turning and looking directly at the lieutenant. "I . . . don't understand."

The lieutenant stared at him, his own eyes angry. "I kept thinking about what you said—about how I'd feel if it were my wife. In all that's happened not one of you Cherokees has fought back. As far as I'm concerned that's the bravest and most admirable decision I've known anyone to make. But your nonviolence has gained you nothing, and I know by your own actions and the condition you were in when they brought you here that you deserve to be able to avenge your family's abuse. I feel responsible myself. I should have gone to get her sooner."

Adam stared at him in disbelief, still unsure of what the man meant to do. "How am I to get my vengeance?"

The lieutenant removed his canteen and opened it, pouring water on top of Adam's head and splashing it into his face. "You settle down and I just might bring you some food and water later tonight," he said loudly. "If not, you can go hungry and thirsty and rot right here on this pole!"

He recapped the canteen. "Douglas Means is camped hardly more than a mile from here," he went on in a lower voice. "Just over that low ridge to your left. Means is a captain now. His tent is bigger than the others, with a Georgia state flag perched on top of it. As far as I could tell he sleeps alone. You'll have to be strong enough to do the deed tonight after dark. I hope you are. It's your last chance. He's moving on tomorrow. I can't furnish you with anything other than a knife—no gun. And if you can get to him it must be done quietly. I'll let you go after dark. If you get back here before morning, I'll recuff you and swear you were here all night. If you don't make it back, I won't cover for you, understand? You'll be on your own. But I need your promise that you'll not get me involved. I'm told the word of a Cherokee can be trusted, and you're supposed to be one of the most important Cherokees, right up there with John Ross."

"I . . . don't know what to say." Adam trembled with joy and relief, and with the excitement of knowing he had a chance to avenge the wrongs done to his family. "Of course you have my word. But I . . . I don't even know your name."

"Renfro. Martin Renfro. I'm from Missouri." He mounted his horse, looking down at Adam. "There are some men on this earth who do not deserve to live. Douglas Means is one of them. I may not be able to stop what is happening to the Cherokee, but I can stop men like Means from making it worse. I'd do it with my own hands, but I'm a federal soldier and we are not at war with the Georgia Militia. I'd never get away with it. Besides, Georgia is already screaming that the federal government has no right to send in men. I'll be back later tonight. You just go along with anything I do in the morning, and act surprised when the Militia ride in here yelling that one of their own was killed. At least I hope that's what they'll be saying." He turned his horse and trotted it toward the prison camp.

Adam watched him go, then sat back and looked up at the sky. "You have answered my prayers, Maker of

Breath," he whispered. "You have sent one of your servants to help me. Thank you, Esaugetuh Emissee." He swallowed back tears. He must not think of Andrea—not yet. He must think only of vengeance. He must be strong. His body was weakened from the grueling beatings and the mistreatment he'd received since that awful moment when Douglas Means had burst into their bedroom. That seemed like days ago now, but it had been only this morning. How could one day bring so much change to a man's life? Poor Andrea! How he longed to go to her. But the lieutenant was right. People must see him cuffed. If he was still there in the morning . . . He actually grinned.

"This will be a good day after all," he whispered. Douglas Means! He must think only of Douglas Means now, of how much he hated the man, of how good it would feel to sink a knife into him and watch him gasp for breath. He would have to be very careful not to get caught. It occurred to him that this might be some sort of trick to get him hung and out of the way, but something in the lieutenant's eyes bespoke sincerity. He knew that what was happening was not the fault of individuals like Martin Renfro. It was all due to politics and power pulls, to outside factors that often affected people like the lieutenant as drastically as it affected the Indians. The man was doing his job, but found it distasteful. It was his appointed duty, nonetheless.

Adam curled up against the post to rest. He needed all the strength he could muster. In his condition it would not be easy wrestling down Douglas Means. He must have a plan. He would force himself not to think about Andrea right now, except for the horrible wrong that had been done her. It ripped his heart to pieces to think of her being abused, but that was good fuel for the fires of vengeance. And he dared not think about going to her then, holding her, comforting her. There would be time for that. For now there was only time to hate, to think about his wife being wronged. His need for vengeance would give him the strength to do what he must.

* * *

Mosquitoes buzzed around Adam's ears and eyes in the still night, and he felt crazed with the need to see Andrea and the need to kill Douglas Means. Now he wondered if the lieutenant would keep his promise about giving him the chance for revenge. His arms ached from being chained over his head, and a cracked rib brought continued piercing pain to his side. His face was so bruised he was more black than brown. But his emotional pain far outweighed his physical pain. There would be time later to give in to the effects of the physical abuse. Now someone must pay. He prayed over and over that Lieutenant Renfro had meant what he'd said. But the moon was rising, and the time was at hand.

Finally he saw someone approach, carrying a lantern. The sounds of the night were strange now, for Adam and others had been thrown into a state of shock by their sudden transportation to this hot place, a spot deliberately chosen because it had few trees. He could hear soft weeping from inside the prison camp, mixed with waves of hymn singing. But there was no wind, and for some reason, not even the sound of singing insects, only the buzzing of mosquitoes that bit at him. His guard sat close by, almost asleep, as approaching boots made a crunching sound against the dry earth.

"Simmons!" It was the lieutenant's voice. Adam's guard jumped awake and stood up to salute.

"Yes, sir."

"Is that how you guard prisoners?"

"I . . . he's chained, sir . . . and just one man—"

"One or a dozen, you stay awake when you're guarding them!"

"Yes, sir."

"Go on back to your bedroll if you're so tired. And you'll answer for this."

"Y-yes, sir. Shall I send out another man?"

"Forget it. I can't sleep anyway, what with all that wailing and hymn singing. Those Indians sure have religion." He glanced at Adam. "Which is more than I can say for this devil sitting here."

"He's been pretty quiet, sir."

"That's when you watch them the closest. Go on back now."

The private saluted and hurried off, and Renfro set the lantern down, keeping it distant enough so that Adam was not in the light. He waited until the private was well out of sight, then moved over to where Adam sat in the darkness.

"I hope to hell you understand the chance I'm taking," he said quietly. He felt for the locks on Adam's chains, slid a key into them.

"I do. I will be forever in your debt."

"Well, I am forever in yours if you keep my name out of it, Chandler," the lieutenant replied quietly.

Adam's hands dropped down when the cuffs were loosened, and he grimaced with pain. The lieutenant quickly began to rub Adam's hands vigorously, to bring the life back into them.

"You're in bad shape, but I'm figuring your desire for revenge will give you what strength you need." He felt inside his jacket and then pushed something into Adam's palm. Adam recognized the feel of a good, balanced knife. "This thing has a hell of a blade on it. Use it well, my friend. It's the best I can do for you. Tomorrow, if you make it back, I'll see that you get a clean shirt and some kind of shoes." He took hold of Adam's shoulder and helped him to stand. Adam faced him in the moonlight, sliding the knife into his belt and then rubbing one arm with the other.

"How do you know I will even come back? Perhaps I will run away."

He could see the lieutenant's grin. "And leave your abused wife and little sons behind? I doubt Adam Chandler would do that."

Adam swallowed back the lump in his throat. "Of course I would not. I am just surprised that you trust me."

"I've heard enough about you to trust you. You and that John Ross and some others handled your struggle brilliantly. As far as I'm concerned you were right all the way down the line. A lot of people feel that way. But there is a lot of power involved in politics. Now get going. I figure a half-hour to forty-five minutes to get there in your condition. Once you're over that far ridge, you'll see the lights of their camp. Means' tent is near the foot of the ridge. Look for the Georgia flag. And make it quick. I figure you'll be gone three hours and be back here before dawn breaks." He squeezed Adam's shoulder. "Good luck, Chandler."

Adam put a hand over Renfro's. "You are a gift from the Maker of Breath. I honor you, Lieutenant Renfro."

"Just get going."

Adam nodded and hurried off into the darkness, limping on badly bruised and swollen feet. The doctor's promise to bring something for his feet had not been kept. But it didn't matter. There were more important things to tend to than his painful feet.

One thing Adam Chandler knew was the land he'd lived in all his life. He had ridden through these mountains and valleys, walked them, loved them. This particular place where they had been brought to be held for departure was not totally unfamiliar to him, and almost like an animal he made his way ·through underbrush and over rocks, quietly, a stealthy cat on the prowl. His eyes adjusted to the moonlight, and his heart beat with frantic excitement. Douglas Means! The man had raped his sister, had had his mother whipped. He had raped his wife. The thought brought a horrible black pain to his heart and he suddenly felt weak. Andrea! Poor sweet Andrea! No! He must not weaken. He must get this done. There would be time later for all the healing.

He scrambled up the ridge and grinned when he saw the lights below. Renfro was right. The man had not lied. Adam headed down under the cover of darkness, toward the largest tent. A light still burned inside it, but the entire camp was quiet. Adam crept closer. He could not go inside until Douglas blew out the lamp, or his shadow would be seen. But he had to be sure that when he struck Douglas would be killed and not someone else.

He stayed in the shadows then, setting his knife aside and removing his pants. He was naked then, for there had not even been time that morning to put on underwear, and he was still shirtless. If this deed was to be done with a knife, there would be blood, and he didn't want any on his clothes. He'd have to wash off before dressing again so that no blood would be on him when he returned to camp and was found sitting at the post in the morning. He laid his pants aside and picked up the knife, wriggled on his belly toward the back of the tent, slithered right up to the edge of it.

The back of the tent was in darkness, and no one saw him. Very carefully Adam lifted the bottom of the tent wall, just a crack. He lowered his head down to peer inside, and then trembled at the sight of Douglas Means, sitting at a makeshift desk and writing something. Means was clad only in his underwear, for the night was hot and humid. Suddenly he called out to one of his men, and someone entered. Adam quickly lowered the hem of the tent.

"Get this letter off to my folks. They're not far away, but they don't even know I'm in the area. I want them to know I'll be by to see them as soon as we've rounded up the last of these bastards."

"Yes, sir." There was a moment of silence. "What happened to the white woman, sir? I thought you were going to keep—"

"Some son-of-a-bitching Federal came in here and took her. I decided not to argue about it. I had my fun with the slut before they got here anyway."

"She was a pretty one. We were hoping to get a share of her."

"Well, you can't have everything, Sloan."

Both men laughed, and Adam trembled with rage. Andrea! He moved back into the shadows, struggling to control his urge to cry out his anger. There was more conversation, and the second man finally left. Then Adam sat and waited. It seemed hours rather than minutes before the lamp finally went out. Still Adam waited. He would let Douglas Means drift off.

An owl hooted somewhere, and mosquitoes buzzed at his bare skin. In the distance the men seated around a campfire laughed. That was good. Their attention was distracted by whiskey. Adam waited nearly an hour before moving in. Then he quietly cut the rope that was tied to a stake at the center of the back wall of the tent. It was not a supporting stake, only one that made the wall stiffer. He grinned at the ease with which the knife cut through the rope. Renfro had given him a good weapon.

His every move was made with almost total silence. The Indian in him came to the forefront, ancient warrior ways taking over. He had never killed before, but there was a first time for everything and he would not regret this. He slithered under the tent wall, now loosened enough to be raised to let him through. Douglas snored peacefully as Adam lay on the ground and let his eyes adjust to the darkness of the tent until he could make out the cot and the body on it. Finally he crawled toward the cot, realizing that the first blow would have to be one that kept Douglas Means from crying out. His thirst for vengeance made him crave to make the man suffer. He remembered the vow he had made to Douglas Means the night the man had ridden in to break up the Cherokee celebration dance. He would keep that vow tonight.

Adam stood up then, feeling brave and sure. He looked down at Douglas's sleeping body and wondered how a man who had done such hideous things could sleep so well at night. Now he would sleep forever. He leaned close and clamped a big hand over Douglas's nose and mouth. "Wake up, my friend!" he whispered.

Douglas awakened instantly, at first confused and unable to breathe. In the next moment, before he could cry out, a big blade was rammed into his Adam's apple and upward, cutting the vocal cords but not cutting a vital artery. In the dim light Adam could see the man's mouth open, but no sound came out. Something dark ran over his throat, and Adam knew it was blood. His satisfaction had never been sweeter. Douglas reached up to him as though to fight him off, but Adam rammed the blade again, once into each shoulder, quickly, deliberately, bringing horrible pain, but Douglas could not scream. The man's arms went limp, and Adam leaned close to him.

"You made a bad decision when you raped my wife, Douglas Means," he hissed into Douglas's ear. "I warned you not to touch her. I told you once what would happen, didn't I? Do you remember what I told you, Douglas Means?"

Means's body began to shake violently. His eyes were so wide that Adam could see the whites of them. He grinned. "Yes, Douglas. I told you you would cry out with the pain of it, but that you would not be able to scream, because your own privates would be stuffed into your mouth. I do not break my promises, Douglas. You should have remembered. I am a man of my word."

An odd gurgling sound came from Douglas's throat, not loud enough to alert the laughing, joking men outside. Adam ran his knife through the man's underwear and a moment later the deed was done. He held up his prize for a moment then shoved hard. Never had he known such a feeling of victory and pleasure. Finally! Finally he could settle something according to the old ways! How wonderful it must have felt to be a warrior!

"I told you you would choke to death on these, you slimy white scum!" He waited a moment, not caring that every minute was risky. He wanted to see the pain and terror in Douglas Means's eyes, wanted him to stay alive and suffer as long as possible. After several minutes of watching him shake violently, Adam raised his knife and drove it into Douglas's heart. Blood raced out, some splashing onto Adam's arm. His hands were already covered with its warmth, but he didn't even care. He wanted to bathe in it. He yanked out the knife then. Douglas Means lay silent—forever.

Adam quickly felt his way to the barrel of water he'd seen inside the tent when he'd peeked into the tent earlier. He dipped the knife into it, then set it aside and dipped in his hands, washing his arms and face and chest. He quickly wiped himself off with a blanket, picked up the knife, and scurried out under the black wall of the tent. He searched for his pants, found them, and disappeared into the night.

He ran hard then. He had crossed a shallow creek on the way to the militia camp. He found it again and jumped into it, wallowing in the water. To get off any blood that might be on him, he rubbed sand over his face and body and through his hair, then rinsed and rinsed. That done, he picked up his pants again and ran on. He had been gone more than the three hours alotted, he was sure. He had not expected Means to take so long to turn out the lamp and go to sleep. But it was still very dark.

He wanted to leap with joy. The feeling of victory, the taste of revenge, was the most glorious thing he had ever experienced. Finally he had been allowed to fight back!

He slowed down when he neared the post. Someone still sat by it and the lantern was still lit. He snuck closer, wanting to be sure the man was Renfro. When he saw that it was he walked to the post, which was still in shadow.

"I am back," he said quietly.

Renfro jumped slightly, but forced himself not to make any sudden movements. He got up slowly and walked into the shadows.

"Did you do it?"

"I did. I am a happy man this night, in spite of the terrible things that happened this day. I will be grateful to you for the rest of my life."

"Sit down and I'll cuff you. I know it hurts and I hate to do it, but I'll let you loose later tomorrow and you can go to your wife."

Adam reached out and felt for the man's hand, then put the knife into it. "Here. Hide this. When you get it in the light, make sure there is no blood on it. I washed myself in a stream, and the air dried me as I ran back. I have to put my pants back on. I took them off so I would not get blood on them."

"A good idea." The soldier's hand brushed the still-damp gauze around Adam's injured ribs. "What about this? There may be blood on this gauze."

"I did not think of that. Cut it off of me and burn it! Do not let anyone see you."

The lieutenant quickly ripped off the gauze and Adam grunted with pain.

"What about my tracks?"

"I thought of that. I'm having a herd of Cherokee cattle brought in closer to camp in the morning, to scatter a few thousand cattle tracks over your own. No one will be able to track you any farther than the edge of camp, if you are tracked at all, for you will be found cuffed to this pole."

Adam quickly dressed and sat down. He let Renfro cuff and chain him. "I was getting a little worried. You were gone a long time," Renfro said.

"I had to wait until he blew out the lamp and went to sleep."

Renfro stood up and threw a blanket over him. "Just play along with me in the morning. I may have to be rough on you."

"It does not matter now. Do whatever you want. It is worth it to have this peace inside of me."

"I happen to be very glad myself that you got your revenge. By the way, the doctor fixed up your wife as best he could—the cuts and all. She's been asking for you. I assured her you were all right, but that I could not let you go. I wouldn't tell her what you've done, nor your mother or anyone. Maybe later, when you get out West you can tell them. But your wife is in a bad state, and she might blurt something out unintentionally if you tell her."

"I understand."

"We've done all we can for the sick and injured ones. We move out in a few days, I'm afraid, and there will be no doctor. I'm sorry."

"Don't tell me the militia will take over."

"No. Some new troops are coming in. Seems the government has decided to change the guard often so none of us gets too friendly with any of you. How's that for a laugh? At any rate, we're supposed to stop doctoring you. If you're lucky the missionaries will send a doctor. In the meantime there will be no one."

"You don't have to explain. I know it is not your doing."

The lieutenant sighed deeply. "I'll come by for you in the morning. I'm sending another man out to watch you come daylight. Good-bye, Chandler."

"Good-bye, Renfro. God go with you."

"And with you."

The lieutenant left, and Adam sank wearily against the post, intense fatigue suddenly overwhelming him. Everything hurt now that he was allowed to feel the pain, to give in to it. He thought about Andrea. Tears came, and he rested his head against an upraised arm and wept. It was over. He would not go home again.

Adam awoke to shouts and the thunder of hooves. He opened bloodshot eyes to see a man standing near him, but looking toward the distant ridge. Adam scrambled to his knees, his heart tightening. Were the militia coming? Would they find him out? For a moment he could not see well, for a herd of cattle had just rumbled through. Choking dust rolled over him and he put his head down. "Please, give me some . . . water," he groaned to his guard.

The young man glanced at him, then back through the dust. He reached down and picked up a canteen, bringing it to Adam. "Put your head back and open your mouth. I don't like Indians drinking out of my canteen."

Adam did as he was told, gasping with relief at the refreshing wetness. Now more pain was setting in. His joints were stiff, his side ached fiercely. His face was black and green, and dull aches persisted in his groin and lower back. His wrists were swollen and bloody. But none of that mattered now. He remembered his deed of the night before, and it was a wonderful memory. Still, he could not help but worry about the men who now approached from the distance. The dust began to clear, and his guard capped the canteen.

"Looks like militia coming," he commented.

Adam watched, and much as it hurt, he began to tug at his chains again, as though fiercely angry that he was still restrained. It was important to put on a good act. The men came closer, and to his relief Lieutenant Renfro was with them.

"There! I told you!" he was shouting. "The devil has been chained to that post all night! Unless his spirit can exit his body and go out and kill his enemies, there is no way this man could have done it!"

Adam stared at them with wild eyes as they rode closer. "What! Done what!" he shouted. "What do these sons-of-bitches think I did!"

"Someone murdered our major last night—Major Means! It was a bloody, heathen, brutal murder. By God no white man would kill another white man that way!"

Adam just grinned through clenched teeth. "Means? He is dead?" He threw back his head and laughed. "Good! It serves the bastard right! Find the man who did it, and I will shake his hand!"

One of the militia men kicked out, his boot landing in Adam's face and sending him flying against the post. "You heathen bastard! Who else would have reason to do it?"

"This man has been here all night!" Adam's guard spoke up. "I took over guarding him before the sun even rose this morning, and he was right here."

"Look at his wrists!" Renfro put in. "There is barely any skin left on them. Last night he got wild as a she-cat. That's why I chained the other wrist also. Does that look like a man who could sneak off and kill a militia man in the middle of the night? What did he do, drag the pole with him? The man has been chained to that pole since he was brought here yesterday."

One of the militia men dismounted, as did Renfro. The Georgia man walked up to Adam, jerked him up by the hair of the head. He studied him closely, pushing him back and looking over his body and pants, staring at the blackened skin on his chest.

"Your own men beat the hell out of this man yesterday,"

Renfro put in. "For God's sake, look at him! He's hardly in shape to go running off to kill someone."

The militia man stepped back. "These Indians have a strength that doesn't quit sometimes." He rubbed a bristly beard. "Still in all, between those wounds and those chains—"

Adam spit at him. "Georgia pig!" he muttered. "Except you do not have the brains of a pig!"

Renfro slammed a fist into his face. Adam's body jerked, for his arms were still pinned over his head and he could not go down. "You keep your mouth shut," Renfro ordered.

"Never!" Adam growled. "Go find your murderer, militia man! Maybe there is a sympathizer among your own men . . . someone who is angry that Douglas Means raped a white woman . . . committed a crime against your own kind!"

The militia man frowned, seeming to consider the statement. He looked back at his men. "No way!" one of them declared. "What was done to the major was Indian things. No white man cuts off another white man's privates."

The lieutenant struggled to keep from showing his shock. He had not expected such brutality, yet how could he blame Adam?

"Maybe somebody just wanted us to think it was an Indian."

"You may never know, Sergeant," Renfro put in. "But there is no sense in looking here. Everyone here has been confined under tight security, and this man has been in cuffs constantly. This camp is in complete order, Sergeant. I suggest you get back to yours and make sure it is the same. I am sorry about your major, but I'll not have you making the federals look bad just for your own gain."

"We followed tracks over the ridge!"

"Fine. Maybe whoever it was wanted you to find those tracks. If you think it was one of the people here, go and find him. There are three thousand people in this holding camp, Sergeant, well-guarded, starving, sick, tired, hopeless people. If you think you can pick out the killer from among them, be my guest."

The sergeant glowered at him. "You Federals think you're so high and mighty. You'd, by God, better keep a good watch on those lice, Lieutenant." His eyes shifted to Adam. "Especially that one."

"I'll tend to my job and you tend to yours. But I suggest you do it with a little less brutality, Sergeant. You've blackened Georgia's name enough these past few years. These people have to go now. Let them go in dignity."

"There is no such thing as dignity for a Cherokee," the militia man sneered. He eyed Adam carefully once more, then turned to remount his horse. "You're a damned lucky man, Chandler. We had some right entertaining things in mind for the major's murderer."

"I hope the bastard is never caught," Adam sneered. "Maybe he's a ghost killer. Maybe he'll come and kill all of you. Maybe you'll be next, Sergeant!"

Renfro's booted foot struck Adam's ankle, making him cry out. "I told you to keep quiet, Chandler! The sooner you quiet down, the sooner you can be with your family."

The sergeant backed his horse, looking suddenly uncomfortable. He didn't like Adam Chandler's talk of a ghost killer. He and his men would not sleep well this next night. If the murderer was not Adam Chandler, then who was it? Was he waiting in the hills to strike again?

"We're moving our camp away from here," he told Renfro. "We'll report this, but I don't know what else to do. I'll send men to tell the major's parents about his death. Then we'll head up into the hills and root out some of those that took to the caves. We'll be gone by this afternoon. I'll not make camp in that same spot another night."

"As you wish, Sergeant." Renfro remounted, and ordered the young guard to stay put until he returned. As the militia men left, Adam shouted that they were cowards, afraid of ghosts. He turned then and sat back against the post, laughing, feeling like a crazy man, wondering if perhaps he truly had lost some of his faculties.

It was close to an hour before Renfro came back and announced to the guard that he was taking Adam inside the compound to be with his family.

"But, sir . . . he's so wild," the guard protested.

"We have plenty of men. This man has suffered enough. Now that the man who raped his wife is dead, we have no reason to believe he will try to escape to go after him. His wife needs him badly. Perhaps being with his family will help calm him down."

Adam grinned. "Finally! Hurry and get me out of these damned cuffs before my hands fall off, damn you!"

"You behave yourself, or I'll cuff both hands and ankles next time, understand? I want your promise, Chandler."

Adam sneered at him. "I will not cause trouble, soldier. Just let me be with my wife."

Renfro bent close and unlocked the chains and cuffs, and when Adam's arms dropped, he writhed in pain. The guard watched warily. "You can go back to camp, Miller," Renfro told the guard. "I'll handle this."

"But, sir—"

"I didn't get to be a lieutenant by not being able to handle one man, Miller. Now get going!"

"Yes, sir." The young man saluted and left. Renfro took his rifle from his horse and then helped Adam to his feet.

"Can you walk all right?"

"I think so," Adam muttered. "Please . . . take me to her."

"Walk ahead of me. You're under my guard, remember?"

Adam stumbled toward the camp.

"You cut off his privates?" Renfro asked quietly.

"I stuffed them in his mouth!" Adam hissed.

"My God, man, I didn't expect that."

"She was my wife. She has been mine and only mine since she was fourteen years old. No man touches my wife!"

"That is obvious." Renfro grinned a little. "I've read about you, Chandler. I've followed this Cherokee thing closer than you know. That's partly why I volunteered for this unpleasant duty. Now that morning is here, I am wondering where my mind was yesterday, letting you go like that. I think it's time I got out of Georgia."

Adam stopped and turned around. "I don't know how to thank you. I have known you one day, yet I consider you a friend."

"Turn around and be a little more belligerent," Renfro warned. Adam turned back around and Renfro pushed at him with the butt of his rifle. "We can't start acting like friends. I'm sorry."

"I know."

"Is it true you're a Harvard graduate?"

"It is true. My family was once very wealthy. We had much land, a fine home and many slaves. All was stolen from us. I have almost nothing left."

They neared pine posts that formed the gate to the prison camp. "Hold up," Renfro told him. Adam halted and the soldier walked around to face him, speaking quietly. "My father is a lawyer, up in Independence, Missouri. I'm going to tell him about you. I don't know what you're in for, or what you'll do when you get out West, but it won't be easy. If you need help, need a job, get in touch with him—Michael Renfro."

"He would give employment to an Indian?"

"Sure he would. We aren't all Indian haters, you know. Your own experience with Northerners a few years ago should tell you that."

Adam's eyes teared, and he swallowed. "I will think about it. The first thing I must do is stay with my people and help them. But I made myself a promise, that one day I will be wealthy again and buy back my land, legally."

Renfro nodded. "I understand, and I wish you luck. Now I suggest you brace yourself for a blow from behind when you go through the gate. I have to give you a proper chastising to make sure you behave yourself."

Adam wanted to smile, but knew he dared not. Renfro

walked behind him and shoved him again. Guards opened the gate at the lieutenant's command, and as soon as Adam was through it Renfro slammed the rifle butt into his back, making him fall forward.

"Just a warning, Chandler," he said loudly. "Behave yourself inside and you can stay with your family. Cause trouble or incite others to make trouble, and you'll go right back out to that post!" He looked at the guards. "One of you take him to his wife and family—over in the southeast corner. And watch him. I think he's calmed down enough to stay with the others, but if he starts anything, put him back in chains."

He turned and left, and two men helped Adam to stand up, half dragging him through a maze of sad Cherokees, most of them silent, some singing hymns. Before they went far two young boys ran toward them.

"Father! Father!"

They reached Adam simultaneously and he went to his knees, hugging them both and weeping. "Thank God," he murmured.

"Mommy's hurt, Father. You gotta come. She cries for you all the time."

Adam wondered how much more he could suffer without giving up. Andrea! It was his fault she had suffered so much. How could he ever forgive himself?

"Take me to your mother," he said to his sons in a weak voice. He managed to get to his feet. "My sons can take me," he told the guards. "Don't worry, I won't make trouble. I just want to see my wife."

The guards exchanged doubtful looks, then one of them shrugged. "He's in too bad shape to make much trouble for now. Let him go to the woman." The second man lowered his gun.

"You mind what you do, Chandler," he warned. Then the two men walked off.

Adam leaned on his sons, who were really too small to support their big father. But he knew they wanted to think they were helping him, knew the terror they must have felt since seeing him beaten and their mother dragged off. He grasped their shoulders and held on as they walked.

"Everything will be all right now, boys. We're together. I won't leave you again, and neither will your mother. Whatever happens, we'll be together."

They headed through the sea of mournful faces, toward a place where a makeshift sun shield had been created from sticks and a piece of a cloth. It shaded a white woman, who lay on her stomach, a light blanket over her. "Andrea!" Adam groaned.

CHAPTER TWENTY-THREE

"Adam!" Her voice was small and weak, but she raised her arm and he caught hold of her hand, bent down, and kissed her cheek.

"My God, Andrea, forgive me," he groaned, breaking into tears. "I tried . . . to stop them."

Her own tears came then, and her body shook. "I thought . . . they'd killed you . . . thought they were lying . . . when they said you were alive."

"Nobody can kill me when I know you need me." He raised up slightly, tears streaming down his bruised face, and he touched her hair, noticing her face was bruised. "My God, what did that bastard do to you?"

Her sobs wrenched his heart, yet she clung to his hand with amazing strength. "I thought I could bear it . . . be strong . . . God, Adam, I'm not yours anymore—"

"Stop that!" He bent close again and smoothed back her hair. He kissed her cheek, her tears. "You are mine and only mine." He wiped at his eyes. "You always were and you always will be. Nothing can change that—nothing! You said that yourself, remember? You did nothing wrong. It was Douglas Means who did something wrong. He is led by the devil, and now he is dead!"

She blinked and quieted somewhat. Adam kept kissing her, talking low in her ear. "Yes, he is dead. I do not know who did it, but someone killed him, and he can never hurt you again, do you hear me? He can never hurt you or Ruth or anyone else again. The man who wronged you is dead, and now we must go on, for Jonas and John. We can't let this destroy us, Andrea. So much lies ahead. We need each other."

For several minutes they wept, unable to control their emotions. Then Rose came to kneel beside her son. "Adam, you should lie down. You are badly wounded. We were so afraid those men would beat you to death."

He remained bent over Andrea, crying like a child, and Jonas and John stood on the other side of their mother, both of them sniffling.

"Please, Adam."

"No," he groaned. "I am all right."

"Adam, you . . . have to rest," Andrea sobbed. "How badly . . . are you hurt?"

"I can take it. It is you I am concerned about."

She had thought perhaps he would treat her differently, love her less. But he was with her, dear, sweet, gentle Adam, her Cherokee man. He was badly hurt, but he cared only about her. She tried to sit up, but was too sore. Her confused mind whirled with ugly memories and the horror of Douglas Means. She could have stood the beating. But the other . . . Her whole body shuddered again. Was it true? Was the man really dead and unable to hurt her again? What had happened?

"Adam, what happened . . . to him? Are you sure he's dead?"

"I am very sure!" he hissed. "He died as horrible a death as such a man deserves."

She felt a chill at his words. Something was wrong. How was he so sure? Yet for the moment it didn't matter. Everything hurt too much. The memories were too ugly and painful. She didn't want to know right now just how Douglas Means died—only that he really was dead. She didn't have to be afraid of him any longer.

"Adam, at least lie down. You can lie next to Andrea if you wish. She needs you to hold her, and you need to rest."

He finally straightened, threw his head back, and whispered a prayer in the Cherokee tongue to the Maker of

Breath. Then he turned to his mother. "He is dead!" he told her through gritted teeth. "And I celebrate his death!"

She frowned. "Who are you talking about?"

His eyes were wild and gleaming. "Douglas Means," he answered.

Her eyes widened. "How do you know this?"

He was tempted to shout out that he had killed the man, but no one must know, not even his family could know until they were safely West. "Militia men came this morning. They tried to accuse me of killing him, but I was chained to that post all night. I do not know who did it, but he is a good man!"

Adam's mother watched him carefully, her eyes dropping to his black, swollen wrists. It couldn't be. Surely he really had been chained all night.

"Do not let the hatred I see in your eyes eat at you, my son," she told him. "Always you have been my fine son, a good man who—"

"Good?" He turned and spat. "What did being good do for me, Mother?" He waved his arm around, indicating his family. "It got me this—a tortured wife, terrified children, an abused mother and sister, poverty! I am tired of being good, Mother, and when we get to the hated land where they are sending us, there are some traitors who will die for not standing with us!"

He was different, as though the beating had kicked meanness into his blood. She could not know that there was a thing that fed his hatred. He had tasted blood himself, another man's blood. He had killed, and it had felt good and right. His wife and family had been cruelly used, and there were more to blame than Douglas Means. They would all pay.

"Lie down beside Andrea, my son. Speak no more of hatred and killing for now. Neither she nor your sons need to hear such talk. We are told that John Ross is yet in Washington, pleading for a postponement of our trip West until the autumn when it is cooler. In this heat it is bad enough just to sit here. It would be worse on us to be traveling."

397

He looked up at the hot sky, then around at the withered, hopeless people who sat in little bunches, tending to their own. "They deliberately chose a hot, open place for us." He swallowed. "Look at them. They fought so hard, remained peaceful, obeyed the laws, made no trouble for anyone; yet look at them now. And this is only the beginning. We have a long journey ahead of us."

She reached out and hesitantly touched his hand. "Yes, son. For now you must rest. I have a special ointment the doctor gave me for Andrea's back. Later more must be put on her wounds. I will let you do it. She would be soothed by your touch."

His heart tightened. "My touch? I can only hope the day will come when she will want me to touch her again."

Rose's eyes teared. "She will want you to touch her. Love can overcome many things, Adam."

His stricken look tore at her heart. "I will lie down beside her. There is nothing more I can do for now."

Adam's mother studied the badly bruised ribs, then frowned. "Where are your gauze wrappings?"

He met her eyes. "What wrappings?"

"The doctor told us you had injured ribs and that he had wrapped them."

Adam looked down, ran a hand over his stomach. "I . . . took them off."

"Why!"

"I just did!" he snapped. "What does it matter why! I wanted to hurt! I did not want any help!"

She sighed deeply. "I do not understand. There is something you are not telling me, my son. But it does not matter for now. I am glad they released you so we could be together. Please make no trouble. It would be hard on Andrea if they took you away again. She has cried so much for you, was more worried for you than for herself."

Adam turned back to his wife, smoothing her hair again. "It was the same for me." His eyes teared again. "My poor Andrea! Everything is so different than when we used to talk under the oak tree . . . isn't it?" He leaned down and kissed her forehead. "I promise you that one day you will again live like a queen, Andrea Chandler. You'll have a fine home and servants, and we will be free to go and sit under the oak tree. I swear it to Esaugetuh Emissee.''

Andrea trained her thoughts on the oak tree, on being fourteen again and lying in the arms of her sixteen-year-old Cherokee boy. "Adam," she whimpered. How she loved him! Yet she wondered if she would ever again be able to lie beneath him and enjoy that sweet kind of love. Before she had been only his. Now Douglas Means had soiled her and she wanted to die, for Adam Chandler was the only man she had ever loved or had ever wanted. And the terrible journey west was before them. Could things ever again be the same between them?

He lay down beside her then, gently slipping one arm under her face so that she could rest her head against his shoulder. Adam, her sweet, beautiful Adam. It was a start.

Recovery was not easy in the hot, unsanitary camp. Insufficient provisions had been made for such a large number of people. Water was scarce, and the outhouses, overused, were hot and swarming with flies. All dignity had been stripped from the proud Cherokee, as had most of their belongings. As Andrea and Adam slowly recovered from their physical afflictions, they worried about the children, for cholera was beginning to strike the camp. There was not time to talk about each other, about Andrea's ordeal; there was no privacy for touching and holding and finding one another again. The heat was oppressive, the food half-spoiled; and despondency prevailed, as they all sat waiting in the hated prison camp for cooler weather for traveling.

The cholera spread. Many died, including Ruth's and James's four-month-old son. Little Charles Adam was buried in the hills behind the camp, and there was no consoling Ruth. Throughout the camp the wailing of other mothers could be heard, the crying of hungry children, and the constant hymn singing.

The most dangerous disease, however, was not cholera or measles or dysentery; a much more dangerous disease was among them, an emotional disease—hopelessness and depression. To be so confined is the greatest destroyer of the Indian, and it was destroying the Cherokee. Many of the old ones or sick ones willed their own deaths, refusing to eat or drink, choosing to die on their beloved mother soil rather than to leave it.

And through it all Andrea saw a part of her own husband dying. In his attitude toward her he remained steadfast, his sweet affection and gentle understanding the only things that helped her keep her sanity. But she felt a hardness growing in him, a bitterness that made him constantly talk about getting revenge for what was happening to his family and his people. The focus of his hatred began to shift from the government to those who had given up early and had turned tail to run to Indian Territory, those who had not stood with him and John Ross and the majority of the Cherokee who had so bravely fought to stay in their beloved land. Often she saw him talking in little groups with some of the other rebellious young men. James had joined them, his sorrow over his lost son bringing to him frightening changes that made him seem like a different man. Adam seldom spoke of John Ross anymore, but turned his attentions to the traitors—men like John Ridge, Elias Boudinot, and Luke Cloud. He especially talked of Luke Cloud, and of how he would finish what he'd started with the man once they got to Indian Territory.

"He will pay for my sister's rape and my mother's, too—and for my father's death. That snake sank a knife into me, and there is no doubt in my mind that he intended to kill me." He spoke the words more than once, often after drinking the whiskey smuggled into camp by white traders. Andrea wanted to object to the whiskey and to his growing thirst for revenge, for both frightened her. They threatened his safety. Yet she loved him so, knew how he was suffering; and after her own horrible rape, she wanted only his acceptance and love. How could she start chastising him, turn into a complaining woman? Life was bad enough in this horrible camp. Why should she make things more miserable for him? If the whiskey helped him in some way, she would let him drink it.

Finally the night before departure came. It was nearly October. Many had already died, and many more were sick. It would be a long, hard journey, and all knew that great numbers would die on the way. Thousands were in other camps like their own. Most were destitute. The government had waited until they had used up most of their own money for food and supplies before giving out rations. A few had been allowed to take along some cattle and horses, and Adam had managed to locate two of his own horses. He and Andrea would ride, a son riding with each of them. They would pull their meager belongings on the travois Adam had made. Luckily James had a wagon. Ruth and Rose would ride in that, along with whatever old and feeble ones could fit into it amid their belongings. Many more would not be as fortunate. Many would walk. And Andrea knew that she and Adam would both spend a lot of time walking while they let others ride for a while.

Now she and Adam lay together, looking up at a full moon and listening to night sounds. She felt his body jerk suddenly, and she started to sit up, but he grabbed her close and broke into quiet but bitter sobbing. There was nothing she could say to him, nothing she could do for him but let him hold her. Her own tears would not come. She would save them until they were settled in Indian Territory. They clung to one another, each thinking it would have been impossible to survive this without the other. Andrea held Adam tightly and looked past him to Rose, who was standing at the fence, looking out. Her heart ached to think of what must be passing through that woman's mind—thoughts of the happy, prosperous, and loving years here in the land of her people, of her fine home and happy family. Tomorrow Rose would not only leave her beloved homeland, but she would probably never see her husband's grave again. At least Jonas Chandler would stay behind.

It would someday be called the Trail of Tears. History books would touch on the subject only lightly, and in the years to come many Americans would not even hear about it or ever learn the tragic story of the Cherokee. Close to a thousand miles were covered, during the bitterest cold experienced in Illinois and Missouri in many years. The Cherokees struggled through icy waters and thick mud, dust choking them or cold rain soaking them to the skin. Pneumonia took many, cholera and measles took more, and others died of dehydration caused by violent dysentery. Rose Chandler died of pneumonia, and Adam buried his mother somewhere in Illinois. It worried Andrea that he did not weep. He was turning away from feelings now, his hardness becoming more evident.

They had not made love since the night before the militia had come to their home and Douglas Means had dragged her away. There had not been the time nor the opportunity, nor had they even had the desire.

Sometimes that frightened her. She knew that in some respects she needed to make love—to know she could be a woman for him again, to know he still wanted her, to remind herself that Adam was her first man and that Douglas Means had not really touched her at all. Wasn't that what Adam had told her once? Long before Douglas Means had so brutally taken her Adam had told her if a man ever touched her that way, she should never feel soiled, for without her willingness, she had not been touched at all. And surely by now Adam needed to make love to her, not out of a man's need for the physical pleasure, but to reclaim her for himself.

But it would be a long time before such a thing could come to be, and she was terrified that perhaps they could never recapture the innocent happiness they had once known. He was so changed that sometimes it was difficult to remember the Adam she had married—the young Cherokee boy swinging in the great oak tree and teasing her, the young man who had touched her in secret places so that she wanted to surrender all to him and to be used however he chose.

On and on they trudged, some falling in their tracks and dying there. Federal troops accompanied them part of the way. Sometimes state militia men took over. Almost no aid was offered. No doctors were provided. But along the way a few concerned citizens offered food and shelter. Wagons broke down and people had to double up. The cold was hard on them, for the Cherokee were accustomed to the mild, humid Georgia winters. Most did not even have the proper clothing for a truly cold winter. They spent the nights in tents and under wagons, some just lying on blankets on the cold ground. By the time they began to trickle into Indian Territory in the spring of 1839, four thousand Cherokees had died along the Trail of Tears.

But the journey of the Cherokee to a new land was historically important. The controversy stirred by their long and proud fight had created a division between North and South. Bitterness had been seeded, and would grow. Northerners regarded Southerners as people who took advantage of the oppressed, used them for their own gain; people who considered the white man superior and counted those of another color worth no more than animals. The South viewed Northerners as pious hypocrites, who would treat the Indian and the Negro no better if the opportunity arose. The North had factories, but the South had only its plantations and its cotton. Its economy required land, and so the Indians had to go. In the South slavery made growing cotton more profitable. The rumbling dissatisfaction on both sides would grow to a roar twenty years later, then explode into a Civil War.

But for now the Southerners considered the book closed on the Cherokee. By the time the Indians reached their new "home," their beloved land in the northern mountains of Georgia had been overrun by whites who had taken over homes and buildings of the Cherokee, their land and their fine, fat cattle. And while these whites enjoyed a green, lush spring in Georgia, amid tall trees and cool mountains, the Cherokee were enjoying a different spring—the days too hot for so early in the year, the trees scarce, the soil new and unturned. They would be starting over again, with few, if any, advantages. But to start over takes spirit, and they had no spirit now. They stared, dumbfounded, at the wide, open prairies of Indian Territory, having little idea as to what to do next. Most of them were still too full of grief over loved ones lost along the way.

PART III

"... a crime is projected that confounds our under-standings by its magnitude, a crime that really deprives us as well as the Cherokees of a country, for how could we call the conspiracy that should crush these poor Indians our government, or the land that was cursed by their parting and dying imprecations our country anymore? You, sir, will bring down that renowned chair on which you sit into infamy if your seal is set to this instrument of perfidy, and the name of this nation, hitherto the sweet omen of religion and liberty, will stink to the world."

—Ralph Waldo Emerson, letter to President Van Buren regarding the signing of the questionable treaty permitting the removal of the Cherokee from Georgia.

CHAPTER TWENTY-FOUR

The rain poured down, and the roof of their little sod house dripped. They lived on approximately fifty acres near the new Cherokee town of Tahlequah. Adam hated it, hated the land, the town, hated himself. He sat on the bed with a bottle of whiskey, watching Andrea, who was stirring the rabbit stew atop a wood-burning stove. Jonas and John played near the doorway, taking turns standing under a water drip and letting it hit their heads. Adam was beginning to wonder how his wife could possibly love him enough to stay with him now. She could have a much easier life. All she had to do was take the boys and leave him for some white farmer in the North.

He swallowed more whiskey. He didn't feel like going out into the rain to check on the few head of cattle the government had been so kind as to provide. He hardly cared whether or not the potatoes were sprouting or the corn was growing. This was not really his land. If the government gave him the whole of the West, from the Mississippi to the Pacific Ocean, he could not call it home. Home was in Georgia. Hard as he struggled to make it work here in this barren land, he could not find the spirit to pick himself up and start over. What he had done so far had been only for Andrea and his sons, to put food on the table and to earn the pitiful amount they might get for a few cattle and some corn and potatoes on the market come fall. He had managed to save and hide enough money to buy Andrea the stove and a decent bed. And he had some left, but he kept it buried for emergencies. If this first year brought drought or a wave of crop-eating grasshoppers or disease among the cattle, that emergency could mean the end of what was left of the once-wealthy Chandler family.

He took another swallow of whiskey. All he cared about right now was the warm, strong feeling the whiskey gave him. It relaxed him and made him feel good in spite of what had happened. And there was at least one thing to look forward to on this night. The meeting. Andrea didn't know about them. Perhaps she suspected, but she didn't say anything. At the meetings he was happy, powerful, a leader. The young full-bloods spoke of many ways to get even with those who were already here when they arrived—men like Luke Cloud, who now ran a trading post in Indian Territory. Adam was sure he'd built the place on government money—money he'd gotten for being a traitor.

Luke Cloud would pay! Adam had tasted blood once, and it was sweet. He would taste it again. It was important now to stay together, to be strong. If this was where they were to live out their lives, then they would protect this new home. They would keep out the white man; they would chase out the Cherokees who had betrayed them. And if anyone came to this place and told them they must leave, they would no longer be nonviolent. They would fight! Here they would make their own laws. If this was to be Indian country, then it would stay Indian country, and the old Cherokee Blood Law would be followed.

Andrea turned to look at him, and he saw the disappointment in her eyes as he drank more whiskey. He knew she didn't like him to drink it, but she never said anything. He had failed her in her hour of need, had let her fall into the hands of Douglas Means. He had promised her that would not happen, and he would never forgive himself. Surely she blamed him. He would lose her anyway, so he might as well drink the whiskey. He thought of making love to her, but he could not. He was too full of hatred, and too full of sorrow for her catastrophe. Surely she didn't want him to touch her now. She had not asked, and he had not offered, even though he wanted to ravage her, reclaim her, prove to himself that she belonged only to Adam Chandler.

"The stew is ready," she said quietly.

He set the bottle aside and sat down at their homemade table in the small, one-room house of dirt. "I don't want much," he told her. "I'm leaving soon."

She set a bowl in front of him, then just stood there a moment. "Adam, where do you go at night? I get scared when you're away. I wish you would stay here."

"I have to go. You needn't be afraid. There is no Georgia Militia here, and Douglas Means is dead. It is the traitors who came here before us who have to be afraid now." He took a bite of stew and she sat down across from him, studying him warily.

"You never told me what happened to Douglas."

He looked at her almost defensively.

"It's all right," she assured him. "If there is one thing I've learned in the last few months, it's to be strong, to never look back. It's all right to talk about it."

He looked back down at his stew, bit a piece of bread and poked at the meat and carrots. "He's dead, that's all. He died violently, the way a man like him should die. Your violation has been avenged—properly."

She swallowed. "The way you say it, it sounds like you did it yourself."

He swallowed and, putting down his fork and bread, met her eyes. How he loved the beautiful blue pools of sweetness that looked back at him. He still shuddered with rage at the thought of Douglas Means ravaging her, beating her, shaming her. "I did," he said calmly.

She stiffened, paling slightly. She saw his dark eyes turn victorious, saw him straighten a little and hold up his chin like a proud warrior.

"I told him once what would happen to him if he ever touched you," he declared. "I do not make promises

409

without keeping them. Someone who felt sorry for me let me go that night. I came back before the sun was up and was again chained to the post. No one even knew I was gone. I assure you Douglas Means died a terrible death, choking on his own filthy manpart!"

She paled more and looked down, and he got up and walked to the bed, picking up the bottle and taking another swallow. "My woman has been avenged," he added. "I do not regret one moment of it. If circumstances had been different, I would have taken much longer to kill him, enjoying his screams and his bulging eyes. I now know the sweetness of victory as my warrior ancestors once knew it."

He set down the bottle and turned to her. She sat trembling, then broke into tears. She could not totally blame him for doing what he had done, but she feared what that one taste of blood was doing to him, combined with the hopelessness of this new life. She could bear anything, as long as Adam was always Adam. But he was different when he talked of blood and traitors and revenge.

Suddenly he was beside her, grasping her arms in strong hands and lifting her. "Look at me, Andrea," he told her.

She raised watery eyes to meet his dark ones. So handsome he was—more handsome with every passing year. His wounds had healed, but it seemed that as he regained lost weight and became stronger, he became harder. "What do you think of this uncivilized warrior who enjoys the taste of another man's blood, my white woman? What do you think now of Adam Chandler, who likes his whiskey and cares not for his stinking, worthless farm? What do you think of your new husband?"

"Adam, don't!" she begged. "None of this matters to me. I could live anywhere—under any circumstances—as long as I am with you. But I need the Adam I married, not the Adam I am looking at now. Don't let this destroy you, please! I love you so much. And we all need you . . . your sons need you."

"Need me? What good am I to you now? Once I could

have given you the world, made you a queen. And I wanted to give you everything. Then they came and took it all. How can you stay with your Cherokee man now?" He almost sneered as he let go of her and turned away.

Andrea choked back a sob. "Adam . . . don't you love me anymore?"

He turned back, tears on his cheeks. "Love you? Why do you think I risked getting hung to kill Douglas Means?"

"Oh, Adam, don't you understand what it's doing to you? You're so bitter . . . so hard. I'm afraid for you—for us. I'm afraid you'll go out some night and get into some kind of terrible trouble. And I'm afraid I'm losing the sweet, happy, gentle Cherokee boy I used to meet under the oak tree."

He stared at her for a long, silent moment. "That is gone, Andrea. I realize it, but I don't think you do yet. I failed you in every way a man can fail his woman. The only happiness I know is in a bottle, and when I take part in ancient Cherokee rituals at the meeting, I feel the old power come into my blood."

She took a handkerchief from an apron pocket and wiped her eyes as Jonas and John darted out into the rain to let it soak them, for it was a hot day. The boys pulled off their clothes and began to wrestle in the mud, but their parents did not hear their squeals of laughter. Already the children were adjusting to this new life. It was the older people who could not forget their homeland; who had the hardest struggle here in this barren place.

"Once you found happiness in my arms, Adam," Andrea told him. "Our love was strong, and I believe it still is. I believe it's strong enough to bring the old Adam back to me. I need you. We made many promises, Adam, and one you made to me was that someday you would be wealthy again—that you would come out of this, use your intelligence and education to make something of yourself and secure a fine home for your family. You promised that one day you would buy back your own land, and we could go to the oak tree again and sit and talk, that no one could ever again take it away from us."

"I did not know then what would happen, that it would be this bad, that you would be violated and shamed, that my mother would die and my sister would lose her son, that we would be living in a house of dirt!"

"I can bear it all as long as I have you. I need you!" Andrea's voice rose slightly then, in desperation. "Don't go away tonight, Adam, please! Stay here. Maybe we could . . . could truly be man and wife again." She reddened, looking down. "I . . . need to know, Adam. Surely you do, too."

He stepped closer, the whiskey making his blood hot. She wanted him! She'd said so! Yet he was sure he was losing her. He grasped her hair, forcing her to look up at him. "I avenged your rape, and I shall finish that vengeance by reclaiming you for myself," he told her, his voice husky with desire. He met her lips, but in his need his kiss was almost violent. He pressed his hardness against her, then lifted her slightly, carrying her to the bed and falling onto it with her still in his arms. His mouth never left hers, but his kiss was bruising her lips and his hands were moving over her too urgently, too demandingly, bringing back ugly memories; for he was behaving almost as badly as her own rapist had.

This was not what she had meant. The old Adam, the gentle, sweet Adam who had touched her so perfectly, so softly—that was what she wanted. If he were the old Adam, she might be able to give herself again, to enjoy this act, for it would be with her Adam, her precious Adam, whom she loved with her whole being. But this was not that man, and his actions provoked only fear and horrible memories.

His lips left her mouth and traveled over her neck as he tore at the bodice of her dress to expose a breast.

"Adam, stop it!" she shouted frantically. "What are you doing!"

"I am doing what you want me to do," he groaned, his mouth covering a nipple.

"Adam, not this way . . ." She began to struggle then,

412

pushing at him. "The children . . . they could come in."

"Let them." He pulled her dress farther down. "I want you and I shall have you."

"Adam, I didn't mean . . . for it to be like this."

He met her lips again, tore at her dress. And all Andrea could see was Douglas Means, his hideous face hovering over hers, his hands ripping her clothing, hurting her, violating her, shaming her. She screamed. "No." Again. A loud, long no. She scratched her husband's face. Andrea's sudden screams and the pain occasioned by her scratching startled Adam and he stiffened. She pulled away from him then, begging him not to hurt her, screaming something about a whip. He realized with horror that she was remembering, and worse, that this woman he loved had reexperienced that horror at his own hands. Why had he done this thing? Her first time must be beautiful, slow, gentle.

She lay weeping and curled up, and the boys came running in, naked and dripping, staring at their mother. John Ross ran up to her then, started to cry.

"Mommy! Don't cry again, Mommy!"

Adam climbed off the bed, horrified at what he had done. He threw on a cape. "I . . . didn't mean . . ." He stared at his shivering wife. Surely he had lost her for good now. But how he wanted her! Why had he gone about it that way? Why couldn't he like himself anymore? If only he could feel useful again, alive. But only whiskey made him feel that way. He had vowed once that he would never drink it, having seen what it had done to so many of his friends. But now he understood. "I have a meeting to go to," he told her. Feeling helpless and unable to do anything for his wife, he then disappeared into the rain.

Andrea shooed the boys out the door to do their chores; then she stood watching the pink morning sky. Adam had not come home all night. The ache in her heart was worse than any she had yet experienced, for of all her losses,

413

losing him would be the most unbearable. If only he had been more gentle the night before, perhaps they would have awakened together this morning, lying in each other's arms the way they used to do. If only she could have been stronger. Perhaps she should have let him have his way, yet it would have been like lying with a stranger. She could not bear that feeling—not now.

Tears started to come, and she took a deep breath to ward them off. She had cried so much the past few months that she wondered where all the water came from. She should be dried up. She watched the rising sun. If the tears didn't dry her up, this land would. It was hot and barren and she hated it. But she could love it if her husband would just be the man she had married. She only hated this land for what it was doing to Adam.

She turned to go inside when she saw a lone rider approaching, and her heart quickened. Perhaps it was Adam. But as the horse came closer, she saw that the rider was a woman—a white woman, who wore a bright yellow dress and a feathered hat. Even from a distance, Andrea could see that she was wearing expensive but poorly coordinated clothes. A gaudy necklace flashed in the morning sun, yet the woman rode a fine black mare.

Andrea watched and waited. The rider seemed to be coming straight to her humble house, and as she came closer, Andrea's heart tightened. The woman looked familiar, yet she could not quite place her. When she was very near, she smiled through painted lips, her eyelids so heavy with black shadowing that Andrea wondered how she kept them open.

"Andrea! It's been so long! I can't believe it. You've hardly changed!"

Andrea just stared, horror building inside her. Mary Means! Why on earth was she here in Indian Territory! And how did she dare come to visit? What had happened to her? She looked like a prostitute.

Mary slid down from the horse, her smile cold, her eyes insincere, just like Douglas's. She sauntered close, looking

Andrea over as if her childhood friend were now a piece of dirt.

"Looks like your fancy Indian man didn't do so well by you after all," she mocked. She glanced at the sod house. "Kind of a comedown from that fancy brick mansion where you first slept with him, isn't it? Or was it on the ridge that he first got under your skirts?"

Andrea stiffened, anger overcoming her horror. "What are you doing here, Mary?"

Mary Means looked back at her and tried to smile warmly. "I'm sorry, Andrea. I didn't mean to say that. I thought maybe we could be friends again."

Andrea struggled not to lash out and scratch the woman's face. "Friends?" She shook with rage. "Was it a friend who told my parents I was meeting an Indian boy on the ridge? Was it a friend who caused me to be sent away to a horrible place, where they took away my baby!"

Mary's eyes widened. "Baby! You had a baby back then?"

Andrea stepped forward this time, and Mary stepped back. "Yes. I had a son by Adam when I was barely sixteen years old. They took him away from me, and we searched but could never find him. That was twelve years ago! And I do not have one waking moment when he is not on my mind, I have not ceased to pray for my lost son! How dare you speak of friendship! And what in God's name are you doing out here in Indian Territory? You've no reason to be here!"

The woman's eyes hardened slightly. "Why, Andy, I never told on you. What makes you think I did that?"

"I'm not a fool, Mary Means! But it's done with now. Why are you here?"

Mary folded her arms and strutted around, looking over the sod house again. "I've come to lead an exciting life, Andrea. Douglas told me a lot about boys and girls and such things . . . taught me a lot, too."

Andrea shuddered at the mention of Douglas Means. This woman was bringing that memory back, and she wanted to scream.

"I decided it sounded like fun, so I made some trips to the other side of the ridge . . . learned a lot from those Cherokee boys. I swear they're built bigger than the white ones, but then I've enjoyed some fine white men, too."

Andrea felt sick. "Why are you telling me all this? I can't believe you're here at all. Please go, Mary."

"Oh, but you asked me why I was here. I'm just trying to explain, Andy."

"Don't call me that. No one calls me that now."

Mary laughed lightly. "You always hated that name, didn't you?" She shrugged. "At any rate, several men later I decided I was a fool to be giving them so much pleasure for free, so I started charging. Douglas invited me to Atlanta, and helped me set up there. I worked in a very fine house, took in only the richest customers. I made a real bundle, Andy. I'm a rich woman."

Andrea looked at her with contempt. "A rich prostitute."

Mary just laughed. "Of course I'm a prostitute! Do you think the title bothers me? I'm proud of it. That is the reason I'm here. When I used to go over the ridge to the Cherokee boys, one of my favorites was Luke Cloud." She paused, then strutted back to her horse.

Andrea frowned, suddenly realizing she must be careful what she said. Something was happening and it involved Luke Cloud and the meetings Adam had been attending. This woman was after something.

"Luke is a married man," she told Mary.

Mary laughed harder then. "They're the worst! How do you know your Adam has never rolled in the hay with a willing girl while he's been married to you?"

Andrea reddened with anger. "It was not necessary," she said haughtily. "I kept him busy." Mary stiffened and Andrea grinned. "I have the best one of them all. You hate that, don't you, Mary Means? Of the whole Cherokee tribe, I have the finest man."

Mary grasped her horse's bridle and glowered at Andrea.

416

"He's not so great. He got in a fight with my Luke one night, and Luke won."

"Won? Adam nearly beat him to death. But your cowardly Luke Cloud pulled a knife on my husband. Adam didn't even see the knife until it was plunged into him. It could have killed him. Luke's a coward and a snake!"

Now Mary was red. Her eyes turned to narrow, gray slits. "Luke wrote for me to come here—paid me well to get here. He's going to help me pick out some young Cherokee girls to take back with me. The white businessmen of Atlanta like the Indian girls the best. I'll make big money off of them." She held up her chin haughtily. "Luke is a rich man—because he was smart enough to come here before the government forced the rest of you out. If your Adam was as smart as he's supposed to be, he'd have come early. He'd be rich just like Luke. Now it will be a struggle, and the dumb ones like your Adam will be eating out of the hands of the smart ones like Luke. If it weren't for Luke's supply store and his willingness to give credit, the rest of you wouldn't survive! I came out here looking for Cherokee girls—the hopeless ones who see a better life in a whorehouse. Some may not be willing, but their parents will gladly sell them for enough money to keep from starving to death!"

Andrea slapped her hard. Mary cried out and made a fist, but stopped herself from striking. Andrea looked so angry that Mary was actually afraid of her.

"Get off my land!" Andrea was shaking with rage.

"Your land?" Mary turned and mounted up. "Government land. This will never really be your land. Indians can't own land, and neither can their slutty white wives. Don't you look down on me, Andrea Chandler. You've been spreading your legs for that Indian bastard a lot longer than I've been at it." She backed her horse. "Luke Cloud is a good business partner," she added. "I don't want anything to happen to him. And I'll tell you something else. He's going to help me find out what

417

happened to my brother. Poor Douglas died a horrible death, and I know a Cherokee did it. Luke will find out! And when he does, I'll see to it that man is hung! I came here to tell you Luke knows your husband and some others are up to something. They resent the smart ones who came here early. So you tell Adam Chandler he'd better keep his nose out of Luke Cloud's business. And you tell him I intend to find out what happened to my brother! Once I do I'll be leaving here—with plenty of young, fresh Cherokee girls for the fine Atlanta men whose wallets are as fat as their bellies! And you're no better than I am, Andrea Chandler! You were laying with an Indian man at fourteen, and you had his bastard son." She tossed her head. "Maybe you were never even legally married. Maybe those two little breeds I see feeding the chickens over there are also bastards!"

"Get out," Andrea screamed. She picked up a stone, and Mary whirled her horse and galloped off. Andrea threw the stone after her, but missed. She clutched her head in her hands, shaking, all the ugliness of Douglas Means brought back through his hideous sister. How could the little girl she had once called her best friend have turned out this way? Where had everything gone wrong? And Adam! What had Mary meant about Adam keeping his nose out of Luke's business? What was Adam up to when he was gone so many nights? He shared nothing with her anymore. He kept everything to himself and refused to talk about his absences. But she'd heard rumors of secret meetings of full-bloods and something about the old Cherokee Blood Law. Was there some way for Luke to find out about Douglas Means? Who had let Adam loose that night to go and commit such a hideous murder? Adam! Adam had killed, and somehow she knew he would kill again.

She picked up a hoe and walked blindly to a potato field. She had to keep busy. She didn't dare stop now or she would lose her mind. Where was Adam? Why didn't he come home?

Hours passed, and she kept the children busy with

chores, then gave them their spelling lessons. The government had promised schools and teachers for the children once they arrived, but so far such promises had not been kept. None of the promises had been kept. Rations and supplies came too late, and meat was worthless. The Cherokee suppliers, men like Luke Cloud, charged ridiculous prices to their own poor kindred, then dared to gloat about their wealth.

It was early afternoon before Adam finally showed up. He looked tired, his eyes were bloodshot, his shirt open. She stood at the doorway waiting. Their eyes held, and she saw the sorrow in his.

"I'm sorry," he said in a husky voice. "I never meant for it . . . to be like that."

For a brief moment she saw a flash of the old Adam. "It's all right."

"No it isn't!" He looked away. "I just . . . I love you so damned much, Andrea. I feel us slipping apart, and it scares me."

"It doesn't have to happen. Just don't change, Adam. And . . . try to stay away from the whiskey."

He shook his head. "I need it."

"No you don't. You don't need it, Adam! All you need is your own pride, your own education and your God-given intelligence."

"I have no pride left," he said quietly, turning back to face her. "My education couldn't help me keep my land. My intelligence was worth nothing. The only way I can even think of being proud again is to feel like a man. I was a man when I killed Douglas Means, and I'll be even more of a man when I—" He stopped then, and her heart raced. What was he up to?

He dismounted then, and came closer to her. "When I have rid myself of the hatred, Andrea, only then can I be a man for you in the night. The hatred makes me . . ." He breathed deeply and reached out, pulling her close. "I'm sorry, Andrea. I did a terrible thing last night. I get so angry . . . and then I need the whiskey and it all just comes out in stupid ways."

419

She hugged him tightly, glad to have him home safe. "Just don't stop loving me, Adam."

"Never. I could never stop loving you. I didn't come home because I was ashamed. I drank all night, and then I was in such bad shape this morning I couldn't come right away. I stayed with James and Ruth."

She broke into tears of relief, for she'd been sure he'd gone to another secret meeting, perhaps had gone out to kill someone. "Oh, Adam, promise me you'll stay here tonight."

"I will." His whole body trembled. "Andrea, I am so sorry for all of it—for the dirt house, no money, and—"

"Adam, don't. It doesn't matter to me, as long as you love me. I get so scared when you're gone. I've heard rumors . . . about secret meetings, about full-bloods plotting against the traitors." She looked up at him. "Adam, a terrible thing happened this morning. You must be careful!"

He frowned. "What do you mean?"

"Mary Means was here!"

His eyes widened. "Mary Means!"

"She's a prostitute—in Atlanta. She does business with Luke Cloud, and she said Luke is going to supply her with young Cherokee girls to take back to Atlanta. She was awful, Adam. She came here just to sneer at me and show me what she is now. She's ugly and painted and horrible. I wanted to kill her."

He grasped her arms firmly, suddenly changing again. "Mary Means is here to buy Cherokee girls through Luke Cloud?"

Instantly she regretted telling him. "Adam, what are you thinking?"

He turned and mounted his horse. "Adam, wait! You promised!"

"I will be back."

"Adam, she said she's also trying to find out who killed Douglas. She said Luke was going to help her find out! Adam, she's dangerous! Stay out of it!"

"She will not take innocent Cherokee girls and turn

them into whores!" he roared. "I have to talk to someone. I will be back in a while, I promise!"

"Adam, don't leave!"

He rode off then toward Tahlequah. Just the mention of Mary Means and Luke Cloud brought fury to his soul. Months of hatred were coming to a head. It was time to do something.

CHAPTER TWENTY-FIVE

Andrea awoke with a start. She had thought she would be unable to sleep, yet the constant worry of the past few weeks had exhausted her, and when she had lain on the bed as she waited for Adam, she had drifted off. But it had not been a restful sleep. Her nerves were frayed, and she was pained by the memory of how Adam had left.

She stared into darkness, sensing something wrong but not sure what. There was a strange cracking sound somewhere far in the distance, then an explosion.

"Adam!" she whispered. She jumped up and reached for the flint. It had not been completely dark when she had lain down, but now she felt it was very late.

She lit the lamp and turned it up, then checked on the boys, who slept peacefully in their own small bed, half-sprawled over each other. She smiled, wondering if she would ever have been able to bear everything without the knowledge that she must keep going for the sake of her sons. Briefly she allowed herself to think about her first son—Nathan, they still called him. She hoped that perhaps he was better off wherever he was than living here in this desolate land. Yet she could not help but suspect that he was not.

She picked up the rifle Adam always left for her. Whatever her husband was up to, it was not good. She opened the door and stepped outside, then gasped at the glowing sky. Orange flames could be seen easily from the town, only two miles distant over treeless land. Was all of Tahlequah burning, or just part of it? Considering the location of the flames, she was certain one building that was burning was Luke Cloud's trading post.

"My God, Adam," she groaned. "Where are you! What have you done!" It had to stop somewhere, or Adam Chandler would end up in prison or hanged. He might be shot by his enemies, or they might do harm to his family. Being taken from his natural habitat and put on the defensive had brought back Adam's warrior instincts. But these were not the old days, and his need for revenge could not go on forever. After all the amazing progress the Cherokees had made in the past thirty years, they now seemed to be going backward, back to old beliefs and rituals, back to physical conflict over territory and for revenge, only this time they did not fight other Indian tribes or the white man. This time they fought each other, and there could be no sadder ending to such a proud and intelligent people.

She waited for what seemed hours, huddled near the door, watching the orange sky. She feared for her own life, and wondered what had happened and whether someone was after Adam. Finally the flames died down, and the sky was not so well lit. She went back inside then and bolted the door, almost laughing to herself at how easily someone could break into her little sod house. The door and its frame were the only really solid items in the makeshift home. She wondered if, and when, she would ever have a real house again, whether she and Adam would ever live like normal people. She sat down at the table and picked up her Bible, keeping her gun beside her—waiting. A mantel clock they had salvaged from their belongings ticked nearby on a small table. The ticks seemed to grow louder with each passing minute, and she tried to ignore them.

Finally she heard an approaching horse. She set the Bible aside and picked up the rifle. The horse stopped, and in the next moment someone knocked on the door.

"Who is it?"

"It's me—Adam. Hurry up. I am hurt."

She set the rifle aside and hurried to the door, letting him in. Her eyes widened at the sight of him. He was black from smoke and his left arm was bleeding. "Adam! Dear God, what happened!"

He sat down on a chair. "Some people died tonight," he said quietly. "That is all I can tell you. It is over now. The traitors will bother us no more. At least there has been some retribution for having to live in this miserable place!"

"Adam, what have you done?" She quickly began to heat some water.

"I don't want to talk about it. The less you know, the better. It is bad enough that you know I killed Douglas Means. I only told you because I needed you to know that I avenged your violation."

She swallowed back tears. Going over to him, she unbuttoned his shirt, helped him slip it off. "What happened to your arm?"

He sighed deeply. "Someone shot at me."

She looked at him with terrified eyes and he actually grinned, something she had not seen him do for a long time. "Don't worry. It won't happen again."

Jonas woke up and rubbed his eyes. "Father?" He sat up. "Father, you're hurt!"

"Lie back down, son. I will be all right." He grimaced as Andrea dabbed at the flesh wound with a wet cloth. "Get me some whiskey."

She hesitated. "It isn't that bad."

"I don't mean for pain. I just need it. After what I have been through tonight I need a drink."

Her lips set tight in anger. She got out a bottle and set it on the table, harder than necessary. "Don't you realize that you're falling into the pit many of your friends have fallen into by drinking this stuff? It will destroy you, Adam. It might destroy both of us!"

He just gave her a playful wink. "You worry too much. It is time now to stop worrying." He uncorked the bottle with his teeth, spit out the cork, and then took a swallow.

She said nothing more. The water warmed and she washed the wound and, taking the whiskey from his hand, doused it on the open flesh. He jerked but made no sound, then watched her as she began to bandage his arm.

"I think you enjoyed that, Mrs. Chandler."

She met his dark eyes. Why was it so difficult to stay angry with him? There were moments when he seemed like the playful, teasing Adam she had met under the oak tree. "Maybe I did," she answered. "You deserved it. You'd better wash all that black off the rest of you. You'll not come to bed the way you are now."

He reached up and touched her face. "I promised I would be here tonight, and here I am."

She tried to remain angry. "Barely. Another hour and it will be dawn." She tied off the bandage. "There. That's the best I can do. Thank God it wasn't more serious. There isn't a doctor for miles, and none that would treat a Cherokee at that."

"We'll get a doctor here, one way or another. The missionaries will send one. Someday we will be well settled and everything will be like it was at New Echota." His voice choked on the last word and he swallowed more whiskey. "Yes, sir, you'll see. It will be wonderful again. I will build you a fine house here, make a little money on my farming, and—"

"You promised to build me a house on our land in Georgia. You said that you would build yourself up again and buy back your land legally. What happened to that promise, Adam? You're capable of making it happen. At least the Adam I once knew was capable of it. Now you speak of being a little farmer in the middle of nowhere. You're giving up, Adam. You could do great things."

He broke into a bitter laugh. "Oh, yes. There is so much opportunity out there for young Cherokee men. All doors are open. We are welcome wherever we go." He got up and undressed. "It was all a dream I once thought could come true. I don't believe it anymore." He threw down his clothes, leaving on only his underwear, then slugged down more whiskey. "I am tired, Andrea. I need to forget

426

what happened tonight." He sat down on the bed and sighed wearily. "Sometimes I think about taking my life. Maybe it would be better for you and the boys if I were dead. You could go north, probably find yourself a nice farmer or even a wealthy businessman to marry. You are still young, and more beautiful than ever."

She soaped up a washcloth and washed his face and neck. "There would be no purpose to my own life without you. Don't talk foolishly, Adam." She toweled off his face. "I love you. I need my man, and the boys need their father. How can you think I could ever love another man after loving you?"

He leaned forward and kissed her forehead. "You're too good for the likes of me, Andrea Chandler."

She put down the towel and took his hand. "No, I'm not. That's the way I've felt about you all these years. I worship you, Adam. I'm proud of your intelligence and education, proud of your strength and pride, your courage. Just be my Adam. And leave the whiskey alone, Adam. Everything could change if you would stop drinking."

He pulled his hand out of hers. "I love you, Andrea, but don't tell your man what he can and cannot do."

She paled and her chest ached. He had never before made such a statement to her. A lump swelled in her throat and she turned away, blinking back tears as she opened the door and carried the water outside to dump it. By the time she had finished cleaning up, he was sprawled on the bed in a deep, exhausted sleep.

She walked closer to the bed, staring down at his hard, muscular body. Yes. she could lie beneath him again, if he would touch her and make love to her the way he used to do. But her worst fear was being realized. Adam Chandler would not be brought down by his human enemies. He would be brought down by his own feeling of inadequacy, his own guilt, his own despair, all of which led him to the brown bottle. How many other strong young men had she seen destroyed by the firewater?

She broke into tears as she sat down beside him and

gently pulled the bottle from his hand. Setting the whiskey aside, she leaned down to kiss his cheek, to touch his thick, dark hair. He was nearly thirty now, and she would soon be twenty-eight. In all their years together, there had been so few moments of true peace and happiness. How she wished they could go back, even just for a little while, to the oak tree, to the special love they had found there.

She undressed and crawled into bed beside him, resting her head against his shoulder. "Sleep well, my warrior," she said softly. "God save you from yourself."

Adam fell deeper and deeper into the brown bottle, and Andrea did not know how to stop him. She, Jonas and John did much of the harvesting, meager as the crops were, for Adam was usually too drunk to help. He even sold some of their badly needed food in order to buy more whiskey. Andrea watched helplessly. He spoke no more of what had happened the night of the fire, but she knew from stories that had circulated what must have happened. Luke Cloud was dead, and the fancy woman who had been found with him had been run out of town, her life threatened. Others had been killed that night, all Cherokees who had come west before the great forced migration, most of them wealthy by the time the rest of the Cherokees arrived. The worst news was that John Ridge and Elias Boudinot had both been murdered for signing the treaty and speaking for Removal. There were still a few threats and some unrest, but Adam seldom went out at night anymore. Andrea could only wonder how many murders he had committed himself.

She did not doubt that he had had a hand in killing Luke Cloud, who'd been beaten and left to die in the flames of his own trading post. Yet knowing what the man had been up to, she could not feel sorry for him, nor could she fully blame Adam. But all the killing and hatred had led him to the whiskey, and now he seemed to be on a road from which there was no turning back.

Summer and autumn passed, then came winter, a long,

cold winter that sometimes left them buried in their little sod house. Andrea tried to think up games for the children, ways to keep busy, while Adam sat and drank. Sometimes he read, but not nearly as much as he once did. And never did he mention making love, nor did he try to do it. There were moments when she sensed he was considering it, but he would always back away, as though he were unworthy of touching her. And her own ordeal with Douglas Means had left her too ashamed to make any brazen advances toward her husband. Their days of playful, teasing sex were over, and the beautiful physical love they had once shared seemed ended. She wondered how much longer it would be before the marriage itself ended, for she lived with a stranger now, and her agony knew no bounds.

In the spring Adam spent more time in town than at home, and was of little help in planting a new crop. James did much of the plowing, a difficult task, for he had his own farm to tend to. Andrea now knew that for survival she would have to leave her husband and take refuge with a Northern mission. The thought of leaving Adam tore at her. How could she truly do it? Yet how could they keep going this way? Perhaps if she left him he would stop drinking in order to get her back. Her decision finally came after a two-night absence, nights she knew he had spent in Tahlequah, perhaps even sleeping with some of the young Cherokee girls who were now prostitutes, having lost all their pride after being repeatedly raped by Georgia Militia. Adam had killed to prevent young Cherokee girls from being drawn into prostitution, but that was now happening right on their own reservation; for hopelessness ran rampant throughout Indian Territory, not just among the Cherokees, but also the Creeks, Choctaws, and Seminoles. To Andrea it seemed the whole world was coming to an end. Those Cherokees who had survived the Trail of Tears were now destroying themselves.

A few had managed to hang on and were slowly rebuilding a life. Andrea had always thought Adam would be one of them. But now that hope was dwindling.

Toward evening of the third day he finally came home, but he was so drunk he half fell off his horse. He greeted her with a grin, placed his hands on her shoulders and leaned over to kiss her. But his breath repulsed her, and she knocked his hands away. "Where have you been? I smell perfume mixed in with that whiskey breath! Cheap perfume—the kind whores use."

His eyes moved over her. "Better the whores than you. I don't deserve to lie in bed with my beloved wife any longer."

"Stop it, Adam! I can't take anymore. I keep waiting for you to find your pride again. You said you'd find it if you got your revenge. You got it, and you've gone downhill ever since! If you want to be a man, then stop drinking!"

He grasped her arm. "I told you once not to tell me what to do."

"I'll tell you whatever I like! I love you. I can't just sit and watch you destroy yourself, Adam! I need you. Your sons need you. This farm needs you. You say you failed us before. But you didn't. You were more man than I could ever want. But what I'm looking at now is no man! You've become so weak that you let whiskey rule your life!"

The blow came too quick for her to be prepared. She felt herself falling sideways into a chest of drawers, and her ears rang. Her face was instantly hot and stinging, and for a moment she could not even grasp what he had done. She fought to get her breath, realizing with horror that he had hit her. Adam had hit her! Beautiful, sweet Adam had hit her. It seemed incredible. Never had she had to be afraid of such a thing. Never had she once considered that Adam Chandler would hit her.

She heard a choking sound near her then and someone was lifting her, holding her. "Andrea! Andrea! My God, Andrea, forgive me. Forgive me! Help me, Andrea."

It took her a moment to regain her senses, and all the while he gently kissed her puffed, red cheek and held her so tightly she could barely breathe.

"I . . . want to stop, Andrea, really I do," he groaned. "I . . . don't know . . . how! I've lost myself. I see faces . . .

430

faces of men I have killed . . . faces of militia men . . . my father . . . my mother. I hear screams . . . and see him . . . raping you. The whiskey . . . makes it all go away."

She decided that was the time to be firm. Perhaps his hitting her was the best thing that could have happened.

"You've got to stop, Adam," she told him with a note of finality. "If you don't, I'll leave you. I can't live this way anymore. I need you . . . but not the Adam who is holding me now. I need my husband back. He left me somewhere along the Trail of Tears."

He held her against his trembling body for a long time, then pulled back, putting a hand to her swollen face. Tears ran down his cheeks. "What should I do, Andrea?"

She dropped her eyes and pulled away. "I don't know, Adam. Whatever it is, you have to do it alone. All I know is that I have lost my husband." She turned away and he made a groaning sound and ran out. In the next moment she heard his horse gallop off, and she felt a grief almost as heavy as if he had died.

Six weeks passed with no word. Andrea spent most of the time with James and Ruth, but she felt in the way at their place. Ruth was pregnant again, and James seemed to be coming around better than some of the others. He tended his farm faithfully, and both he and Ruth were glad to give Andrea and the boys shelter. But it was too much of a burden for them. Since Andrea had no idea whether Adam would come back, she had to make a decision, and she began to pack her few possessions for the trip north to the Methodist mission. At least there she would have shelter until she decided how she was to survive. Adam might be drunk, or he might have killed himself. How she would manage to go on, she wasn't sure, for she blamed herself for letting him go away that awful night. She should have stopped him. He'd needed her and she had failed him. At the time it had seemed right to turn away from him, but now she was not so sure, and her agony was almost unbearable. If it were not for Jonas and John,

431

Andrea would have found it impossible to go on living.

Adam! What had happened to their beautiful love? There had been a time when she'd been so sure it could not die, and for her own part it had not. But it was not today's Adam that she still loved. She still loved the proud, intelligent, fiery Cherokee man she had married, not the broken, weak man he had become because of the whiskey.

Jonas was ten now, and John Ross was nearly nine. She had taught them as best she could, but neither of them had yet had any formal schooling. At least at the mission they could get that for the time being. Soon schools would be built right here in Indian Territory, but she could not wait, at least not without Adam. If he were here . . . But it was no use wishing or hoping. The brown bottle had been too powerful for him.

She set two carpetbags near the door and started to pack the dishes. So little was left from the grand estate Adam and Jonas Chandler had once owned. And she had nothing left from her childhood. Pain went through her at the thought of her dead mother and of the secret the woman had lived with for so many years. Life was so strange, so often ruled by fate and restricted by lies. But her love for Adam Chandler had never been a lie. It was the most real, the most beautiful experience she would ever know, and in spite of all she had been through she did not regret it. If it were not for the whiskey and for the bitterness in his own heart, that love could still be as beautiful as it was in the beginning.

She heard a horse then, and her heart quickened. Suddenly chilled, she stood frozen in place. Could she hope it was her husband? Moments later she heard Jonas and John shouting, "Father! Father! Where did you go?"

Andrea felt limp and nervous, suddenly wondered how she looked; for outside she could hear Adam laughing and talking to his sons, in a way she had not heard him talk and laugh in months. He almost sounded like the old Adam.

"Where is your mommy?" he was asking.

"She's in the house. She is packing things to go away,"

Jonas told him. "Don't let her go, Father. We want to stay here by Aunt Ruth and Uncle James. And if she goes away we might not see you anymore."

There was a moment of silence. "Don't you worry. Your mommy isn't going anywhere." His voice was still cheerful. He wasn't angry. "You two run over to Aunt Ruth's and tell her I am back and I want you to stay there for a while. She will understand. I will go and talk to mommy."

There was a moment of playful laughter, then silence. Andrea clung to the back of a wooden chair, feeling as nervous as when she had first met Adam Chandler and had been overwhelmed by his handsomeness and his charm.

When the door opened, her heart skipped a beat at the sight of him. He was clean and neat, wearing tight-fitting black pants and a white shirt with a ruffled front. His wavy dark hair was neatly cut, making a neat contour around his collar. And his eyes were bright, not dull and red; his smile was quick, the old smile of the old Adam. At that moment he seemed more handsome than he had ever been since she'd met him fourteen years earlier. His eyes ran over her in the old, teasing way, that provocative way that made Andrea feel under his power.

He closed the door. "The boys say you're going away."

"I . . ." She swallowed. "I had to do something. We've no money—"

He held up a finger. "Wrong, Mrs. Chandler. Everything is going to be different from now on. I hope you'll stay long enough to let me prove it."

"I don't understand. Where have you been?"

He stepped closer. "I will tell you. But first I wish you would let me hold you."

Her tears came then, and she fell into his arms. "Oh, Adam, where did you go? I felt like it was my fault. I thought you . . . killed yourself or something awful had happened to you."

"What happened was your fault, and it was good. You are a smart woman and a beautiful, wonderful, devoted wife, and you've put up with hell this past year." He kissed her hair. "God, forgive me, Andrea, especially for hitting you. When I did that, I knew I had lost myself and that I would lose you and my sons if I didn't change."

She hugged him tightly. Did she dare believe this was really happening, that she had her old Adam back? Yet here he was, holding her, apologizing, telling her he had changed. She leaned back and looked up at him, and his lips met hers then in a hungry kiss, a passionate kiss, the kind of kiss neither had offered the other since they'd been torn from their home over a year ago. And they had not made love since that had happened. Both had a hunger long buried. Both had something to prove to themselves—and to each other. Could they find that sweet passion they had known under the oak tree? Could they rekindle that wonder, that glory? It was a silly question. One heated kiss told them the answer, and there was one thing they must do before they did any more talking. One aspect of their marriage had been neglected far too long.

Adam showered her with kisses, and she whispered his name over and over. He felt her apprehension, knew what her memories were like. But he knew he would erase them and reclaim his woman. It was over now. He had avenged her; all the hatred and bitterness was out of him.

Andrea was soon lost in a swirl of tender kisses and whispered Cherokee words of love. Strong arms carried her to the bed, gentle hands undressed her, warm lips explored, tasted, caressed; loving her so gently, so perfectly, in the way Adam Chandler used to love her. His body was somehow naked then, hot and trembling. How he needed her! And she needed him! It was ecstasy to be lying beneath her handsome Cherokee man again, letting him possess her, claim her, love her. They laughed and cried, teasing at one moment, serious the next, touching, enjoying. She opened herself to him and he came inside, pushing, wanting, erasing all bad memories. She wondered how this act could be so horrifying with one man, and so beautiful with another. Yet there had been a time when she'd thought she could never again enjoy such pleasure.

She arched up to him, wanting to give and give; he drove deep and hard, wanting to do the same, reminding himself that he was her first man. Andrea Chandler's virginity belonged only to him; he was the only man she had been willing to entrust with her body and heart.

It had all been so quick, almost frantic. At one moment he was standing at the door; the next he was invading her, one with her. Love had won out after all, and Andrea's heart had never known such joy. Was it only minutes, or was it hours that they lay there sharing bodies, moist skin against moist skin, silken touches and tender kisses throwing them both into rapture unlike any they had shared.

His life poured into her then, and he cried out with the ecstasy of the moment, then released a long sigh and rolled onto his side, keeping her in his arms. He pulled the blankets over them and Andrea snuggled close, savoring every beautiful moment, feeling once again sheltered and protected—Adam was home.

"I've been to Independence," he told her. "I will tell you everything about what happened the night I killed Douglas Means. It is over now, and things have calmed down. Nothing more can happen, for only you and one other person know. I have already seen that person—and his father."

She frowned, pulling back to meet his dark eyes. "Adam, what on earth—"

He put his fingers to her lips. "When they took us to the holding camp, the Federal in charge had heard of my work in the fight to stay in Georgia. He felt sorry for me, the way they had beaten me and all. You were probably in too bad a way then to remember him. At my request he went to the militia camp and sought you out. He brought you back, and when he saw how you had been treated, he was very angry, especially since you were white. He understood my manly feelings, my need for revenge." Adam sighed and pulled her close. "I was like a crazy man then, Andrea. I felt I had failed you, and the only way to make it up to you was to kill Douglas Means. The lieutenant understood. He

435

is a good man, a man of compassion. He stood guard over me that night, and after dark he let me go and gave me a knife, told me where I could find Douglas Means. I left my clothes behind so I would not get blood on them. Then I killed him, and I washed myself in a creek before returning. The lieutenant chained me back up, and when the militia came in the morning he told them I had been there all night. There was no way to prove otherwise, and it was obvious that in the chains I could do nothing."

She kissed his chest. "But what does that have to do with Independence?"

He grinned. "That is the best part. The lieutenant's name is Martin Renfro, and he is from Independence. His father is an attorney there. Martin told me before he left the prison camp that if I was ever in bad need, I should come there and his father would give me a job as an apprentice. He had heard I was Harvard educated. I wasn't sure he was really serious about his father giving a job to a Cherokee Indian. But considering what was happening to me here, I knew the only way I could get back on my feet was to leave this place and use my education—get back to work with books and laws—use my brains again instead of dousing them with whiskey. Others have been able to get on their feet right here, like James has. But I can't get used to it here, Andrea. And most of the others can't either. It will be a long struggle, but I decided that I should use the education for which my father paid so dearly. So I went to Independence."

She hugged him tightly. "Oh, Adam, you got the job?"

He wound his fingers in her golden hair. "Yes. Martin's father is a very gracious man. Now I understand why his son is such a fine man. Martin was there himself and is preparing to finish his own schooling. He is out of the Army now. He is a good man and will be a reliable friend. At any rate, I wrote up some briefs for his father, who was very impressed by how quickly I got them finished, considering that I was unfamiliar with the cases involved. He paid me for that work and gave me an advance so I might return and then go back to work under him for one

436

year." Adam pulled back, touching her face with a big hand. "I am going back, Andrea. I will work hard, and I will send you money regularly, some for you and some for Ruth and James, to cover the cost of letting you stay with them. And in a few months, when I am sure it will all work out, I'll find us a place to live and send for you. But at first, I think I would like to work very long hours and just take a room for sleeping. I want to prove myself quickly, Andrea, perhaps be a full-fledged lawyer much sooner than most. Then I can slow down a little and you can come there. At first there will be little time for my family, and you would be all alone in a strange city. I want to break the children in gently to that new life, be with them as much as I can at first. Will you wait here for a few months? I promise it will not be too long, perhaps six or eight months."

She put a hand over his. "It will seem like forever, but considering the reason for our separation, I'll do whatever you want. Just knowing I have my old Adam back is all I need." She was afraid to ask, but knew she had to. "What about the whiskey, Adam?"

He shook his head. "The first week was bad. I have not touched a drop since I left here that night. I knew getting off it was the first thing I had to do. But I was miserable. The pain and the bad dreams were terrible. I stayed alone on the prairie, sometimes rolling in the buffalo grass and feeling like a crazy man. After a few days it got better, but I was shaking all the time. By the time I got to Independence I was over it." He kissed her forehead. "No more whiskey, Andrea. I promise you. And I renew the other promises I made. Someday I will be a wealthy attorney, and I will find a way to legally buy back my land. We will go back to Georgia wealthy and successful, Andrea Chandler, and I will open a law practice there, and we will live in a grand brick home and go and sit under the oak tree whenever we choose."

"Oh, Adam, do you really think we can go back, after all the things that happened there? Maybe it's best to stay in Independence."

"No. Things will change. The hatred will die down.

And I will offer your father or whoever else owns the place by then so much money it would be impossible to turn it down." He grinned. "Only they will not know it is Adam Chandler who wants to buy it. I will send a white man to represent me. Even if we do not move there right away, it will feel good knowing I own that land again. But we will be rich enough to take our time deciding. This I promise you, my beautiful and elegant wife."

She laughed lightly. "Adam, it's all so wonderful. I can't believe it."

His eyes teared. "God sent Martin Renfro to me on that terrible day, I am sure of it. He let me get my revenge, and then he opened a path by which I could find my way back out of hell. I know I will be successful, Andrea. I am too determined to fail. And once I am a licensed attorney, I will do all I can to continue to help the Cherokee, for I see more troubles in the future. The white man will not stop at Indian Territory, Andrea. He will go on through, all the way to California. More Indians will suffer what we suffered in Georgia, and much of this Indian Territory they have given us will be taken away. The wilder Indians, those who ride the plains and hunt the buffalo, will suffer just as we did; they will be pushed onto reservations. I see it all happening, and there will be no stopping it. But I have an education, and I intend to show them just how resilient and successful an Indian can be."

She leaned forward and kissed his lips. "And I know you'll do it." Her eyes teared. "Oh, Adam, I'm so happy. I'm so proud of you. But it will be hard, waiting."

"I will write often, and I will make love to you in my dreams."

Their eyes held. It had been so long. So long . . . There was so much to make up for, so much to experience all over again. Their love had been reawakened, along with their passion. She was suddenly fourteen again, and he was sixteen, and they lay under the great, protective arms of the oak tree. He moved on top of her then, parting her lips with a tender kiss. After this long, they must be one again, only this time they would make love slowly. They would take their time and enjoy every tiny touch. The sweet scent of lovemaking, of heated bodies, filled the small sod house. To Andrea it was like the aroma of spring flowers. She did not see the sod house at all. She looked up as he entered her, and she saw only golden leaves and a blue sky beyond.

The letters came regularly, and it had been a long time since Andrea had been so happy. Adam was working hard, certain that soon he would be licensed and a full partner in the Michael Renfro's law practice. The firm would be called Renfro and Son, Attorneys at Law, for Martin would join his father in another few months. Andrea could not remember Martin Renfro. She only remembered that soldiers had come and taken her away from Douglas Means. But she wished she could remember this man, and she sent him a note thanking him for his offering Adam employment.

More displaced Indians flooded into Indian Territory, and the influx of Eastern Indians pushed at the Plains Indians already entrenched in the Western lands. New rivalries began to take shape, and sometimes there were skirmishes between the Eastern and Western tribes. Andrea found it ironic that the once-flourishing Cherokee were now reverting to old warrior ways at times, going back on all that they had achieved in Georgia, yet starting all over again.

And many were surviving, many were building. A school was opened in the autumn of 1840. Jonas and John attended it. Ruth gave birth to a baby girl, named Rose after her dead grandmother, and James's farm began to take shape and realize a profit. Adam sent money regularly to help all of them, and Andrea could finally again hope that at last they would be able to start a new life and live the way a family should.

In the beginning she never wondered whether or not she would have stayed with Adam Chandler, married him, if she had known what would happen. There was no question in her mind. She would do it all over again if she were taken back and knew what she knew now. For she was the wife of Adam Chandler, and that was all that mattered. He had fathered their two beautiful sons, now eleven and ten; and a third son. Nathan Peter would be fourteen now. Fourteen. If he was alive, Andrea was sure he was just as smart and handsome as his brothers. Would the pain of never knowing him ever leave her? She thought not, but it seemed now that if she was ever to meet him, it would have to be after death. But she would not think about that now. There were too many good things happening; there was too happy a future ahead of them now. For the time being she could not and would not look back on all the pain and loss. She must look forward.

Finally in the spring of 1841 came the letter she'd been waiting for. He had passed his exam and was an attorney. He had found a small but comfortable home to rent and he was coming for her to take her to Independence. Within two weeks Adam would be there, holding her again, making love to her again. How she had missed him! What a long, lonely winter it had been. Now he was coming, and they would leave their little sod house behind them. She had not even lived in it for several weeks. Over the winter James had built a frame house for Ruth, and for the first time in nearly two years they all lived in a real house again, a family. Little Rose was a year old, fat and happy, already walking, and Ruth was pregnant again. Life was good, so very, very good.

And so when tragedy struck again, it was harder to take than all the other tragedies put together, for Andrea was about to face the worst horror of her life. On a night in mid-June, 1841, her newly happy world came crashing down around her. It started with the sound of rumbling hooves, and the faint sound of war whoops. It was early morning, and Andrea had just finished dressing. Everyone else still slept, none of them yet hearing the horses. Andrea looked toward the door. Although she had never seen the wild, savage kind of Indians she'd heard lived west of the Cherokee settlements, she knew instinctively that she was hearing their cries. Indians! But far different from the gentle Cherokees she knew so well. The Plains Indians lived as the Cherokee had, before they'd become educated and Christianized.

She yelled for James. Already the yipping and thundering horses could be heard all around the house.

CHAPTER TWENTY-SIX

Andrea tugged again at her leather bindings. But the pain it brought to her swollen wrists and ankles was almost unbearable. They rode, day after day, her wrists bound behind her, her ankles secured under the big Appaloosa, her body tied against the cruel Comanche man who carried her on his horse. Her confusion and terror were boundless, and her physical condition was getting progressively worse. At first she had refused to let her head rest against the greased back of the dark Indian who was her apparent "owner." But now she was so weary she could not help but let her head drop forward. Her mouth was parched, her stomach a tight little ball of hunger.

Why? Why had they come? And why only to Ruth and James's house, chopping their way through the door, terrorizing all of them, then taking only her and no one else. The children, thank God, had been left untouched, and Ruth had not been harmed, though James had suffered a blow from a club. Andrea could only hope he would be all right. But the Indians had come right to her, had dragged her out despite kicks and screams and the terrified crying of her sons.

That had been nearly a week ago. Since then they had ridden hard, stopping only to relieve themselves and eat. They fed her little, gave her hardly any water, and laughed at her when she urinated. But they had not raped her or even touched her in that way. It was as though they had some kind of mission, as though they were delivering her somewhere. Andrea could only speculate because she did not understand their language. To their village? Would she become the captive of some Comanche chief, to be used in horrible ways and then tortured to death? And why? She could not begin to imagine a reason for any of this. Her captors apparently had not needed food or anything else. Nothing had been taken from James and Ruth.

Adam would be home by now. He would be at the house, happy and eager, ready to take her and the boys to Independence. Poor Adam! What would this do to him? He had such big plans. Would this destroy them? Would he turn to the bottle again when he found her missing? Surely he would come after her—try to find her. Of course he would! She took hope in the thought. Adam would find her, and whatever had been done with her, it wouldn't matter. He would still love her. He would take her to Independence and they would be happy together. She had to be positive. She had to think of Adam and the boys, or she would lose her mind.

It was hard to believe that Adam's own ancestors had once been this uncivilized, this cruel, this hard. These Comanche men were nearly naked, their bodies painted grotesquely, and they carried an array of weapons. Andrea loved and lived with an Indian, yet these Indian men terrified her. She could not understand a thing they said, and only occasionally did she note any feeling of compassion in any of them. The one who kept her with him constantly would at times give her some extra food when the others were not looking, and he always made sure she was kept warm at night, sleeping right beside her with plenty of blankets, but not touching her rudely. She knew that while she was with him, nothing horrible would happen to her, but he refused to unloose her leather bindings, and he stared when she relieved herself. Finally she got used to the stares and the laughter and ignored them. She had a slight hope that the one who looked after her would somehow turn around and help her, but that was dashed when they finally rode into the camp where she saw several men—white men.

Andrea shivered, even though the day was hot. She knew instinctively what was happening, yet she also knew if she screamed and ran she would be killed. She had to stay alive—somehow—for surely Adam would come. But how would he find her?

They rode past a row of white women, some young, some old, all tied, their clothes torn, their hair a tangled mess, their faces dirty and tear-stained. Some were crying even that moment. Several wagons and horses were about, and a couple of campfires. Men talked and drank and laughed, dirty, sweaty, unshaved men. One man walked up to a crying girl and slapped her hard, telling her to shut up.

Andrea was certain she would join the others, and be earmarked for some strange, horrible fate. She had been singled out. There were other white women around Tahlequah. Why her? That was the one thing she could not understand.

Her Comanche captor dismounted. Untying the strap around the horse, he pulled her off, letting her fall to the ground. She just lay there while men came up to the Comanches, speaking in sign language and Comanche both. One of the white men turned and looked at an enclosed wagon. "Mary!" he called. "Come on out here and make sure this is the right one."

Mary? Andrea's heart pounded. It couldn't be! She sat up and stared toward the enclosed wagon. A woman climbed out, a woman with mousy brown hair and steely gray eyes. She was wearing a red, low-cut dress, and her eyes were heavily painted. She sauntered toward Andrea, smiling more widely as she came closer. Andrea glared back at her. She needed to ask no questions. This had all been planned.

Mary looked her over, then laughed lightly. "Your precious Adam should never have killed my Luke." She sneered. "Now he will pay dearly." She reached down and ripped open the front of Andrea's dress. "There you go, boys, have a look!" she told the men, overjoyed at the look of shame and horror on Andrea's face. "She's the one, all right. Don't you think the Mexican men will pay a pretty penny to get a mouthful of those nice white breasts and to do whatever else they want with this pretty white girl?"

They all laughed. Then one of them went to a long box, from which he took a rifle. He held it out to Andrea's captor. So, these men paid Indians with rifles, and probably whiskey, to kidnap white women. The cost of the whiskey and rifles was probably nothing compared to what they got paid for the women down in Mexico.

Andrea turned over to hide her breast, struggling not to vomit. Adam! He had to come. He had to!

Mary bent down, still laughing. "You always thought you were so high and mighty, Andy. What do you think now?" She pushed Andrea over onto her back, then yanked off the rest of her clothes, while the men whooped and laughed. Throwing the torn dress aside, she then sauntered around Andrea's naked body. "This business of selling my body to men has made me a rich woman, Andy. And I'm getting even richer dealing in the sale of other women to men who would give everything they own to bed a beautiful white woman. You will notice that most of my captives are pretty blondes. They're the favorites of Mexicans—blonde and redheads. You'll be a prize package. Who knows? Maybe you'll be as rich as me someday, when you learn to like it and we can trust you enough to keep you off the drugs."

Andrea wondered how she managed to breathe. Never had such horror run through her. Drugs? What did she mean? Mary bent closer to her face then.

"You'll be taken to a grand Mexican whorehouse, Miss Uppity Chandler, and you'll give yourself to every Mexican who comes along and is willing to pay for you—because you'll have no choice. There are certain drugs we can give you to make you wild for it. You'll see. It won't be so bad. Might be the most wonderful experience you've ever had. Before long you won't even think about your precious Adam anymore. Compared to what you'll be doing, sleeping with him will seem boring."

Andrea stared into the face of the woman who had once been her best friend. "You bitch!" she hissed. "You ugly, filthy, worthless whore! Adam Chandler will come for me!"

"Of course he will. And he'll find you—or at least he'll think it's you. By the time he gets here, I'd say a dead body would be pretty unrecognizable, wouldn't you? I mean, rotting out here in the sun for over a week, maybe longer, picked over by buzzards."

Andrea swallowed back vomit. "What are you talking about?"

Mary laughed lightly and stood up. She walked over and picked up Andrea's dress and underwear. Then she pulled off her shoes and removed the locket that hung around her neck—the locket Adam had sent her from Independence.

"Please don't take that!" Andrea whimpered.

Mary kicked her hard in the side. "Shut up!" She sauntered over to the other women, studying them closely, then called to one of her men. "I think this one here resembles her the most, don't you?"

The man looked from the terrified young girl to Andrea. "I'd say so . . . they're just about the same build . . . a mite skinny but plenty of flesh in the right places." He reached out and fondled the girl's breasts and she cringed away.

"Take her away from camp and strip her. Do what you want with her, Lonny; then I want you to kill her. Put Andrea Chandler's torn dress on her. Leave the underwear beside her, but put the shoes on her and put the locket around her neck. Pick up everything else—anything that is not Andrea's, and bring it back here. We'll burn up those clothes. Then we'll leave the body here. By the time Adam Chandler comes along, if he happens to be smart enough to track her this far, he'll find the body, with his locket around its neck. It'll be so bloated he won't be able to tell if it's really her, but he'll have to think it is." She turned to Andrea and grinned. "He'll bury it and leave. And little Andy will be under my control for the rest of her miserable life."

447

Andrea could not believe what she was seeing and hearing and feeling. The horror of it was beyond reality. The poor girl who was to take her place was dragged off screaming and kicking, and Andrea was left naked on the ground, while men talked and laughed and drank, Mary joining them. The Comanches left, with new rifles and plenty of whiskey. An hour or so later, after the horrible screams of the girl chosen to be killed finally stopped, Andrea heard a gunshot. She rested her face against the dry earth and wept, praying that if Adam did not find her she would somehow die soon.

Such country Adam Chandler had never known. So, this was the West. The farther he got from Cherokee country, the worse it got—more barren, hotter, harder, more dangerous. There seemed to be a rattler at every turn, and the sun shone down without mercy. James rode with him, and the two of them using their Indian instincts, they followed the probable course the Comanches had taken with Andrea. At times tracking them seemed almost impossible. Their trail would disappear into streams, and it would take hours to find out where they'd ridden out again. The pursuit was taking too long, and Adam's hopes were dwindling. Even though he was Indian, he did not know this new land. In Georgia, he could find a worm in a pine tree. He could smell out a butterfly in the branches of an oak. But this land was different. A horse's hoof left only a slight impression on the hard earth, and they were tracking native Indians who knew every rock and crag.

"I don't understand it, James." He spoke up for the hundredth time, his voice strained and tired. "Why Andrea? Why did they single her out that way?"

"I wish I knew, Adam." James's heart was heavy, for he had been unable to fight so many Comanches. His ear and the side of his face were still bruised from the blow of a heavy club. "I guess there could be a hundred reasons. There has been a lot of raiding along the borders of Cherokee land, by Plains Indians who feel we are infringing on their territory. To them the taking of a woman is the supreme insult, the best way to get back at their enemies."

"Then why not a Cherokee woman? Why a white woman?"

"Maybe they thought she was worth more. The more she is worth, the greater the insult."

Adam sighed and rubbed at tired eyes. "Do you think she is still alive?"

James could not look at him. "From the things we have been hearing, she would be better off if she were not. The Comanches are not kind to their captives. But perhaps she is some kind of slave. Perhaps she still lives."

Adam stared out over the quiet, hazy horizon, into miles and miles of nothingness. There was not a sound in this country, not even bird calls or the singing of insects. It was as though all life had vanished and they were on some other planet.

"We'll never find her. I don't know how much longer to keep searching, or even if we're following the right tracks anymore. And I'm keeping you from your farm. But I have to go on . . . a little longer."

He hunched over and wept. Andrea! All his plans, his hard work, his dreams. What was he to do if he didn't find her? There was no law in this land, no one to help, no one to turn to. The West was wild and untamed, and such vastness could swallow up one tiny woman. Andrea! Andrea! He couldn't live without her. Not now! Not after all they had been through! And what had she suffered at the hands of the Comanches? Wondering about that, he could not help but think she might be better off if she were dead. But how could he go on if she was? How much was a man supposed to take? If only he could go back, to the days of their youth, to the oak tree. He had waited so long to come home, settled and successful, to hold her and take her and the children to their little house in Independence where they would be a family again. He could no longer control the tears. He leaned forward as he sat his horse, his shoulders shaking. From above, he and James were just two small dots in the middle of a vast, untamed, cruel land.

It was another week before they saw the vultures circling silently, their black ugliness spelling death. Adam pulled up his horse and James rode up beside him. They stared out from a great mesa to the place far below where the remains of a body lay, something blue beside it. Adam had been told that Andrea had worn a blue dress the morning she'd been taken. Still, it all seemed too impossible.

"What do you think, James?"

"I don't know. We'd better go and see. But those vultures won't like it. They're already picking at the body."

Adam gritted his teeth. "Worthless, stinking country! How can anything be this big and desolate? How is a person to get help in a land like this? If that is my Andrea—" He made an odd choking sound, then headed his horse down the embankment, chancing its dangerous steepness. Rocks slid and tumbled, but his sure-footed mount did not lose its footing. James followed, but more slowly.

"Adam, wait for me! Adam, keep a hold on yourself!" He knew that if the body was Andrea's Adam Chandler would be like a crazy man, but Adam was soon far ahead of him. His horse reared as vultures dove at it. Nonetheless, pulling his rifle from its boot, Adam jumped off, and ran toward the body. As his horse ran off, he shot wildly at the birds, screaming at them, fighting them off. James caught up, dismounted, and fired along with Adam until the vultures left alive flew to rocky perches to wait.

Adam went to his knees near the swollen, smelly carcass. The only thing recognizable was the blue dress and what looked like blond hair. The eyes were missing, the face chewed beyond recognition. He stared, moaning and rocking.

James approached the body, making a face at the smell. His stomach churned, yet he knew they had to know for sure. He picked up a piece of underwear that lay nearby, then dropped it again. When he stared down at the dress, he swallowed back his horror. "It's the dress . . . she was wearing." He bent a little closer. "My God! Goddamn!" He turned away, his voice choked. "She's got the locket on, Adam—the locket you sent her a few weeks ago."

A strange guttural sound came from Adam. He threw back his head and screamed Andrea's name, then turned around and vomited.

Andrea and the others were herded into the plush parlor of the fancy whorehouse. Only five girls were left. Those not pretty or shapely enough had been used by the Comancheros along the way, then killed. The stark cruelty of it had left Andrea dazed. She had no idea where she was, except that she was supposed to be in Mexico. A fat Mexican woman with painted lips was looking her over.

"You did well, Mary. I will pay you much gold for these lovelies, and I, in turn, will make much money from them." She grasped Andrea's face and turned it back and forth. "High cheekbones, lovely blue eyes. When she is cleaned up and her hair fixed nice—"

"My husband will find you," Andrea said, her voice dull. How many times had she said it? "Somehow, someday, he will find you, and Mary Means. It would be better for you both if you let me go."

"Is that so?" The fat woman laughed hard, and opened the flimsy robe Andrea had been given to wear. When she touched a breast, Andrea jerked away. "Let him come," the woman declared with a strong Mexican accent. "By the time he finds you, if he ever does, he will no longer want you. Is your husband handsome? Huh? Maybe he will do business with one of my other girls." She laughed then, and Andrea's terror came out in a growling scream. She reached out and scratched the woman's face, and the woman slapped her hard, knocking her down. "Take her upstairs," she told someone. "Give her the drug. Soon she will beg us to send her customers, for it is the only way she will get the drug which she will learn to crave."

Hands lifted Andrea, but all the mistreatment she'd suffered over the past several weeks had left her too weak to fight any further than that sudden lashing out at the fat woman. She groaned Adam's name, but he was not there.

All the other horrors she had suffered had been bearable, because she had had Adam. Now she was alone, and how would he find her in this strange, desolate land? And if he found the dead girl Mary Means had left behind in Andrea's dress, perhaps he would never come at all. Adam! There would be no Independence, no little house, no happy home. And her sons! Her precious sons! How could she live at all without her babies, for that was what they still seemed to her. Who would take care of them? Someone flopped her onto a bed, and a strong-smelling cloth was pushed over her face and held there until she had no thoughts at all.

Such blackness Adam Chandler had never known. Losing his land had been one thing, but losing Andrea . . . How could this happen? Why was God punishing him so? Or was it just a matter of fate? Perhaps fate was something even God could not control. All he could see was the young, fourteen-year-old girl who had given herself to him with such sweet abandon under the great oak tree. The oak tree. He had promised her he would one day own that land again and he would take her to it. Perhaps now that could only happen in the afterlife.

Again he cut himself, this time down the arm. He wanted to hurt. He needed to hurt. He had asked James to leave him, and he sat alone on a rocky ledge. It overlooked the lonely little grave in which they had buried Andrea. Some ancient instinct had led him to strip and to cut himself in mourning.

What was he to do now, without Andrea? They had struggled so hard together against the horrors of the Trail of Tears, against his own drunkenness and his vengeful killings, against poverty. She had urged him to use his education to bring back his pride and wealth, to give him the hope of buying back his land. He had worked so hard in Independence, just for her. For Andrea. Everything had been so perfect. He would have taken her and the boys back to Independence and they would have had a good life.

Why? Why had this happened? Over and over he asked himself this question, but was unable to come up with any kind of answer except that someone had retaliated for what he had done to the traitors who'd first arrived in Indian Territory. But even that did not make sense. Everything was peaceful among the Cherokee now. There was still some bitterness, but it had not erupted into violence. And Andrea was always a favorite, well liked by all of them. If there was vengeance to be sought, it should be vengeance against him, not Andrea.

But perhaps it was simply fate after all. There had been a lot of raiding along the borders. James had said so. Now that the Cherokees were done fighting among themselves, they had the Plains Indians to fight. In a sense he could not blame the Western Indians. What had happened to the Cherokees was now happening to them. It was their turn to fight for their land. The raids were just one way of telling the Cherokees and other Eastern Indians to stay out of their territory, and to them stealing women was the ultimate insult. Perhaps when they'd seen a white woman living among the Cherokee, they'd become enraged and had taken her for spite. Who could know? And it didn't matter anymore. Andrea was dead, and he could not go after the entire Comanche Nation, much as he would like to. Someone else needed him—his sons, his precious sons.

He rolled onto his back, letting the hot Texas sun beat down on his bleeding body. He wished he could die! He longed for whiskey. But because of his sons, he dared not grant himself either desire. For the sake of Andrea's love, and because the boys were a part of her, he must somehow go on. He could hear her, telling him that the boys needed him, hear their own young voices, see their joyous faces as they ran to greet him when he came home. They'd been sure he could find their mother. And he had. But he'd been too late. How could he live with that? So much suffering.

Now this. Perhaps if he had been home . . .

The tears came again, deep, wrenching sobs that hurt his stomach and chest. He screamed out her name, and it echoed against canyon walls and through the dead, hot land where her body lay. James waited in the shadow of an overhanging rock, and he doubled over and wept at the pitiful shout, understanding Adam's anguish. He could only hope the boys would give Adam an incentive to carry on.

Dusk fell; then darkness came. James made a small fire and waited. It was quiet on the ridge top. He hoped Adam Chandler had not killed himself. The night was silent, with not even a stirring of the air. Indeed, the silence was so heavy that it actually hurt James's ears. When he awoke in the morning, Adam was standing over him, his nearly naked body covered with blood, his eyes bloodshot and wild. James stared, rubbing his eyes and slowly rising, his first thought of wilder Indians, because of the way Adam looked at that moment.

"Adam?"

"Let's go home," he replied quietly.

"Are you . . . all right?"

"I will never be all right. But my sons have been through enough. I'll not desert them. It's bad enough that I go home without their mother."

His voice was cool and quiet, all his grief and despair now buried somewhere in the deep recesses of his mind.

"What are you going to do, Adam?"

"Go home to my sons. I will tell them . . . I found their mother . . . very sick . . . and that she told them she loved them and to be good boys . . . that she'd see them in the afterlife." He swallowed. "I made Andrea a promise, James. I promised I would get back my land, and I will."

"You can't go back anymore, Adam."

"I am going back!" Adam snapped. "One way or another I'll own that land again, and I'll go sit under our oak tree, and she'll be with me. I'll feel her there. She'll be with me."

James sighed, forcing back his own tears. "Whatever

you want, Adam. You're right about the boys. They need you. And Andrea would want you to be strong, to get rich and get that land back, just as she'd want you to take care of the boys and make fine men of them."

Adam stared at a distant mountain. "I will never love that way again. Never. I would prefer to die now. It is only for her that I go back to my sons. Our first son was taken from her, and that just about broke her heart. It would be a disgrace to her memory if I abandoned Jonas and John Ross. For now I must be glad that I have something that is a part of her, two sons who carry her blood." His eyes went to James. "Will you watch over them for another year or two? I need some time, and they should be a little older before coming to Independence. I will be very busy, but I will send you money. I will visit them often, and as soon as possible, I will take them back with me so we can all be together."

"You know Ruth and I will take care of them as long as necessary. They're fine boys."

Adam grinned sadly. "Fine because of her. She was a good mother, taught them well. For her sake I will see that they get the best schooling in Independence, or maybe St. Louis. I am thinking of going to St. Louis soon, to open my own practice. It is a bigger city, with more businesses. And it is farther east, closer to the universities where I intend to send my sons." His eyes hardened. "They will be educated, James, and Indian or not, they will do whatever the hell they want with their lives! They will be successful, and they will show the white sons of bitches what an Indian can do! And if they want to marry white women, they will marry them without going through the hell Andrea and I were put through. All we ever wanted was to be left alone . . . to just share our love freely . . . to be one and to—" His voice choked and he turned away. "Let's break camp and head for home."

He said no more. They packed their gear and mounted up, then rode out to look once more at the grave. A breeze kicked up the sand and swirled it around the makeshift headstone.

"One day no one will even realize there is a grave here," Adam groaned. "It isn't right . . . leaving her here all alone."

"Her spirit isn't here, Adam. Just her bones. Her spirit is with you, in your heart, and through your sons she will always live."

Adam's body shook with grief, and he turned his face away. He reined his horse around then, and headed north. He would not look back. He could not. Andrea! How did a man go on after losing his lover, his friend, his reason for living?

CHAPTER TWENTY-SEVEN

There was nothing for Andrea now but mere existence, and the craving to breathe and drink the blessed drugs that kept her from reality. She had no concept of time anymore, and hardly realized that five years had passed since that dreadful morning when the Comanches had come. Had there ever been another life? Men ravaged and abused her, mostly Mexicans, some white, all rude and revolting. At first she had fought, despite the drugs that were supposed to make her more submissive. But starvation, beatings, and being constantly tied while more drugs were given her soon took their toll. She stopped fighting. And now she would do anything they told her in order to have the drugs; without them, her pain and the torture to her body was unbearable.

Sometimes fat Rosa would withhold the drugs just for punishment—for not showing a customer enough pleasure, or perhaps for crying. Andrea stopped crying. There was no room now for love or any other kind of feeling. There was room only for the drugs. Occasionally she would remember . . . a man . . . a handsome, dark Cherokee man who had been gentle and loving. Adam? Yes, that was his name. Adam. Sweet Adam. At times the memory would become very clear, and she could see him vividly, feel him holding her, look up and see golden leaves. But when she remembered, she knew he must think her dead, and she also knew that it was best now that he did consider her dead, for she might as well be. There was nothing left of Andrea Chandler for Adam Chandler to love. No matter what happened now, she could never go back. She was a used, destroyed woman, a far cry from the young Andrea who had once lain under the great oak with her Cherokee boy. The oak tree, innocence, youth, carefree days in the Cherokee land were all gone.

And sometimes she would remember the faces of two little boys, so sweet, so trusting, so loving. Were they hers? Of course! Little Jonas and John Ross. Her sons! Oh, how it hurt to remember! She wanted to go to her sons and hold them. How long had it been? Who was taking care of them? She should be doing that. That was when the tears came, bringing severe punishment by Rosa. But Andrea couldn't hold them back. And the pain in her heart was even worse when a third face tried to appear in her memory, a blurred little face. Whose was it? Who was the third little boy who tried to come to her mind? She struggled to remember, but the drugs had clouded her mind, making clear recollections few and far between.

She had often contemplated suicide, especially when first brought here and thrust into the horrors of forced prostitution. But she had always been tied. Even so, a deep inner strength had not let her give up on life. She had held onto the distant hope that somehow she would wake up in Adam Chandler's arms, that all of this would be some kind of nightmare. She had told herself she must hang on for Adam, yet as the years passed, she could not always remember who he was. And when she did, she realized it was foolish to ever hope to see him again, for even if he should find her, things could never be the same. Not now. Not ever again. But she would think of him with great, wrenching grief. He had gone through so much hell— losing his land, his parents; falling into drunkenness. But he had worked so hard to overcome it all, only to come home and find her gone.

Where was he now? What was he doing? And what about the boys? How much time had passed? How old were they?

Such vivid memories came to her about every three months now. Most of her time was spent in a daze, while men pawed over her, used her; and she pretended to like it, just so Rosa would bring her more of the strange concoction that kept her floating in that blessed world of unreality, where she did not have to feel or think or care. She knew that sometimes Rosa stood and watched while men used her, laughing and making dirty remarks. Andrea had dared to object once, and had been punished with a beating and the withdrawal of the strange drinks and the burning incense until she had screamed and begged for the drugs to take away her terrible pain. She never again complained.

At first the real Andrea had struggled violently against what was happening to her, clinging to sweet memories of Adam, fighting the drugs and the attacks by Rosa's male customers. But finally all reality left her, except for those occasional moments when memories came to tease and haunt her and make her cry.

It was gone now . . . all gone. Even if she were to come out of this drugged state and be released, there was no going back. A woman did not go back to hearth and family after doing what she had been forced to do. What decent man would have her? Certainly not Adam Chandler, so beautiful, so tender, so intelligent and honorable. And she was not worthy to be a mother to her sons now. She wondered if Adam had remarried and some other woman was raising her boys. She could not blame him if that was the case, yet the thought of Adam loving another, lying with another . . .

How horribly painful was the memory of being in Adam's arms! Painful because she knew it could never be that way again. And it was painful to think of him loving another, giving himself to another. Adam! He belonged to her! He was her husband! But no. He could not be her husband now. She was spoiled and worthless. The wicked Mary Means had seen to that. She had punished Adam Chandler in the worst way, by stealing his wife and then letting him think she was dead. And she had punished

Andrea by forcing her into this horrible sexual slavery.

She was wicked, more wicked even than her brother. Because of her, Andrea Chandler had turned into a pitiful, begging whore, who panicked every time Rosa threatened to take away the drugs. Yet something inside her still made her want to fight sometimes; a part of her still clung to the old Andrea. But such feelings were being buried deeper and deeper. They had almost vanished now. All hope of Adam coming for her was gone, as was all hope of ever again leading a normal life. If she was lucky, death would come to claim her. The sooner, the better. There was nothing else to wish for.

"*Siyu, asgaya,*" she muttered as another man came into the room, grinning, bending over her. Rosa was there, too, putting something strong-smelling over her nose again.

"You be a good little girl now for this man," she said with her strong Mexican accent. Then she laughed, the ugly laugh that Andrea hated.

The man laughed as well, and hands moved over her. Memories of Adam and her sons faded then, and she became just a thing, just a body existing somewhere in Mexico. Was it summer? Winter? How old was she now? It didn't matter. Perhaps soon she would awake, look up and see the great branches of a golden oak, and know she had died and was finally released from this hell.

Adam stopped on his way inside to adjust the hook that held the sign bearing his name: Adam Chandler, Esquire. He gently ran a hand over the carving. How proud Andrea would have been, and his mother and father as well. But they were all dead now, victims of hatred and greed and violence. The pain tore at his heart again, and he wondered if he would ever really get over those black years of struggle and exile and whiskey.

He thought again about Lorraine. Lorraine Drake. She had come to him as a client, to settle a detail in her late husband's will. Their business relationship had grown into a friendship and he'd been her escort on a few evenings out. Lorraine was pretty, a thirty-year-old childless widow, and she was lonely. Adam knew that she loved him, and he had strong feelings for her. But another woman still occupied his heart, refusing to make room for someone new. For twenty years he had held Andrea there, treasured her, loved her. Her death had not changed that. And he was sure Lorraine sensed his feelings, sure that Lorraine struggled with a similar problem, for she had loved her husband very much. Perhaps because of their mutual understanding, their own affection could grow and someday he could allow himself to love again—to love Lorraine, maybe even marry her.

Still, to marry again, to lie with a woman out of love, seemed some kind of betrayal of Andrea. If only he could get over that feeling. There had been many easy women, whores for the most part, who had gladly accommodated the handsome, successful, and lonely attorney. But that was different. He hadn't given them anything but his body. They were merely a means of physical relief. But to totally devote himself to a woman, that was hard, though he knew if he kept seeing Lorraine, he would have to attempt it eventually. Perhaps he should just stop seeing her. To care again, risk losing again, was too frightening. He had been hurt far too deeply, had suffered too much, to risk any more damage to his heart. He had only now begun to face the fact that Andrea really was dead.

Still, something haunted him. Something ate at him. At night he could hear Andrea calling to him, but he knew it was just her spirit, yearning to be with him. Someday, in death, they would be together again. He had considered making his own death come early, by his own hand. But there were the boys to consider. They had suffered so much that to end his life might destroy them. They were such fine, handsome, strong boys. Jonas was sixteen now, dark and handsome, tall and broad like his father; a bright young man ready for college. John Ross was nearly fifteen, with fair hair and blue eyes, as big as his father but closely resembling his mother in coloring and looks. To look at him brought an ache to Adam's heart.

John Ross was more quiet than Jonas, more even tempered, quicker to smile. Both boys were a source of great pride for Adam, and as brothers they were very close, having suffered so much together. The latest horror, the loss of their mother five years ago, had left John Ross totally silent for two years. Adam had taken him to specialists, but to no avail. Only after being brought to St. Louis, sent to a special school, and settled in their home there did the boy finally begin to talk again. Now he was doing well in school, and in another year or two he, too, would attend college. Jonas was intent on being an attorney like his father, but John Ross wanted to be a doctor. He intended to go back to Indian Territory and work among the Cherokee, a decision that made Adam burst with pride.

How wonderfully complete the family would be now if Andrea could be with them. This was what she had dreamed of. This was what she had wanted so much. And he had done it all for her, out of respect for her memory. After her death, he'd cared about nothing, but he'd struggled to make fine, educated, respectable men of his sons—for her sake. This is what she would have wanted. Andrea! Andrea!

He turned away from the sign and went inside the neat, brick building that was his office. Today he would sign the agreement with Attorney Michael Renfro—another dream come true for Andrea. If only she could be here to know he was buying back the land! No man could have worked harder or saved harder than Adam Chandler had over the past five years—investing, doubling his money, using his brilliant mind to pinch every penny so that now he was very rich, just as he had promised Andrea he would be. He often represented large businesses, who overlooked his being Indian because he was a damned good attorney and won cases for them. The money had multiplied, and now he had enough. If only Andrea could be here, she would laugh and he would hold her, and together they would celebrate.

Her father was dead now, if he could be called her father.

Ethel Means had also died, leaving only Wilson Means to run the huge farm. He had run it poorly and was bankrupt. Adam could not be more delighted. With Douglas Means dead and Mary Means off whoring, there was no one in the family who was interested in taking over the farm.

Adam went into his office and sat down behind a grand, oak desk. Yes, he knew all about the farm and what was happening. He had sent a spy to investigate the situation. Now the time was right, and he would keep his promise, whether he ever went to live on the place or not. He was buying back the Chandler farm! Michael Renfro would be the buyer on paper, for Indians could not own land. But it was Adam's money that would be used, and today he and Michael would sign their own secret agreement, signifying that the land actually belonged to Adam Chandler.

Adam leaned back and lit a pipe, thinking about his good friend. Renfro had been much more than a business acquaintance or an interested party who had given him a job. He had been the best friend a man could have. He and his son Martin had helped Adam through the first agonies of Andrea's death, talking to him, keeping him busy, not allowing him to drink. It now seemed like a hundred years ago, that night when Martin Renfro had helped Adam get away to kill Douglas Means. With Andrea dead, the deed seemed pointless, yet Adam did not regret it. He only wished he could have made the man suffer longer.

His thoughts wandered then to the oak tree. Things had come full circle. He'd got his revenge, and he'd got his land back. But there was no Andrea to share it with. He would love to take Jonas and John Ross to the farm, take them up the ridge to the oak tree and tell them all about how he'd met their mother there. But he knew it would be far too painful without Andrea at his side. And how could he take Lorraine there? It would mean nothing to her. No. He could not go back, not this way. His victory was a bitter one. For now he would let the land sit, or perhaps lease it out to a neighboring farmer. That would have to be done through Michael Renfro, the "paper" owner. Someday, when Renfro died, the farm would be willed to Adam Chandler, and he could legally and openly own it. Maybe then it wouldn't matter anymore to whites that an Indian owned land.

It would not be easy going back, now or later. There were so many memories . . . so many memories. The laughter in their household when he was a small boy . . . his father's happy face and his mother's beautiful one . . . chasing Ruth and teasing her until she cried out to her mother . . . the first time he broke a horse, roped a steer.

But most of all he remembered the oak tree, and all the times he'd gone to it alone to think, to pray, to plan his future; little knowing that someday everything would be taken from him. A lump rose in his throat when he remembered the first time Andrea had come there, his stifled laughter as he'd hid from her and watched her come up to hug the tree. Andrea. He could close his eyes and see her gold hair, her blue eyes; he could feel the softness of her skin, taste her sweetness, feel his lips against hers.

Why had he wasted that last year on drink? He'd almost lost her, and it sickened him now that he'd neglected her after all she'd been through to stay with him. He'd been so full of bitterness and hatred, and he'd taken it out on the one person he'd loved most. Those last three days they'd spent together before he went to Independence had been so beautiful, so forgiving, so filled with ecstasy and joy. He'd finally found himself, finally made her proud of him again. He'd finally found a way to get back everything for her. Now she was not here to share in his success.

It was so hard to keep going, so hard to care. But he had to do it, for her sake. She would want him to achieve, would want him to do all he could for the boys—to give them a good life. He hoped her kidnapping and death would not have disastrous effects on poor Jonas and John Ross. Now that John Ross had snapped out of his silent mourning, he was working hard and learning fast. He would make a good doctor. He was a bright boy, a young man with great compassion and gentleness. And Jonas was fiery and stubborn, a fine combination for a good attorney. Yes, they would do well. And he would help them all the way, for Andrea. How he loved them! They had come from seed he'd planted in Andrea's womb through love and ecstasy, and birthing them had not been easy for her. Then, of course, there was the third son . . . the one poor Andrea had never seen . . . the one she grieved for all those years. Perhaps they were together now. Perhaps the boy had died and was finally with his mother.

He got up then and walked to a window, to stare out at the streets of St. Louis. He should go back to Indian Territory and see Ruth and James. They had two more children now, two sons. Their little daughter was nearly six already. The Cherokee were more settled now, many of them slowly finding themselves again, slowly rekindling their pride, building farms, rising up from poverty and depression. He'd worked so hard to help them keep their land, but it had been to no avail; and so much had gone out of him that it hurt too much to go back there very often, especially without Andrea. For the present he could not even go back to the old farm in Georgia.

He was feeling lost and alone. He'd done well here in St. Louis, through very hard work and a quick intelligence that soon won him a reputation for seldom losing a case. It had been hard at first, because he was Indian, but the state could not deny him a license to practice for he'd passed his exams with almost perfect scores. He had since proven himself many times in the courtroom. He'd had to fight harder than a young white attorney, but he'd won. Yes, he'd won. He had everything now . . . except Andrea. His chest tightened and he took a deep breath. The sky had clouded, and raindrops picked at the window. The door to his office opened then.

"Can I get you anything, Mr. Chandler?"

He turned to the apprentice who did his secretarial work. The young man was eager and bright, and although he was white, he respected Adam and Adam sensed it.

465

Walking to his desk, Adam set his pipe in an ashtray. "I don't think so, David. Did you do those case studies yesterday as I asked?"

"Yes, sir." The young man came closer then, speaking quietly. "Sir, there's a man outside who wants to see you. I told him you seldom see anyone before ten o'clock, that you always do your reading and so forth first. He has no appointment."

Adam frowned, sat down in his chair. "What's his name?"

"Stephen, sir. Just Stephen. He didn't give me a last name, and he didn't even say what it was about. He said you'd know once he talked to you, that you'd be glad to see him."

Adam sighed and ran a hand through his hair. "I don't know any Stephen. Tell him to come back later this morning. If he's going to be rude enough not to state his problem or even give his last name, then I can be rude enough to refuse to see him until later. He should have made an appointment anyway."

He turned to some papers, but David did not leave the room. Adam finally glanced up at him, noting a strange, nervous look about him. "Well? I told you what to do. Why in hell are you just standing there?"

"Sir, this young man . . ." He looked at Adam intently for a moment. "Sir, it's very strange."

"What's very strange?" Adam leaned back again, looking annoyed.

"Well, sir, he . . . he looks an awful lot like you. Fact is, Mr. Chandler, he could be your twin, only younger, of course. I swear it, sir. When he first walked in, I wondered how you'd got back outside. I thought it was you coming in."

Adam frowned, a faint flutter rippling through his body, a suspicion he could not even name moving through his blood. He knew he was thinking something he dared not think, and his heart pounded harder. "Send him in," he said calmly.

"Yes, sir."

David left and Adam stared at the doorway. Moments later a tall, broad, handsome young man walked in. He was dressed in a neat but inexpensive suit, and looked as though he'd spent his last penny on something decent so he'd look nice for his appointment. The youth walked a few steps from the doorway, then just stopped and stared. Adam stared back at him, dumbfounded, for he looked just like the young Adam Chandler Andrea had loved and married.

Both men just gaped, surprised at how much they resembled one another. Then Adam slowly rose, his instincts telling him all he needed to know. His legs felt weak. The young man swallowed, his eyes watery.

"You are . . . Adam Chandler?"

Adam nodded.

The young man took a deep breath, visibly shaken. "I . . . am your son."

Pain shot through Adam's chest, so fierce that it made him bend over. The young man stepped closer. "Are . . . are you all right? Maybe I shouldn't have—"

"It's all right," Adam broke in. He slowly straightened, his own eyes brimming with tears. "My God!" He let his gaze run over this young man, strong, handsome, dark. He did not doubt the young man was telling the truth. "My God!" he whispered again. It was overwhelming. Here stood a piece of the past, a gift from Andrea—the son she had never seen, the son she had borne alone, the son they had searched for so long but could never find. A tear found its way down his cheek. "If only . . . your mother could be here."

The boy swallowed, his own tears beginning to flow then. "They told me, at the Cherokee settlement, what happened. I went there first . . . met your sister. My aunt, I guess. She told me about my mother, where I could find you and my . . . my brothers . . . if I may call them that. I only regret that I didn't come sooner. I was afraid to come . . . afraid you would be angry . . . that there was some reason you gave me away to the orphanage."

"Orphanage!" Adam moved from behind his desk. "My

467

God, boy, we searched and searched for you. Your mother's parents had her sent away because she loved an Indian. I didn't even know she was pregnant! Her baby was taken from her. By the time she got back to me it was done. We searched and searched, but she didn't even know where it was they had kept her. No one would tell us. We tried, Nathan. For years your mother pined over you, loved you, worried about you. It's just so . . . so ironic that you show up now. She's gone." His chest convulsed in a sob and he quickly wiped his eyes.

"You . . . called me Nathan."

Adam nodded, then ran a shaking hand through his hair. When he spoke his voice was choked. "We . . . named you. We refused to . . . forget that you existed . . . somewhere."

He met the boy's eyes and saw the loneliness in them. What kind of hell had his son been through? Where had he been?

"I stole my file . . . found out your names," the young man told him. "When I was eighteen, they let me out. I was confused. I'd never been in the outside world. I was scared to try to find you at first . . . but I didn't know what else to do . . . where to go. I just need some help getting started. I don't have much education. If you could get me started somehow at some kind of work, I'd get out of your life if you want me to. Maybe it's too late to be showing up. I just need . . . a little help."

Adam stepped closer, grasped the boy's shoulders. They faced each other, practically twins, except that Adam was slightly taller. "Help? Did you really think if you walked in here I would just give you a few dollars and send you on your way? My God, son—Nathan . . . Stephen, whatever you wish to be called—you're my son. My son! You're my first-born son, the child Andrea cried over so many nights. Did you think I'd let you just walk back out of my life? Seeing you is like . . . like Andrea has come back to me. You have to stay—live with me and your brothers. You're a part of us. You're—" He broke down then, embracing the young man. "My God, if only Andrea were here," he

468

groaned. "Andrea! Andrea!"

They embraced for several seconds, neither of them able to speak. For the first time in his life Stephen began to understand what it was like to be loved. Someone had embraced him with genuine feeling, and even though he was nineteen and full grown, he suddenly felt like a lost little boy enjoying the warm protection of his father's arms. He had been prepared to hate this man, had not been sure what Adam's reaction would be. But Ruth had told him what had happened, when he'd gone to Indian Territory to find his father. On his way to St. Louis he had wept bitterly over the mother he'd never known, for surely she had loved him. And now there was no doubt in his mind that she must have loved the man who held him, for she had suffered greatly but had remained true to him. He wished he could have known his mother.

Adam finally released him and pulled a handkerchief from his vest pocket. "We have so much to talk about," he told the young man as he wiped his eyes. "So much. I'll close the office for today, have David cancel everything. We're going home, Nathan. I'll send for your brothers right away."

Brothers. The word sounded good to Stephen. Family! A real family, after all those black years of working fourteen to eighteen hours a day in the miserable factories, hardly ever seeing the light of day, never knowing love, seeing friends die of horrible injuries, seeing little boys keel over right at their machines and die from overwork.

"It will be hard for me to answer to Nathan, sir, but if that's what you prefer—"

Adam interrupted. "You're used to Stephen. We'll just call you Stephen Nathan Peter Chandler, and I'll get used to calling you Stephen."

Stephen wiped his eyes. "I can really use your last name then?"

Adam smiled sadly. "You're my son, aren't you? Of course you can use my last name. It's yours legally. All I have to do is look at you to know you're telling the truth. I feel like I'm looking into a mirror. And your brothers will welcome you with open arms, I guarantee. Your mother and I always talked about you as though you'd come in the door at any moment. They know they have an older brother, and they'll be just as happy to see you in the flesh as I am." He blew his nose. "What a day this would be if your mother were alive. My God, I'd love to see her face." He choked up, then said, "It's been five years, Stephen. Five years since I last saw her. Sometimes it seems like it was yesterday. I . . . loved your mother very much." He met the boy's eyes. "I never tricked her, Stephen. I loved her. I wanted to marry her, but her parents wouldn't allow it. When they found out we were seeing each other, they had her sent away. I didn't lay eyes on her again for three years. By then she'd had you and they had taken you away from her. She never knew where. But she loved you—we both loved you, prayed for you. As soon as she returned, she came to me and we married, against her parents' wishes. We had two more sons. Then there was all that hell—my father's death, our land taken away from us, my mother beaten and raped, my sister, too. And your mother . . ." He stopped and sighed. "There is so much to tell you, so much I want to know about you. I'll close up here and we'll go home."

Stephen watched him put a few things away. Home. Did he really have a home? Would he really fit in there after all these years? "Sir, I . . . you're so . . . successful. Everything I hear about you . . . your intelligence and education . . . I can hardly read and write. They didn't teach me those things. I had to ask a friend to read your file to me because I couldn't make out the names. I can't hold an important job. Are you sure you want me around?"

Adam glanced at him, realizing how awkward and uncertain the boy must feel. His son, yet a stranger. He closed a drawer. "You are a Chandler, Stephen. You'll learn fast. In no time at all I'll have you ready for a university, if you so choose. And I'm buying back my land in Georgia. I'll explain that later. At any rate, we'll all go back there someday. We'll farm, raise cattle, have a fine home there. I promised your mother I'd get that land back, and I got it! Someday you boys will marry, and you can live there the rest of your lives if you want—farm, or teach, or practice law—do whatever you want. Young John Ross wants to be a doctor and might end up doctoring in Indian Territory. You'll have many options, Stephen. I'll see that you get an education, and you can take it from there. If you don't want that, I don't give a damn if you never read a word. You're here. You're home. You're my son, and a part of Andrea. All our years together she wept over you. I wouldn't have cared if you'd walked in here with two heads and no arms. I'd be just as happy as I am right now."

David tapped on the door and opened it, a tray in his hands. "Sir, I thought you might like—"

"David!" Adam interrupted. "I want you to meet someone." He walked around his desk and put an arm around Stephen. "David, this is Stephen Nathan Peter Chandler, my first-born son."

David's eyes widened and he stared from son to father. Adam had spoken often about Nathan. David could not help but feel his employer's joy, and he grinned broadly. "Congratulations, Mr. Chandler! You found him!" He shook Adam's hand, then Stephen's.

"I didn't find him, David." Adam looked at his son, admiring the boy's ability to find his way west, his determination to find his parents. "He found me," he finished. He turned to David then. "I won't be in for the rest of the day. I'm taking Stephen home. We have a lot to talk about."

"Of course, Mr. Chandler. I'll take care of everything."

"Thank you, David." Adam took a deep breath and looked Stephen over again. "Ruth must have just about had a heart attack when she saw you standing in her doorway," he said with a grin.

Stephen smiled back. "She had a real strange look on her face. I think at first she thought I was you, but she knew that couldn't be because I was so much younger. She's awfully pretty, sir. And a nice woman."

Adam nodded. "My sister has had more than her share of grief, as most Cherokees have. I still work for the People,

Stephen. I stay abreast of the latest Congressional moves, file petitions for them, see that their rights in Indian Territory are protected as much as possible." His eyes teared. "It's been a long, long road, Stephen. Twenty years ago I fell in love with a beautiful little girl named Andrea Sanders. Her hair was golden and her eyes were blue as the sky. She was only fourteen and I was only sixteen." His eyes teared again. "But by God, I loved her, Stephen. You are the result of that love. That makes you very special, very special."

He put his arm out and Stephen walked up to him. As they walked out together, David shook his head. "Too bad Mrs. Chandler can't be here," he mumbled. "What a day this would have been for her."

CHAPTER TWENTY-EIGHT

Two years passed, and the summer of 1848 found Stephen, at twenty-one, managing a supply store in St. Louis. Eighteen-year-old Jonas and seventeen-year-old John Ross were both home from universities in the East, and Jonas was a temporary apprentice in his father's law firm. The land in Georgia was being leased to neighboring farmers, but it was still Adam's dream to go back someday. He just didn't have the courage to return without Andrea. He had been promising the boys for years that they would go back, but he was having trouble keeping that promise. It had been seven years, and still he could not seem to function completely without Andrea. Everything he did was still for her, even though she was dead.

His sons, his friends, his relatives—all had chastised him for letting Lorraine Drake slip through his fingers. They wanted him to be happy, to find love again. And he almost had, with Lorraine. But a deeper love had kept him silent and distant, so distant that another man had come into Lorraine's life. He knew his sons and the others had loved Andrea dearly, but they seemed better able to face her death. They felt that life must go on, and they simply wanted their father to be happy. They didn't denigrate Andrea's memory, but they were worried about him because he immersed himself in work, taking on difficult cases and working so late into the night that he fell asleep from exhaustion.

But that was the only way he could sleep at all, for he was plagued by a feeling of guilt over Andrea's fate, even after all these years. If only he had brought her north with him right away, if only he hadn't spent that last year drinking and being so rude to her, perhaps she'd be alive. He had been tempted many times to go back to the bottle, but he'd always seen her sad eyes, begging him not to drink.

And there were the boys to think of. He had a flourishing practice. He did not want to lose it all and jeopardize their futures. He'd made flimsy attempts at establishing a social life, occasionally taking a woman to the theater, the opera, or dinner. But none of them could hold a candle to Andrea, not in looks, not in charm, not in strength of character. Even Lorraine hadn't filled the emptiness in his heart. Only Andrea had all the qualities he wanted in a woman.

Perhaps he had been a fool to let Lorraine get away from him. Probably so. Finding a good woman was not easy. Lorraine had been a good woman, and she had understood his loneliness. She had been a good friend, too. But when he'd kissed her, touched her, his passion was not aroused as it had been with Andrea. Maybe that was the way it was supposed to be. Maybe a man could love that way only once. Maybe he was searching for the impossible. It didn't matter now. Lorraine had married someone else.

Still, fate will have its way, and that same summer Adam discovered the reason his God had not allowed another woman to come into his life. In June a young Cherokee girl came to visit him at his office. Hers was a visit Adam Chandler would remember for the rest of his life. The girl had an air about her that indicated she had once been innocent and was still too young to have lost that innocence. But when she stepped into his office, her pretty young face was hard, her lips were painted, and her cheeks were reddened with so much rouge that they looked ridiculous. Adam watched her curiously, standing up and nodding. "Miss Reed, I believe?"

She stood several feet from his desk, seeming to be afraid of him, eying him carefully. "That's the name I gave outside," she said quietly. "I don't want anyone to know my real name."

Adam frowned. "If I am to be your attorney, I have to know—"

"I didn't come here for that," she interrupted quickly. "I came because . . . because of Mary Means."

Adam's heart tightened. How he hated the Means woman! His eyes immediately clouded and his face hardened. "If you're here to ask me to help that woman—"

"No! It isn't that, Mr. Chandler. Mary is dead."

Adam stared at her, totally confused now as to why this woman should be here. He sat down wearily. "Have a seat, Miss Reed, or whatever your name is."

She stepped a little closer. "I . . . want your promise . . . that you'll do me no harm."

He leaned forward, resting his elbows on his desk. "Why in hell would I harm you?"

"Promise me! I'm Cherokee, just like you. You . . . you wouldn't harm a Cherokee girl, would you?"

His eyes ran over her pretty form, and he thought it a waste for such a young girl to be what she obviously was. "You have my promise, but I can't imagine why you need it."

She came even closer, cautiously sitting down on the chair near his desk. "I have something to tell you. I just thought . . . maybe you'd be upset when I tell you and you might hurt me. I only came because of Mary's dying request."

His eyebrows arched. "Request? Mary Means sent you to me with a request?" He laughed lightly, but it was a bitter laugh. "I take it you were one of the Cherokee girls she ended up recruiting?"

The girl looked down at her lap. "What else is there for us now?"

"Pride. There is Cherokee pride—and strength!" he shot back. "You're a pretty girl. Why in God's name did you turn to the likes of Mary Means?"

Her dark eyes flashed when she raised her head to look back at him. "I was eleven years old when the militia came, Mr. Chandler! They killed my parents, and they took me out behind the house and showed me everything there was to know about men—all eight of them! A girl has no pride left after that!" Her voice broke and Adam looked away.

"I'm sorry," he said quietly, feeling sick.

"Yes. We all have our burdens from those terrible times, don't we?" Her voice was shaking. "You have your own burdens, so I was told. I . . . I came here to . . . relieve you of your greatest burden, Mr. Chandler, and to do something Mary asked me to do as she lay on her deathbed. I guess she thought if she did one good thing, it might get her to heaven after all. She was scared . . . scared to death of what would happen to her after death. She wanted to . . . right some wrongs."

Adam turned to face her then, Andrea suddenly coming to mind. Andrea. Mary Means! Why had he never thought of it before? This had something to do with Andrea! Why else would this girl be afraid to tell him whatever it was she had to tell? He stared at her, his eyes widening. "Mary Means! It was her, wasn't it? She planned that raid, didn't she?" His eyes smoldered, and the girl gripped the chair arms. "Didn't she!" he growled. "Did she think telling someone on her deathbed would clear her of guilt? Did she think that would right what happened to my Andrea?" He rose from his chair, shaking. "Do you want to know how I found her—bloated and rotting in the Texas desert, her eyes plucked out by buzzards!"

He came around the desk toward the girl, and she cringed. "Your wife isn't dead, Mr. Chandler! She isn't dead! She's alive—in Mexico! The girl you found wasn't her!"

Adam stopped dead in his tracks, his jaw flexing in anger and disbelief. Was this some kind of trick? Andrea? Alive? He gritted his teeth, went quickly to the girl, and grasped the front of her dress. She squealed as he jerked her right out of the chair and shook her.

"What do you mean! What do you mean, coming in

here after all these years and telling me my wife is alive! Why now? Why didn't someone tell me before?" He slammed her against the wall, and Jonas came running in at the sound of all the commotion.

"Father!"

"Where! Where is Andrea?" Adam was shouting, as the girl pushed at him. "Where in Mexico? What did that bitch do with my wife!"

"Father, what are you doing?" Jonas rushed up to him, pulling at his arms, while the girl cried and covered her face. "Father, let go of her! You're hurting her!"

David rushed in then, and he and Jonas each grasped Adam, but Adam Chandler was a powerful man, again the same, wild man who had been hard to hold back the day the militia came and raided their cabin. He would not let go of the girl, and pushed her hard against the wall while Jonas and David tried with all their might to make him let go. He was squeezing the breath out of her, and she began to scratch his face.

"She says your mother is alive! Alive, somewhere in Mexico! The little bitch! She's known it all this time."

"No! No, that isn't true!" The girl gasped for breath. "I just found out . . . from Mary . . . before she died! Please believe me! I came here . . . to help you find her!" Her face started to turn blue. "You . . . promised . . . not to . . . hurt me!"

"Father, let go of her! If she is telling the truth you must let her talk!"

Adam finally released the girl. As she slumped to the floor, choking and gasping, he turned away and bent over, so consumed by shock that he felt ill. Andrea! Andrea! What in God's name was she doing in Mexico? And if it was Mary Means who— "My God!" he moaned, clinging to his desk.

David helped the girl to a chair, and Jonas took Adam's arm. "Father, sit down. I will get you a drink." He led Adam around the desk and seated him while David stayed beside the girl, patting her shoulder. She was crying and holding her chest, and her painted cheeks were smearing because of her tears. For a moment the office was quiet, and Jonas poured four small glasses of bourbon. Handing one to the girl and setting one on the desk in front of his father, he picked up one for himself and gave one to David. "Go close the door, David, but stay in here in case I need you."

The young man nodded and walked over to close the door, while Adam raised wild, red eyes to look at Julia Reed, or so she called herself. The girl stared back, frightened, as she raised the drink to her lips with a shaking hand. Adam swallowed his bourbon in one gulp.

"Start talking, Miss Reed." He glowered. "And you'd better, by God, be telling the truth or I'll kill you!"

Jonas looked at his father in surprise, but said nothing. Adam Chandler was in no mood to be chastised by his own son. David stood by, totally confused.

"I suppose you expect money for your information," Adam sneered.

The girl blinked back tears and shook her head. "No. I told you . . . why I am what I am, Mr. Chandler," she said in a shaking voice. "I'm . . . not bad . . . like you think. I don't want to be bad. It just . . . happened. After the militia . . . I couldn't . . ." She took another sip of the bourbon and Adam sighed, then held his head in his hands.

"I know," he said quietly. "We've all suffered—me, my sons, my mother, my sister, my father . . . young girls like yourself. We're all still living with it. Tell me what you came to tell me, Miss Reed, from the beginning. I won't hurt you."

He sat there quietly then, not looking at her, only holding his head and looking like a broken man. If Andrea was in Mexico . . .

"Mary Means ran the house where I worked . . . down in Austin, Texas. She came to the Cherokee settlement a couple of years ago, found me working in a saloon there . . . said she'd see that I got rich off the white men down in Texas." The girl swallowed some more of the whiskey. "She told me later how . . . how you and some

478

others ran her out of Cherokee Territory a few years back . . . killed Luke Cloud and all.''

Jonas glanced at his father. He had never known everything that had happened during those terrible times after they'd arrived in Indian Territory, but he remembered that his father had been gone a lot, had drunk a lot. He loved his father dearly, and had never blamed him for any of it. In his later years he'd understood what had really happened to his poor mother at the hands of the militia. How could his father help but be full of hatred.

"Mary Means hated you," Julia Reed continued, watching Adam carefully. "She wanted to hurt you somehow. She could never prove anything against you, and I think . . . I think she was kind of jealous, too. Sometimes she talked about you like you were special to her. I think she . . . was attracted to you . . . a long time ago . . . when she and your wife were young . . . back in Georgia. I could tell by the way she talked that she was jealous of your wife." The girl sniffed and rubbed at her eyes. "I knew Mary also dealt with Comancheros and sold women into white slavery in Mexico. I tried to pretend I didn't know. She was bad, Mr. Chandler. It took me a while to realize how bad. It wasn't so bad using girls like me. But she had innocent white women kidnapped to be sold down in Mexico. And you're right . . . she's the one who had the Comanches take your wife."

Adam raised dark, agony-filled eyes to meet hers.

"I swear I never knew any of this until just a few weeks ago, Mr. Chandler!" the girl hastened to add. "Mary got some kind of disease that ate her up . . . made her all thin. Her hair fell out, and at the last, she was in a lot of pain. She got scared then . . . knew she was dying. I helped take care of her. And this one day she took my hand and held it real tight, said she'd been bad and was scared of going to hell. She said she didn't want to go there . . . and she thought if she did a nice thing for somebody, maybe she'd be saved. That's when she told me . . . about your wife . . . about Andrea. She was sold, Mr. Chandler . . . to a . . . to a house of prostitution down in Mexico. I've heard of it. Women are taken there and drugged . . . drugged so much that their minds and memories leave them and they don't even know what they're doing. The Mexican men pay a lot of money for the white women . . . especially the ones with blue eyes and blond hair."

Jonas turned away, his stomach churning, but Adam struggled to stay in control. "I found my wife lying dead in the Texas sun . . . years ago," he told the girl, his voice gruff with emotion.

Julia shook her head. "No, sir. That wasn't your wife. Mary had a girl raped and killed, had your wife's dress put on her, had your wife's locket put around her neck. She knew that by the time you found the body, if you tracked her that far, all you could recognize would be the clothes and the locket. The girl had blond hair like your wife's. Mary figured you'd think Andrea was dead. She was going to tell you one day . . . send you a letter . . . just to be mean. Let you know your wife has been a . . . a whore for years down in Mexico."

He slowly rose, anger emanating from his body until it seemed to permeate the room. "Don't you call my wife a whore," he said in a near whisper. "A woman drugged and forced is not a whore! How dare you call my Andrea a whore, you little slut!"

He headed toward her. "Father, don't!" Adam stopped, meeting his son's eyes. "If she hadn't come here, we never would have known. Don't hurt her, Father. Find out where mother is and free her."

Adam looked at the girl again, his emotions mixed. He hated her, yet he felt sorry for her. She was just another tragic product of the Trail of Tears. "Why don't you go back to Cherokee country and stop what you are doing?"

"It is too late," she said quietly, hanging her head.

"It is never too late! Ask my sister. She was raped, too, but she is married now and has three children. And it is not too late for my wife! I will find her and take her away from that horror!"

The girl wrung her hands. "I do not even know if she still lives. Mary said as far as she knew, Andrea Chandler

480

was still alive. She asked me to come and tell you . . . so you could go and get her. She was being kept in Chihuahua . . . at a place called Rosa's. It is—was—very popular. I do not know if anything happened to it in the war."

Adam looked at Jonas. "The war! Troops have been coming through here on their way to Mexico for a year now."

"General Scott is riding into Mexico right now, Father, to take Mexico City. This is a bad time for Americans to be riding into Mexico. We are officially at war."

Adam's eyes lit up. "War or no war, we're going down there to get your mother. Bring your brothers here right away."

Jonas smiled a little. "You didn't need to tell me. I'll be back within the hour." Their eyes held a moment, both wanting to weep from the combination of joy and sorrow. Andrea might still be alive, but how would they find her?

Adam studied his three sons, all tall, strong, brave young men. Stephen, engaged to be married, was doing well at the supply store, and was soon to be part owner. But that would not stop him from going to Mexico. It was his mother he was going after, the mother he had never seen, and his heart raced with anticipation.

Jonas would forgo returning to the university until he knew his mother was safe, and John Ross would do the same.

"David will take care of my affairs while I'm gone and will find others to fill in for me," Adam declared. "You all know why you're here. I'm sure Jonas explained on the way."

"When do we leave?" Stephen asked anxiously.

"Tomorrow, if possible. We need supplies. Stephen, I've made up a list. I want you to take it and fill it at your store. We all have good, sturdy mounts, but we should have a couple of pack mules. Jonas, see to it."

"I will."

Adam leaned back, eying each of them. "We might have problems. Mexico is in turmoil right now. But you all know how to use rifles and handguns, and when it comes to using your fists, just do what comes naturally. You're all strong men."

"It's our mother we're going after. We can handle anything that comes along," Jonas replied.

"I would fight an army to get her," John Ross added.

Adam smiled sadly, his eyes filling with tears. "I know you would. We all would. Just let them try to stop the Chandler men, right?"

"Right." Stephen lit a thin cigar. He'd fit in right away, all Chandler, learning quickly. He was good with numbers and had helped the owner of the supply store bring himself back from near bankruptcy. With a generous loan from Adam, he was now going to buy into the store, and he was in love with the owner's daughter. He was turning into a confident, proud young man.

Adam sighed and leaned forward, resting his elbows on his desk. "You had all better think about how we might find your mother. She might be so doped up she won't even know us. God only knows what she looks like or what she's been through. It won't be a pretty picture. And when we get her out of there and into safer country, I want you three to leave us alone. I'll pick a remote place where I can be alone with her and stay with her until the drugs are out of her system. It will be very painful for her, and not something she'd want you three to watch. I know Andrea. She'll want to be well and cleaned up before seeing her sons again." He turned his eyes to Stephen. "Especially you. The way I figure it, she won't want to come back at all at first. She'll feel worthless. Maybe she won't even want to live. You're my trump card. When I tell her you're with us now, she won't be able to resist."

The young man smiled. "I hope you're right. All I dreamed about when I was being raised in that orphanage was someday seeing my mother."

Adam nodded. "I know." His eyes went to his other two sons. "Both of you know Spanish and so do I. And we all have dark skin, but you, John Ross. You have that light hair and blue eyes. I'll just have to say that this Mexican—me—had a white slave once and you are the result."

"Mexican?"

Adam grinned. "What safer way to travel in Mexico than as Mexicans? We'll dress like Mexicans, we're dark like Mexicans, and three of us know Spanish. Stephen will just have to keep quiet."

They all laughed. "That's a good idea, Father. I never thought of that," Jonas put in. "Sure we'd look Mexican."

"If anyone comments about our American saddle gear, or our rifles, we'll just say we stole them. Why not? Mexicans do it all the time. And this is war. A man can do anything in war, right?"

"*Sí, amigo*," John Ross answered.

"Very good, son," Adam answered with a smile. "We might as well get used to talking in Spanish. I want no slip-ups. Everybody get plenty of rest tonight. You'll need it. Tomorrow we'll take a steamboat down the Mississippi to Louisiana, then ride straight west through Louisiana and Texas. Chihuahua is just a little south and west of the western edge of Texas, almost directly south of El Paso." He stood up. "Stephen, take John Ross with you to help you with the supplies." He handed a list to his son. "I'll meet you back at the house. Right now I'm going to a church to pray that we find your mother alive and well. And I'm telling all of you that no matter how we find her, I love her just as much as I ever did. I've loved her since she was fourteen years old, and nothing that has happened to her can change that. I expect all of you to love and respect her as your mother, no matter what."

"Did you think we wouldn't?" Jonas asked. "You don't know us very well if you did."

Adam's eyes teared. "I didn't really think you wouldn't. Let's get going. Mexico is a hell of a long way from here." He moved around the desk, and the four men hugged each other quietly. None of them had dry eyes. They were going to Mexico, and woe to any man who tried to stop them from coming back with Andrea Chandler.

CHAPTER TWENTY-NINE

All three Chandler sons were surprised by their father's relentless push onward. He never seemed to tire. His strength and determination were undying, and they were seeing a side of him that had not come to the fore since his vicious struggle to save Andrea the day the militia came. But Jonas and John Ross had been much younger then, their memory of that day and of their father's animallike fighting vague now. Stephen had never seen his father this way—determined, hard, untiring. Adam's years of a successful attorney had not softened him, and the three of them sometimes had a hard time keeping up. He rode until they thought they would fall out of their saddles. Saddle sores plagued them for the first few days, but when they thought they should be making camp, Adam kept going, until well after dark.

Adam seemed undaunted by the rigorous schedule, and none of the boys complained. Their father was going after the woman he loved, and he could not let age or weariness stop him. Every day was important. And in spite of the sad purpose of their journey, they all knew it was good for them. This was the first time all four Chandler men had come together in one cause, the first time in many months they had been able to be together for any length of time.

A closeness began to develop; it ran much deeper than anything they had experienced before. There was something about the silent, lonely Texas prairie that drew them together as brothers, sons, and father in a new and special way. They were four against the elements, against the wolves, against the night and its dangers—four men with one purpose, to find a special woman and take her home. They were together, even the first-born that the others had thought they would never see. The family must be complete now. Someone was missing—a woman, a mother, a wife.

On and on they rode, over mile after mile of open territory, past red rock canyons and dried up arroyos, avoiding towns and keeping to the back country. Each morning they checked their boots for lizards and snakes, and always they watched for Indians, especially Comanches, who might try to kill them and steal their horses.

They were well armed, wearing crossed leather belts of ammunition and carrying pistols. Adam and Jonas preferred Paterson Walker Colts; John Ross and Stephen preferred the "Texas Arm," a different type of Paterson Colt. All four carried two repeating rifles and large hunting knives. Two pack mules toted plenty of water and the supplies, and they had to be carefully guarded. Each man took a turn standing night guard on a two-hour shift, and no one complained about this or any other assigned duty.

"We'll have to be extra careful on the way back," Adam told them one quiet night. Millions of stars glittered in a black sky, and wolves howled in the distance. "We're strong bait with these horses and guns, and having a woman along will make us even more tempting." He lit a thin cigar. "Once I get your mother out of that place, I'll be damned if any Comanche renegades or white trash are going to get their hands on her. I'll shoot her myself before I let another man touch her or let any more harm come to her."

They all sat around a crackling campfire, smoking, watching the shadows. Stephen swallowed a lump in his throat. "How did you meet her, Father? You never really told me, except that she was fourteen."

Adam sipped at coffee from a tin cup. "I met her in a

special place—a secret place I used to call my own. There was a ridge on the border of my father's farm, and at the top of that ridge there was an oak tree, the biggest oak you'll ever see. I used to go there a lot, called the tree my own. Then one day your mother came riding up there on her pony. She lived on the other side of the ridge. That ridge was kind of a divider between Cherokee country and the whites' farms. Her father had just moved there, and she was exploring. She saw the tree and walked up and touched it." Adam smiled. "She asked it how old it was, talking to it like the little girl she was. I was hiding in the tree, and I answered in a deep voice, as though the tree were talking. You should have seen the look on her face."

Stephen laughed lightly and the others grinned. "She jumped back and stared up," Adam continued. "I swung down like a monkey, scared her to death. She just stared at me with those wide, blue eyes. The sun shone just right on her yellow hair, and a sixteen-year-old Cherokee boy was instantly in love. I wanted that girl to be my very own and nobody else's, but she looked at this Indian boy like I was some kind of creature from another world. 'Are you Cherokee?' she asked, like I was something rare or perhaps extinct." He sighed deeply and puffed on the cigar. "But she started meeting me up there on the ridge, under the oak tree. We were good friends at first, but before long we were more than that . . . two kids in love. We didn't care that she was white and I was Indian, or that we had to keep our meetings secret because her parents would disapprove. We were going to wait for the right time to tell them . . . but some things can't wait when you're that age and in love and people are trying to keep you apart. Before I could stop myself I was making love to her. I just wanted her to be mine . . . to be her first." He threw the cigar into the flames. "And I was not just her first; I was the only man she ever loved, the only man she willingly gave herself to. Douglas Means never really touched her. And neither have those men in Mexico." His voice died off. "Andrea Sanders belongs to me," he said in a quiet, broken voice. "To Adam Chandler, and no one else. She suffered many things because of her love for me. Her parents sent her to an awful place where she was whipped and forced to work long hours. It was there they took you from her, Stephen. She stayed with me while we went from riches to poverty, through a militia rape, the Trail of Tears—even during the time when I was drunk more than I was sober and I was involved in vengeful killings." He laid back against his saddle. "Those vengeful killings have come around to haunt me. If I hadn't been involved in them, Mary Means wouldn't have done what she did to get back at me. Killing for vengeance never really ends, my sons. Remember that. It just goes on and on, and now Andrea has suffered for what I did. I'll never forgive myself for all she's been through."

"You can't blame yourself, Father," Jonas declared. "It all started with the white man's injustice, the government's underhanded methods of getting us out of Georgia. A lot of people learned to hate them. You weren't the only one. Many suffered. And you suffered. I remember how badly they beat you. And I remember you were gone a lot when we still lived in Georgia, helping John Ross fight the legal battle so we could stay."

Adam closed his eyes. "I used to believe we really would win, Jonas. So did thousands of others. That's the sad part. We all thought we would win. We couldn't believe they would really make us go, especially in the hideous way it finally happened. What the government did to the Cherokees, the Creek, the Choctaws, and the Seminoles— it will remain with this land. The government will be plagued by Indian problems for hundreds of years because what they did was wrong, plain wrong. But it will be done again—to these wild Plains Indians. You mark my words. The white man will do it again, and the question of Indian rights will never really be solved, because everything the government does to the Indian will go against all conscience, against all the white man's religious beliefs. And when a man defies his own deepest beliefs, he never quite gets over it. Don't ever go against what you know is right, not any of you. We all suffered because I fought for what I knew was right, but I don't have to live with the memory of going against my beliefs, of turning tail and running without even trying to keep what was rightfully mine. Now I've come full circle. That land is mine again, and someday we're all going back there. I'll show you that oak tree, where Stephen was conceived . . . out of love, not lust. And when we go there your mother will be with us, I promise. And don't ever think your mother was bad for meeting me there under that tree. She was just a sweet little girl in love. She put all her trust in me." He rubbed at his eyes. "I've betrayed that trust so many times."

"You never betrayed her, Father," John Ross said quickly. "It was outside forces that made everything happen. You never betrayed her." He stood up. "It's my turn to keep watch. You'd better get some sleep, Father."

"That's not always an easy thing to do."

"Not for any of us," Stephen put in. He lay back against his saddle.

"Keep your eyes and ears open, John Ross," Adam called out. "Draw on those Indian instincts we civilized redmen have kept buried for too long. They're still there, somewhere. Just concentrate on the night sounds and let the Indian in you take over. We can't let any wild Comanches outdo a Cherokee."

"Don't worry about that," the young man answered from the dark. "What about our white blood?"

Adam pulled a blanket over himself. "Seeing as how it's from your mother, I wouldn't worry. She's a strong woman. Her white blood can't do you any harm. By the way, in the morning we'd better put on our Mexican clothing. We're getting close to the Rio Grande. We've been through hell's furnace, snake country, Comanche country—every bitchy kind of country you can name. But in a few days we'll be in Mexico, and soon after Chihuahua. Let's be real careful. We don't want anything to go wrong now."

He rubbed at his lips. They were dry and cracked. This land was certainly a far cry from the warm, moist green of Georgia. How he missed it! The blue mountains and the big, hardwood trees . . . and Andrea. Did he dare think he could have it all again—Andrea, his three sons, Georgia? He was afraid to dream about it, but could not help doing so. He fell asleep and envisioned the oak tree, all five of them standing under it and looking up into its glorious golden branches.

They rode down the dusty street, watched from beneath sombreros, chickens clucking and scattering before their oncoming horses. One man sat near a well in the center of town, playing a guitar and humming to himself, and a buxom young woman sauntered across the street in front of them so that they had to slow their horses. She looked up at the handsome men on the fine steeds and gave them a coy smile.

Adam nodded. *"Señorita*, where can a man get a cold drink in this town," he asked in Spanish.

She pointed to a saloon farther down the street and giggled.

Adam flashed her a handsome smile. *"Muchas gracias, señorita."*

She watched as they rode on, walking beside them for a ways and smiling at Jonas, who took great pleasure in viewing the huge breasts revealed by her low-cut dress. If it were not for the gravity of their purpose, he would have struck up an acquaintance with the eager-looking Mexican girl.

They approached the saloon, eying every building on the way but seeing nothing called Rosa's. Adam dismounted and tied his horse. "Wait out here," he told his sons. He adjusted his poncho so that access to his handgun was unhindered by it, then walked inside. A sea of dark eyes turned to this stranger, as Adam walked up to the bar and ordered whiskey in Spanish. The bartender eyed him cautiously, then poured him a shot. Adam paid for it with Mexican coins, then leaned closer.

"I am looking for a place called Rosa's. Do you know of it?"

The bartender looked around warily, before studying Adam's dark eyes. "Why do you want to know of this place?"

Adam grinned. "Why do you think? Any Mexican with money knows he can get a white woman there, no?" He spoke in perfect Spanish. The bartender grinned.

"I have been there myself. Blue eyes, green eyes, red hair, gold hair." He rolled his eyes. "It is like being in heaven, *señor.*"

Adam nodded, forcing himself to hide his horror. Perhaps this very man had . . . No. He must stay calm. "I have heard the same. I am a rich man, and I am here with my sons. They need to learn about women. It would be exciting for them to learn with white women. It is my gift to them for coming into manhood. Where can I find this place?"

The bartender frowned. "It is feared Americans will come down here and try to take their women out of these places, now that the American soldiers are invading Mexico. You would not be some sort of spy?"

Adam snickered. "I assure you, my intentions are strictly pleasure, *señor.* My sons wait outside at this very moment. Come and see if you don't believe me."

The bartender waved him off. "It is all right. You just do not look all Mexican, that's all."

Adam slugged down his whiskey. "Don't you realize there are many Mexicans who carry European blood? How many Mexicans are pure Mexican? How many Apaches are pure Apache, hmmm? Of course I am not pure Mexican. There is Spanish blood somewhere back there, and a little Apache. Maybe an Apache ancestor captured a pretty Mexican girl once, huh?" He laughed and held out his shot glass.

The bartender chuckled and poured another shot. "*Sí, señor.* I understand." He set down the bottle. "Rosa's place is a big house about a quarter-mile north of town. It is painted all white with green trim, and is kept very neat. The wealthy customers like it clean. The women are also clean." He leaned closer. "Some are drugged, you know.

With strange drugs that make them crazy for a man." He shook his head. "A man has to have a good heart to go to that place. He will get much exercise." He chuckled and walked away, and Adam slugged down the second shot. It tasted good. He'd stayed away from whiskey for a long time now. It was hard to drink it without wanting more, but he had only drunk it to fit in and not be suspected. Suddenly the thought of these men groveling over Andrea made him want to turn and shoot at every man in the place and then drink down a whole bottle of the blessed whiskey. But he had to think of Andrea. His drunkenness had been part of the reason he'd lost her in the first place. He wouldn't allow it to inhibit him now. He fought the desire for more and walked out, mounting his horse.

"Let's go, boys." He turned his horse and rode south, and his sons followed.

The fat, aging Mexican woman opened her door gladly, grinning excitedly at the four fine-looking men who waited outside. One was obviously older, but just as handsome and well built as the young ones. Four good-looking, wealthy Mexicans! This would be a good day. So far no Americans had come to raid her. No soldiers had taken away her white women. Now most of the American soldiers were much farther south, heading for Mexico City. She was safe.

She greeted the four men with a happy grin, and Adam Chandler and his sons entered the parlor behind her mountainous form. Everything was red velvet, the carpeting, the upholstery, the drapes. Three white women languished on sofas and loveseats, their breasts billowing from ruffled dresses. The one with red hair smiled at Adam as she pulled her dress nearly to her hips to reveal slender white thighs.

"And what can we do for you fine-looking men today?" Rosa said to them. "For the right price, we have the finest wines and liquors, and of course, the finest women. There are more upstairs if one of our ladies here does not please you." Rosa breathed deeply, eagerly as she eyed the younger men. She stepped closer to John Ross, running a hand along his arm. "This one seems very young. Perhaps he is . . . inexperienced?"

John Ross jerked away, and the woman frowned. "My son is new to this," Adam said quickly. He noticed an armed Mexican standing in one corner of the room, another near the doorway. "Perhaps an older woman who is very understanding would be better for him. Can you bring them all down here for us to look at?"

He spoke Castilian Spanish, and Rosa was sure he was a very wealthy Mexican. If she could please him, perhaps he and his sons would return often, paying the best in gold coin for her finest women. "Ah, come with me, *señor*. There are six rooms upstairs, with a beauty in each one. Two are occupied right now. We will have to knock first, and perhaps you will have to wait a few minutes before they can serve you. Would you like some wine before you go up?"

Adam looked at his sons and grinned. "No. They are too anxious. Perhaps afterward . . . a bath and wine would be nice then."

Rosa laughed and, hoisting her hefty body past them, started up a grand, red-carpeted staircase. "Come then!"

The Chandlers followed, Adam's heart pounding wildly with dread and anticipation. Andrea! Had she really been forced to work in this hellish place? And what had the white women downstairs been like when they'd been brought here? A couple of them had a hauntingly innocent look to them, but their eyes were glazed and staring, as though they were not in this world. He followed a huffing, puffing Rosa to the top of the stairs, where another armed man stood guard.

Rosa led them to the first door, and the boys looked away as she opened it, afraid their own mother would be inside, perhaps nude and involved in some hideous sexual act. "She is too dark," they heard their father say. They moved to the next door, and Adam cleared his throat before commenting on the woman's beauty, his signal to them that it was not their mother inside. After seeing every girl upstairs, Adam turned to his sons. "Well, boys, it's your choice," he told them in Spanish. Even Stephen knew the signal words, for he'd been drilled in them. They had not found their mother. It was time for more drastic action.

Stephen whirled then, cocking and aiming a handgun at the guard upstairs, while Adam whipped out his gun and aimed it at Rosa's nose. As he shoved the fat woman against a wall, Jonas and John Ross moved to the head of the stairs, to watch the unwitting guards down below. Stephen held a finger to his lips, warning the man upstairs not to make a sound, and then motioning for him to take out his gun and drop it.

"I'm looking for Andrea Chandler," Adam said in a near whisper to Rosa. She stared cross-eyed at his gun. "Where is she!"

"I . . . I don't know."

"Don't you lie to me, you fat bitch!" Adam hissed, pushing the gun hard against her nose. "Mary Means brought her here about seven years ago—a pretty blond woman. She'd been married to a Cherokee man!"

Rosa's eyes moved to his face. "Y-you?"

"Where is she? You tell me, fat lady, or there will be a big hole in your ugly face where your nose used to be!"

The woman swallowed. "She . . . she is with the used ones . . . the crazy ones . . . downstairs."

He grasped her hair. "What do you mean, crazy ones?"

"Downstairs . . . we put the girls there who . . . are too used . . . or too crazy from the drugs. The poor men can visit them . . . for a few coins. They are no longer . . . any good to the rich men. Downstairs . . . through a kitchen door to the cellar . . . they are chained to cots down there."

Adam's eyes widened with rage. Then he swung the gun hard. Rosa was no woman to feel sorry for. He smashed the barrel across her face, and she screamed just before it hit her. As her huge body slumped to the floor, the two guards downstairs charged up the staircase, guns drawn.

The man Stephen had been guarding lunged at him.

Stephen fired point-blank, and the Mexican's body lurched backward. Then everything else happened in a matter of only one or two seconds. Jonas and Adam both fired at the two guards coming up the stairs. One fired back, clipping the top of Adam's shoulder and ripping his poncho. A bloodstain immediately appeared as Adam's body was jolted by the hit.

"Father!" Jonas gasped.

"I'm all right! Come on!" Adam headed down the stairs, past the bodies of the two Mexican men they had shot on the stairway, caring little if they were dead or alive. The house was full of screaming and running women as the three Chandler sons followed their father down a hallway to a kitchen at the back of the house. Two more men made an appearance then, barging out of the kitchen door. Adam yelled for the boys to look out, then ducked to the side as the two Mexicans opened fire. Jonas dove under a table and came up with it, tossing it into one of the men and knocking him backward. Adam fired at the second man, catching him in the side of the face, while Stephen yanked the gun from the first man's hand and hit him over the head with it.

The four Chandlers barged into the kitchen then. Women ducked and ran. The three in the parlor had already run outside for help. There was no time to waste. Adam began to open doors until he found the one that led to a stairway going down into a room dimly lit by lanterns. "Stay here and keep watch!"

He headed below, feeling sick with dread and horror. The small cellar room had a damp stench. Eight cots sat in two rows, each with a naked woman chained to it. Three men stood up, yelling in Spanish. "Get the hell out of here before I blow you all to pieces!" Adam ordered.

They all grabbed for their clothes, cursing in Spanish but afraid of the wild-looking man who had come barging into the little room. They fell over each other getting to the stairway, and Adam frantically checked each cot, wanting to find Andrea yet almost hoping she would not be there.

"Andrea? Andrea?" He checked each woman, shooting

off her chains as he did and wishing he could help them all. But he could not. It had to be . . . A gut-wrenching groan came from his lips then and he struggled not to vomit. A frail wisp of a woman with blond hair lay in the farthest corner on unwashed sheets, her eyes sunken and staring, her face so thin and hollow that at first he could not be sure. He took down a lamp and held it closer, and the tiny brown birthmark near her left breast told him who it was. "Andrea," he groaned.

"Father, hurry!" John Ross shouted. "We have to get out of here. Stephen has the horses at the back door! More men are coming!"

Adam set down the lamp, horrible sobs wanting to come. But there was no time for anything now but getting her out. He quickly shot off the chains and wrapped her in the sheets. With horror, he noticed how light she was when he picked her up; she felt like a skeleton. He covered her face, not wanting the boys to see her until he could clean her up and bring her back to reality. He hurried up the stairs then, regretting having to leave the other women behind. Jonas and John Ross stared wide-eyed at the wrapped body, tears in their eyes.

"It is she . . . our mother?" John Ross seemed afraid to ask.

"It is. She's alive. Let's go."

They hurried out the back way then. Adam handed Andrea to Jonas while he mounted up. Then Jonas handed her up to him, wanting to scream at how light she was, wanting to kill and kill for what had been done to her. He mounted his own horse then, and they rode north. The men behind them were shouting and firing, but none tried to follow. A bullet whizzed past Stephen, skinning his right calf, but soon they were out of range. They rode hard toward the mountains, where they had left the pack mules, to the place Adam had already decided to take Andrea if he found her alive. It was a little hidden valley with green grass and a stream of fresh, clear mountain water. There they could be alone until she was ready to face the world once more . . . and her sons. God was with them this time. No one followed.

To Andrea it all seemed simply a vague dream. Had it been Adam's voice that called to her? No. Too many years had gone by. He would never find her now. And besides, it was hard to remember sometimes who Adam was. There were moments when she remembered him very clearly, and her precious sons. She would cry then, cry until she was sick. Then memory would leave her, especially after Rosa put the smelly cloth over her mouth, or lit the strange incense, or gave her something to swallow. Then her only memory was of hands using her rudely, of bad breath and ugly laughter. Sometimes she had actually wanted the strange men who came to see her. It was the liquid Rosa gave her that made her want them. She fought it, but could not. And finally she begged for it, took men willingly for it, for she could not live with the pain she felt when she could not have the blessed liquid or smell the wonderful incense. She remembered Adam then with sorrow, for she could never go back. Things could never be the same.

But now the dream of hearing his voice, feeling him hold her, seemed so real, so real. The voice became more clear, the arms more sure. Sometimes she sensed fresh air and sunshine. Someone bathed her, said beautiful words to her, said something about an oak tree. But then the pain came, the horrible pain that made her scream and writhe, curse and fight whoever it was who held her and would not let her have the blessed liquid or smell the wonderful incense. He was cruel, so cruel! She begged for it, offered her body for it, but he refused. Sometimes she could hear him crying; sometimes he held and rocked her, telling her pretty things; sometimes he just said her name over and over—Andrea. Andrea.

Hours turned into days, days of screaming agony until reality finally began to take hold of her abused body and tortured mind. "I know how bad it is, *agiya*," he was

497

telling her. "I went through a terrible time when I decided never again to drink the whiskey. This I know is even worse, but you can make it, Andrea. You are strong. You are my Andrea. We have survived so many things. We can survive this. I will help you. I will hold you until the pain is gone."

How many days had they been there? How many days had passed before she opened her eyes and saw him for the first time, sitting near her, shirtless, bent over a campfire. Adam! He was older. He looked so tired. It all came to her then—all of it. The memories. The horrible, horrible memories. How could she ever be worthy to look at him again, let alone touch him? How had he found her, and why? Why would he bother now? How could he possibly love her? She had to get away! She threw off her blanket and started to run, but a moment later someone caught her. She screamed and kicked wildly. "No! No! No! Don't touch me! Don't look at me!"

"It's all right! It's all right, Andrea!"

He held her so tightly she could not budge. Then he carried her back to the campfire, where she fought and fought until she was limp from exhaustion. Her agony finally came out of her in wrenching sobs and fits of vomiting. And all the while he held her. He would not let go of her for a moment. He smoothed her hair back when she was sick, washed her face, gave her fresh water with which to rinse her mouth.

"Go away! Leave me here!" she begged. "You don't know what I've done."

"I know everything. My God, Andrea, I thought you were dead! I buried a woman I thought was you, and my life has been empty ever since. When I heard you were alive—"

"How? How did you find out?" She kept her head bent, her hands over her face. How could she ever, ever face him?

"It doesn't matter now. It doesn't matter, Andrea. All that matters is you are alive, and I have found you. And if only you can forgive me for allowing any of this to happen . . ." He choked up and broke into tears himself, then grasped her tight against himself. Turning her and pinning her face against his chest, he wept, rocking her, begging her forgiveness for not taking her with him to Independence, for his drinking, for that last terrible year when he was cruel to her.

She slowly allowed herself to cling to him, breathing in the old, familiar scent that was all man, all Adam Chandler. Adam! After all she had been through, it was he who was sitting there begging forgiveness. How could he hold her this way? How could he still love her? Yet he said over and over. "I love you. I love you. Nothing can change that, Andrea. Not anything." How could she believe those words? "I don't drink now, Andrea. I'm a successful attorney in St. Louis. I've bought back the land, Andrea, all of it. It's all ours now, if we want to go back. I want to take the boys there. I want to show them the oak tree. Please, Andrea, don't let it end now, not after all of this, not after finding you again. Don't give up. We have to go back to the oak tree, you and me and our sons. They came with me, Andrea. They love you so much. They want their mother back."

"I can't go back," she sobbed. "I'm ugly . . . and used. I'm not . . . the same anymore."

"Yes you are. You are! You will always be the same to me . . . my sweet little Andrea . . . the innocent child I claimed under the oak tree. I always think of you that way and I always will. Please, Andrea, let's live the rest of our years in peace. We can now. It's all over. All the ugliness is over."

She hung limp in his arms. "I wish I could just die," she groaned.

He kept rocking her, patting her hair. "Oh no you don't. If you really wanted to die, you would have let yourself die back there. You would have found a way. But you knew that as long as I lived, I might come and find you. You lived for me, Andrea, and for our sons. Don't give up now. Now you have more reason than ever to live." He kissed her hair, her face, taking it in his hands and forcing her to look at him. He studied her thin face and hollow eyes lovingly, seeing the beauty that would return as soon as she gained some weight and could smile again. "I did not bring just two sons down here with me, Andrea. I brought three sons."

Her body convulsed in a sob, and she just stared at him. "I . . . don't understand."

"One calls himself Stephen. We called him Nathan."

Her sobbing subsided, and a look of desperate hope came into her eyes. "No!"

"Yes. He was released from an orphanage where he'd been held like a prisoner and forced to work in factories until he was eighteen. Then he came to find his father and mother. He'd found out he was part Cherokee, so he went to Cherokee country first and learned where I was and what had happened to you. He found me, and he has been with us ever since. He is buying into a supply store, Andrea. He is a fine young man, and will marry soon. He is twenty years old now—a tall, strong young man. When you see him, you will think you are seeing me when we first met, for he is like my twin. I knew the moment he walked into my office he was my son. And his fondest dream, his most heartfelt prayer is to meet his real mother. Do not disappoint your first-born son, Andrea. And do not pass up this chance to finally know him yourself."

"My God," she whispered. "My son!"

Adam nodded, and she flung her arms around his neck then, weeping bitterly. He let her cry. She needed to cry . . . and cry. But he would win her back. Slowly but surely she would be his Andrea again, and they would be a family. It didn't matter if she might be unable to let him make love to her again. That would come in time. All that mattered was that she was here, in his arms, his Andrea. They had truly come full circle. Someday they would go home, to Georgia, to the Cherokee hills, to the oak tree. He had kept his promise. Over twenty years had passed since he'd met little Andrea Sanders under that tree, and to him she had not changed.

"Do not cry, *agiya*. It is over now. We will go home.

Your sons wait for you not far from here—all three of them."

She clung tightly to him. It was real! Adam was here, holding her. He still loved her, and her son, her first-born son had found his father and brothers. "Adam, I'm scared," she sobbed. "How can I face them? How?"

He smiled sadly, kissing her hair, rocking her. "It will be easy. You are their mother. A son never stops loving his mother, and one of your sons has never even known his mother. There is nothing more he wants in the whole world than to see you, *agiya*. We all love you. They came with me through hellish terrain and Comanche country to find you. Does a man do that for someone he does not love? Even now Mexican soldiers could be after us, so we have hidden ourselves well." He pulled away slightly, kissing her forehead. "Let me fix your hair. I brought perfume and powders and a couple of your prettiest dresses. Let's go see our sons, Andrea."

She hung her head. "But I'm so . . . thin, and I must look—"

He took her chin gently and raised it. "Look at me, *agiya*."

She raised sky-blue eyes to meet his dark ones. It was the first time she had allowed herself to look directly at him, and in that moment she knew nothing had changed. How beautiful he still was, and there was so much love in those dark, hypnotic eyes. It seemed impossible he could still love her.

"When a man loves a woman, he does not love her only if everything goes right and all is perfect. If he loves her, he loves her." He kissed her lips, gently, ever so gently. "One day you will again know the beauty of that love, the beauty of a kiss, the beauty of touching—all the things we once shared, *agiya*. If it takes a month, a year, five years, it does not matter. It will happen, because nothing can change our love for each other."

"But, Adam—"

He put his fingers to her lips. "Your husband has

spoken. Do you think we went through all that hell just to find you and leave you here? We love you. You are a Chandler. You belong with us. Now let's get you dressed. Don't you want to see your sons?"

Her lips quivered. "I don't even know . . . how old they are," she said softly.

He smoothed back her hair. "Stephen—that's what our Nathan calls himself—he is nearly twenty-one. Jonas is eighteen and John Ross is close to seventeen."

Tears of love and sorrow slipped down her cheeks. "Grown! All grown."

He brushed at the tears. "Never too grown to love and need their mother. Come now. Stop crying so your eyes won't be all red."

"I can't . . . stop. I'll never stop."

"Yes you will." He kissed her cheek. "We are going to have the peaceful, comfortable life I promised you so many years ago, Andrea. Finally we will be happy and together. It is not too late for us. Come now. Let's fix you up, then go to our sons and get the hell out of this country." He helped her up and walked her back toward their camp. "We have a pretty little house in St. Louis. We'll stay there a while. And then we just might go back to Georgia. I have everything now—my sons, my wife, my land. We're going back, Andrea. We're going to go and sit under that oak tree, just you and me, like when we met."

She leaned on him. Adam. This was Adam. This was real.

"I hope they come pretty soon," John Ross mumbled, poking at the fire with a stick. "I want to get out of this country and go back to St. Louis."

"You and me both," Jonas answered, lighting a cigar.

John Ross sighed. "What do you think she's like? Father wouldn't even let us look at her."

Jonas blinked back tears. "She must have been pretty bad. He handed her to me to hold while he got on his horse and it was like holding a—" he choked up—"a damned bag of bones. It makes me sick," he hissed.

John Ross threw the stick aside. "At least we found her. If anybody can help her, Father sure can. He sure loves her a lot."

Jonas smiled sadly. "Don't we all? I hope I can find somebody someday I'd love that much."

Stephen had been several feet away, quietly watching the horizon. He came over to them then and sat down. "You two, do you think . . . well, do you think . . . she'll like me?" They both looked at him in surprise. "Well, I mean . . . she's never met me or anything."

Jonas burst into laughter then, and John Ross snickered. Stephen scowled. "What's so funny?"

"Jesus, Stephen, what a dumb question! You're her son!" Jonas sobered then, realizing Stephen had been serious. He punched his arm. "Hey, brother, as far back as I can remember our mother and father talked about you, wondered about you. Mom cried over you I don't know how many times. She gave birth to you. Of course she'll like you. Fact is, Father was probably right. I know how much she loves me and John Ross, but like Father said, you're the trump card. The way she must be feeling, well, she might just want to die or something. But when Father tells her you're with us, hell, how can she resist that?" He puffed on his cigar and then threw it aside before reaching over to squeeze Stephen's arm. "Stephen, she's going to be pretty low." He looked at John Ross. "Look, we all have to make her know how much she's loved, and show her that she's just as respected and honored as she ever was. Let's help Father get her back to normal, and let's surround her with so much love that she can't turn away from it or consider something dumb like killing herself."

John Ross looked at him in surprise. "Do you think she would?"

Jonas shrugged. "Who knows what goes through the mind of a woman who's been in the kind of hellhole she was in? We can't let her see any doubt in our eyes, understand? There can't be any doubt. The best way to get her back to normal is to just surround her with love.

Father will need our help for a while."

John Ross picked up a stone and threw it. "That won't be hard."

Stephen sighed. "I don't know about you two, but I'm nervous as hell."

Jonas and John Ross looked at each other. "Hey, John, remember when we used to wrestle in the mud back in Indian Territory and Mom used to get so mad at us?"

John Ross nodded and Jonas winked. In the next instant they both landed into Stephen and the match was on. The young men tumbled and growled and laughed, rolling in the dust like children. After several minutes of scrambling and twisting, Stephen picked up the smaller John, hoisting him across his shoulders and standing up, yelling like a victor. He whirled his brother around, then stopped cold. There, close by, stood Adam, with a frail-looking but beautiful woman.

"Mother," he whispered. He let go of John Ross, and the boy landed hard on the ground.

"Hey, I'll get you for—"

John Ross saw her then. Jonas was already walking up to her. He hesitated when he reached her, his eyes full of tears. He ran a hand through his hair.

"I'm a mess," he told her awkwardly. "We didn't know . . ." He swallowed back a lump in his throat. "Mom!" He reached out and hugged her close then, breaking into tears. John Ross was beside them now. He glanced at his father, who smiled as though to tell him she'd be all right. He put a hand on her shoulder.

"Mom?"

She reached out then, and was soon hugging both of her sons, weeping because they were full grown and she'd missed all those years.

"Hell, we still need our mom," John Ross told her, kissing her cheek. "You're gonna be okay, aren't you? You'll come home with us and we'll all be together."

They hugged each other and cried for several seconds. Then Adam glanced at Stephen, who stood back, watching them nervously. He broke in on all the hugging,

504

and took Andrea's arm. "Jonas, John Ross, somebody is waiting to meet his mother."

Both boys pulled away, sniffing and wiping at their eyes, and Adam walked Andrea closer to Stephen, who just stared at her. She was beautiful, more beautiful than he had pictured. So, this was his mysterious mother, the cat who had had the kitten that was taken from her, the woman who had sacrificed so much for his father.

"Stephen, this is your mother," Adam was saying.

Andrea just stared at her first-born. Adam! It was like seeing the young Adam she had first met. Here he stood! But of course this was their son! How handsome and tall and beautiful he was, the son she had never known! If only she could have cradled him in her arms when he was a baby, loved and protected him. What horrors had this son experienced?

"I'm . . . so sorry, Stephen," she said in a near whisper. "They took you against my will. I wanted you."

He nodded and swallowed. "I know."

In the next moment she reached out to him. But he was so tall and strong it was he who held her, so tightly she could barely breathe. "Mother, my mother," he whispered. It was all she needed to hear.

They climbed the ridge together, two people ravaged by injustice, but finding strength in their love, and in experiencing this final victory.

"Do you think it will still be there?" Andrea asked.

Adam squeezed her hand. "Of course it will. Man can change the laws, Andrea, but he cannot change the land." He kept a firm hold of her frail hand. He had got her the best medical care available in St. Louis. There would never be any more children, but she would be all right, in time. And they had their handsome, successful sons, Jonas, John Ross, and Stephen, precious Stephen. Now Adam led Andrea to the place where they had known sweet, pure, innocent love, so many years ago. They had left the horses tied below and now made the ascent, their hearts pounding with dread that for some reason someone might have cut down the tree. Below them, on the very location of Jonas Chandler's burned-out home, sat a new one, a fine, two-story, brick structure, expensively decorated and furnished. Andrea had servants to help take care of it. They had come full circle, and Adam Chandler once again traveled often to Washington, continuing the legal battle for fair treatment of the thousands of Cherokee who now lived in Indian Territory. Perhaps one day more of them could return to this, their beloved homeland.

Now it came into view, its sprawling, golden branches stretched out as though to defy time and man. Andrea ran to touch it, pressing her face against the rough bark and weeping. The oak tree still stood. Adam walked around beneath it, looking up, stretching out his arms and thanking *Esaugetuh Emissee*. And his heart was strengthened in knowing man had removed the Cherokee from this place in body only. But no law on earth could govern the spirit. His eyes filled with tears, and he smiled. "I got it back, Father, just like I promised," he said softly. "I have come home."

"It affords me sincere pleasure to apprise the Congress of the entire removal of the Cherokee Nation of Indians to their new homes west of the Missisippi. The measures authorized by Congress at its last session have had the happiest effects. By an agreement concluded with them by the commanding general in that country, their removal has been principally under the conduct of their own chiefs, and they have emigrated without any apparent reluctance."

—President Van Buren's message to Congress in December, 1838.

Across America lie the buried bones of the Indian, from the Atlantic to the Pacific, Iroquois and Cherokee; Cheyenne and Nez Perce. In truth, all of America's soil was once sacred to these people. It remains so. Beneath the concrete walks and heaven-bound skyscrapers lie their bones, quietly waiting. For the day will surely come when the real American will again walk this continent and call it his own. Perhaps it will be in another time . . . perhaps after the "war of wars." But it will happen. The Indian will return to his sacred lands, and never again will they be taken from him. It is the ultimate dream of all remaining full-blooded Indians that one day their ancestors will rise, their bones will be fleshed out, and they will walk again. The cities will vanish, the green grass will return. The waters will flow clean again, and the earth will abound with buffalo and all sorts of wild game. Those will be happy times, good times, an age of plenty. All Indians wait patiently for this moment. And it will come. . . .

From the Author...

I hope you have enjoyed my story. I will be glad to send you a newsletter listing other books I have written, and upcoming novels, as well as personal information about myself. Simply write me in care of ZEBRA BOOKS, 475 PARK AVENUE SOUTH, NEW YORK, NEW YORK 10016. I answer all letters and enjoy hearing from my readers. Please be sure to include a self-addressed, stamped envelope with your letter. Thank you.

ROMANCE REIGNS
WITH ZEBRA BOOKS!

SILVER ROSE (2275, $3.95)
by Penelope Neri

Fleeing her lecherous boss, Silver Dupres disguised herself as a boy and joined an expedition to chart the wild Colorado River. But with one glance at Jesse Wilder, the explorers' rugged, towering scout, Silver knew she'd have to abandon her protective masquerade or else be consumed by her raging unfulfilled desire!

STARLIT ECSTASY (2134, $3.95)
by Phoebe Conn

Cold-hearted heiress Alicia Caldwell swore that Rafael Ramirez, San Francisco's most successful attorney, would never win her money . . . or her love. But before she could refuse him, she was shamelessly clasped against Rafael's muscular chest and hungrily matching his relentless ardor!

LOVING LIES (2034, $3.95)
by Penelope Neri

When she agreed to wed Joel McCaleb, Seraphina wanted nothing more than to gain her best friend's inheritance. But then she saw the virile stranger . . . and the green-eyed beauty knew she'd never be able to escape the rapture of his kiss and the sweet agony of his caress.

EMERALD FIRE (1963, $3.95)
by Phoebe Conn

When his brother died for loving gorgeous Bianca Antonelli, Evan Sinclair swore to find the killer by seducing the tempress who lured him to his death. But once the blond witch willingly surrendered all he sought, Evan's lust for revenge gave way to the desire for unrestrained rapture.

SEA JEWEL (1888, $3.95)
by Penelope Neri

Hot-tempered Alaric had long planned the humiliation of Freya, the daughter of the most hated foe. He'd make the wench from across the ocean his lowly bedchamber slave—but he never suspected she would become the mistress of his heart, his treasured SEA JEWEL.

Available wherever paperbacks are sold, or order direct from the Publisher. Send cover price plus 50¢ per copy for mailing and handling to Zebra Books, Dept. 2253, 475 Park Avenue South, New York, N.Y. 10016. Residents of New York, New Jersey and Pennsylvania must include sales tax. DO NOT SEND CASH.